BEC MCMASTER

MISSION: IMPROPER

LON
THE BLUE
NR
CONSPIRACY

ALSO AVAILABLE BY BEC MCMASTER

LONDON STEAMPUNK SERIES
Kiss Of Steel
Heart Of Iron
My Lady Quicksilver
Forged By Desire
Of Silk And Steam
Novellas in same series:
Tarnished Knight
The Curious Case Of The Clockwork Menace

LONDON STEAMPUNK: THE BLUE BLOOD CONSPIRACY
Mission: Improper
The Mech Who Loved Me (Coming 2017)

DARK ARTS SERIES
Shadowbound
Hexbound

BURNED LANDS SERIES
Nobody's Hero
The Last True Hero

SHORT STORIES
The Many Lives Of Hadley Monroe

CHAPTER ONE

London, 1883

THE INVITATION CONTAINED an address and two words: *Come alone.*

Caleb Byrnes had found it earlier that morning, in the middle of his bed in the Nighthawks Guild headquarters, a place that he'd previously considered impenetrable. Not only were the Nighthawks comprised of rogue blue bloods—those afflicted with the craving virus, whose infection had *not* been sanctioned by the aristocrats who'd once ruled London—but they were also thief-takers and bounty hunters. An intruder should have been heard, or smelled, or spotted before they got within five yards of the place. And if they hadn't been, then the guild was protected with all manner of mechanical devices. It was a virtual labyrinth. To his knowledge, nobody had ever broken in successfully.

His curiosity was aroused.

Or perhaps that was just a side effect of the fact that the invitation smelled quite liberally of perfume.

Someone had just dared him.

Someone who knew enough about him to know what piqued his interest.

Someone female.

If there was one thing that Byrnes desired above all else it was a mystery, or a chase. The hunt was everything to him, whether he was hunting miscreants over the rooftops of London, vampires causing mayhem, or women.

It was only once the chase was done that he grew bored, and considering that it had been a good year since he'd had a decent pursuit or case—that actress from the theatre, or the so-called Vampire of Drury Lane—he figured he was due.

Hence why he was here, at the address listed.

Lifting the invitation to his face, Byrnes breathed in the scent, and stared up at the nondescript Georgian townhouse in front of him that threatened to blend in to all of the others along the street. If he hadn't owned preternatural senses, the perfume would have been subtle, that of lilies floating in the wind past him. As it was he could make out the tiny trace notes of oils and chemicals, of solvents and preservatives, and something faintly musky that he couldn't quite identify.

Lifting his hand to knock, Byrnes paused as skirts swished behind him along the footpath.

"Goodness, Byrnes, is that you?" Ava MacLaren asked, coming directly to a halt behind him.

Not his intended pursuit, though Ava certainly could have delivered the invitation, as she too was a Nighthawk, and therefore had the means to enter his room. The scent was wrong however. Ava was engine oil, blood, and chemicals, masked by the faint trace of rose perfume she sometimes wore.

"Indeed it is." Byrnes raked a glance over her, and missed nothing—including the gold-engraved invitation trailing from her fingers. His eyes narrowed. "What are you doing here?"

Three years ago, Ava had been the victim of a madman who performed clockwork experiments on women, a case that had left her with a thick, ragged scar down her chest, a mechanical heart, and a case of the craving virus. Her parents had thought her dead, and there was no place in the world for a female blue blood such as herself, so she'd ended up staying at the guild and taking a position there in the laboratories with Fitz. In three short years, she'd become quite adept at crime scene investigation, whereas Fitz still fainted at the sight of blood.

Had Ava received the same invitation? The thought irritated him a little, for he'd thought this to be *his* mystery. However, he saw Ava as a friend—one of the few he truly owned—so he pushed the thought away.

"Same reason, perhaps, as yours." Ava lifted the invitation ruefully, juggling her parasol in her other hand. "I received this but an hour ago. It sounded urgent."

"Urgent?"

Ava offered him the piece of parchment.

To the Divine Miss McLaren. An offer awaits you, if you dare. Come immediately.

Ava's cheeks colored. "I thought—perhaps—an admirer. I was just curious...."

"You should be more careful," Byrnes said with a frown, turning it over to find the same address listed. "What if it hadn't been? What if someone with nefarious intentions sent this to you instead?"

"They still might have nefarious intentions," she suggested.

"Yes, but my virtue is nonexistent, and everyone knows it. So I doubt they'd have invited me."

Ava rolled her pretty green eyes. She was used to his humor, though she often told him it was lacking. "I'm a blue blood, Byrnes. There's not a lot that could kill me, and considering my heart is made of metal, perhaps not even a stake through that, hmm? And you've taught me how to protect myself. I deemed it an acceptable risk."

True. Blue bloods were exceedingly difficult to kill, thanks to the craving virus, which could heal most injuries. That didn't mean that killing one was impossible, and Ava had already suffered enough in life.

Byrnes looked up at the building. "They still might have dangerous intentions. You should let me go first."

"I should," Ava said, swinging her parasol with a dangerous glint in her eyes, "but I'm not going to. For goodness sakes, Byrnes, I'm not a debutante. Besides, I have this—"

The parasol swung toward him, and Byrnes tensed, ready for anything. "I'm not certain I've fully recovered from the last ingenious device. What does this one do?"

Her eyes glittered, and she slid her hand toward some trigger on the handle. The tip of it was pressed directly against his chest. "Want to find out?"

"On second thought, I don't want to know," he replied, moving it swiftly away from him.

Ava laughed. "Trust me. Nobody wants to be on the receiving end of my electromagnetic discombobulating device. Talk about sweeping men off their feet...."

"After you, then," he said, and knocked on the door again.

The second his knock died down, the door swung inwards.

A butler appeared, impeccable in black. "Good morning, Master Byrnes. Miss McLaren."

Byrnes hadn't heard him so much as breathing. "I believe you have the advantage of us…." He didn't like not being the one in the know.

"My name is Herbert. Please come in. You're expected."

Herbert's eyes were far too watchful for a mere servant, and the way he moved was… disturbingly graceful. Then there was the pale skin. Could just be a result of London's perpetual cloud coverage, but it might also be sign of a blue blood. Byrne's eyes narrowed, one hand dropping to the knife sheathed at his side as he stepped past. If he didn't know any better, he would have classified the butler as dangerous.

"Oh, thank you," Ava told the butler, holding out her parasol.

Byrnes intercepted it and tossed it toward the fellow.

Herbert snatched the parasol out of the air, moving faster than the eye could see. The butler froze, then returned Byrnes's narrowed glare with a bland one. "Let me put this away for you, Miss McLaren."

Huh.

Byrnes didn't take his eyes off the man as he stepped inside, until the fellow turned to the coatrack.

Ava gave him a look. "Byrnes," she mouthed.

He let a smile stretch over his lips. "For a rogue blue blood, Herbert, you seem to have escaped the fate of the rest of us."

Which was either an offer to join the Nighthawks, the Coldrush Guards that protected the queen, or death. Although "offer" could be considered too charitable a word. The aristocratic Echelon had once guarded their blue blood status as a privilege, reserved only for the best. They didn't take kindly to accidental infections.

"I still serve, Master Byrnes. However, my particular skills were noticed by one who can bypass certain rules."

Which narrowed the field considerably. The plot thickened.

"The others are gathered in the library," Herbert said, gesturing them toward the stairs.

"Others?" Byrnes glanced up. He could hear murmurs from above.

"The rest of the company, sir." Herbert returned a bland smile that told him nothing. "If you'll join them, I'll send for refreshments—"

"Do you know the purpose of this meeting? Who's hosting it? Who's—"

"All shall be revealed, sir. Perhaps some blud-wein for the lady?"

"Please," Byrnes replied, then offered Ava his arm to escort her up the stairs.

"What do you think is going on?" she whispered, her flyaway blonde curls brushing against his shoulder.

"I don't have a bloody clue," he replied. "Who are the others? What could they want with a pair of Nighthawks? A case?" He shook his head. "No. They wouldn't have requested your presence, and they would have applied for the commission through the guild master. Plus I'm fairly certain Herbert could handle something like that himself."

"Do you think he's—"

"Very dangerous, I suspect."

That widened her eyes. Ava gave a delicate sniff. "Not a case, then. I cannot smell any blood. Only... lilies."

Lilies. His gut clenched, and his gaze raked the foyer. That at least, boded well. There was something mingled with the scent now though, something almost musky.

Byrnes frowned, as a slither of warning lit down his spine, but Ava tugged on his arm and drew him toward the library. He lost whatever train of thought instinct had served up.

"You seem distracted," she noted.

"Something on my mind." The curiosity was almost *itching* on his skin. Who was the woman who'd delivered the invitation? "Here we are."

Byrnes threw the doors open to the library, drawing the attention of three sets of eyes from within. Two men eyed each other across the expanse of the room, one an enormous bruiser with black hair and evil blue eyes, and the other a young lad who bore evidence of the craving virus on his pale skin and the faint gilded tones of his hair. The higher a man's craving virus levels, the more his skin and hair paled. The distance of almost five feet parted the two men, and the lad looked both cocky and amused, as if he'd been picking a fight with the brute.

The woman leaning against the curtains rolled her eyes. She was everything elegant, with loose black hair swept into a chignon, and a sweeping fall of violet skirts. Beautiful, but ultimately uninteresting, as Byrnes could detect an Oriental perfume about her, not the one he was hunting for.

"So who the hell are you?" The black-haired giant demanded, staring up at them from an armchair with his boot hooked up on his other knee.

"This would be Master Byrnes, of the Nighthawks," said the woman by the window, crossing her arms with amused disdain, "and Miss Ava McLaren, I presume?"

Byrnes and Ava exchanged a glance. Ava looked a little discomfited by the strange man's animosity, but tipped her chin up. "I believe you have the advantage of us—"

The lady strode forward, her skirts swishing about her legs as she clasped Ava's hand and squeezed it gently. "My apologies. You may call me Gemma Townsend. Information is an interest of mine, and female blue bloods are so rare that I've made a note of them. I believe you to be the third located in London proper? The Duchess of Casavian, Lady Peregrine of the Nighthawks—and yourself?"

"There's one more," the lad muttered, "but she... she ain't likely to be known."

Byrnes eyed him. "Charlie Todd?" He recognized the boy as one of the rookery lads who ran with Blade, the Devil of Whitechapel, though the little bugger had grown. They were almost of a height now.

The young man grinned and shook his hand. "The one and only."

The Nighthawks occasionally had dealings in the rookeries, and ever since the corrupt prince consort had been dethroned, Blade had become a common sight around town. The Hero of the Realm, the commoners called him, thanks to his part in the revolution that overthrew the prince consort. More like the devil, Byrnes thought privately. But Charlie was Blade's ward, and had passed on information before. Trustworthy enough, which, considering Byrnes's trust in others only went so far, meant a lot.

"More fuckin' blue bloods," the dark-haired man said under his breath. "Like we don't already have enough in here."

"Kincaid," Gemma warned.

Ava stiffened, and Byrnes strolled toward the window, hands clasped behind him. "By the scent of oil and the whir of clockwork, I presume you're a mech."

The word had once been an insult, before the Uprising of 1880. Humans had been considered cattle, useful only for their blood, and mechs—those with mechanical limbs or clockwork organs—even less. Once, there had been a line in the sand: blue bloods versus humans and mechs. Taxes to be paid in blood. Mechs to be imprisoned in the enclaves, where they worked metal to repay the gift of their clockwork organs or mechanical limbs.

Times had changed, or at least, they were changing. Old hatreds, however, still lingered.

"Aye, I'm a mech. What of it?" Kincaid asked, in a low, threatening tone as he found his feet. Byrnes had an inch on the bastard, but Kincaid more than made up for that in breadth. Muscle rippled beneath his coat and bulged as the brute flexed his forearms.

Byrnes simply clasped his hands behind him and stared back. Ava would no doubt tell him later that he was causing trouble, but sometimes he simply couldn't help himself. "Nothing really. It explains a great deal." Then he turned away and ran his fingertips over the shelves, as though dismissing the man.

"Aye, well—"

"Mr. Kincaid," Gemma mocked. "Pray don't tell me that blue bloods make you uneasy."

Kincaid's voice flattened. "Not really. They tend to bleed just as well as any other, only takes a bit more sticking to finish the job."

"Gentlemen," Ava said firmly. When he looked at her, she arched a brow behind her steel-rimmed spectacles. "Byrnes." This was said somewhat more warmly, with just a touch of exasperation.

He held his arms out, as if to say, *what?*

"Well, don't you all wonder why we're here?" Ava asked, including them all in her look. "I don't think picking fights with each other is conducive to anyone's cause."

"But hardly unexpected," Gemma declared, with a faint snort of amusement. "After all, what happens when you put four blue bloods and a mech in a room together?"

"That sounds like the beginning of a good joke," Charlie Todd declared.

"I just hope it's not on us." Ava sounded nervous.

"Only thing is, we're missing one particular species, if we want it to have a truly decent punch line," Gemma replied.

"A verwulfen?" Charlie said with a grin.

The only one who didn't find that thought amusing was Byrnes. His gut dropped through his boots at the word. *No.*

"Let us hope not," Gemma said. "We already have one hothead."

It continued, but Byrnes's attention had been caught by something else. He could hear footsteps padding behind the closed doors at the far corner of the room, and a slither of shadow darkened the door briefly, softening the air with scent.

Lilies.

And something else... something that was becoming clearer as the day continued, as if the overpowering scent of perfume was wearing away, leaving a musky hint of something else. Something... all woman.

No. Hell, no.

Every nerve in his body grew tight. Byrnes stalked toward the door on silent feet, pressing his fingertips against the paneling.

"Fuck me," Kincaid muttered.

From Ava, "Well, it stands to reason. Verwulfen were cleared by the treaty too, you know—"

"And what would we need one of them for? It's not like this is a frigging alliance of any sort—"

Every one of Byrnes's hunting senses was alight. His mystery was beginning to clear up, and it was drawing a conclusion that he didn't particularly like. Not at all.

A light, husky laugh mocked him through the door, and then movement danced in the room beyond. Going. His prey was going.

Byrnes slipped through the doors before he could think about it.

There was no one there. Only another door, swinging shut slowly, and her scent, becoming obnoxiously clearer the closer he got to her. He knew that scent hiding beneath the perfume. It had driven him crazy a year ago, when someone—the Nighthawks' guild master—had this smashing idea about pairing him with an outside bounty hunter on a case nobody could seem to solve. His bloody case. The case *he* couldn't solve.

"Just work with her, Byrnes. She's good at what she does, and she's an even better tracker than you are." Garrett's voice echoed in his memory.

Byrnes grit his teeth. Garrett had known he worked better alone. He always had, and it got on every one of his last nerves to know that not only could he *not* find the answer in this particular case, but that they expected that *she* would.

They'd lasted an entire day working together.

And then it became a competition.

"Bet I catch the killer first," that husky voice whispered in his mind.

"I bet you I do," he'd shot back, and stepped toward her, into her space. "And when I do, you're going to get down on your knees and—"

"And?" she'd drawled, straightening a little, her eyes lighting with a challenging fire.

It changed what he'd meant to say. "And kiss my boots" had been his intention. That was not what had come out. The instant he'd stated his intentions she'd taken a step toward him, closing that last inch between them, and reached up to whisper in his ear.

"Be careful what you wish for, Byrnes." A mocking finger traced over his shirt so lightly he barely felt it, yet the not-quite touch sent a shiver through him, and their eyes had met then, as something more than words had been exchanged. "I don't think you'll want my teeth anywhere near your balls." A smile that gripped his cock like a vise. "Not that that will ever happen, but it does add a certain little incentive toward the case. When I bring this bastard in, I have my own terms, and you'll meet them."

"Name them." The shock of his sudden interest had flared through him, and he'd caught her wrist, stopping her hand just above the waistband of his leather breeches.

"If I solve the case, then I get to tie you to my bed, and do anything I desire to you. Anything at all."

A mistake. He should have made her be more specific, but just at that moment she'd flexed her wrist in his grasp and raked her fingernail over the leather protecting his cock.

"Done," he'd said. After all, he'd never lost before.

If there was one person who could get into his room at the guild and leave that taunting note, knowing just knowing how much it would get his itch going, it was her.

The devil in disguise.

Pushing open the doors to the next room, he came to a halt. It too was empty.

And then someone spoke. Someone he knew all too well.

"Looking for something? Or is it someone?" said an amused voice from the side.

Her.

Byrnes met a pair of eyes that were lit from within with a bronze glow. She hadn't changed one inch from that debacle last year, where he'd been left tied to his bed, naked, with a lovely little message written across his chest in ink, which all of his fellow Nighthawks had found absolutely hilarious.

"Ingrid," he said.

"Did you miss me?"

CHAPTER TWO

"MISS YOU?" Byrnes stated flatly, though the gleam in his blue eyes wasn't cold. Not at all. He took a menacing step toward her before pausing, his lean form falling into absolute stillness.

Ingrid Miller smiled. She'd worked with Byrnes for only two weeks—or worked against him, perhaps, when he'd declared that he didn't need her and could find the suspect before she could—but in that time she'd come to know him well enough to predict him.

He hated emotional displays, especially in himself. His control was absolute. And she'd just caused him to break both of those self-governed rules.

Call it the devil on her shoulder, but when it came to Byrnes, she absolutely could not help herself.

"Miss you?" he repeated. "Why yes... I believe I did. I have a little debt to repay."

"A *little* debt?" Ingrid glanced at him from beneath her lashes in a most un-Ingrid-like way. "What a curious choice of words."

Instantly his gaze flattened, and she laughed.

"I searched for you," he said stiffly.

"Did you?"

"I spent months looking for you."

"You wouldn't have found me, no matter how much time you spent looking for me." *You wouldn't have found me, because I wasn't here.* Not that her quest to Norway had been successful, even with all of the lovely bounty money she'd earned by bringing in the so-called Vampire of Drury Lane all by herself. The humor drained out of her, but she managed to keep her smile on her face.

Some mysteries took time.

She certainly wasn't giving up on this one. And now Ingrid had received this offer, with more money on the table, should her work prove satisfactory to the Duke of Malloryn. More money meant more informants she could pay, more searchers she could employ. She'd find the family she'd been stolen from all those years ago. One day.

She just had to be patient.

"Where did you go after the Drury Lane case? You weren't in London. You weren't in any of the towns nearby. You weren't even in bloody Scotland!"

"That's not really any of your business."

"Oh, I think it is." Byrnes was in her space. They were of a height, especially with her in her heeled boots, but she never felt unfeminine around him, the way she sometimes felt with other men. Byrnes always challenged her to be an equal, and that look in his eye had always made her feel distinctly feminine.

"You left me naked and bound to my bed. I've been thinking about what I'd do to you to repay the debt for the last year." His voice dropped. "Oh, and Ingrid, I've had time to get very creative about it."

"Poor Caleb. It sounds like I got to you."

He *hated* it when she called him Caleb. His teeth ground together, and he reached out to cup her cheek. One thumb brushed against her cheek, then lower, to her mouth, sinking into her plush lower lip and pressing just firmly enough to rouse a fire in her blood. Byrnes leaned closer. "That happens when a woman makes certain promises, and then reneges upon them."

"I promised to get you naked," she whispered around the press of his thumb. "You were naked, if I recall. We never agreed upon anything else."

"You wrote on me."

"It was a lovely little poem. There was a young Nighthawk from Matlock; Who had a fairly significant—"

"I remember," he growled under his breath, blue eyes alighting with fury and desire.

Ingrid's smile deepened. "I'm certain you do."

I am going to repay this debt tenfold, his eyes seemed to say.

You can certainly try, replied her smile.

That made his eyes narrow.

"Miss me, Byrnes?" she murmured, her voice dropping to a whisper as her body softened toward his. The devil always had this effect upon her. "It certainly sounds like it."

"Only because I mean revenge, Miller."

Miller. God knew she'd missed that, strangely enough. Ingrid's smile softened and she bit the thumb that still lingered on her lip. The heat in his gaze turned intense, and he sucked in a sharp breath.

"Admit it," she said, sucking his thumb gently. One of her hands curled in the lapel of his coat as she drew free of his hand. "It was more than revenge."

The look on his face told her everything. *Everything.*

A part of her wanted to grab a fistful of his hair and yank his mouth down to hers. The second she did, they'd be upon each other, Byrnes slamming her back into the wall, and Ingrid lifting her legs to wrap around his lean waist.

She knew it, because that's precisely what had happened the one time she'd dared to kiss him. The vision sent a shiver of need straight through her, as if she could remember every second of that moment, every self-destructive instinct that had driven her to throw herself into the abyss of desire.

No, their interest in each other had never been the problem. It was the fact that she couldn't trust him.

Ingrid stepped back, crossing her arms over her chest. Sometimes she was tempted to reach out and touch, but the warier part of her knew it would get burned when it came to Byrnes. Far easier to keep him at arm's length and pretend this was merely desire between them.

"One day, Miller," he said, noting the way in which she'd disengaged, "One day you're going to pay your dues—"

"But until then," a male voice said behind them, "would it be at all possible for the pair of you to join us?"

They staggered apart with a start of surprise. The Duke of Malloryn stood in the doorway, both hands holding the doors wide open, and from the look on Byrnes's face she hadn't been the only one taken unawares.

Which was almost unforgivable, considering the two of them had the greatest hunting senses of anyone in the house.

"Of course." Ingrid recovered smoothly. "After you, your Grace."

Malloryn's icy gaze raked over the pair of them, "This had better not become a problem."

"Of course not," Ingrid replied.

"Because if it does…." Malloryn didn't need to add anything else as he turned to head back to the library.

And she needed this job too much to disobey.

"Revenge is going to be very sweet," Byrnes whispered in her ear as he brushed past.

She followed him, feeling that little thrill tingling through her blood, unable to stop herself from whispering, "Just remember: two can play at that game."

Malloryn shot them both a cool glance as they entered the library, but Ingrid merely smiled and took a seat next to a young woman with blond curls, who looked at Byrnes, and then at her with a slightly shocked expression.

"Ladies," Malloryn called, taking the center of the room. "Gentlemen. May we begin?"

"As you all know," Malloryn said, standing with easy authority by the wall, "three years ago the prince consort was overthrown by his queen and society went through quite an upheaval. Humans and mechs had their rights restored"—this with a tip of the head to the burly Kincaid—"and Echelon society was changed forever."

"Aye," said Kincaid. "Bluebirds fuckin' sang, and everybody lived happily ever after. 'Til the Packenham Riots, and the burnings in Manchester, and the disappearances in Begby Square."

Malloryn smiled. It wasn't friendly at all. "Like I said, everything has changed. Some changes have been well received. Some have not. The queen and the ruling Council of Dukes would like to think that Britain is on its way to greatness but others seem not to hold that same opinion. That's why this team has been called together.

"Someone in particular means to cause trouble for the monarchy and they're using the populace to do so. The Packenham Riots weren't just circumstance. Someone murdered that poor young mech and before her blood had even cooled, there were pamphlets being circulated in the streets, which makes me think it was planned. I want to get to the bottom of who is stirring trouble before another riot breaks loose. And that's where all of you come in."

"I had friends as died in the Packenham Riots," Kincaid said. "Why should I help you? Your Echelon used your Cyclops war machines to mow down half the mob that day."

"A mistake, in hindsight," Malloryn admitted. "And you're not helping *me*. I don't even particularly want you on this team. You're a hothead and I don't entirely trust you, but you came highly recommended by my friend the Duchess of Casavian, and I need someone with a particular skill set that's hard to find. You fit that description."

"And what's in it for me?" Kincaid demanded.

"For you? A comfortable wage and the help of one of my best inventors for that project you've been working upon," Malloryn replied. "Someone who has recently passed his Bio-mech examinations with the Royal Mechanics Society."

Kincaid reeled back as if struck and Byrnes sipped his blud-wein. Bio-mechanics dealt directly with the application of mechanical limbs and organs that were fused directly to a man or woman's flesh as if they were one. Oh, there were cruder mech limbs in circulation, but only those within the Royal Society knew how to deal with the process called fusion.

Which meant that Kincaid needed some sort of limb or organ that crude mechwork couldn't cover, and was shocked to realize that Malloryn knew of it. For himself though? Or someone he knew?

Bio-mech was ridiculously expensive. If Malloryn could gift that so negligently, then what else could he offer the rest of them?

Byrnes's heart raced. Bio-mech, medical technology… was there an answer for his mother's fate? "And the rest of us? What can you do for us?"

"You all have something you want and I have the means to provide it. But we can discuss that later. In private." Malloryn gestured to the mysterious woman at his side, the one in blood red silk. "This is my colleague, Isabella Rouchard, the Baroness Schröder. She will be in charge of this team."

Charlie Todd stuck his hand in the air. "Arguments aside… what team? Why precisely are we here? To find the instigators of the riots? That was over a year ago."

Isabella Rouchard leaned on the back of her chair, every inch of her thick black hair tamed into an elegant chignon. "The queen has tasked Malloryn with putting together a team of highly skilled participants to discover who is behind these incidents that threaten national security. We have… information networks, but we need more. We need people who can deal with and contain threats, and are equipped to both delve directly to the heart of a mystery, and then handle it."

"Why would you choose us?" Kincaid asked.

Malloryn shuffled some files on his desk. "Don't assume that you haven't been thoroughly vetted. All of you came recommended to me by various members of the Council of Dukes who rule this city. I have spies—I don't need more of them. But what I don't have," he said, picking up the files and gesturing toward Byrnes, "is someone trained to investigate." One of the files hit the desk and that gaze turned to Ingrid. "Someone who works private commissions to find what others can't find and has ties to the verwulfen community; someone who understands the mech world,"—this at Kincaid— "someone who knows the rookeries and how to steal the eyes from a man's sockets." Charlie Todd. "An inventor trained in detailing crime scene investigations." Ava. His hard blue gaze turned to Miss Townsend. "And—"

"Someone you swore you'd never work with again," Gemma Townsend said softly, her challenging gaze locked on Malloryn's.

There was a moment's pause as the two of them stared at each other.

"Someone experienced in the arts of espionage," Malloryn corrected emotionlessly, dropping the final file onto the desk.

Miss Townsend looked away, as if there was far more to it than that.

Interesting.

"There are others who have already been briefed on the situation," Malloryn said. "In my absence the baroness will be the leader of this group and you will report directly to her. Jack Fairchild is our resident inventor, whom Miss McLaren will be working with, and Herbert will handle… security. Anything else?"

Every single hand in the room went up, but Malloryn ignored them as he circled the room and gestured to the baroness. "If you would, Isabella. It's easier if I show them."

The baroness wheeled a screen into place and Malloryn flicked a switch on the projector at the back of the room.

Byrnes leaned forward in his chair as a photograph appeared: a street, middle class by the look of it, with abandoned handcarts and steam cabs sitting under a line of washing. He recognized the place immediately and that old thrill tickled through his veins. Begby Square. An unsolved case. There was nothing more interesting than a riddle that remained unsolved.

That alone might convince him to go along with this.

"The Packenham riots were just the beginning. In March, an entire street of people vanished near Begby Square. Despite Nighthawk assistance not a single person has been recovered out of fifty-three. Nobody knows where the Begby Square people are, or what happened to them. In most of the houses dishes lay covered with half-eaten dinners, and washing was hung to dry as though it were a normal day. Only a single baby remained behind, crying in his crib. No blood, minimal signs of violence such as scattered dishes, and no tracks or scent trail. It all happened within the space of two hours, just as evening fell on March sixteenth."

Malloryn flicked the slide. A sandy arena sprang to view, spattered with blackened shadows of blood and covered in bodies. "The Devil's Pit, beneath the Barking Dog Tavern on the outskirts of Whitechapel. The entire crowd was slaughtered, and most of the combatants. Nobody knows who did it, but the doors were locked from the outside. Considering the location we left the scene to Blade, the Devil of Whitechapel, to solve. So far, he's got nothing. No scent, no tracks, just slaughter."

Byrnes's interest sharpened. He'd heard nothing of this, but that was not unusual. The Devil of Whitechapel was a force of his own, and had been part of the consortium that overthrew the prince consort during the revolution. He policed his own territories with his gang of ruffians, and Nighthawks were rarely invited in. Charlie

Todd, however, didn't look surprised, and he was one of Blade's lieutenants.

Something caught his attention as Malloryn flicked through several slides from the fighting pits. "Wait a minute," Byrnes called. "Go back to that previous slide. *There.*" He pointed. "That black flag painted on the wall, with the letters above it... that symbol was on the walls at Begby Square."

"Very good. So it was." Malloryn pressed the slides forward. More images, more chaos. "The same symbol appears on the nearby walls at the St. Andrew's Church in Holborn, where the local congregation was attempting to rebuild the church now that the laws against humans practicing religion have been relaxed." A photograph showed a man crucified outside the burning church. "The newly ordained priest, Joseph Cannon. Or should I say, the late Reverend Joseph Cannon. The symbol also appeared at the abandoned King Street enclaves last month, where fourteen mechs lay crushed in the machinery. All of them had worked there in the past, and there was no reason for them to be there once the project was abandoned."

"Four incidents in London," Byrnes mused.

"That we know of," Malloryn hastily corrected. "Since March this year."

"Traditionally, a black flag has been a symbol of anarchy," Ingrid said with a frown. "What do the letters painted above them say?"

Malloryn flicked hastily through the slides until he showed a closer view of the symbol. "Sometimes it reads SOG. Sometimes it is simply the number zero. At the enclaves, it was a numeral three."

"Which means?" Ingrid asked.

Malloryn leaned back, crossing his arms over his chest. "That's what I am interested in discovering. People are growing scared and there is a rumor on the streets that the queen's new rule isn't so different to the prince consort's. All of the progress that the queen and the Council of Dukes have made in the past three years to improve the city and create peace between the factions and species has been obliterated."

"No scent," Kincaid said. "Slaughter... that sounds like a blue blood to me. Any of your pasty-faced lords unaccounted for?"

"No member of the Echelon did this—"

"How do you know it's not a member of the Echelon?" Kincaid demanded.

"Because information is currency, and I'm the type of person who is extremely rich in information. No one blue blood *could* do this.

"Every time the queen and the Council of Dukes make a proclamation—such as the reformation of the Anti-Religious Act—someone goes out and wreaks havoc against the very thing that we are trying to improve. I've seen broadsheets stating that the queen rules that people can gather at houses of worship again, then goes and slaughters the lot of them, just to prove that they can't. People are scared," Malloryn said, resting his hip on the edge of his desk. "And when people become scared, trouble starts to occur.

"I need to know who is doing this and my traditional network isn't coming up with answers. In short order, that's why you're all sitting here. You have been invited to form a company of elite agents to protect the queen and the people of the city. Are you in?"

"What if we're not?" Kincaid's voice roughened.

"I'm fairly certain that Jem Whitlow was your cousin, was he not?" Malloryn lifted a folder from his desk and flipped through it, though Byrnes was fairly certain that

Malloryn had the information memorized. "Whitlow spent eleven years in the King Street enclaves before helping you march on the Ivory Tower to cast the prince consort down. Imagine that... eleven years in hell, then three blissful years of freedom before someone crushes him beneath a manufacturing machine—"

"I know what eleven years of hell in the enclaves feel like," Kincaid snapped. "I don't have to imagine it."

"Don't you want to find out who killed him?" Malloryn arched a brow.

Silence. The entire group focused on the burly mech.

"The enclaves are mine," Kincaid finally said, his jaw jutting pugnaciously. "I get to hunt the bastards as did this."

"Done." Malloryn gave no sign of satisfaction other than a slight heaviness around his eyelids. "Everybody else?"

"Aye," both Byrnes and Ingrid said at the same time. They shot each other a sharp look as the others echoed them.

"What do we call ourselves?" Charlie called.

"Malloryn's Henchmen?" This from Gemma.

"The Merry Men—and Women," Charlie Todd countered.

"Malloryn's Misfits?" suggested Gemma again.

Malloryn did not quite roll his eyes. "I'm sure you'll all think of something." Grabbing a stack of files, he and Isabella began handing them out to people. "Byrnes, I know you're familiar with the Begby case. I want you back on it."

Byrnes stared hungrily at the images on the screen, the bloody and broken bodies in the enclaves. Then he sighed. "It's a cold scene, sir. Seven months cold, to be precise."

"True." Malloryn's eyes glittered. "But *these* disappearances aren't. Same type of scene, same kind of mayhem. Happened last night." Sliding a folder across the table toward Byrnes, he straightened. "We move fast, we keep it quiet, and we stop whoever is doing this before the general public finds out about it."

Byrnes dragged the file toward him with his fingertips. A case, one that nobody had been able to solve last time. Intriguing.

Byrnes lifted the edge of the folder as Malloryn muttered something.

"Hell, no," Ingrid stated flatly.

That made him look up. He'd missed something.

"You brought down the Vampire of Drury Lane," Malloryn replied. "Your expertise is exceedingly valuable, and you and Byrnes should make one hell of a team."

Team. Everything in him went on point. Like bloody hell. This was his case. His—

"I would rather spend the rest of my days knitting," Ingrid stated, crossing her arms. "There's no way I'll work with Byrnes."

Byrnes slowly tilted his head to look at her. That stubborn mouth was set in a line he remembered only too clearly and suddenly his brain kicked into gear. A flash of memory cut through his emotions: of himself lying naked on his bed, finally forced to concede and yell for help once he realized he couldn't get free of the silk stockings binding him to the bed. "Sounds like an excellent idea," he found himself saying, and suddenly he was the recipient of every stare in the room.

"It— What—?" Ingrid demanded. "Are you mad? Or drunk? We very nearly killed each other last time."

"Think about it, Ingrid. My experience, my skills at deduction married with your strength, and your skills at tracking, so much better than mine," Byrnes said, watching her eyes narrow as he laid it on thick. *Oh yes, my dear. Now you're catching on.* "Who else could handle such a case?"

"Anybody in this room."

"What's wrong?" Byrnes taunted, letting silence fill the gap, until the moment had stretched out long enough. "Scared?"

Ingrid's almond-shaped eyes narrowed to thin slits. They really were beautiful, though at the moment, they were practically incinerating. "Of you? I don't think so."

"Excellent," Malloryn interceded. "Consider yourself enlisted, ladies and gentlemen. You're now protectors of the realm. I'll give the rest of you your own assignments the second these two stop arguing with each other, and then I need some eyes on the ground at the Venetian Gardens scene. Understood?"

CHAPTER THREE

LIGHTS FLOODED THE Venetian Gardens, a dirigible flooding the scene with sweeping light as it hovered over the walled pleasure gardens. It was one of the latest improvements to the Nighthawks' ability to fight crime, but Byrnes personally thought it a waste of taxpayers' money. He much preferred an on-foot hunt with the scent of a criminal in his nostrils, and pavement under his feet.

Reporters hovered like vultures, the flashbulbs of their cameras hammering his retinas as he tipped his head to the pair of Nighthawks on duty at the gates. "Brasham, Copeland. What have we got?"

"Not sure, Byrnes," Copeland said with a scowl. "The bloody Duke of Malloryn won't let us in, so we've been set to nursemaid the gates until his 'elite' unit arrives."

Byrnes eyed the reporters. "Someone seems to think this is a major case. Have you heard anything?"

"Thirty or forty people vanished from the Grand Pavilion"—Brasham clicked his fingers—"like smoke. The Earl of Carrington was hosting some sort of party there. When sunrise started to come up, the manager of the gardens realized that his blue blood guests ought to be departing soon if they were going to beat the sun home, so he opened the door and... nothing. Apparently."

"An earl." That was going to be bothersome. The aristocratic Echelon might no longer be in charge of the city, but they could make things difficult if they wished to. "No wonder the *London Standard* is haunting us."

"I thought it might have been your pretty eyes they were captivated with," Ingrid said, appearing at his side with little fanfare. "Are we going in or not?"

Copeland's eyes widened as he took her in, bearing all the hallmarks of masculine appreciation. "Ma'am. Unfortunately we've got orders to—"

"Keep the scene's integrity preserved," Ingrid finished, practically batting her eyelashes at the man. "Until Malloryn's unit gets here."

"Ah, yes, ma'am." Copeland's stance softened, a smile flickering over his mouth.

Byrnes bared his teeth. It might have passed for a smile. He hoped. "Well, I think we're the elite unit you're waiting for." Tugging a sealed letter from his waistcoat pocket, he shoved it in Copeland's face before the bloody idiot could fall at Ingrid's feet in worship.

"What have you gotten yourself into, Byrnes?" Brasham asked, taking the letter off a flummoxed Copeland and examining it.

He smiled. "Trouble, hopefully."

"Only you would say such a thing." Brasham shook his head. "Through you go."

Grabbing Ingrid's hand, Byrnes tucked it in the crook of his arm and escorted her through. Ava and Charlie followed, Ava lugging her precious carpetbag along with her.

"Keep your mind on the job," he told Ingrid as the gates shut behind them. "Copeland doesn't deserve your games."

That earned him an arched brow. "Who said they were games? He has pretty eyes. And *you're* the one that insisted that I play your partner. If you cannot handle it, Byrnes, then do be a dear and speak up."

He was going to throttle her. Slowly. Or maybe kiss her. He hadn't quite decided.

"This way." Ingrid swept under his arm and headed across the grass, shooting him a knowing glance as she went. "Some of us want to see the scene of the crime."

The Venetian Gardens had been crafted for pleasure. Both upper and lower classes could buy their ticket in, and there were often fireworks, acrobatic shows, and pavilions where parties could be hosted. Broad canals crisscrossed the sprawling gardens and white lacquered gondolas sat in a row at the boarding docks, bobbing up and down in the breeze as they waited for night to fall and passengers to come.

"Which way is the Grand Pavilion?" Byrnes asked.

"You've never been to the Venetian Gardens?" Charlie Todd seemed surprised.

"Not really my sort of affair," Byrnes replied.

"He's more interested in gambling dens than in garden parties," Ava added, with a *tsk* of disapproval under her breath.

"Oh, but this place is so much more than that. This way," Charlie called, heading toward a huge pavilion that was circled by Georgian pillars. It dominated the grassy space, and French doors opened on all sides to reveal the room within.

"Anyone approaching the pavilion should have been seen," Byrnes noted.

"It was dark," Charlie replied, raking the roofline. He pointed. "If I were going to enter unseen, I'd use those trees for cover, then climb them to get to the roof."

"That doesn't negate the fact that the grass surrounding it provides inadequate coverage," Byrnes shot back. Bad enough working with Ingrid, let alone all three of them.

"Let me look inside," Charlie replied. "There's got to be a way that someone got in and out—with all the guests—without being seen by the staff."

"If Carrington was an earl, then there's high chance he was a blue blood," Byrnes said, looking around. Not every single member of the Echelon had been infected with the craving virus that had once been considered an elite privilege, but most of the upper nobility were. Or the males, at least. Females were considered too prone to hysteria and overruling passions to be able to control themselves should they suffer from the bloodlust. Accidents happened, of course, and there were both rogue blue bloods like himself, whose existence hadn't been sanctioned, and a handful of female blue bloods.

"He *was* a blue blood," Ava said, flipping through her notes. "It was in the earlier report at Malloryn's."

A man fidgeted by the entrance to the pavilion, his stained fingers holding a half-smoked cigarette, though his glazed eyes stared at nothing.

Byrnes held out his hand. "Caleb Byrnes, Nighthawk."

"Silas Compton," the fellow greeted, "I'm the manager of the Venetian Gardens."

"We'll leave you to it," Ingrid murmured, taking Charlie and Ava inside with her.

Byrnes watched them go. "You're the one who found the earl and his guests missing?"

"Aye." Compton ground his cigarette out among the stubby corpses of several other half-finished blunts. Though his clothes were distinctly upper class, his hair was rumpled and signs of disorder streaked through, with his crooked tie and an inch of shirt that hung loose at his waist.

Clearly bothered by the ordeal.

Byrnes flipped open his notebook, filing that away for future notice. "Do we know how many guests were in attendance?"

"Got the register from the gates," Compton announced. "Thirty-two of them remained at this late hour, sir. Including the Earl. Plus there were eight attendants from the Venetian Gardens, taking away the food platters and the glasses."

"So forty people are missing altogether?" Byrnes glanced up from the notes he was writing. "Sounds like a small private party for an earl."

"Birthday party, by all accounts. Carrington's pockets are shallow, according to gossip." Compton shrugged. "Been hit hard by the Revolution and the new laws."

"I would have thought the Pavilion to be expensive to hire."

"It is. Not as bad as some, but appearances have to be kept, sir."

"So Carrington was trying to balance the party between affordable, but stylish enough to pretend he didn't care about that sort of thing. Minimal guests, not a lot of food and drinks, that sort of thing?"

"Aye."

Byrnes looked around. "You saw nothing?"

"Nothing out of the ordinary," Compton replied. "And I've been racking my brain, sir. The doors were open and guests trickled out to watch the fireworks, then they went back inside. By the time I came around to alert everyone to dawn's imminent arrival, the doors were locked and nobody was there. Nothing but... a trace amount of blood, though that could have been from their own private flasks. The only person I saw leave was a beautiful woman who exited the party ten minutes before I came. I only noticed her because I was overseeing the arrival of crates of blud-wein at the time."

"Can you describe her?"

"Dressed in white, I think. Pale hair. Blonde, perhaps? I didn't take much notice, sorry sir. We were running short of blud-wein, so I was attempting to sort out that mess."

"And you didn't hear anything?" Byrnes paused with his pen pressed against his notebook.

"Nothing, but then that might have been the fireworks. There was also another party over the eastern side, and the gondolas were busy with other guests."

Byrnes assessed his notes. "If you think of anything else, let me know," he said, handing the fellow his card.

Then he was free to enter the pavilion.

The room was eerily silent. A table by the wall held a row of champagne glasses stacked in a pyramid, and champagne lay flatly in the glasses. Ice buckets still held half-drunk bottles of blud-wein, judging by the coppery scent of it. There'd been an automaton orchestra in the corner, but they'd long since wound down, the automata caught in frozen tableaux over their instruments. Their glass eyes made him shudder. They alone might have been witness to whatever had happened in here, but nobody would ever know what they'd seen.

"Over here, Byrnes," Ava called.

The three of them were gathered in the northern corner. Someone had painted a bloody "0" on the gauzy curtains that surrounded the room. There were several blood spatters on the marble floors, but no other signs of a skirmish.

"Do you think that's some kind of symbol of ownership?" Ingrid asked, staring at it.

"Possibly." Every now and then he and the Nighthawks worked a case that was clearly committed by the same person. They all tended to have their signature tricks. Byrnes frowned, running his finger through the blood and then rubbing his fingers together. "It's tacky in some areas, but mostly dry."

"Not fresh then," Charlie said, his nostrils flaring and his eyes darkening to a bottomless black before he turned away from the curtains and forced the *hunger* back down.

The *hunger* had never overruled him before, but Byrnes knew that other blue bloods sometimes struggled with its grip. "Is it going to be a problem?" he asked quietly, and Charlie shot him a sideways look before shaking it off.

"No time for dinner this morning," he muttered, his hand delving inside his pocket for a flask of blood. "That's all."

"So we have forty people who are missing," Byrnes commented, looking around. "And an empty room, with minimum signs of a struggle. How did forty people just vanish? That's what we need to know."

"Through the roof?" Ingrid suggested dubiously.

"People would have seen them leaving," he pointed out, then looked around.

"Underground. It had to be through a tunnel. Perhaps there's an entrance to Undertown here," Charlie suggested.

"Perhaps." Byrnes shoved a table out of the way. Nothing beneath it. "Undertown was formed where the Eastern link of the Underground project collapsed. That's a long way from here."

Charlie grinned at him. "You think like a Nighthawk, Byrnes. I'm a thief from Whitechapel. There's not a section of London that's inaccessible from below. There are tunnels, sewers, underground rivers, old plague pits... It's an entire world down there."

"How do you think we ran the revolution?" Ingrid snorted, shoving aside a rug.

And he was forced to remember that she'd once been a humanist, one of the founding members of the revolution that tore the prince consort from his throne.

"I'll leave you to it," Ava said, scraping some sort of residue into a small glass vial that she had tugged from her carpetbag. "My place is not scampering through tunnels. I'll try and work out what this smoky residue is. It's dirtied the floor in areas."

The three of them crawled across the room, shoving chairs and tables out of the way and peeling back rugs. Byrnes used his knife to feel around the edges of the large floor tiles, keeping an eye on the other two.

"Got anything?" Byrnes called, watching as the lad paced a rug on the floors, sniffing at the air.

Charlie flipped the rug out of the way, his face lighting up. "This tile is loose! I can smell blood."

Byrnes crossed to his side and used his knife to feel the edges of the tile. It wiggled upwards. Clearly loose. "It's moving!"

Charlie slipped his fingers under the edge of the tile as Byrnes pried it clear of the floor, and together they eased it aside. Beneath it was a grate.

Hauling the grate out of the stone, Charlie set it aside with a ringing sound, wincing. "It's heavy."

"Which means our perpetrator is either supernaturally strong, or they used a mechanical contraption to shift it," Ingrid said.

"And someone stayed behind to ease the rug over the grate again." Byrnes considered what Compton had told him. "Actually, Compton said a beautiful woman left the party nearly ten minutes before he discovered the missing persons. She might have replaced the rug. I'll check the guest list to see how many women were on it."

Charlie knelt beside the grate, peering into the darkness. "The scent of blood's clearer here."

Fine. "Ladies first." Byrnes gestured.

Ingrid lowered herself through the manhole and vanished with a splash. One of the things he admired most about her was her willingness to do what needed to be done in the pursuit of a killer. She hadn't even flinched at the scent wafting up out of the tunnel, and her knee-high boots and leather breeches meant she was dressed for the occasion.

"Youth before age," Charlie said with a wink, and disappeared after her.

"You all right here, Ava?" Byrnes called.

"Fine." She waved a hand, absorbed in some kind of chemical test she was performing.

Byrnes stepped through the open grate and landed in a splash of water. The predator inside him reared its head, his vision cutting through a dozen colors, and ending up in shades of black and gray as it intensified.

Some blue bloods had trouble dealing with the other side of the craving virus: the darkness, the hunger. Instead of trying to control his darker side, Byrnes had learned to use it to hunt, and thus assuage the urge to kill. If he glutted his predator half on the thrill of the chase, then most of the time it left him alone.

Just one problem now: he wasn't focusing on blood, or the scent of whoever had done this... No, all he could smell were lilies, and the heated musk of Ingrid's skin. His gaze locked on her, as though she were the prey.

Focus. Byrnes curled his fingers into fists and closed his eyes, forcing himself to hone in on the droplets of blood in the water. It was more difficult than he'd expected.

"I can smell several different perfumes," Ingrid announced, splashing forward through the gloom. She tripped on something and caught herself. "Appears to be some sort of... tracks... underneath. Rail tracks?"

"Not wide enough," Charlie replied, peering through the murky water. Enough light gleamed through grates set at varying intervals along the tunnel for them to be able to see. "Perhaps closer to what you get in a mine, or in Undertown, when you're using wheeled carriages to carry heavy objects."

"Whatever it is, it's under ten inches of water," Byrnes pointed out. "So it hasn't been used for a long time."

"Can you smell that?" Charlie asked, his nostrils wrinkling up, as they splashed along.

"All I'm getting is that perfume." Byrnes knew he was a good hunter, but the rookery lad just *might* own better senses than he did.

"Smells sweet," Ingrid murmured, her amber eyes a beacon in the dark.

"And kind of rancid," Charlie muttered.

They moved silently through the tunnels, just in case whoever had done this was still here.

"The scent of blood's getting stronger." Byrnes waded ahead, one hand on his knife, as he tracked the scent. "It's— Oh."

A woman floated facedown in the shallow pool of water. Above her, the grate allowed weak sunlight through it, highlighting the edges of her rose-colored silk gown. A gown that was stained and bloody.

Byrnes slowly rolled her over. Her abdomen was torn apart, like a feral dog had been at it, and so was her throat. Blood spooled through the water, heading in at least three different directions.

"Why did they kill her?" Byrnes gently levered the woman out of the water and onto a ledge.

"Looks like an animal attack," Charlie said. "Maybe."

"Whatever it was," Ingrid pointed out, gesturing to the fractured ribs, "it was strong. Blue blood?"

The throat was torn open, but a blue blood's feed was generally cleaner. Without sharp teeth, most blue blood lords preferred to use a thin razor to open the vein, and a chemical in their saliva caused the wound to clot enough to begin healing once they were finished. "Don't think so. No blue blood that I've ever seen anyway. They wouldn't have gone for the abdomen—tear the wrong organ, and it sours the blood. No, they'd have gone for throat, or thigh, or wrist, any of the major arteries."

"Even in the bloodlust?" she asked.

"Even then," he confirmed. "It's instinctual. Could a verwulfen have done this?"

Ingrid chewed her lip. "Yes. I don't know why they would though. If they were suffering from a fit of *berserkergang*, they'd have kept tearing their enemy apart, limb from limb. A gut wound like this is not a technique we'd usually employ." She knelt closer, examining the ragged edges. "These look like sharp teeth marks, like... fangs. And despite what the superstitious whisper, verwulfen don't change shape. Our hearts beat with the heart of the wolf, but our bodies always remain human."

"So we're looking for something with fangs," Byrnes mused, "which counts out a blue blood."

"Vampire?" Charlie whispered, and all of them stilled.

The hairs on the back on Byrnes's neck lifted, but a quick glance showed that they were alone. Just his body reacting to the word. Even so, he rubbed a hand across his nape, soothing the skin. "I hope not."

A vampire was rare; the final end stages of the craving virus finally overtaking a blue blood and turning him into something... else. Something wiry and maggot-pale and purely destructive. Ever since a rash of vampires had haunted the city in the 1700s, no blue blood was allowed to exist past a craving virus count of 80 percent. They were executed instead.

"If it was a vampire, they wouldn't have taken the people," Ingrid pointed out in a soft voice. Even she felt it. "We'd have walked into a bloodbath in the pavilion, and the trail of bloody wreckage would have been easy to follow. A vampire doesn't hide itself, or its acts. It's not smart enough to see past prey. It just kills."

"And it doesn't stop," Charlie whispered.

There was nothing more to see here. Byrnes scowled. "Let's follow the trail a little longer, then get the body back to Ava. She assists Dr. Gibson with the autopsies at the guild, so I'm certain she can give us more information. We need to know what killed this woman, and why."

Byrnes took the lead. Sometimes all he could go by was the splash of blood against the walls. At other times, it was the muddy stir of water. A great many people had either been carried or forced to march through here.

It took another half hour to realize what was slowing Ingrid's and Charlie's steps. Byrnes stood at the crossroads of four intersecting tunnels with his hands on his hips.

"They're long gone," he said, "and the water is washing the blood trail in other directions." His jaw hardened. "We've lost them."

"I don't like to agree," Ingrid replied cautiously, "but... I'm getting nothing. We might not even be following their trail anymore."

"What we do know," Charlie pointed out, "is that they used the sewer system to get in and out of the Venetian Gardens. This was a planned assault then, and they could have gone anywhere."

"How could forty people go missing?" Byrnes mused, noticing the warm presence that stepped up to his side.

"I don't know," Ingrid replied, sharing a sideways glance with him. A shared case—something to focus on—had taken most of the animosity out of her behavior.

And his, he had to admit. If he were being generous, Ingrid was an excellent person to work with—smart, hardworking, well skilled, and someone who didn't slow him down. "Especially when half of them had to be blue bloods. Not so easy to take down."

"Not so easy to take down," she agreed. "So how did they do it?"

CHAPTER FOUR

SINKING ONTO THE ottoman in Malloryn's library, Ingrid sighed. She should have been looking at the guest list, but she couldn't stop her hand from delving into her pocket, and unfurling the small telegram she had stashed there. Its edges were rumpled, thanks to extensive use ever since she'd received it three days ago.

Tracked down Bergen family. I'm sorry. Not your family. Don't have other leads. Request next directive? Cease looking? Detective Maddeslow.

Ingrid fingered the worn edges of the telegram. *Cease looking.* He might as well have cut out her heart. What could she do? This job for Malloryn would give her so much money, perhaps enough to complete her search, but how could she continue when she didn't even have a single idea of where to look?

When she'd first begun looking for the family whom she'd been stolen from, she'd had so much hope inside her. It was dulled now. Barely a glimmer. Too many years had passed since she'd been kidnapped by English raiders, in the snow near her Norwegian home. And she'd been four. Far too young to recall enough details to track them.

"Where are you?" she whispered, half to herself.

Looking up at the sound of footsteps, she shoved the telegram into her pocket, and only relaxed when Ava McLaren entered the room. The young woman's mess of blonde curls was gathered back into a neat chignon, and she wore a plain gown of grass green, with her laboratory apron over the top of it. Something ticked as Ava settled on the sofa across from her, and it was so quiet that Ingrid thought it a clock, or a pocket watch, except Ingrid had been studying the young woman today and could sense neither of those objects about her person.

"Well, I've found something," Ava said, tugging a small object from her apron pocket and tossing it in the air. It was a clockwork ball. "This was at the crime scene. It's a Doeppler orb, designed to release a pressurized gas once the timer releases the clockwork lock on the mechanism. They were first used in that blood frenzy case the Nighthawks investigated a few years ago. The gas drove several blue blood lords to commit terrible murders against their servants and families."

Ingrid knew the case. Several of the mechs who had worked with the humanists she'd run with had created the orb before going off on their own to mount a half-baked scheme against the ruling Echelon. Ingrid set the lists aside in interest. "Do you think that's what happened to that girl? Did a blue blood dip into the blood frenzy and tear her apart?"

"I'm not sure. It doesn't have the same chemical components as the blood frenzy gas, and it didn't affect me in that way. I've been speaking to your friend, Jack, down in the laboratory, and neither of us can identify the gas, but after I took a sniff, I had the most unusual sense of dizziness. It doesn't effect your friend Jack, and I think it has to do with the fact that he's human and I'm a blue blood."

"You actually smelled a gas that was notorious for driving blue bloods insane?"

"I took precautions," Ava replied.

"I should hope so." Ingrid slid closer, examining the orb. "So you think this was used to incapacitate the blue bloods? Somehow?"

"Possibly," Ava replied. "I only found one, so the kidnappers might have collected them following the assault."

"Which argues for quite a few people involved."

Ava's gaze grew distant. "This is quite a dilemma, isn't it? I knew the moment Malloryn was involved that we were facing something big, but it frightens me somewhat to think of how important this work could be."

Ingrid turned the clockwork ball over in her hand. The two halves had popped open, but when she pressed them together, they fit back neatly. "The general public don't know the particulars of the blood frenzy cases," she said, slowly. "Only the humanists who were involved, the mechs who stole the device, and the Nighthawks who investigated were aware of what this is, and how it was used."

Ava's gaze lifted to hers. "You think whoever is involved in this is someone that we know? Or who has some connection to the blood frenzy case?"

"It has to be someone who knew what a Doeppler orb could do." Ingrid turned her head on an angle, her thoughts scattering as the ticking became louder. "What *is* that ticking sound?"

Ava froze. "Ah, that's my heart."

"Heart?"

The young woman looked away in distress. "I have a clockwork heart, Miss Miller. Not by choice, however."

Sometimes Ingrid was perceptive enough to pick up on certain emotions, and the look on Ava's face told her not to press. "My apologies for bringing it up. And you may call me Ingrid. I'm not used to polite company, and 'Miss Miller' sounds like you're speaking to someone else."

"Oh?"

Ingrid smiled. "I've spent most of the last decade skulking in and out of back alleys and taverns, or in the tunnels of Undertown. I'm more at home with people cussing at me rather than playing polite."

Ava's expression softened. "Well, I've been with the Nighthawks for three and a half years, so I guess that I'm more accustomed to people cussing at me too."

"People?" Ingrid asked. "Or just Byrnes?"

Ava laughed and patted a hair into place. "Actually, he's the exception. He's terribly polite when it comes to me, though I've heard him speak when he thinks I'm not around."

A little fluttery feeling ignited in her chest. She couldn't quite describe it, but it had something to do with how polite Byrnes was to Ava. "Oh. That's... nice of him."

"I'll attempt the autopsy on that girl in a minute, so we should know more by this evening," Ava said, standing and heading for the door. "But Kincaid found something at the enclaves and wants me to have a look at it first." She stifled a yawn, and Ingrid realized that Ava, as a blue blood, would most likely be sleeping through the day if not for this mission.

"You're going to be pursuing the lab work here then?" Ingrid asked, following the other woman.

"It suits me. It's what I've been doing for the past three years at the guild, and I've never been very good in the field." Ava grimaced. "My heart has limited capacity for pumping blood, and I can exert myself only to a certain point, which makes field work out of the question."

Don't ask. Don't ask. Don't ask. She wanted to, however. She'd never heard of a clockwork heart. Most mechs had mechanical limbs, or other less complicated internal organs, like chest pumps instead of lungs. How could you keep someone alive whilst you installed a new mechanical heart inside them?

"Well, that sounds like an ideal pursuit for you," Ingrid said, swallowing the question down. "You'll most likely be spending some time with Jack then?"

"We've already begun working together. He's claimed the basement laboratory, but he's allowed me a small space."

"He would." This time Ingrid's smile was genuine. Jack was the older brother she'd never had. "Don't let him push you around. He'll use charm and smiles to get what he wants, but make no mistake, he's demanding." A thought occurred. "If you think that Jack's overdoing it... will you let me know?"

"You care for him?"

"He's part of the only family I've known," Ingrid admitted. Along with Rosa, the Duchess of Bleight, and young Jeremy, who'd set up as a candlemaker's apprentice. The three of them shared blood in truth, however, whilst she had merely been adopted into the fold when all four of them had escaped a madman.

"Oh." Ava glanced sideways at her and Ingrid realized she'd been sounding out how well Ingrid was involved with Jack.

"It's not like that," she hastily assured the blonde. "Jack's a brother, not... well, not like that." Nor was he likely to be interested in Ava, but Ingrid thought she'd best keep that to herself. "Do you know where Byrnes went?"

Another look. One that slammed through her like a punch as she realized precisely what it entailed. Oh, hell. It wasn't Jack whom Ava was interested in, after all. Ava had feelings for Byrnes, and was clearly aware of the... complex relationship between he and Ingrid.

But the pretty young woman merely smiled, an expression that didn't quite reach her eyes. "He's returned to the guild for the rest of the afternoon. Said something about examining the guild records from the blood frenzy case."

"You told him about the orbs?"

Ava rolled her eyes. "He was hovering in the laboratory. I didn't particularly have a choice."

"Byrnes thinks the orb might have something to do with the woman we found, doesn't he?" And he was following a lead without her. Ingrid's blood heated. This was supposed to be *their* case. Not just his. It was happening again.

Ava shrugged. "I personally disagree. A preliminary glance showed that you were correct. The woman's wounds were caused by fangs, of perhaps an inch in length. No blue blood has fangs." Consternation flickered over her heart-shaped face. "Though some do file their teeth into sharpened points. Still... The length is almost half an inch long, so it couldn't be a blue blood."

"Then we still have no idea what did this." Frustration burned through her. When she got her hands on him....

"No," Ava said with a sigh. "But we know what didn't."

Ingrid clunked down the stairs to the laboratory that was located in the cellars. She and her friend, Jack, had been called in three days ago to help Malloryn set up this network, and Jack had been poking around down there ever since.

Good God, if she'd known what Malloryn intended when she set out to deliver his invitations, she'd have balked. Last night as she lay in the dark in her bed staring at the ceiling, she'd finally accepted the fact that she would have to work with Byrnes in the company. She'd even told herself to buck up, because with half a dozen spies in the group, what were the chances that she'd have to spend much time with him?

She hadn't expected Malloryn to partner them together.

"Are you there, Jack?" she called, gathering her skirts as she thudded down the stairs. Jack was her lodestone, her emotional compass, and right now she was far too vexed to think straight. The typical verwulfen curse. Her kind were driven by their emotions and thrived in a state of fury, or even passion. It drove them, gave them their strength—but it could also prove crippling if one wasn't able to control it. Right now, she wanted to punch her fist through the wall, but that would only tear the skin on her knuckles and smash a brick or two into powder.

You are not ruled by the beast. You control it, not the other way around.

If she repeated it to herself enough, she might even start to believe it.

Boxes and crates crowded the benches, and Jack muttered under his breath as he limped through the darkness. "Down the end here! Give us a lift, will you?"

Ingrid grabbed the box he'd indicated and carried it toward him.

Jack turned, his breathing mask hanging loose under his chin. Evidently the air down here didn't affect his lungs too much, which was a good sign. It scared her when he suffered one of his attacks, and they'd been coming far too frequently for her liking of late.

He took one look at her eyes and started. "What is it? What's set you off?"

Her eyes were hot, and she knew that the amber irises were flaring a dramatic bronze with her mood. There was no point even trying to hide it, and Ingrid trusted Jack. Ingrid dumped the crate on the bench, growling under her breath. "Malloryn's given me a new partner."

"Oh?" Jack crossed his arms over his flamboyant waistcoat, though he moved slowly. Once, a long time ago, the man who'd put Ingrid in a cage had poured acid all over Jack's skin. Ingrid hadn't expected him to survive, not with all of those runnels and scarred pits in his flesh, but he had. Jack was a survivor, just like her. But the damage made him stiff, and ginger to the touch. "Anyone I know?"

"Caleb Byrnes."

Watching her in a sidelong fashion, Jack slid the crate lid open. "Not a name I'm familiar with."

Ingrid hadn't told him. She hadn't told anyone about what had happened a year ago, though Jack's sister Rosa had somehow found out about it. Most likely through her husband, Lynch, who used to be the guild master of the Nighthawks. "He's a Nighthawk."

"One of the new recruits, eh? You don't care for him?" Jack hefted a microscope, wincing under the strain.

Ingrid stepped forward quickly and lifted it easily out of its nest of straw.

"Thanks," Jack told her, red spots heating his cheeks. "So why does the Nighthawk bother you?"

Ingrid slid onto the bench and let her feet dangle. "I've met him before. We worked together last year during the Vampire of Drury Lane case."

"Ah."

"Ah?"

"I remember that case," he replied, wiping his hands on his pants. "You weren't at all yourself for nearly two weeks. I wondered what had set you off. Or more importantly, who."

"It's not the who, so much as the how. He makes me... so angry." Which wasn't quite the truth.

"Angry, or uncertain?"

Ingrid shot him a dark look. "Curse you. Both. I don't know what he makes me feel." Too small for her own skin, irritable, competitive... nervous.

"What does he look like?" Jack moved to pour her a brandy, which was her poison of choice.

"He's a little taller than I and ridiculously muscled." Or at least if her memory could be believed. "Lean, dangerous-looking, the type of blue eyes that can pin you on the spot and make you feel naked."

"Handsome?"

Incredibly so. "If one is interested in dark-haired men, then yes."

"Here's to handsome dark-haired men, then." Jack smiled, as he clinked his glass against hers.

Ingrid threw the brandy back. "There was... a bit of a moment between us last year."

"I'd guessed that. Do tell."

"We made a bet," she said, then filled him in on the details, including the fact that she'd left Byrnes tied to his bed. Naked.

Jack's eyebrows were both halfway to his hairline. "Good God. What were you thinking?" A laugh escaped him, then another. "Or were you?"

"It's not bloody funny," she said, which of course set him off laughing again. "I was quite prepared to enjoy what I'd started until he opened that fat mouth of his and said something along the lines of 'I knew I'd get you on your knees eventually,' and then of course I reacted badly." She groaned. "It was not my finest hour, but he... I... God, stop it, will you!"

Jack leaned against the bench, wiping his eyes. One last wheeze of laughter escaped him, then he tried to sober. "So what are you going to do?"

"I have to work with him, clearly," she said. "Whilst keeping him at arm's length. And that's if I don't kill him first. He's already headed off to follow his own leads."

"How vexing. Are you going to let him get away with it?"

"Absolutely not." She crossed her arms over her chest. "I am not going to let that man get under my skin ever again. I swear."

"You could just go to bed with him and burn this curiosity out of your blood, you know."

"What? Don't be ridiculous. And there is no 'curiosity.'" But her cheeks heated.

"Liar," Jack replied.

Ingrid lifted her head as noise rasped above them. "And that sounds like a saw. Ava must be starting the autopsy. I wanted to be there to see it."

"Just in case you learn some interesting little tidbit that might give you the head start on Byrnes?" Jack's smile was pure innocence.

"It's tempting, I agree. Then I remember there's a dead woman upstairs who will never get to return home to her family, and it reminds me that there are more important things to life than rivalry." Ingrid sighed as a woman's half-remembered face sprang to mind, a face that looked like hers. Sometimes she wondered if she were only imagining those bronze eyes and dark hair, or whether it truly was a memory. "What if this poor girl has children at home, Jack? Or a husband waiting for her?"

"You're thinking of your parents. You'll find them one day, Ingrid."

She merely shrugged. There'd been a letter the other day, telling her that her latest investigator's lead had turned to nothing. Again. Hope couldn't burn bright forever, but if she couldn't find her own parents, then at least she could bring the dead girl home to hers. "I have to find the people who did this so I can help lay that poor woman to rest. And if that means working with Byrnes, then I can lay aside my pride for the moment."

"Just be careful. If that woman was torn apart by some sort of animal, then you might be dealing with more than you can handle. You're not invincible, Ingrid, though you might be damned hard to kill."

Ingrid paused to brush a kiss across his cheek. "I love you too. But you can be an old fusspot at times."

Back at the guild, Byrnes finally collapsed into his sheets after a long fruitless search through the archives. The only comparison between the cases was the use of Doeppler orbs to dispel the gas, and the fact that people had died. Once again, if the killer had been a blue blood in a blood frenzy, then they wouldn't have stopped. There would have been more bodies, more blood.

Not a trail that vanished.

His lead had shriveled into nothing.

So what else did they have? What did the Begby Square disappearances have in common with the Venetian Gardens, besides the missing people?

No signs of a struggle. That wasn't much use, and Ava was working on that. An unidentified body, ravaged by... something. No lead there. Not yet. His mind threw up an image of the flag that had been painted in blood.

There'd been a black flag painted on the walls near Begby Square. The same letter there too, a "0."

He couldn't shake the feeling that he'd seen that black flag symbol before. The more he worried at it, like a dog with a bone, the more convinced he became.

But where, damn it?

He was just falling off to sleep when he finally realized where he'd seen it.

Byrnes's eyes shot open. "Debney."

CHAPTER
FIVE

IT WAS THE early hours of the following morning before the door to Debney's bedroom opened and the young viscount staggered in, kicking the door shut with one boot even as he tried to remove his striped coat. And failed. Debney staggered, looking down as though somewhat perplexed by the way his elbow simply wouldn't bend out of the way.

Bloody hell. He was soused.

"A good night by the look of it, Debney," Byrnes said, stretching in the chair he'd been napping in. Every Nighthawk knew how to snatch a few winks of sleep here and there when they were on a case.

Debney nearly jumped out of his pale skin, tripping over a pair of boots that had been left on the floor and knocking a tray of cologne off the top of his vanity. It bounced, luckily. "Blood and ashes, Caleb! Give a man a fit next time.... What are you doing skulking about in my bedchamber?" Sneering slightly, he used the tip of his boot to lift the baseboard quilt around the hem of his bed. "No murderers tucked under 'ere, eh?"

"By the look of it, nothing but cobwebs and dust." Byrnes took a sniff. "Were you *swimming* in a vat of brandy?"

Clearly the viscount had been participating in a rather dedicated spree of dissipation if he was coming home this late after the sun had risen, but Byrnes had smelled gin hovels in Whitechapel whose scent was less inclined to knock him off his feet.

Debney sprawled back on the bed, lifting his heel. "'Ere. Help me get these off."

Byrnes stood and took a slow circuit of the room, trying to breathe through his mouth. "I'm not your valet, Francis. Get them off yourself." Picking up one of the sprawled bottles of cologne, he ignored the young viscount and took an experimental sniff, then recoiled. How anybody could wear so many chemicals astounded him. You wouldn't be able to smell anything else.

Slight improvement on Debney though.

Debney grunted, and then a boot hit the floor. With a sigh, he collapsed back on the bed. "So what do you want?"

Taking the jug of water on the washstand, Byrnes poured a glass, then crossed to the bed, considering the state of the viscount. "I need to ask you some questions about something, and I can't explain why."

Debney sighed, his eyelids fluttering closed. Byrnes threw the glass of water in his face.

"Jesus!" Debney came up, wide-eyed and wet. "You sodding bastard!" He looked down at himself, hands held wide. "What was that for?"

"To wake you up." Byrnes put the glass aside, then dragged his chair around and resettled in it. Tugging a piece of paper from his pocket, he held up the photograph of the Begby Square black flag. "Have you seen this symbol before?"

He'd thought that nothing would sober Debney up at this rate, but the second the viscount saw the picture, his face paled even further and his Adam's apple bobbed in his throat. "Put that away. I'm going to cast up my accounts."

Byrnes complied, watching as his half brother stumbled to the basin and retched. Hell. He rubbed at his temples. "I know I saw an invitation with that symbol embossed upon it on your desk a few months ago."

Debney spat and rinsed then turned, giving him a frightened look. "I don't know what you're working on. I don't care. But if you go digging into that symbol, then you won't find whatever puzzle piece you're looking for. You'll simply die, Caleb."

Well, now. Byrnes took his chair again, resting his elbows on his knees. "You know who's behind it."

Debney shook his head. "Don't. I beg of you. If they find out I told you about it—"

"How are they going to find out? Nobody knows of the connection between us." A connection he'd be quite pleased to keep quiet forever.

"They'll find out. They always do," Debney protested.

"Who are they?"

"Caleb—"

"If you think I'm going to leave this alone, then you don't know me very well," Byrnes replied. "I can make your life hell, Francis. Besides..." His eyes narrowed to thin slits. "You owe me."

"I always bloody owe you," Debney snapped, pacing the room. "When will it end? You cannot keep calling in this debt! Do you think that if I could go back and change things, then I wouldn't? I would. I swear, I would. I'd have sent word to the Council that his craving virus levels were high. Or I'd have... stood up to him—"

"If you could go back, you'd cower behind your mother's skirts the same way you did then." An abrupt slice of the hand cut the young lord off in his tracks. "Let's not pretend any different."

"He always—"

"We're *not* talking about your father," Byrnes countered, and the crack of his voice startled Debney into silence. "Not now. Not ever."

Sullen and starting to shake now, Debney stared at him belligerently. "Unless you want something," he said, "and use him to browbeat me into complying. And he's your father too! This is the last time, Caleb. The last. I do this, and I don't owe you anything else. Do you understand?"

"Perfectly. Tell me what I need to know and I'll never bother you again."

Something about Debney's eyes caught his attention. A sudden, stricken expression.

"What's wrong?" he demanded.

"It doesn't matter." The viscount collapsed on the bed. "It's not like you'd care anyway, or as if I mean anything to you."

Byrnes stared at him.

Debney saw his perplexed look and laughed. "Look at you. Not even a hint of consternation. You just want to know about your precious black flag. It wouldn't bother you to walk away and never look back, would it?"

For the first time, Byrnes felt some stir of emotion, hot and bloody. He'd been trying not to think about it, but this house—and all the memories it contained—disconcerted him. "No. It wouldn't."

Debney looked away. "They're called the Sons of Gilead. Don't ask me why. I'm hardly in favor at the moment."

S.O. G. Everything inside him lit on fire. "Who are they?"

"A group of disgruntled Echelon lords who don't like the new world order the queen has presented us with."

"Names?"

Debney's nostrils flared. "Caleb—"

"Who are you protecting? Yourself? Your friends? Are they involved?"

"I don't have any friends, curse you. Look around. I'm certain it hasn't escaped your notice that I'm distinctly short of a valet at the moment. I had to let my thrall go earlier this year too—I couldn't afford to pay her the pin money the queen insists every thrall must receive, thanks to her new laws, so Elsie had to return to her father. In the eyes of the Echelon I'm in dun territory. Creditors keep hounding me, and my so-called friends seem to have vanished off the face of the earth. My mother's dead, my brother wants nothing to do with me, and even though old Henslow and his wife are still here, I'm fairly certain I'm going to have to let them go by the end of the year too.

"You know what?" Debney seemed to find some strength from somewhere. "Who am I protecting? Myself? What a joke. There's nothing *to* protect. Maybe if they killed me it'd be a bloody relief. I'll even do you a favor— consider it one for the road before we part. There's an invitation around here somewhere for a house party this weekend at Lord Ulbricht's country home. The bloody SOG are throwing some kind of party for young disaffected lordlings like me. I dismissed it, for I'm not an idiot—it's a recruiting drive if ever I've seen one, and I'd really rather not be caught between the ruling Council of Dukes and the SOG—but I'll give it to you. It's on the secretary there, I think."

Byrnes examined him for a moment longer. They'd never truly been brothers and he despised most of what Debney was, but there was a sense of hopelessness in his half brother's face. This was the most impassioned Debney had ever been. "You're not going to do anything stupid, are you?"

"Why? Worried you'd be called in to identify the body? I'm sure such a thing would only be an inconvenience for you."

Byrnes eyed the stiff way Debney sat. "I don't wish you ill. I've never wished you ill. It would... grieve me to see you dead."

Debney raked a hand over his face, the sneer vanishing as something more akin to hopelessness filled his expression. "I'm not going to do anything suicidal. I'll leave that to you and your mad scheme to confront Ulbricht and his cronies." Looking up, his voice softened. "They're dangerous, Caleb. Those who speak out against them or threaten to reveal their secrets have a tendency to go missing. And we're talking about dukes and barons here, people in positions of power. If you think that your Nighthawk status protects you, then you're wrong."

"I'm used to dealing with dangerous people," he replied, crossing to the secretary and rifling through the piled up invitations there. He finally found the one he wanted and tapped the invitation against his thigh as he turned back to Debney. "It's made out in your name."

"Of course." Debney frowned, then understanding dawned. "You can't use it *yourself*."

"Why not?" Undercover work was one of his fortes. "Just how large is this gathering going to be?"

"It doesn't matter how large it will be." Debney's gaze raked over him. "You're not.... You wouldn't fit in. They'd spot you from a mile away."

Byrnes looked down at himself. "I mustn't have realized that my rogue blue blood status was emblazoned on my forehead. I might, however, need to borrow some clothes—"

"It's not the clothes, or the fact that your infection was unapproved," Debney protested. "Christ, Caleb, it's the attitude, it's everything—even the calluses on your hands. You don't look like some idle aristocrat, and you never will."

Which wasn't something that had ever bothered him. Byrnes arched a brow.

"You look like you kill people for a living." Debney interpreted the look correctly.

"Part of the job description sometimes. I don't do it for fun."

Debney threw his hands up in the air. "Fine. Try your luck. I don't know why I should care. Just—if you're caught—then you need to make it abundantly clear that you stole that invitation from my house. I know nothing."

Melodramatic Debney. Byrnes laughed under his breath. "I know nothing. I know what I'm doing, Francis." Heading toward the door, he paused, then added softly, "Thank you."

"Wonders never cease," Debney muttered.

It wasn't the first time someone had mentioned something along those lines. With a wry smile, Byrnes reached for the door, listening to the sounds of Debney shifting on the bed.

"Before you go... how is Nanny?"

And there went his equilibrium. "The same. Nothing ever changes."

"I miss her." There was a note of quivering hesitancy in Debney's voice. "She was the only one who ever cared, you know? She always made me feel like I belonged to her just as much as you did. Out of all the people I've lost, she's the one I miss the most."

That vacant stare, the way his mother looked at him as though he was a stranger.... His smile evaporated and Byrnes bowed his head for just a moment. "So do I," he said bleakly, and stepped through the door. "Get some rest and sober up, Francis. You're of no good to yourself like this and from the looks of it you need to be."

Ingrid stretched in her bed, wondering what had woken her.

The sharp rap came again.

Ingrid froze for a single, heart-tripping moment, and then Byrnes popped the lock on her window, and lifted the sash. "Good afternoon."

Ingrid let herself slump back onto her bed. "I must have missed the moment I invited you into my lodgings, Byrnes."

"Oh? Miller, I thought that invitation ensued the moment you broke in to mine? And I *did* knock. Good to see you're awake."

"Barely," she growled, tossing aside her blankets and thanking God her cotton nightgown stretched to her knees. "What would you do if I told you to get out?"

He blinked. Looked back at the window. "Get out, I suppose. Though I came here prepared to share information, and it's rather awkward to shout through the glass."

Information.... That was unexpected. "I suppose you tracked me home last night?"

"Not really. I followed your scent trail early this morning from Malloryn's." His gaze slipped away from her as she stood, an unexpected gesture of chivalry.

But then, there was no challenge in this, and she hadn't invited him to view her bare legs, or the possible flashes of skin he'd easily make out through the thin cotton nightgown she wore. Crossing to the slatted timber screen, Ingrid considered his turned back. Byrnes would insist on an invitation. That was the only way he could tell if he was winning this game or not.

And now she was in a rather interesting position of power.

Ingrid flicked her honey-brown hair behind her shoulders, watching him over the top of the screen. "It's safe to look."

Byrnes turned around just as she shimmied out of her nightgown. Cotton pooled around her bare feet and despite his immaculate control, his gaze dropped, eyes flaring wide, as though he hadn't expected it. The heat in his gaze sent a delicious shiver through her, despite the screen between them. Only the tops of her shoulders were revealed, and no doubt her feet and ankles, but she was still naked. An odd mix of nervousness and excitement sent butterflies scattering through her abdomen.

Byrnes looked away as though he felt it too, taking in the bare state of the room. "You know, I overheard Malloryn offering rooms at Baker Street to Charlie Todd, and Kincaid. You could stay there."

Ingrid splashed her face with water from the jug by the basin, then scrubbed her hair away from her face. "This is *my* set of rooms, Byrnes. I don't want to lodge with Malloryn."

"What are all the rat traps for?"

Ingrid barely suppressed a shudder. "Rats."

"You need a cat."

"I would have one, but for some strange reason they don't like my scent."

"Strange." He almost smiled. "It quite sets my hair on edge too."

She ignored that. "You're up early. I didn't think you'd be out and about during the day." That pale skin burned too easily, after all, and the bright sunlight half blinded him. Byrnes didn't like the vulnerability of day. That was one thing she'd learned in their previous encounter.

"Haven't been to sleep yet." He was trying not to look at her. And failing.

Ingrid dragged her green silk robe around her shoulders. Not that she was uncomfortable. She'd always been comfortable in her own skin. It was just... him. Knotting it around her waist, she stepped out from behind the screen. Byrnes looked at the nightgown still on the floor, and then back at her.

"What?"

His eyes gained that lazy, heated quality that she remembered from when she'd pressed him down onto his bed and licked a line up the center of his naked chest. Right before she tied him to his bed with her stockings. "Nothing."

Liar.

They were both back there, in that moment. Only, those memories were juxtaposed against reality: he was surely wondering if she was naked beneath the robe, right here, right now, and Ingrid was having trouble forgetting the sensation of his skin beneath her palms as she'd taken the chance to explore that night.

Soft. Cool to the touch. Like stroking her hands down silk.

Her fingers curled into fists. She was still angry with him. "So did you learn anything in the Nighthawks archives?"

"How did—? Ava," he guessed.

Ingrid crossed to her vanity and brushed out her hair. "Congratulations. You've set a new record. Not even twelve hours, and you were already going behind my back with information."

His dark form stepped into view in the mirror, but Ingrid concentrated on her hair. It was either that or throw the hairbrush at him. And Rosa had given her the bone-backed brush. It was precious to her. Byrnes was not.

"You're annoyed."

"One would think you a prime investigator," she replied mockingly. "Picking up on the mood so swiftly."

"My apologies. It's instinct. I had a thought and followed it through to its conclusion. I don't work with others. Not well. You know that. But I'm here now. Apology... accepted?" That voice turned as smoky as sun-warmed honey.

The brush caught on a particular knot, and she focused on it, tugging gently. Then the image of that pale, blank face from the autopsy penetrated her memory again. Imogen Moore. They had a name now. And a cause of death. And poor Imogen needed more than for Ingrid to risk this case thanks to her pride. She sighed. "You're not the only one with information, Byrnes. You share yours, and I'll share mine."

Reaching inside his pocket, he produced an invitation, complete with gold curlicue writing. "I know what the letters SOG stand for."

What? Ingrid put the brush down and reached for the invitation, but Byrnes withdrew it sharply.

"Ah-ah," he said, sauntering back across the room. The black leather of his nighthawks uniform did marvelous things for his anatomy. "Mine. I found it."

"Where? And how?"

"I remembered seeing a black flag symbol like the one we encountered yesterday on a piece of paper on Viscount Debney's desk one day. He told me that the Sons of Gilead are an anti-establishment group of Echelon lords, interested in returning to the status quo where blue blood lords rule over the human rabble and can own as many blood-slaves as they like. They use a black flag on all of their correspondence."

"A symbol of anarchy," she muttered, then shook her head. "I don't see the point of their cause. Nobody would stand for a return to the 'good old days.' All of the downtrodden have had three long glorious years to realize what freedom means. They'd fight to the death to keep it from slipping through their fingers again."

"It's the Echelon. Inconsequential details like the lower masses resenting such a return to the 'old glory days' mean nothing to them. They probably haven't even wondered what they'd be up against. They're led by a Lord Ulbricht. I don't know much about him, but Debney's terrified they'll crucify him. Seems to think that if I attend the party I'm practically begging to get myself killed."

"We," she corrected.

There was a pause as he digested this. "My clue," he reminded her. "My invitation."

"Don't make this mistake again."

"What mistake?"

"This is precisely the way we set about last time." Somehow she managed to keep her vicious verwulfen temper in check. Somehow. "You began to hoard clues and

I was forced to work by myself. Need I remind you what happened, Sir Leather-britches?"

"No, you need not." His gaze dipped, just briefly, a quick glance that scored over the naked skin of her collarbones where the robe dipped. "I'm fairly certain I recall—in exact detail, mind you—what happened last year. Could you please put some bloody clothes on?"

"What's wrong, Byrnes?" She sank into her chair, her robe sliding up her bare thighs as she crossed one knee over the other. A thrill of heat slid through her veins as she met his gaze with a challenge in her own. "Anyone would think you hadn't seen a naked woman before."

"Anyone would think this an invitation," he reminded her, his nostrils flaring.

"Well, it's not."

"I know," he growled. "That's part of the problem. And I'm trying to behave, Miller. I'm trying to be a gentleman. I know I'm not allowed to touch. But this is both distracting"—he captured the end of her robe—"and tempting."

Ingrid captured his hand before he could tug at her robe. Every inch of her body said *yes*. It was only the part of her that was still capable of rational thinking that knew this was a bad idea. "You want revenge."

"Hmm, that wasn't a no."

"No, it wasn't." She'd concede that, even if she wasn't entirely certain what it was. "I'm thinking about it."

Byrnes's eyes flared with heat, the black of his pupils overtaking the blue of his irises, as the craving hunger within him flooded to the surface.

He eased closer, reaching out to brush a lock of hair off her shoulder, his fingers grazing the silk of her robe and sending a ripple of sensation through her. "I want you naked and writing beneath me, my dear. I want... everything."

Hell. If she'd thought her body complicit in his seduction before, then she'd severely underestimated the effect he had on her. Her entire body ached. And she was... tempted. "What makes you think I'd trust you?"

The edge of his mouth curled up. "Then give me some rules to play by, my dear. Challenge me. I'll prove myself worthy."

The thought captured her attention. A challenge. *Yes.* "Three challenges," she interrupted breathily. "Prove yourself trustworthy, and I'll give you a reward after each challenge is completed."

"Be specific."

So he hadn't let that go. She tugged the silken tie of her robe from his grasp and leaned closer. "I will. But all in good time, Byrnes. You wouldn't want to rush me. I know you're not interested in anything that can be won easily."

He smiled and held his hands up, giving her an innocent expression. "Fine. I'll await your first challenge then. Just... don't be too long, Ingrid. Now, you were saying... about the case? I showed you mine, after all...."

True. Curse him. Ingrid dragged her robe closed.

"Thank you," Byrnes murmured, and sat on her bed. A clear foot of space separated their knees. "That was distracting me."

It was meant to. But she looked away. "Ava finished the autopsy a few hours ago."

"I know."

"The girl's name was Imogen Moore. She's the niece of some baron, hoping to make a thrall contract with a powerful lord." Though the practice personally affronted her, Ingrid knew that not all young ladies were as privileged as she was, to be in command of her own life. For a young girl in society, perhaps becoming some blue blood lord's personal blood flask was the best option they had. And the fact that they earned pin money and gowns and jewels from their protectors probably made it seem a glamorous proposition. Probably. "Unfortunately Imogen attended the wrong party at the wrong time. Ava's certain the wounds to her abdomen were what killed her, and she's also fairly certain that they don't belong to a knife, an animal, or anything else she can imagine. The closest she could come to explaining it was presuming it was some sort of handheld threshing machine."

Byrnes scratched at his jaw. "Looked like teeth marks to me. What's your point? What's new about this?"

"Think about it, Byrnes," she said, leaning back in her chair. "If this SOG had anything to do with it, then why would they kill a girl of their own class? Or kidnap an entire party full of blue blood lords? How does that affect their cause?"

That got his attention. "Maybe Carrington knew something. Or maybe the partygoers were arguing against the status quo."

"I did a little digging. Carrington was a vocal supporter of the prince consort before the queen overthrew him. His finances took a blow thanks to the revolution. I'd imagine that if this SOG does have something to do with the disappearances, then he'd be a prime candidate for one of their members."

"Go on."

"So why attack a group of people belonging to their own class? And what would a group of disaffected lords be doing tramping through sewers? How would they even know what was down there?"

Byrnes frowned. "You're blowing holes in my theory."

"It's a nice theory." She shrugged. "And deserves looking into. Maybe the black flag symbol is purely coincidence... but maybe it's not. We just have to put the pieces together. Which is why you need me."

His back straightened. "Miller—"

"The party should reveal more about this mysterious SOG." Ingrid crossed toward the screen, snagging her shirt and protective overcorset off the edge of a chair.

"And I'll tell you everything you need to know—"

"I'm coming, Byrnes."

"No, you're not." He stood, tucking the invitation firmly within his pocket. "You didn't get a chance to read the fine print, but I'm not telling you when or where. I might be able to slip beneath their notice, Miller, but you're very clearly verwulfen. As far as they're concerned you're an animal, and far beneath their notice. You'll stand out like a sore thumb, and contrary to popular opinion..." He held up a finger to stall her protests. "I don't want you getting hurt because some blue blood lords decide they want to play games with you."

She glared at him over the screen, because he was mostly right. "I'll think of a way."

"As for today," he continued, as though she hadn't spoken, "I'm planning on informing the Moore family of Imogen's passing, and seeing if they know anything more about Carrington, or this Ulbricht fellow. What are your plans?"

"I'd love to tell you, but then I'd have to kill you." With a smirk over the top of the screen, she dropped the robe. His eyes turned flat, his nostrils flaring as she slipped into her shortened chemise. "May the best agent win, Byrnes."

After all, two could play this game, and Ingrid was weary of his lone wolf attitude. "Now get out, and let me wash and dress."

"I could stay," he replied with a half-amused smile. "Button up those hard to reach places for you."

"I could also rip your arm out of its socket," she told him mildly. "But I'm not going to. Though I am tempted."

Byrnes wisely beat a strategic retreat as Ingrid set to thinking. Just because he didn't want her along on this mission into Ulbricht's home didn't mean that she couldn't be there.

CHAPTER SIX

THE SUMMONS TO Debney's house appeared early that afternoon. Curious, but not entirely surprised, Byrnes complied.

"Change of heart?" he called, appearing in Debney's study where the lord was scribbling something furiously on a piece of paper.

Debney started, spattering ink across the page he'd been working upon. "Can you not use the front door, like everyone else?"

"The point is subterfuge," Byrnes replied, resting his hip against the desk and trying to see what his half brother had been writing. "I don't particularly want anybody seeing me waltz in and out, and neither should you. I'm a known Nighthawk, and you're a very convenient source of information. You look like hell."

"Thank you." Debney pushed away from his desk, rubbing at the bridge of his nose. "I'm not entirely certain whether I've been manipulated, or whether I've had an attack of conscience."

"Oh?"

"I'm coming to the house party."

That was interesting, but also not exactly what he'd planned. Debney would be cannon fodder at best, and if Byrnes was to work at optimum, then he couldn't be watching over his shoulder all the time, trying to keep an eye on his wayward brother. "If you don't wish to go, then you don't have to. I don't need you, Debney."

"No, but I do," came a sultry voice from the door, and then, with a swish of skirts, Ingrid appeared.

Like hell. "I don't—" And then his mind stopped working as he saw her for the first time.

The tall, lean huntress had vanished, replaced by a woman in a flattering black jacket, open over a dove-gray corset and bustle that swept up on one side to reveal the midnight-blue sweep of skirts beneath. There were bows. Ribbons. Frills. A hat cocked on top of a mass of gorgeous, polished honey-brown curls. She was even carrying a white-and-blue-striped parasol, though the design looked almost like something Ava had created.

Their eyes met. She was wearing that intense expression—almost as if he were prey at that moment—the one that made his hackles rise. Ingrid's slow smile was dangerous.

The French had a word for it: *la femme fatale*.

Byrnes' eyes narrowed, and he belatedly realized his mouth was hanging open. "No," he said, turning and placing his hands flatly on the desktop, as he captured Debney's gaze. "I don't know how she managed to convince you to do this, but it's not going ahead. We stick with my plan."

"Which includes you waltzing through the doors at Lord Ulbricht's estate and pretending to hobnob with the Echelon?" Ingrid snorted, crossing her arms under her breasts. "Even the blindest member of the Echelon would spot you for a wolf in their midst the second you appeared. You wouldn't pull it off."

"And you would?" A vein ticked in his temple. She was doing this on purpose, using her stance to turn her bust to best example. If she wasn't careful she was going to spill out of that dress.

And he was having trouble looking her in the eye.

"Debney looks the part," she said. "The invitation is in his name, and quite frankly, unless he wants Malloryn on his heels, then he needs to comply with this case."

"You *threatened* him?"

"I reminded him of the consequences. There's a reward, in case you haven't being paying attention."

And Debney needed money.

"You'll get him killed," Byrnes growled.

"That's why I'm going." Walking smoothly, she trailed her fingers along the desk, stalking behind Debney. "I can keep an eye on him to protect him, while you're sneaking around the estate. It's perfect."

If a blue blood could sweat, Debney looked like he'd be doing it. "Wasn't my idea."

Byrnes didn't take his gaze off her. "Oh, I guessed that. I should never have told you."

"*Au contraire*, you should have told me from the start, and we could have come up with a feasible plan together. I might have allowed you to work *my* case." Ingrid leaned over the desk. "As it is, I might still allow you to join us. Someone needs to play valet."

Might? *Might?* Byrnes rested his knuckles on the mahogany and loomed closer until her breath brushed his cheek. "I thought you were chasing up that theory about the Doeppler orbs."

"Jack's still looking into it for me. Results should be due in around twenty-four hours, and oh, look, I seem to have the time to fit in a side excursion."

"No."

"Give me one good reason," Ingrid countered, her voice thickening and the bronze rings around her pupils flaring.

Usually a good time for any sane man to run. Verwulfen were rash, passionate creatures, and he'd since learned that Ingrid was dangerous when her verwulfen nature was roused. "Because I said so."

She leaned toward him and there was a heat in her eyes that indicated she was one second away from pouncing upon him.

He crossed his arms over his chest. *Oh yes, my dear. Anytime you're ready, I can take you.*

Debney cleared his throat. "Just in case anyone is interested in my opinion, I've decided that I'm only going if Ingrid goes, and I'm the one with the invitation. She can pretend to be my mistress."

Ingrid brushed a piece of nonexistent fluff off her sleeve.

"Be reasonable, Caleb." Debney's expression was long-suffering. "It's a better idea than your own. You've only got your back up because someone else came up with it. And I'm not going to risk my hide without at least two people to watch my back."

"I can circle the ballroom while you're skulking about Ulbricht's study," Ingrid countered. "Three sets of eyes, instead of one."

Maneuvering him like a chess piece. "I'm not Debney. You'll need to work harder than that to convince me."

"What makes you think I need to convince you?"

"The fact that you're trying."

"How about this, then? First challenge," Ingrid said softly, meeting his gaze. "Prove to me that you're worth the risk. Prove to me that you can compromise when you need to. I'm not interested in... selfishness, Caleb."

Every muscle in his body locked into stone. She was accepting his dare. But— No! Not like this. "Miller."

"You won't get another chance." Those dark lashes fluttered down, obscuring her amber gaze.

He stood arrested. Frustration clashed with sheer want. If he didn't submit, then she'd no doubt never let him so much as touch her. Oh, she'd trapped him so neatly. He was furious. And aroused. "The prize had better be worth it."

"I'll let you know what I'll consider." Ingrid's smile held satisfaction: his statement was pure capitulation. Pushing away from the desk, she took her seat in the corner, crossing her legs.

God. Damn. It.

Debney coughed, reminding them off his presence. "So we're all going, then?"

Byrnes gave a curt nod. "Let me go get my things and send for the dirigible. My lord." He shot one last glare at Ingrid as he strode from the room.

Patience. Just a little patience, and she could be his.

They borrowed the dirigible from the Nighthawks Guild, though Ingrid wasn't entirely certain whether *borrowed* was the precise term to use.

Byrnes ushered them aboard a little too swiftly, and insisted on speaking to the captain privately, dropping his voice just low enough to make it difficult for her to hear.

"Well, I'm going to freshen up," Debney said with a yawn. "It's at least an hour to the air docks near Ulbricht's manor. And I'll need all of my wits about me tonight. Are you coming?"

"In a moment," she replied, crossing her arms over her chest. "Just... curious about something."

Debney's glance shifted between the two of them and he made to say something, then clearly thought better of it and scurried away.

Byrnes was definitely up to something. Close proximity last year had given her most of his tells, and when Byrnes smiled like that and made an effort to be affable, he was up to no good. Charm did not come naturally to him, as usually he saw little point in it.

Despite her feelings about Byrnes, it was one of the things she almost admired about him. Charm was all well and good, but at least you knew exactly where you stood with him. Most of the time.

"Something amusing?" Byrnes arched an eyebrow at her as he finished up with the captain and sauntered over.

"A private thought. I might tell you later, if I feel like it. I also might not." Ingrid pushed away from the paneling she'd been leaning against. "So... just how difficult are you going to be to work with tonight?"

Byrnes opened a door in the passageway, revealing a private chamber. Those blue eyes were smoky. "I'm on my best behavior, aren't I?"

Ingrid stepped closer and slid sideways through the door, not taking her eyes off him for a moment. "That's because you want something."

His sudden smile took her by surprise, so blinding in its intensity. "You always think I have ulterior motives."

"You always do," she countered.

"Mmm." His smile softened. "Give me a moment to get changed, and then I'll return to plot with you." His gaze slid down over her curves. "Unless you don't mind if I change here?"

Ingrid smiled, tilting her shoulder toward him flirtatiously as she slipped her fingers around the door. "Tempting, truly it is, but the last time you ended up getting naked in front of me, it didn't end well, did it?"

Then she shut the door in his face and went looking for a drink.

Hers wasn't the only transformation.

Byrnes's hair swept in a sleek line across his forehead from the layer of pomade and gleamed in the gaslight from the dirigible's chandelier. He'd borrowed Debney's previous valet's set of tails, and the black velvet coat looked almost touchable. A crisp white bow tie completed the look, rendering him almost tamed in appearance, though the sleek way in which he moved gave hint to the predator within. Anyone who mistook Byrnes for something he was not would have his teeth handed to them.

It should help. Servants were practically wallpaper at these events. Nobody would be looking for a Nighthawk in the kitchens.

Ingrid sprawled in her chair, resting her chin on her hand as she watched him pour himself a drink. "Time to plot?"

"Time to plot," he confirmed, sinking into the chair opposite her.

The drone of the engines throbbed through the floor beneath her boots, and her own glass vibrated on the small table beside her. Ingrid downed the remaining brandy in her glass in one swallow.

"Very well," she said, sitting forward on the edge of the seat as she laid out the small set of maps that she'd found earlier that day. "Airfields are here, in the small town of Kew-on-Upton. Ulbricht's manor is here." Her finger stabbed the map as she set about detailing their arrival and their escape paths should all not go according to plan.

"It will go according to plan," Byrnes countered. "We get in, you and Debney distract the group and see what you can hear, while I go sneaking about the back hallways."

"Still," she replied, "it never hurts to know your options."

"Always so methodical, my dear."

"One of us has to be." She continued on, detailing the layout of the manor from what she'd learned from Debney. "Any questions?"

"I spoke to Debney about what to expect. You'll be the center of attention," Byrnes warned, fetching the blud-wein and the brandy. Ingrid idly watched him move, because the man looked damned good in black. "Four years ago verwulfen were still outlawed and considered slaves. In London you might have the protection of the Reformation of Verwulfen Bill, but the group we're joining are considered outdated even among Echelon standards, so expect slurs and certain jibes. I'll do my best to protect you, but you may have to simply ignore the worst. Though you bring an exotic element to the group, I'm not entirely certain how they'll accept your position as Debney's mistress."

If some blue blood lord thought he was going to put his hands on her, then she'd disavow them of the notion, but words and slurs were nothing new. Ingrid shrugged. "If someone gets too friendly, I'll make certain they understand the situation," she said. "The rest is... nothing new."

After all, she'd spent nearly half her life in a cage being spat upon and taken out only to be bloodied in a ring, where her sole aim was simply to survive. Words couldn't hurt her anymore.

Indeed, ever since Will Carver's law had been announced just over three years ago and she'd been allowed onto the streets of London as a free woman, she'd found such a prospect the more frightening situation. Leaving the dark shadows of Undertown—where she, Rosa, Jack, and the rest of the humanists had once discovered sanctuary—made her feel uncomfortably out of place. She was still getting used to daylight, open spaces, and blending in to a crowd, as though there was nothing out of the ordinary about her. Freedom was terrifying in a way that oppression never had been.

But she'd be damned if she'd admit that.

Byrnes looked away, tapping his fingers on the edge of the chair. "I'm not going to be difficult to work with tonight," he said suddenly, and then their eyes met. "This is not the time nor the place for the two of us to be clashing. Ulbricht and the Echelon can be dangerous, and they've no liking for your kind or what you represent for them."

She breathed out a laugh. "So it's a truce then?"

"A truce."

Ingrid's smile faded. "You must be worried about me."

His look said it all, really. Ingrid downed another finger of brandy. "There's a possibility that they won't even know what I am. As soon as we land, I intend to use the occipital lenses that hide the bronze in my eyes."

"And your scent?"

"A liberal dousing of perfume," she replied. "Blue bloods like you have exquisite sense of smell, but in my experience the Echelon lords are too used to wearing colognes and perfumes. It dulls their senses."

"Like your letter," he murmured, standing and heading for the small travelling case he'd brought. "The one you left on my pillow. I could barely smell you at all. Here," he said, opening the case. "We might as well finish the remaining preparations, if you're going to start disguising yourself."

She watched him gather up a handful of devices. "It's quite convenient having the Nighthawks at your beck and call, isn't it? Did you raid their equipment store on your way out?"

"I'm testing some new experiments for Fitz," he corrected, "the guild's weapons master."

"Does Fitz know this?"

That earned her a rare smile. "Hold still. And wear this at all times," Byrnes told her, brushing the honey-brown curls on the left side of her head behind her ear. Ingrid's pulse hammered as he gently eased the small brass device inside her ear and fitted it carefully. Byrnes looked up from beneath thick lashes, as if he'd noticed. That touch gentled, tracing the delicate curve of her ear. Then his gaze dipped, the back of his fingers twisting to brush against the delicate skin of her throat. Right over the flutter of her pulse.

"Byrnes," she breathed, though it was a token protest.

Hunger flooded through his eyes, turning them darker, until only blackness remained. Byrnes leaned closer, his breath buffeting her jaw, and—

Ingrid caught his wrist, breathing hard. She knew what he was thinking, what he'd intended. And so did he, judging by the sharp realization in his eyes as he blinked. The darkness fled, leaving only the alpine clearness of his blue irises, but it unnerved her. Blue bloods only reacted like that when their hunger was in ascendancy. "You haven't earned your kiss yet."

"A kiss, is it?"

His voice roughened. "This is a communicator. You'll be able to hear me, and I'll hear what is being said around you too. Once the ball's in full swing, I'm going to explore the grounds a little and see if I can find anything incriminating in Lord Ulbricht's study."

"Can I join you in rifling his study?"

"I'll think about it." Easing out of his squat, the creases of his trousers falling into place, Byrnes turned away, toying with the various items displayed on the table in front of him. Taking the time to compose himself, she thought, remembering that dark glint in his eyes.

The *hunger*. She was still frozen, not quite certain what had just happened. Something unusual, judging by the stiffness of his shoulders.

Once upon a time, she'd despised all blue bloods, considering them nothing but monsters; their inner predator hidden by a sleek exterior that was little more than a facade. Byrnes himself had helped dispel that myth a year ago, when they'd worked together. She'd expected a blue blood, driven by his desires for blood. What she'd gotten was a man who held himself so chillingly composed that the only predator she'd seen within him had been the one who hungered to capture the Vampire of Drury Lane. His needs were sharply focused; his thoughts trained solely on the mission. If anything, she'd found his composure so supreme that it was almost insulting.

Except for the last couple of days, when the bet had been in place, and for the first time she'd seen a man with hunger in his eyes, a man who burned with it.

But not for blood. Never for blood.

"Screamer," he said, turning and handing her a tube-shaped device. Evidently they were pretending nothing had ever happened, which was fine with her. "You press this button, and the device emits a high-pitched noise that will drive a blue blood to his—"

"Jack created these," she told him, taking the device and slipping it down her bodice as she stood, before adjusting the snug fit. The gown was one she'd used in the past for undercover work, though times had been straitened then, and she'd evidently gained weight since. "This is not my first undercover role, Byrnes."

"Just play it safe."

With her heeled slippers on, she was almost on a level with his eyes. Reaching out, Ingrid smoothed her hands down over his lapels. "I cannot quite figure out if you're worried about me, or worried that I'll betray the game before we have it figured out." Though her voice sounded light, she felt that question curl through her. Did he actually care more than he seemed to?

Byrnes's hands captured her wrists. Something flickered in his gaze—consternation? "If we get caught, then we get out as swiftly as we can. It would be an inconvenience, but... not unmanageable."

"You *are* worried about me," she blurted.

"The last time I worked with a partner, I almost got her killed," he admitted with a scowl. Every word sounded as though she were threatening to pull teeth. Clearly he loathed admitting his concern. "I don't work well with others. I never have, and I know that I frustrated you last night when I went behind your back with Debney, but... working in a team has never been one of my strengths. Sometimes I forget to cooperate, and when I find a clue my first instinct is to chase it, not to reconnoiter and plan our next step. It wasn't personal, Ingrid." Grudgingly, he added, "If I were going to work with someone, you seem as good as any of the others I've been partnered with."

Good heavens. That was practically a compliment. She didn't voice it, however, as Byrnes had clearly extended an olive branch toward her. Instead, she shrugged. "Apology accepted. I will warn you though, I do expect better next time."

A sudden flash of smile made him shockingly handsome, then it was gone as he turned his attention back to her earpiece. Ingrid couldn't help feeling as though she'd been jolted by a Leyden jar, however.

Byrnes was a complex man. "Who was she?" she asked, for his tone had softened at the mention of a "her."

"My nighthawk friend, Perry." Byrnes let her wrists go. "As you can imagine, Garrett was quite put out with me."

Perry... Well, that was all right. Ingrid had met the woman and decided that she liked her, thanks to a knife-throwing game when the pair of them had been into Rosa's sherry one night. Besides, Perry was quite happily married to the guild master of the Nighthawks. "It sounded as though you were quite put out with yourself."

"Yes, well." He turned, the tails of his coat flaring. Pouring a glass of blud-wein from Debney's decanter, he drained it in one swallow, and Ingrid enjoyed watching the muscles in his throat work. "I care for Perry. She reminds me of myself, in some ways, and I always.... She always seemed invulnerable to me."

"Until?"

"The day she was not." Byrnes finally looked at her. "Don't get yourself killed. I still have a bet to win and a reward to claim."

Ingrid's breath flushed from her lungs. For a moment, it had almost felt like something else lingered between them, but his words were a good reminder. Byrnes considered life a challenge. If he gave any indication that he cared for her, she would be a fool to believe it.

"Don't worry. I wouldn't want to deprive you of such a challenge."

CHAPTER SEVEN

THE WELCOMING ball was a masquerade.

"No mention of *that* on the invitation," Debney huffed, as though personally affronted, as they waited in the receiving line.

Dozens of gorgeously gowned ladies fluttered their fans, wearing an assortment of hawk masks, and butterflies, or even some masks with clockwork gears turning slowly over their faces. At the door, a footman held a platter of assorted masks for those guests unfortunate enough not to have one, and Ingrid swept up a pretty gold-and-blue concoction of feathers that matched her gown.

Just as she lifted the mask to her face, the lordling in front of her tilted his head to the side, as though scenting something, and went deadly still.

Though the occipital lenses she wore should have hidden her eyes, Ingrid swiftly tied the mask on as he moved off, nudging someone else, who turned to examine her with a cold eye. Both of them had pale silvery-blond hair, as though they were blue bloods well into the Fade. Once upon a time, the Fade had led to a blue blood developing into a vampire, and they'd been executed when their craving virus levels grew too high, but there was some sort of transmutation machine now that helped dilute the craving virus levels in a blue blood's blood.

No blue blood had to fear the Fade anymore.

So why hadn't they used it?

"This way, my dear," Debney said, tucking her hand firmly in his. He stared the pair of lords down, as though daring them to say something to her.

"You know," she murmured, glancing back over her shoulder curiously, "I'm not quite certain why Byrnes dislikes you so. You are quite a charming fellow when you want to be, Debney."

The pair of blue bloods had vanished.

"It's a long story, and I don't take it personally, as Caleb dislikes most people." Those perceptive eyes turned her way. Debney looked like fluff, but was proving to own a shrewd mind behind those insipid blue eyes. "Except, it seems, for some."

"I don't know what you mean." Fanning herself, Ingrid looked away.

"He seems quite taken with you, my dear, if one knows him well enough to know what he's looking for."

A brief spurt of something—hope—flared in her chest, but she swiftly repressed it. That was foolishness of the worst sort. "I'm a challenge to him."

"Mmm," Debney murmured, but he said nothing more.

They swept into the ballroom, and she couldn't stop herself from lifting her eyes to the vaulted ceilings, dripping in gold, and the decadent chandeliers. She'd never seen the like. Dozens of servant drones roamed the ballroom with steam hissing from their exhaust vents. More than one young lady's silk dress was ruined in the wake of the steam, and the room was intolerably hot and humid, considering it was October. Ingrid slipped a glass of chilled champagne from the serving platter on top of one of the drones' heads.

"Ulbricht used to be a scion of the House of Morioch," Debney murmured, guiding her through the crowd. "Owned two of the London enclaves, and had exclusive shipping contracts with the prince consort. He's practically a new-age Croesus."

"So he'd have disliked the fact that the revolution stripped his means of revenue so dramatically." Good heavens, there were even girls dressed in watered white silk that barely covered them. Her eyes narrowed as she saw the matching pearl chokers about their throats, complete with a small metal ring at the front. They were very nearly reminiscent of the slave collars that the Echelon used to put on their blood-slaves. "Isn't that illegal now?"

Debney knew exactly what she was referring to. "Not quite, which basically describes Ulbricht and his ilk. They push every law to the very limit, though they never seem to take that step over the line, leaving the queen with very little recourse. Those girls are most likely paid to surrender to any who desire them for the night. No matter what is asked of them."

Revulsion burned like acid in her throat. This was what she'd fought so hard to prevent during the revolution. It ached to see that the progress she saw everywhere in London was but a facade to these people.

"Relax." Debney patted her hand, which she realized was clenched over his. He didn't quite wince.

"Sorry."

"Don't be." Behind the mask, his eyes seemed suddenly weary. "It's nothing that I didn't flaunt in my heyday." His gaze seemed to take in every girl, but there was no hunger in it. Only shame. "I never questioned it, as it was the way I was raised, but some of the stories you hear...." His voice lowered, almost to a whisper. "Some of the things that you saw."

"Or did?"

"Or did," he admitted softly, and to his credit, did not try to explain away his actions. "You said that you weren't quite sure why Caleb dislikes me." This time he did meet her gaze. "I know. When my father died, I... I found myself lost to freedom for a long time. I never thought of consequences. Not until recently."

Ingrid frowned. "Freedom?"

"My father was not a very nice man, and when you consider that I walked among those that surround us and thought them harmless, well... let us just leave it at that. There." Debney tipped his head toward something behind her. "There he is. Ulbricht."

Applause and cheers tore through the room. Lord Ulbricht appeared at the top of the stairs, impeccable in black, with his pale hair pomaded within an inch of its life. The man wore a thin, well-pruned moustache, and faint lines shadowed his hawklike eyes as he smiled and greeted his guests with a wave.

Ingrid watched him saunter down the staircase, shaking hands with one young lordling and then offering a smile to another. It was surreal, the way such evil wore a pleasant mask. "I'm going to stop this, Debney."

For the first time, her mission—and Malloryn's— suddenly made sense to her. She'd fought so hard with the humanists to destroy the prince consort and see his queen in a position of power. The intervening years of peace and subsequent failed trips to Norway might have dulled her ambition, but this moment reignited her quest again.

Verwulfen, humans, and mechs were free now, but how long would that last? Especially if Ulbricht and his friends had anything to do with it. She was never going to live her life in a cage again.

"Perhaps you'd best look at me," Debney murmured in a nervous tone, patting her hand. "You're drawing attention."

And she was. Her stare had become an almost incinerating glare, and from the swift glance that Ulbricht shot her, she knew she'd captured his notice. Ingrid looked away, sipping at her champagne. "Thank you."

"You're welcome." Debney ushered her through the crowd, and this time Ingrid forced herself to watch everyone.

Ulbricht reached the bottom of the stairs and a woman stepped forward to meet him. White was always something that debutantes wore to symbolize their purity, if they had never been taken as a thrall before, but the fashion had died out recently. Though gowned in a voluminous gown of pearlescent white, with dozens of pearls embroidering her bodice, this woman looked neither innocent nor pure.

A pearl choker dripped from her throat and her mask covered the entire top half of her face, with gauze obliterating even the eyeholes. A glorious swan mask, but something... *something* about her seemed wrong. Perhaps it was the way she surveyed the gathering with the same regard that Ingrid had given to the buffet earlier.

"*What is it?*" Byrnes's voice murmured in her ear, which shocked her. She'd forgotten that he was keeping watch, and had no doubt listened to the entire previous conversation.

She couldn't quite put her finger on it. Exchanging her champagne glass for a fresh one, she put the glass to her lips to disguise the words. "I don't know, but all the hairs on the back of my neck just rose. That woman... on the stairs, in white."

There was a moment's silence.

"*The swan?*"

"Yes." Ingrid shivered. The feeling quite reminded her of a child's chalk scratching over slate and the resulting sound.

"*She seems harmless.*"

"She looks like a predator," Ingrid countered. "Look at the way she's watching all of the blood-slaves in here. It's almost hungry, as though they're naught but cattle to her."

Silence. "*Hmm. You might be right. She's certainly not his plaything. Not with the way she just grabbed his hand.*"

Though they might have been an entire ballroom apart, Ingrid felt as though Byrnes stood at her side, watching as the swan caught Ulbricht's arm and reined him to her side, murmuring swiftly in his ear. Ulbricht looked startled, then followed the swan's gaze to something at Ingrid's left.

When Ingrid turned, all she saw was Debney, clasping hands in welcome with someone in an embroidered green waistcoat.

Ulbricht's smile sharpened as it locked on Debney, and then the pair of them separated, slinking in different directions through the crowd, as though circling Debney.

"Did you just feel a cold shiver down your spine?" Ingrid looked away, masking her words with the glass.

"*I couldn't see what just happened.*" Byrnes's voice had softened. "*Someone intercepted me, wanting more blud-wein. But I'll keep an eye on her.*"

"Don't. Keep an eye on Debney instead. I have a feeling that Ulbricht's up to something."

"*What do you mean?*"

"It's the way he just looked at him."

"What are you saying?"

"What if he's outlived his usefulness?" she murmured.

"Are you certain you're not imagining things?" Byrnes murmured. *"Everyone looks normal to me. And he's safe here, in the ballroom."*

Ingrid looked around. Nobody was focusing on Debney anymore, nor her. People laughed. Ulbricht held court in front of the automaton quartet, and the swan... was nowhere to be seen. She rubbed her arms. "Perhaps I'm on edge. I'm not used to this."

"Take your glass, ma'am?" someone murmured, and as she set her empty glass on the tray, she realized it was Byrnes.

His eyes twinkled behind the plain black velvet domino mask he wore. "Calm down," he murmured. "I'm watching over you *and* Debney. And I have a highly developed recurring pistol in my pocket, packed with firebolt bullets that could tear a blue blood in half."

"Thank you," she replied, cocking her head and then turning away. It wouldn't do to have someone notice that she knew him. "Who did you knock out to steal that costume?" she whispered, fluttering her fan in front of her face.

Byrnes moved away from her. *"Tall fellow. Punches like a brute, but he went down eventually. Not a footman, no matter what he was wearing. Undercover guard, perhaps. Ex-soldier, back from the wars in France. Unusual type of servant at a place like this."*

"You think something smells fishy."

"Something is definitely going on. I can't wait to do some breaking and entering."

"When?"

"Give me a half hour, then meet me in the hallway that leads to the powder room."

"And Debney?"

"Safe here, in public. Nobody would dare touch him, if your little theory proves right."

A strange little flutter went through her. He'd promised to keep an eye on her, but it was surprising how much it meant to know he was here.

She'd never needed anyone to watch her back, but she'd never felt more out of her depth. Debney had been correct. Being verwulfen in this place marked her as lesser, and though she could handle herself, she was still outnumbered. Somehow, they knew what she was.

"There you are," Debney said, making his way through a veritable crush of silk and feathers. "Lord Ulbricht is interested in an introduction."

"Lead on then, darling." She accepted his arm, playing her part.

Up close, Ulbricht was even more imposing than he'd first seemed. He eyed her with a flinty up-and-down, taking a considerable pause at her mask, as though trying to see her irises through the eyeholes. Or was that just her imagination?

"Ulbricht, may I introduce you to Mrs. Inga Miller?" Debney purred, sweeping her forward as though she were a precious gem to display. "Mrs. Miller is a *very* good friend of mine."

Ingrid graced Ulbricht with her most pleasant smile, flashing her teeth. He reminded her of Lord Balfour a little, the man who had bought her as a child and locked her in a cage. Perhaps it was the thin, supercilious smile he returned, or the sneer in his dark eyes, as though she were nothing to him. "A pleasure, my lord." The words were breathy and unctuous, and Ingrid extended her hand for him to greet, forcing him to accept it.

Ulbricht eyed her glove, distaste rampant on his face, but he took it. That enormous hand lifted hers to his lips, his sleeve sliding down, revealing a dark tattoo on the inside of his wrist. "The pleasure is mine, Mrs. Miller."

"What an interesting tattoo, my lord." As he moved to withdraw his hand, she kept hold of it. "What is it meant to represent?"

Ulbricht's lips thinned, but Ingrid could see better now. The shape was that of a rising sun. "Something that interested me, Mrs. Miller." This time, he was more insistent upon withdrawing his hand. "If you will? I have guests to entertain."

Since Ulbricht's earlier cut, most of the Echelon lords seemed to be taking their cues from him and ignoring the pair of them. Girls came and went from the ballroom, vanishing into private parlors with blue blood vultures. Ingrid watched the clock, waiting for time to tick around to her appointed meeting with Byrnes, but she couldn't stop herself from making sure each girl returned.

"The first time I received an invitation to one of these events, I was thrilled," Debney murmured, staring across the room at Ulbricht in a way that she couldn't quite define. "A chance to restore life as I knew it—one where finances weren't quite strained and a man couldn't find himself in trouble for something he'd always done. The balance would be restored. Smashing, I said. And I came, and I watched as they partied, and it was horrible in a way that it had never been before."

"What did they do?"

"There were girls there. 'Do as you wish,' Ulbricht said, as they circled among us. They'd been promised good money for the event, you see. But... telling a blue blood lord to do as he wished meant that her life lay in his hands.

Those who remembered what it was once like... they were insatiable. Men who I knew before the revolution who had never raised a hand against their thralls in the past, or some who even disdained the taking of blood-slaves as a necessary evil, were suddenly men that I didn't know. For three years there have been limits to bloodletting, and punishments for those who stepped over the line, and it were as if Ulbricht took our leashes off for the one night and something emerged that wasn't pleasant."

"The Echelon were always like that. It wasn't as if you didn't know."

"I had changed. For the first time I realized what Caleb saw when he looked at me." Debney's gaze dipped beneath gold-fringed lashes. "A disgrace."

"And what happened to the girl they'd given you?"

"I got her out, of course."

Something didn't quite add up. "Earlier, you said that you'd come to three of these events, and yet they disgust you."

Embarrassment flashed over Debney's face. "I-I.... He made me come again."

"Who? Ulbricht?" It was the first time that Debney had proffered any hint of excuse for his behavior, and it rankled. Or perhaps that was the presence of a pair of young blue bloods forcing one of the 'blood-slaves' into a private curtained alcove of the ballroom, despite the flash of fear that crossed her face. "Did he force you into a carriage by chance? Abduct you at gunpoint?" Ingrid swished away through the crowd before her emotions got the better of her. She was struggling to stand there and watch that poor girl be molested.

And how is this any better than what Debney did? Walking away, because it offends you.... After all, she had no plans to get that girl to safety, even if her instincts seethed within her to do so. Malloryn had even predicted such a conflict when he offered her this job, knowing her nature as he did.

"Ingrid, can you do this?" Malloryn had asked. *"Can you pretend to turn the other cheek for the sake of the greater good? Can you look the other way? For that is the type of work I'm offering you."*

She was verwulfen, and always prey to her heated emotions. In her ignorance—or arrogance, perhaps—she'd shrugged, and claimed that it was what she had always done in her role with the humanists.

This was not the same. Then she'd been in the shadows, spying for Rosa and using her strength to run brief skirmishes, but she'd never played an acting role. She'd always been herself, unabashed in her defiance of the very lords and culture she walked among now. It was one thing to lead humanists against the Echelon, quite another to slip through its ranks and pretend to be something she was not.

"Ingrid, wait!" Debney snagged her elbow, and because she had promised Malloryn she went with him, even though she was feeling a rather violent itch to push Debney over the rail.

"I can do this," she told him flatly.

"I know." He looked both young and old at the moment, and disappointed with himself. "You never gave me a chance to explain. It wasn't... like that."

Tamping down the sudden fury within her, Ingrid slipped inside one of the very alcoves that the young lords were currently using to their advantage. She could smell blood nearby as one of them fed. Soft mewls of discomfort—or something else—mingled with the sound of polite conversation and edged laughter. "Then explain."

"Ulbricht is aware of... some private things about me. He wanted me to invite some of my friends to his gatherings, to enlist them in the SOG, and so he became quite insistent on my attending. I know everybody, you see. That was the one thing I was always very good at. Knowing people, and yet, not really knowing them at all."

With a cough, he continued. "Nobody else is aware... not even Caleb, but I was somewhat indiscreet a few years ago with one of Ulbricht's cousins, and when the relationship broke off, he told Ulbricht everything."

He. Ingrid stared at him, her mind absolutely blank.

"I have certain proclivities," he hurried to explain, seeing her expression, "that are not widely accepted. It's the kind of thing some of these men here would kill me for, if Ulbricht didn't see a use for me."

"You have relationships with men." How had she not noticed? She was well acquainted with Jack, after all.

"It's actually quite amusing." Debney seemed relieved that she hadn't immediately cut him, though he was watching her face intently. "Watching Caleb fret over my attentions to you, as though I pose some kind of threat."

"He does?" *He did?*

"Well, yes." Debney laughed, a little shrilly. "I've never seen him behave so with a woman. He avoids emotional entanglements—he always has—so it's quite amusing to see him so tangled up over you."

There was a faint hint of static in her ear, a muttered curse. Ingrid opened her mouth, then shut it. Debney would probably faint if she told him that Byrnes could hear everything she could through the communicator.

"May I ask, what precisely *is* your relationship with Byrnes?" For there was a familiarity there that was beginning to grow quite obvious.

"We're brothers," Debney said, the words spilling out of him as if one confession suddenly unloosed a tide. "Though he wouldn't call it such."

"*Ingrid,*" Byrnes growled through her earpiece.

"Brothers?" How fascinating. "And how did such a thing come about?"

Debney's face brightened. "Oh, I was three when Nanny came to live with us—or Byrnes's mother, I should s—"

The curtains suddenly wrenched apart and Byrnes stood there. "Are we keeping an eye on Ulbricht, or gossiping like a bunch of little old ladies?"

"Well, it *is* terribly interesting," Ingrid replied.

"If you want to know something, just ask," Byrnes replied coolly. "I detest people gossiping about my life as though I'm not living it."

Touché. Ingrid tilted her head. He was correct: Ulbricht had to be the focus.

At her side, Debney looked like he'd seen a ghost, and made some sort of gasping noise.

Byrnes shot him a disgusted look. "Christ, Francis. It's not as if I didn't know. You followed Christopher Lamb around like a girl with the swoons the summer I turned fifteen. It was fairly obvious to anyone with eyes. And I *am* a Nighthawk. Grant me some credit."

"You never said a word about it," Debney managed to rasp.

"What was there to say? It was your business, not mine." Slipping a hand behind Ingrid's back, Byrnes nudged her toward the ballroom, his voice lowering for her ears only. "Just as my past is *my* business. Stay out of it. Five minutes."

That stung, which was her own fault. She knew better than to develop an interest in him. Pushing past, she tilted an eyebrow at Debney, "So much for your idea that he saw you as some kind of threat. I'm going to mingle."

The target was Ulbricht's study.

Leaving Debney in the ballroom—with strict instructions to stay there in plain sight—Ingrid ghosted up the stairs in search of the ladies' retiring rooms. After she'd powdered her nose she returned to the hallway, and then darted away from the ballroom deeper into the depths of the manor house.

"Where are you, Byrnes?"

"*Come and find me*," he whispered back. "*If you can.*"

So be it. Ingrid breathed in deeply. Blue bloods had no personal scent, but she knew what type of cologne he was wearing tonight, and... there.... A trace of it.

Shadows darkened the halls. There were few lights here, merely fireflies of fuzzy goldenness burning at certain distances along the hall. Ingrid stalked Byrnes's trail, smiling a little with anticipation as the smoky, lemon verbena scent of his cologne grew stronger.

It was darker here and there were no lights at all. The sounds of the party grew muted. Ingrid thought she heard a rustle, and then—

A hand darted out of the shadows, curling around her wrist and drawing her into an alcove by the window. Byrnes snapped the curtains closed with a flick of his hands, pressing her back against the glass of the window. There were books scattered on the low padded bench, inviting a passer-by to sit and rest for a moment, but there was no resting here. Something had caught his attention. Ingrid arched a brow, but he clapped a hand over her mouth, his hard body pressed against hers. She could feel the whisper of his breath against her cheek, and that old thrill went through her. That attraction that she simply couldn't fight. The second he realized she wasn't going to make a noise, he withdrew his hand, pressing one finger against his lips for quiet.

Seconds later she heard it: a pair of footsteps rustling against the rug in the hallway. Tilting her head to the side, she caught a hint of cologne that she recognized, and something else... a scent that made her mouth twist in distaste.

Ulbricht, and someone else.

"Are the preparations all in order?" Ulbricht murmured, and fabric rustled as she shifted.

Byrnes's hand came to rest on her hip, a gentle caress that startled her. Ingrid glanced up from beneath her lashes. She was fairly certain that this was gentlest touch he'd ever laid upon her.

Focus, she told herself sharply.

"Lady Zero is seeing to it now," came the low, terse reply. "What I wouldn't give to see the look on his face when he realizes what is in store for him."

"The Sons of Gilead need to know what happens when one of their own crosses the group." Ulbricht's words were crisp with satisfaction.

"Yes," said the other voice, amused now, "we cannot have any of them thinking for themselves now, can we?"

"You almost sound as though you admire him for his defiance."

"The sheep irritate me. He would have made a good addition to our *elite* order. The rest of them are pawns, to be pushed wherever the Rising Sons deem worthy, with barely a thought in their heads beyond how much they would like a return to the act of taking thralls, or blood-slaves. None of them think beyond their own immediate world and needs."

Ulbricht sneered. "That's what makes the SOG so useful. Their loud, bleating voices hide what's really going on behind the scenes. They'll keep Malloryn's attention long enough for us to do what really needs doing."

"Do you think so?" mused the stranger. "Malloryn's no fool."

"I'm not afraid of Malloryn. He'll get what's coming to him for betraying his own class." Ulbricht sounded disgusted. "But enough of this. We shouldn't be seen together."

Ingrid looked at Byrnes. Both of them were barely breathing.

"I'll meet you at the grotto, once this entire unsavory business is concluded," Ulbricht said, and began to stride away from them, judging by the sound of it.

"If you're not afraid of Malloryn," murmured the stranger to himself, "then you're the fool, Ulbricht."

His footsteps also vanished into the distance, and Ingrid let out the breath she'd been holding. She didn't dare move—to be caught after that revelatory little conversation would be disaster.

But... there was something about being held in the warm darkness of the manor, silent behind their curtains, that made her nervous. Move, and they might be caught. Stay, and she would become victim to the heated lure between her body and Byrnes's.

It was already starting. His breath against her throat; his hands resting easily on her hips, as if they belonged there. Their hearts pounded in the heavy stillness of the night, shockingly loud to her ears. Byrnes listened to the sound of echoing footfalls, intent and focused, but as her face slowly tilted towards his, he looked down, blue eyes gleaming in the faint moonlight as his own awareness flared to life.

They stared at each other.

Hard fingers turned soft on her waist. Byrnes's piercing gaze shuttered beneath a sweep of thick black lashes, and his mouth rested a hairsbreadth away from her temple. It would have been easy to push him away if he'd simply moved toward her, but he didn't. She was growing all too aware of the softening flex of her own hands against his chest, thumbs caressing the hard planes of his pectorals beneath his shirt, tempted to do more, to explore. This gentleness both tempted and confused her.

Their last case had been a haze of arguments, and that one heated kiss when passion had finally overtaken him and he'd thrust her against the wall behind the theatre, taking what they both wanted. Seduction had never owned any part in it.

"If you keep looking at me like that, Ingrid, then we're not going to see the inside of Ulbricht's study at all," Byrnes whispered. His voice told her that the thought wouldn't bother him too much, even as their responsibilities pressed down upon them both.

Ingrid let go of the breath she'd been holding. She'd always been attracted to him. That wasn't the problem. "I believe the hallway sounds empty. Let's go."

A hand caught her wrist, and Ingrid glanced up.

"Later," Byrnes insisted, and his eyes had darkened from that compelling blue to the pure, sweeping darkness of a blue blood's hunger.

Ingrid shook his hand free. "You and I aren't a good combination. We mix like potassium and water."

His teeth gleamed as he smiled. "Explosive?" Pressing closer, he nuzzled the edge of her ear, and a thrill went right through her. "You and I... It would be a night to remember. That's not always such a terrible thing, Ingrid."

"It is when one considers the debris left behind." Like her own shattered heart. She'd always been too intrigued by

him, and knew herself well enough to know that this—
what lay between them—was not the same as the handful
of liaisons that she'd had in the past to assuage her
loneliness.

Byrnes's gaze grew heavy-lidded and sleepy as he
looked at her, and the speculation there was enough to
make her wary. If he looked too hard at her, perhaps he
might see something she thought best kept hidden.

Stupid bloody heart. Longing for something that was
best kept at arm's length.

Ingrid let out an unsteady breath and slipped through
the curtains in a swish of skirts. Byrnes trailed on her heels,
but she knew that discussion had simply been set aside, not
finished.

"This one," Byrnes noted, trying a handle. Locked.

It took a swift jiggle with the lock pick that she'd
hidden in her bodice to get through the latch. Byrnes
remained a cool presence at her back as she slowly turned
the handle and peered inside. Ulbricht's study. Success.
Within seconds, they were both inside, moving like stealthy
shadows. Perfectly in unison, silently understanding every
look they gave each other. A twitch of his brow indicated
that the desk was hers, and Ingrid complied.

This... this was what it could be like between them, if
they truly worked together. Byrnes moved immediately to
the bookshelf, sliding books out, and rifling through them.

If only she could trust his pride and his ability to let
her in.

"Ulbricht has guards on rotation, disguised as
footmen," Byrnes whispered abstractedly, his focus
completely on the mission now, as if by promising her a
"later" he'd been able to entirely compartmentalize his lust.
"I've been timing their routes. We've got ten minutes...."

Glancing at his pocket watch, he amended, "Closer to nine now."

Ingrid let out another breath, and with it the last of her own fragmented thoughts. Time to focus. "Do you think there'll be anything incriminating here?" Piles of paper were neatly shuffled into place on the desk, which gleamed. Ulbricht had fastidious tendencies.

"The problem with the Echelon is that they firmly believe that they're sitting on a throne on top of the world, and that the rest of us are mindless, spineless cattle who couldn't do anything, even if we dared break into their manors and find evidence. I've only ever encountered one blue blood lord who has absolutely nothing of interest in his study, and that's Malloryn."

"You broke into *Malloryn's* study?"

Byrnes gave her a faint frown; a warning to keep her voice down. "I wanted to know more about this covert operation he's running."

"And?"

"Nothing," he responded gruffly, finished with the bookshelf and beginning to search for hidden drawers in the cabinetry. "Though he did have certain traps in place for the unwary, which is interesting. Almost as though he expected someone to go through his things. He's got all the important information hidden away somewhere, and his study at Baker Street is a complete sham, well stocked with treatises on livestock rearing, the best way to feed cows, Bio-mechanics, and welding temperature suggestions for creating mech limbs. Terrifically boring stuff, I kid you not. One would almost suspect him of having some private joke on the rest of the world."

"Or certain spies."

Ingrid sorted through the papers, trying to keep them in their rightful place. Receipts, stock movements, a pile of newspaper clippings featuring incidents where blue blood lords had been stoned in the streets, or executed. She turned her attention to those, pausing for a moment. Not proof of anything, but an interest in the poor hamstrung blue bloods' plight. Clearly where Ulbricht's sympathies lay.

Ingrid lifted a newspaper clipping of the queen's birthday celebrations, frowning as she saw the way someone had stabbed a pair of holes through Queen Alexandra's eyes. "He hates her," she whispered, easing her thumb against the newsprint. "Ulbricht hates the queen."

Byrnes had been running his fingers over the inside of a previously locked cabinet, when he rattled a hidden latch. "Got something," he whispered, and set to work unearthing the small drawer.

"What is it?"

Byrnes withdrew a slim folder from the hidden compartment that he'd unearthed.

"Insurance," Byrnes read off the top of the folder.

"Insurance against what?"

"Subject X," he murmured, reading the document within the folder. "Hmm, something something formula... bloodthirsty... rampage through asylum.... Here we are: 'The debacle with Subject X has created instability at the facility. Though how could we have predicted that he would escape his cell and lay waste to so many of the staff? All evidence indicates that he was responding well to the elixir, and his transformation appeared to be almost complete. Erasmus suspects he has formed an attachment with the Byerly girl, the one who nurses him, so he instructed her to work in another of the wings so as not to distract X. It is believed that the board members will vote for foreclosure of the asylum, possibly destruction of the specimens. I cannot imagine the Duke of—'" He flipped the piece of paper over. "Hmm. That's strange. I wonder if the rest of it slipped out."

"What does that have to do with Ulbricht?"

"I don't know." Setting the folder down, he began hunting through the cabinet with more focus. "But it's caught my interest. Perhaps thanks to the part about 'bloodthirsty rampage' and the hidden compartment. We do have a ravaged body on our hands, after all, and nobody hides something unless it's important."

"Focus, Byrnes. We want information on the SOG. Not scientific experiments." Ingrid continued her sweep of the room, finding a curled up piece of parchment in the fireplace.

Unrolling it revealed several symbols. None of the letters made sense—some sort of odd language, possibly a code, but.... "I've seen this symbol before," she said, tapping the picture. "Tattooed on the inside of Ulbricht's wrist."

Byrnes glanced over, eyes narrowing at the half sun symbol. "I've seen it tonight too, though I cannot remember where. I didn't take much notice of it."

"A half sun," Ingrid murmured, then her eyes lit up. "Or the Rising Sons?"

"What do they have to do with the Sons of Gilead?"

"You heard Ulbricht and his crony in the hall. I think the Sons of Gilead were created to cover the fact that the real faction—these Rising Sons—are up to something. The SOG might think themselves important, but I'd be surprised if they knew just what they were being used for. It's all been talk of recruitment drives and funding down in the ballroom."

"And the Rising Sons? What's their purpose?"

"Anarchy," she whispered, staring into nothing and seeing that photo of the queen with her eyes stabbed out.

"They're up to something, some plot against the queen and Malloryn, and we need to discover what it is before it gets too late."

Ingrid folded the small piece of coded letter, then slipped it inside her corset. Silence strained the air. "What?" she asked, arching a brow and looking up. "I might as well use what I have."

A faint smile played about Byrnes's lips. "I didn't say anything."

"Jack can decode it for me when we return. If it wasn't important, then I think it would be written in plain English."

"Agreed." Byrnes suddenly cocked his head on the side, holding a stalling hand up, and pressing the other one to his earpiece with a frown. Then he was moving in a flurry toward the door. "Debney," he shot over his shoulder. "They've got Debney." A frown drew his brows together. "Ulbricht's there. Something about betraying their sons? Or their—"

His face suddenly paled, and Byrnes pressed the communicator even tighter to his ear. Then he was off, moving toward the door. "He's screaming."

CHAPTER EIGHT

"DAMN IT!" Byrnes paused in the gardens, scenting the air.

There'd been no sign of Debney in the ballroom. Frustration burned through him. He'd been following Debney's cologne trail but it had suddenly vanished as he walked into a scent bomb that obliterated his senses with its sudden intensity.

"Hell." Ingrid reared back as if slapped, and he was reminded that her scent-tracking abilities were even more sensitive than his. "I cannot smell a bloody thing."

Another scream pierced his eardrum: Debney begging someone to stop. Byrnes held the communicator close against his ear, pacing in each direction. Unlike Ingrid's jeweled ear cuff, he'd had to be more surreptitious with the listening device planted on his half brother. Thank God. If it hadn't been planted within Debney's collar, they might have found it, and then Debney would be dead before either of them knew it.

"—*please, please, please... Make it stop! Make it stop!*" Silence filled the sudden void, as Debney gasped.

"*Where's the verwulfen bitch?*" Ulbricht hissed in Byrnes's ear.

"*Don't know,*" Debney cried out. "*I swear I don't know! Last... saw her in the ballroom.*"

"*You're lying.*"

"*I'm not!*" Debney squealed.

"What's happening?" Ingrid demanded, drawing Byrnes back into the here and now with a faint touch against his sleeve.

"They're trying to get him to give us up." Byrnes turned. "Where would they have taken him? They can't be in the manor. Not with all those guests.... Damn it, I thought he'd be safe in public view!"

"What about what Ulbricht said about the grotto?" Ingrid paced to the top of a small hill overlooking the sprawling gardens as she squinted into the night. "There! Byrnes! I can see torchlight!"

She was right. A ring of torches flickered in the distance.

"*Is `there anyone else?*" someone asked through the communicator, in the kind of voice that sent a shiver down his spine.

Byrnes held his breath.

"*No.*" Debney gasped. "*Just her. And me.*"

Debney. You bloody stupid fool. Trying to be a hero.... Byrnes squeezed his eyes shut, then took a deep breath. The debt had just turned the other way. He had to get his half brother out of this. No matter what the cost was.

"Come on. We'll get closer, see what we're up against. Between the two of us, we should be able to handle a few pasty-faced Echelon lords and get Debney out," Ingrid said, overriding the voice in his ear. She grasped a section of her skirt and whirled the fabric away from her body, revealing a pair of slim-fitting leather leggings beneath the skirt and a ruffle at the back that was all that remained of her bustle.

"...*got a special treat in mind for Mrs. Miller*," Ulbricht whispered, in his ear. "*Thou shalt not suffer such filth to live. Is that not correct, Barringale?*"

"*Indeed*," came a sibilant hiss.

Byrnes caught her wrist. "Wait."

Ingrid lifted bronze eyes to his. She'd peeled off her silk gloves, revealing slim leather gauntlets that ended with silver spikes that had been pressed flatly against her fingers but were now extending into deadly points. One punch with them would render a man full of holes. "If we don't hurry—"

"I'm aborting this mission," he said forcefully, "Get out of here. We'll rendezvous at the airfields in Kew-On-Upton. If I don't arrive by dawn, then take the dirigible and return to London."

Ingrid's expression told of her confusion. "What about Debney?"

"I'll bring him out. He's *my* brother, after all."

She searched his gaze, drawing back against his hold. "What did you hear? Byrnes?"

"Nothing."

"You promised we'd work together." Her expression was becoming steely. "And I like Debney. He's quite a decent fellow. He's—"

"This has nothing to do with me not wanting to work with you—"

"Oh, really?"

Damn it, yes! "They've got something planned just for you."

There. It was said. Ingrid paused.

"I don't like the idea of placing you in that situation," he admitted, just as Debney began screaming again. The sound of it was like ice in his veins, but that threat.... He knew men like this, men who'd once tortured verwulfen just because they were different, or because only a verwulfen could stand against a blue blood and hope to survive. He'd even worked one particular case, closing down a set of fighting pits that forced their verwulfen slaves onto hot coals for amusement, or chained them down, allowing blue blood lords to pay for their bodies for the night. Verwulfen would survive almost anything, including being cut open or burned and branded. But just because their bodies could heal, it didn't always mean that their minds did. "Ingrid, I won't risk it. They don't know about me yet, but you—"

"*Get it away from me!*"

Debney. Again.

Ingrid squeezed her eyes shut, then let out a slow breath. When her eyelashes fluttered, he saw the fear evaporating, replaced instead by steely resolve. "I know what they want to do to me, Byrnes. It's nothing I haven't experienced before. I didn't just join this mission for entertainment's sake, but because I believe in it. These men want to bring back a culture and time where I was barely worth spitting at, let alone allowed to live as a person with my own dreams and desires. They need to be stopped, and unfortunately there are only two of us here. Going back for Debney's a risk that I am willing to take, because he is worth it. He is trying to make amends."

He didn't want to let her go, but there was no time to argue, and it was her choice ultimately, not his. "Fine. We go back together, but if we do this, then we do it smartly...."

Ingrid's eyes gleamed as he explained how.

CHAPTER NINE

"ARE THE CHAINS secure?"

Ingrid forced herself to hover at the back of the crowd as someone shouted. Nobody had seen her yet, but they would. Dozens of masked blue bloods stood in a central ring near the grotto's pool, surrounding something that screamed. As the wind drifted, she screwed up her nose. Something smelled rank, almost enough to turn her stomach, and she had barely begun to get her sense of smell back after the chemical bomb.

"Don't do this," Debney begged. "Ulbricht!"

"I name this man guilty of betraying his social order," Ulbricht called. "And leading agents of the Crown against us in order to bring down the Rising Sons. Raise your hands, my friends! Cast your votes! Should he live, or should he die?"

Each member of the crowd thrust forth one fist, thumb out. All of them slowly turned down.

"Death," Ulbricht snarled. She could just make out his face as he whirled on something in the center.

Ingrid strained to see. Debney, trussed and tied? What the hell had they done to him?

Her mind struggled to make sense of the shapes, of the pulley system that was rigged with chains tied to Debney's wrists and ankles, holding his body taut off the ground, as each chain pulled at his limbs—

"*Jesus*," Byrnes whispered, in her ear. Horror filled his voice. "*Ingrid, get out. Get out now!*"

Too late, for the crowd was starting to notice her now. Ingrid pushed her way through them, emerging from the shadows of the cave like some ancient Valkyrie, come for revenge. "Wait!"

Sudden shocked silence greeted her, as almost three dozen blue bloods turned to face her, covered by dark robes and blank face masks. The effect was eerie.

"I deny your vote," she called, standing firm in the wake of their unspoken censure. "I vote for him to live!"

The pressure on Debney's chains eased and he slumped with a whimper, halfway to the ground, looking around for her, his face a mess of white.

"*Run*," he mouthed.

And that was when she saw what was harnessed to the chains. Everything in her ran cold. *Oh shit.*

Vampires.

The stink made sense now. The maggot-white bleached color of their bodies strained in their harnesses at each of the four points of the device, threatening to tear Debney apart. Wiry and lean, with knotted protuberances marching up their spines, vampires were any sane person's worst fear. All that remained of a blue blood once they reached the Fade and color began leeching out of them, they were consumed by nothing but hunger. Strong, fast, vicious, and terribly, terribly bloodthirsty.

Ingrid froze.

She'd never seen one, only ever heard the stories; of martial law settling on London and vampires running loose, leaving rivers of blood in the streets. The Year Of Blood had been over a century ago, but London never forgot. And the part of her that was purely primal began to feel the pulse-thundering tick of prey, sending shivers of fear through her veins, her muscles trembling as if prepared to run.

She knew now what could tear apart that woman in the sewers. But why had it stopped? Once unleashed, a vampire would just keep killing and killing....

"You." Ulbricht was the only one without a mask, and his smile etched pure evil upon his face. "The filth thinks she has a right to vote!"

Laughter roared back at her.

Be brave. Be brave. Ingrid lifted her chin. "I hope you have everything in place," she whispered to Byrnes, swallowing hard.

"*Almost,*" Byrnes promised. "*Are you ready?*"

No. "Yes."

"*The second the Doeppler orbs release, get out.*"

"What about Debney?"

He hesitated.

"I'm not leaving him here," Ingrid told him, glaring at the assembled blue bloods.

"*Then get to Debney and try and release him, but Ingrid... if you can't do it, then you need to retreat. Promise me that?*"

"Promise," she whispered, her heart thudding like a drum.

"*I'll cover your back. Just make sure the hemlock spikes don't hit him. He's too heavy for you to carry and still be able to fight.*"

Feathers ruffled. The swan stepped forth at Ulbricht's side as the mysterious woman swept off her mask.

Cold gray hair glittered beneath the torchlight, so fine and silvery it looked like spun moonlight. The gleam of the woman's pale, translucent blue eyes was shockingly frigid as their eyes met, and suddenly Ingrid remembered that a single woman had walked free of the Venetian Gardens disappearances, a woman with pale hair.

"This trespass demands an answer," the woman called. "What say you, my friends?"

"Hunt," came a resounding cry.

"Hunt!"

"Hunt! Hunt! Hunt!" they all echoed, the shout taken up like tribal war drums.

Everywhere she looked, Ingrid was faced with fists thrusting in the air and vicious, gleeful smiles. Macabre figures circled her, backlit by the flickering torches. Right. Ingrid flipped both of her knives from the wrist gauntlets she wore into her palms.

"You have no right to vote, filth." Ulbricht held his hands up, demanding silence.

And it came, almost as eerie as the menacing shouts had been. The nearest vampire snapped and strained at its harness, sniffing the air and making creepy chittering noises in her direction. It had her scent now, and if blue bloods craved verwulfen blood above all others, then she had no doubt the vampire hungered for it too. Those yellowed fangs were almost an inch long.

"*Ready?*" Byrnes whispered.

"Ready," she said, and crouched low.

Firecrackers started going off, coughing and spluttering as they were launched into the crowd. Small explosions of red and gold light spat as something whined past her ear. Ingrid shoved forward, knifing one blue blood in the back and slashing at another as he wheeled and tried to flee. An explosion sounded, dangerously close to her, and left her ears ringing.

Chaos. Beautiful, glorious chaos.

Ulbricht spun, trying to see what was happening as the torches on the left side of the grotto fell into darkness, one by one.

"*Go*," Byrnes said, and more firework balls began crackling as they were launched into the crowd of blue bloods, their short fuses hissing.

Ingrid sprang into a run, her bustle flapping against her thin leather breeches. Lowering her shoulder, she smashed directly into a blue blood and with a cry he went up over her shoulder. Lashing out with one of her knives, she cut another's throat. He went down as she waded on, but she doubted the blow would kill him. Blue bloods could heal almost anything; only a knife to the heart or decapitation could kill them. Or fire.

Byrnes had been busy, having retrieved the special traveller's bag he'd stashed in their rooms. Whilst she and Debney distracted the Rising Sons, he'd been laying powder trails and planting the Doeppler orbs he'd brought with him. The orbs worked on a timer, releasing a mixture of gases that sent the blue bloods coughing and spluttering, thanks to Ava. Fire raced along the powder trails, igniting the tails of one blue blood's coat, and sending panic through the mob. The last weapon he had on hand was the most dangerous; exploding devices that contained almost a hundred hemlock-studded iron spikes in each ball. Hemlock would momentarily paralyze the blue bloods, although it would barely affect her.

Debney. There! Ingrid felt the wild surge of her blood suddenly heat as the violence and mayhem appealed to her predator nature. Faces began to blur away, becoming mindless shadows that she cut and slashed, and then suddenly she was through the ring of blue bloods into the marble circle cut in the center of the grotto, where Debney strained in his chains.

The swan was between them, one hand on a pulley system, as if she'd been waiting. "All yours, my dear," the woman said, yanking the lever down.

One of Debney's chains sprang free. He yelped, and rolled as he hit the marble, the chains easing. The woman turned and pulled another lever, and steel bit through the chain on his left wrist, snapping it clean off.

Ingrid paused. "Why are you helping us?"

"Oh, I'm not." Another yank, another chain. Only one remained, this time on his left foot. The woman stepped away, crossing toward the vampire. "I promised Ulbricht a hunt, and a hunt he shall get." Withdrawing a slip of brightly colored silk from the bodice of her dress, the woman reached out as if the creature couldn't simply take her hand off, and petted it, waving the silk in front of its face.

Red silk. Her drawers. "You bitch!" She'd been in Ingrid's room, in her things.

Bunching the silk, the woman rubbed it against the vampire's nose. "Easy, easy now, my pet. You'll get a taste," she crooned, smiling at Ingrid as she began to tug on the straps holding the vampire in place. "Soon."

That cut through the rising surge of *berserkergang* that was threatening to overwhelm her. Suddenly Ingrid knew exactly what the woman planned.

"Byrnes!" she snapped, turning and rushing to the final lever.

"*Rather busy*," he panted.

"She's releasing one of the vampires." Ingrid threw all of her weight into the enormous lever, and it barely budged. *What?* She stood back. The woman had yanked it as easily as if it weighed a mere ounce. "It has my scent."

"*I'm doubling back then! Get moving!*"

"It's a vampire, Byrnes." A chill ran through her. Nothing could escape a vampire. Very few things could kill one. During the Year Of Blood, it had taken over a thousand militiamen and half the Echelon to find their nest and destroy them. Numerous buildings had been gutted by fire, and hundreds of civilians were torn apart by the creatures.

"*One problem at a time, Miller. Free Debney.*"

Throwing all of her weight into the lever, she felt it hover on the verge of shifting, and then finally launch down, the last chain on Debney falling apart in two pieces as the guillotine sliced through it.

Something exploded behind her. Blue bloods screamed, then three of them went down. Hemlock bombs. "Debney!"

He was scrambling to get on his feet. "Ready!"

Yanking him up by the arm, she dragged him through the crowd. Byrnes had detailed their escape route to avoid most of the hemlock bombs he'd planted. They ran, Ingrid barging through panicked blue bloods and shoving them out of the way with her verwulfen strength.

Another bomb exploded. Fiery pain lashed her arm as two of the hemlock spikes drove into her flesh, and the flash-fire burn in her blood indicated the loupe virus was attacking the poison with prejudice. It was good to be verwulfen.

Not so good to be a blue blood. Debney jolted, staggering as his right leg suddenly stiffened. "Hit," he gasped, and went down on one knee. "Leave... me...."

Like hell.

Straining under his sagging weight, Ingrid dragged him over her shoulder, and started running up the slope, her thighs burning. Every hair down the back of her neck rose, as if she could feel something hunting her.

Screams broke out behind them. Then a strange fluting trill pierced the air. "Hunt, my pet!" Another low, eerie tone from the flute.

"Byrnes!"

"*Coming!*"

A lithe black shadow broke out of the trees, and Byrnes caught her, wincing as one last hemlock bomb exploded behind them.

"What are we going to do?"

"Can you carry him?" Byrnes glanced over his shoulder, flicking his pistols into his hands.

For a while. She ground her teeth together. "I'll manage."

"Head for the folly. I've planted some more bombs there, on a remote detonating charge." He gave her a shove in the back and turned, both pistols lifting.

Bang. Bang. Bang. Bang. Double barrels spat bullets, the sound shearing through her eardrums. "There are two of them! I've got this one!"

As if the odds could not get any worse.

Panting, with sweat dripping down her face, Ingrid forced her way up the hill toward the marble folly. Something snarled behind her and she threw herself over the edge of *berserkergang*, letting the fury, the fierce rush of the loupe consume her. It fired through her veins, granting her an extra burst of speed, even as the fierce cold-hot rush bled through her veins.

A heavy weight hit her and Debney squealed. Ingrid went to one knee, as a flash of *something* rocketed past. Dumping Debney off her shoulder, she spun just in time to face a nightmare. The vampire had overshot them, but now it loped toward her then paused, as if it sensed that she'd turned, and lifted its head to sniff. Crab-walking sideways, it made a series of high-pitched clicking noises that somehow helped it to see, considering the blind film covering its eyes.

Ingrid moved with it, trying to force it back to the main entrance up the slope. "Come on," she whispered. "Back you go." There was no fear now, only a tempting lure of violence. *Let's see if you bleed.* "Back, you ugly bastard."

Back where the glittering gold hemlock orbs waited, lying forlornly on the grass. In the distance, she could see flames flickering as if something was burning, but Byrnes was nowhere to be seen. The vampire took a single step forward, hopping on three limbs. Nearly there. Nearly.

"Byrnes," she said softly, gaze locked on the vampire as it made one more step. "Anytime you're ready with those detonators."

The golden orbs made a faint clicking noise, and the vampire looked down. Ingrid threw herself behind the folly wall as they exploded. Iron spikes flew past, embedding themselves in the marble, and the vampire gave a high-pitched scream.

"Got you."

Hemlock couldn't be entirely trusted; its effectiveness differed depending on the levels of craving virus in the blood, and a vampire's would be coming in at 100 percent. But it might slow it down, just for a few seconds anyway.

Blades in hand, she launched herself down the slope. The creature was staggering, shaking off the effects of dozens of the iron spikes. Ingrid lashed out, raking her knife through its maggot-pale flesh. Black ichor splashed and it screamed, its claws lashing at her, just as a wave of putrid stench enveloped her. Forcing herself not to gag,

Ingrid sank her second knife into its guts, and wrenched it upward, toward its sternum. *Heart. Where was the heart?*

There. She felt it on the tip of her blade, and the vampire's efforts redoubled, its back claws hooking up between them and raking down her side. Hot blood burned her knuckles; somewhere in the back of her mind she was aware of the pain and the hurt, but the *berserkergang* had her in its grip now. Lashing out, she drove her main knife in deep to join the second one. Again. Again. Then it kicked out, and the force of the blow knocked her feet out from under her.

"Ingrid! Clear!"

Ingrid threw herself aside, relief flooding through her, as Byrnes suddenly appeared, pistols raised.

There were a few moments in his life that had branded themselves on Byrnes's brain; the moment when his mother had fallen that last time, her head striking the edge of the fireplace and making *that sound,* that horrible sound; the memory of cold rain drizzling down his face as he stared impassively at his father's casket and hoped the bastard was rotting in hell; and now Ingrid, backlit against the blaze below, runnels of sweat marking her face.

Blood. And pain in her eyes. And a white blur, moving toward him with impossible speed. Byrnes stepped back, his heel catching on something, his eyes going wide as he fell....

Tumbling onto his back, he jerked the trigger as the vampire launched itself at him. Acid blood sprayed across his face as the pistol retorted, the creature falling heavily across him. Byrnes scrambled backwards, still fighting, still wrestling, until he realized that he was fighting a dead weight.

It was over.

Half of the vampire's head was simply... gone. The firebolt bullets in his pistol had exploded upon impact, and its chest was a mess from where Ingrid had cut it.

"I killed it."

A vampire. He'd killed a *vampire*. Pure bloody luck, that was what it was; the pistol in the right place at the right time, his finger already on the trigger. His heart wouldn't stop racing.

Then the pain of the blood burns washed over him. Vampire blood was like acid. That, and the recollection that he hadn't been alone.

"Ingrid!" Byrnes wiped it off, scoring his sensitive skin and ignoring the flash of pain as he searched for her. Ingrid watched him warily, those amber eyes flaring bronze-hot. She was kneeling, one hand pressed gently to her side.

"Are you hurt?" he demanded.

Ingrid shook her head, staring again at the vampire's body. "Just... shaken."

And she was so rarely shaken. Those long, dexterous hands trembled and blood marred her bodice. She'd never looked so bloody beautiful. Nor so vulnerable.

"And Debney?"

"Alive." She pressed her hands over Debney's chest. Sharp slashes gouged a bloody ruin in his brother's skin.

"Oh, God. I'm dying, aren't I? Caleb? Caleb?" There was a note of panic in Debney's voice as he searched for Byrnes.

"Not dying, Debney. Not today." Byrnes knelt at his brother's side, assessing the damage. "You probably won't even have a scar, courtesy of the craving virus."

"Not dying?" The words gurgled in Debney's throat; an incredulous laugh.

"Not dying."

For some reason, Debney caught his hand. "You came for me."

"Well, you were squealing like a stuck pig in my ear. I couldn't just leave you there." Though he tried to sound disgusted, their eyes met. Byrnes looked away. "No more debt, Francis," he said softly. "You were very brave. If you hadn't lied about my presence, we probably wouldn't have had a chance."

Sitting up with a wince, Debney nodded, looking quite overcome. "What happened to the other vampire? Did you kill them both?"

"She recalled it with her flute." Byrnes ran a hand through his hair.

"Bloody hell." Staggering to his feet, Debney nearly took a swan-dive into a stand of bushes. "Just let me... get my feet under me." He headed off in a slow circle around the folly, shaking off the hemlock.

And then they were alone, the feral need in Ingrid's eyes matching the sensation in his chest. Nearly dead. Both of them.

Want kindled in his veins, fanned to hot flames by the exhilaration of what had just happened. The blaze of post-battle fury brought with it the need for physical release, or simply even the touch of her skin.

Fuck it. He gave in to the urge, closing the distance between them, cupping her face and tilting it up toward him, his thumbs wiping the blood from her cheek. Ingrid made a growling sound in her throat, but he didn't think it was denial. An echo of the lust slamming through him, perhaps.

BEC MCMASTER

"Think I've earned that kiss yet?" It came out rougher than he'd intended. Hell. He wasn't feeling at all himself. Shaky perhaps, in ways that he didn't understand.

Sliding a hand behind his nape, Ingrid yanked his face down, her lips brushing against his and sending an electric shock through him. "I think you've more than earned it."

Then she claimed his mouth in a kiss that lit the very soles of his feet on fire.

A year. An entire year in which he'd yearned for this, dreaming of that last time she'd kissed him and ridden his hips with only her breeches between them and the hot scent of her need dampening the air. Byrnes had locked it all away—every last memory—but he hadn't been able to forget. Not completely. It all surged to the surface, but the sensation of this, the realness of it, blew his memories and his expectations out of the water.

Muscling her backwards, he felt the jolt as her back came up against the marble column of the folly. Kissing each other, their mouths warring, no finesse, only hunger... it burned through him. Sliding his hands down her hips, he rocked against her. Tongues clashed, hers faintly teasing—

"Ahem." Debney made a faint coughing sound behind them.

Byrnes froze. He was going to kill his brother. Slowly and painfully. A thousand ways to do so sprang to mind, even as tension slid through Ingrid's lithe body.

But this wouldn't be his only chance. No. He'd won a precious step toward earning her trust today and this contest of wills between them. He would have her. All he had to do was remain patient.

With a sigh, Byrnes lifted his face, reluctantly releasing her. It hurt to let her go. Darkness slithered through his vision, the hunger—the predator within—asserting itself. *Mine*, it whispered, and Byrnes actually blinked.

126

Then it was gone, his vision sliding through shades of black and gray, until color flooded back into his world and he had to wonder if he'd imagined that.

Because, if he wasn't mistaken, the darker side of his nature had just stamped its claim on the most frustrating woman he knew.

"Let's go." Ingrid's voice was sharper than expected. He could almost hear the sound of her putting up those guarded walls around herself so that he could never, ever get in. "That woman had four vampires. I shouldn't like to wait around to discover if there are any more out there in the dark, hunting us."

"Agreed," he said softly, and shook off the unusual sense of connection that he'd momentarily felt.

That way lay danger.

And Ingrid wasn't the only one who guarded her heart.

CHAPTER TEN

"HOW'S DEBNEY?" Ingrid asked, rapping her knuckles against the door of the passenger cabin that Byrnes occupied.

She paused awkwardly as Byrnes looked up from beneath those thick, indecent black lashes, his blue eyes locking on her with that intensity with which he viewed everything. Something heated lit his gaze, then he returned his attention to his bare arm, which he was wiping the blood from.

Bare arm. Bare chest... rippled abdomen. Ingrid looked away, her gaze locking on his discarded shirt and valet's coat and staying there. Far safer than letting it wander back to the man himself as he tended various wounds. The blood burns from the vampire had long faded, leaving only a reddened mark on his skin, but there were various cuts and bruises. Much like her own, though she hadn't had a chance to tend them. The one along her side burned as the loupe virus fired through her blood.

"Most likely in some sort of alcoholic stupor in the main cabin," Byrnes replied, and she could hear fabric rustling as he dragged his shirt off the chair and slid into it. "I had to force half a bottle of blud-wein into him before he'd even start to make sense." Byrnes suddenly sounded disgusted. "He kept telling me how brave I was to come back for him. And he's in awe of you."

"You *were* brave," she said, deciding to tease him a little. A glance revealed that he was decently covered and struggling impatiently with the buttons on his shirt. "Sweeping in to rescue your brother like that."

Byrnes's eyes narrowed to thin slits and Ingrid crossed toward him, brushing his hands out of the way and doing the buttons up beneath his chin.

"Thank you," he murmured, and their eyes met.

She lowered her hands. "You came back for me too."

Odd words. She felt like she stood on the edge of a precipice with that sentence, and from the uncertain look on his face, he knew it too. This truce was new to both of them.

"Well, I couldn't have you stealing all of the glory," he finally said, as if to settle them safely back within the familiar realms of their relationship. "Single-handedly defying Ulbricht and his cronies; dashing headlong into the reach of four vampires to pull Debney out, and then carrying him over your shoulder. It's almost embarrassing. Had to do something."

"Maybe Debney's been rubbing off on you. You sound half in awe too."

"Well, I did have the other half of the bottle of blud-wein. Garrett's personal stock."

"Why do you enjoy pulling on Garrett's whiskers so much?" she asked, sinking into one of the chairs. She'd met the guild master a year ago when he'd first commissioned her help during the Vampire of Drury Lane case.

"Because I can." Byrnes shrugged and dragged his coat up his arms and over his broad shoulders.

Which wasn't quite the entire truth, she suspected.

"You're bleeding," he declared. "I can smell it on you somewhere."

The wound along her side was painful, but not overwhelming. "I've bandaged it up. Just an idle claw mark or two. Not going to bother you too much?"

Blue bloods, after all, liked blood. A great deal. But Byrnes had always seemed in control of his darker half. Brutally so.

"I can manage it." At that his expression tightened and he scrubbed a hand across his mouth. "Vampires, eh."

"Vampires," she echoed.

"Real actual vampires," he repeated. "Not like that Drury Lane nonsense. Never thought I'd see the day where I didn't actually *want* to hunt something. But hell... what a sight. What a smell." His nose wrinkled. "Want a drink?"

"As long as it doesn't have any blood in it."

"I've had enough to recover," he replied, squatting in front of the liquor cabinet that was built into the side panels of the room. Glass chinked and he straightened, staring down at the bottle in his hand. "Scotch. That ought to take the edge off things."

Pouring them both a glass, he snagged them in his fingers and handed her one, sitting beside her. "To surviving the unsurvivable."

"To killing the unkillable," she added, and their glasses chinked together in companionable camaraderie.

"I've radioed ahead to London, whilst you were tending Debney," Ingrid said. "Given Charlie and Jack the heads-up on what happened. Garrett was looking for you. Something about a missing dirigible the Nighthawks own?"

"Can't imagine where that went," he replied, offering her a slightly rakish smile that stole her breath.

Don't be a fool. It's not the first smile you've ever been given. But Byrnes's smiles were so rare that they were somewhat shocking in their intensity. He had the whitest teeth, and looked as though he intended some sense of mischief when he graced her with a smile like that.

"The captain's having a minor case of the conniptions," she pointed out, sipping her Scotch. She was half tempted to roll her eyes back in her head. *God, that was good.* "He seems to think that he's possibly absconded with the *Nightingale* against orders, though he *seems* to remember seeing some kind of warrant, and he's fairly certain the guild master's signature was on it."

"I'll explain matters." Byrnes stretched his arm across the back of the sofa they shared. "And it was a good forgery. Garrett won't care. He owes me a favor or two."

"I thought it was his new toy?" She pointed out. "Don't men get rather territorial about such things?"

"Toys can be shared. Garrett will huff and puff, then ask me how it flew. If it were his wife, however, that... that would be a different story." Byrnes's voice softened. "There are some lines a man doesn't cross, some belongings that a man doesn't tamper with."

"Perry isn't an object, like a chair," she pointed out. Leaning back against the chair, she let her head loll to the side. He was watching her intently now, his fingers toying with the loose ends of her hair, and the Scotch held negligently in one hand.

Byrnes tugged on a lock of her hair. "Don't be deliberately obtuse. Garrett belongs to her just as much as she belongs to him." His touch softened. "I wonder...."

"What?"

"What it would be like to belong to someone." There was a questioning tone to his voice, but she wasn't about to believe it.

Ingrid's breath caught. She'd walked into this, let her defenses down, and now she was trapped here as Byrnes slid toward her a fraction. "I don't belong to you," she whispered. "And if you think I'm falling for that codswallop, then you're definitely off your game. Caleb Byrnes is a black-hearted rake who lives for the hunt. Not someone who dreams of romance."

"Aren't I? I suppose you know best." That questioning look faded. He smiled again, loose and relaxed, and instantly back to his old self. Definitely up to mischief. "It's a good thing I cannot fool you." The backs of his knuckles brushed against her shoulder. "It would make you far less interesting, if you were too easily seduced."

Ingrid swallowed, her lashes fluttering down as she tracked the movement of his fingers, every muscle in her body tight with anticipation.

She knew better than to trust his touch, or the faint self-mocking tone to his voice. What was she doing?

Something foolish.

Ingrid pushed away and went for the Scotch, snagging her empty glass between her fingers.

"What's wrong?" Byrnes taunted. "A little hot under the collar?"

"Weary of wading through sweet nothings," she shot back as she poured herself another glass. "I'm tired, Byrnes, and your insincerity is hardly convincing. I don't believe you're interested in exploring forever with me, and if I were to offer you one suggestion it would be this: what makes you think I'd want forever either?"

Byrnes stretched one arm along the back of the daybed, looking coolly unruffled. "Is this a negotiation?"

"It's... an exploring of options. You want to bed me," she told him, frustrated by how composed he looked. Perhaps it was that fact that made him so irresistible to her: she wanted to ruffle him, wanted to see him undone, that facade washed away and replaced by the beating heart within him. She knew it was there, that passion. She'd seen it once or twice on their previous case, and it intrigued her.

"Well, I wouldn't say no," he murmured. "You and me... We've already proven we'd be an explosive combination."

"And if you win your three challenges—"

"Of which I am now up to two," he pointed out.

"Of which you are now up to the second challenge," she conceded, "then you may get a chance to do so. Though the first challenge remains open throughout this case, Byrnes. Renege on your promise to work with me, and you may kiss your chance of getting me into bed good-bye."

He considered that, hands clasped between his knees. "Fine."

"Just like that?"

"Just like that." His smile held mischief. "Because it sounds like you want to fuck me too."

Ingrid shrugged, though her body screamed *yes*. It had been a while, and Byrnes was... a little bit of a secret weakness. "I'm not entirely certain yet. I want to make sure you're not playing games with me in response to that situation last year."

And I don't want to find my heart trampled beneath your boots.

She glanced away. If she were being honest with herself, she could admit that it would be easy to fall for him. She'd never met a man so frustrating, so... challenging. For the first time in her life she could be herself with a man, and he actually seemed to like her for it.

"So," she murmured, "give me one good reason why I should give you a chance to get into my bed... and I might seriously consider it."

"Because I make your heart race and your breath catch. And don't bother denying it: I'm a blue blood. I can hear the pulse thumping through your veins."

A smile danced over her lips. "Running from a vampire made my heart race too, Byrnes. Don't flatter yourself."

"You want me."

Ingrid snorted in a most unladylike manner. Toying with Byrnes always brought out this side of her. "Is this a litany you repeat to yourself of nights, or simply the result of your overexaggerated sense of importance?"

"Let's examine the evidence then," he shot back with a devilishly crooked smile. Holding up a finger, he said, "One, you could have simply delivered that letter to the doorman at the guild. Instead you had to sneak in, leave your perfume all through my room—when you never wear it normally—and slip the letter under my pillow."

"Maybe it was to prove to myself that I could, hmm?"

"Or," his voice lowered to a growl, heat flashing through his pretty blue eyes, "maybe it was because you knew how much it would provoke me."

"Maybe," she admitted, sipping her Scotch. "Provoking you *does* get me all hot and bothered."

Those blue eyes glittered and he smiled as he took the empty glass from her and sat it aside. "Two," he continued, as he slid closer to her, "you could barely take your eyes off me before, when you walked in here unannounced."

"You *are* pretty to look at."

All sharp cheekbones, hard, lean body, and dangerous grace.

"Three"—his mouth brushed against her ear—"you wouldn't be keeping me at bay half as much if some part of you didn't crave me."

She bit her lip, a shiver running over her skin. *True.*

"Admit it, Ingrid. You want me in bed with you."

"Maybe I do want you. But would falling into bed with you be worth my while? Convince me, Byrnes."

"And how do I convince you?" The devil had that look in his eye. "Without any practical experience?"

"You've got a tongue," she suggested, sitting back and sliding the toe of her boot up his calf even as she fanned herself with Ulbricht's secret folder. "Use it. Tell me how good it would be."

Again that smile. A little thrill went through her lower abdomen. Byrnes didn't move, however, just looked at her, and that one look communicated all manner of suggestions. "I would like to use my tongue, but I fear communication isn't my best use of it." His gaze slid lower, down over her breasts and then back up again: a slow, heated perusal. "There are other applications where it excels. Right here. Right now. You... naked and wet beneath me—"

Her breath caught. The improvised fan in her hand slowed. "Tempting... but no."

"Damn it, Ingrid." His intensity returned to her. "Why?"

"Because it suits me."

"You like being chased," he accused.

"And you like chasing."

Those fingers drummed on the table for a moment, quick flashes of expression crossing his face one after the other. She could see the moment he settled back into nonchalance, his mouth thinning and his eyebrow arching. "I know it's going to happen, Ingrid. But I can be patient and wait for you to come to terms with this. Even if it takes you weeks."

"And then?" she asked softly. "What happens after we crash and burn?"

That halted the softening of his smile. "We're both adults, Ingrid. When this ends, it doesn't have to be messy."

Ingrid pushed to her feet to head toward the viewing deck. Maybe it was her recent sense of vulnerability following the telegram she'd received, but the idea didn't sit well with her. "Indeed."

Sometimes she wished he didn't have to be so bloody honest all of the time.

Leaving Debney shivering by the dirigible, Ingrid and Byrnes headed toward the main thoroughfare to find him a steam cab.

Byrnes strode with his hands in his pockets at her side, his gaze turned inward as dawn began silvering the sky. He looked faintly ridiculous in Debney's borrowed coat.

"So what's our next move?" Ingrid asked, feeling equally ridiculous. She'd been forced to borrow a pair of pants from Debney and a great cloak that hung around her ankles, covering up what was left of her pretty ball gown. Fur rimmed the collar of the cloak, itching her skin. All she needed was a highwayman's mask.

"Right now?" Byrnes seemed surprised. "As soon as we get back, I'm going to go deliver the coded letter to Malloryn, and then I'm going to get some sleep. It's been a busy couple of days."

"Really?" Ingrid arched a brow. "Considering the coded papers are stuffed down *my* corset, I was planning on giving them to Malloryn to decode myself."

Byrnes gave her a certain look that made her catch her breath just a little. "We shall see about that."

A shadow skittered near her ankle, and Ingrid's heart felt like it leapt through the back of her throat. Leaping forward, she found herself on top of a house's brick wall, balancing precariously, before she could even think about it.

"What is it?" Byrnes's coattails flared as he spun, a knife springing to his hand. Prepared to face danger, he obviously found nothing worth fighting, and cast her a dubious look.

Oh God. She would never live this down. Ingrid shut her eyes as the rodent's smell caught her nostrils. "Nothing. Just a rat."

The expression on his face was almost laughable. "A rat?" Byrnes's voice was soft. He sheathed the knife then extended a hand to help her down.

Ingrid shook her head. A cold flush had sprung through her veins. She didn't want to get down. She hadn't seen where it went. "Just give me a moment, Byrnes."

The way he looked at her, as if making silent calculations in his head, sometimes made her nervous. Like now. Then his face cleared; a decision made. Moving forward, Byrnes swept her into his arms and turned to stride away from the mess in the gutter and the small squeaking she could still hear. A sound that made her feel ill and forced her arms to lock tightly around his neck as she tried to look for the rat.

"Ingrid Miller." Byrnes's voice was as soft as honey, his arms like steel. "Are you going to tell me that you don't hesitate to launch yourself at a vampire, and yet a tiny, insignificant rat sets you quaking?"

"Shut up."

A brief laugh sounded in his throat, his eyes crinkling with amusement. "Worry not, fair maid. I shall save you."

"If you like your teeth where they are, then I would take my advice," she growled.

Byrnes merely laughed again.

Though she'd been hesitant initially, Ingrid forced her body to relax. He was taking her away from the nasty rat, that no doubt had an entire contingent of friends. Some things were worth forgiveness. Resting her head on his shoulder, she let him carry her.

Sensation began to leech into her. Again she felt that kiss, that sense of longing. Again she just wished she could let him do to her what was promised. Ingrid stroked his collar, not daring to do more, but wishing she could. Falling into bed with him should be easy, so why did it feel so hard to take that step?

I don't want to be discarded at the end. Not like that.

Then what was the answer? Because it was going to happen. She and Byrnes were burned in the stars together, a promise made but unfulfilled. She knew she wouldn't have enough willpower to last the distance. Ingrid rubbed the gilt thread of his embroidered collar between her finger and thumb.

Maybe she should just take the plunge now, get it over and done with, and move on herself, before he could?

"So that's what it takes," he said gruffly.

"What do you mean?"

"A little bit of gallantry has you patting me like a cat." He smiled. "I'm learning your weaknesses, Miller."

She sighed. So was she.

And she was starting to be afraid that her most dangerous weakness was one that remained somewhat unrevealed to her.

"Here," Byrnes said, setting her down on the footpath with a faint flourish.

Ingrid patted her cloak into place. "Thank you."

With his hands in his pockets, Byrnes strolled beside her. "Why are you afraid of rats?"

Just the word sent a shudder of dread through her. "I'm not."

"Really?"

Ingrid turned her face away, feeling that queasy sensation return. "I would rather not speak about it." But that didn't mean that she wouldn't remember it. Viktor's face sprang to mind, slack and gaping in the shadows of memory. A little boy, locked in a cage on the ship the English raiders had dragged her to as a child. He'd been half-dead when they put her in the cage next to him, and not quite all-the-way dead when the ship's rats had started eating him. She didn't know how old she'd been—four or five—but she would never forget that moment, or her screams when the rats scurried over Viktor's corpse and nobody came to help her.

Firm hands cupped her cheeks, and suddenly Byrnes's face swam into view, breaking through her waking nightmares; those stark cheekbones, and the harsh slant of his dark brows. "Then I shall not ask."

Ingrid let go of the breath she'd been holding. She'd expected him to push, but was thankful that he didn't.

"Let's go hail that cab," she said, and turned away.

CHAPTER ELEVEN

DEBNEY SHUDDERED, wrapping both hands around the flask of warm mulled blood that Ava had fetched for him. The bloodied gashes at his wrists and ankles where the chains had cut him were gone now, healed by the craving virus, but the night's events had shaken him.

"I don't particularly wish to be alone tonight," he'd told Ingrid, with shadows in his eyes, and so Ingrid had stepped into the steam cab with him and taken him back to Baker Street.

Malloryn was at a ball, according to Isabella Rouchard, squiring his fiancée around town. It was the first Ingrid had heard about his engagement, but from the baroness's tone, she didn't like to press. Some things were easy to guess about the humans surrounding her, and judging from how often Malloryn wore Isabella Rouchard's perfume, she knew she was most likely correct in her assumptions. The woman was his mistress.

Until Malloryn returned, she had nothing to do but sit and wait for Jack to help decipher the coded letter she'd found at Ulbricht's. At least Byrnes had returned to the

Guild of Nighthawks, which gave her some peace of mind about his promised, "later."

"You've a visitor." Jack limped into the workshop with his goggles sitting high on top of his head.

"Oh?" Ingrid asked, caught in the act of fetching a rug to wrap around Debney's shoulders.

Crisp heels rang down the staircase, and Ingrid's heart leapt within her chest as she recognized that step and the purposeful swish of skirts. Rosalind Lynch, the Duchess of Bleight, swept into view, gowned in a deep purple that gleamed beneath the gaslight. As Jack's sister, Rosa shared the same coppery hair and the same stubborn mouth. Calculating brown eyes swept Ingrid from head to toe, and then Rosa came forward to press her lips to Ingrid's cheek.

"My, my," Rosa murmured. "You look lovely in a gown. Or the remnants of one."

"It itches, and I can't breathe," Ingrid replied.

Rosa laughed. "There's my fierce verwulfen friend. I was wondering what this stylish young woman had done to you." She glanced down. "Though she made short work of your skirts, I'm afraid. Is that blood?"

"Not mine."

"It never is." Rosa looked amused. "Want to tell me all about it?"

Guilt flared. *No*. No, she did not. Because whilst Jack might not bat an eyelid over Byrnes's reappearance in Ingrid's life, Rosa knew altogether too much. And fiercely disapproved.

"Jack, will you keep an eye on the viscount for me?" Ingrid murmured, noting the curious look Jack gave Debney. Then she linked arms with Rosa, drawing the duchess back upstairs, toward the parlor. "What are you doing here?"

"I cornered Malloryn at the Parkers' ball," Rosa snorted. "He told me where you were. You haven't been at your rooms for days, though I found Malloryn's invitation in your drawers and recognized the writing."

"Some secret." Ingrid sighed. "And what were you doing going through my private documents?"

Rosa looked amused. "The same thing you were doing when I was working undercover as Lynch's secretary. Trying to keep an eye on you. You haven't been to dinner in an age."

Privacy, she'd learned, was practically impossible when it came to Rosa and her two siblings. All she needed now was young Jeremy showing up and lecturing her about getting involved in dangerous affairs. Which would be somewhat ironic, considering how many times she and Rosa had saved him by the skin of his teeth.

But then, she guessed that turnabout was fair play. Rosa was family, and that meant more to Ingrid than anything in the world. Meddling in each other's lives seemed to be the price they all paid for the warmth and love that they shared. "I've been busy."

"Clearly." Rosa looked around. "Malloryn has a mind like a steel trap," she warned. "Don't get caught in its jaws."

"Brandy?" Ingrid ignored the warning, knowing that Rosa was only worried about her.

"Would love one," Rosa replied, drawing off her gloves as she perused the parlor. One of her hands was entirely mechanical, and Ingrid noticed the easy way Rosa wore it these days, when once she'd hidden it behind a never-ending supply of gloves. Rosa's marriage to Lynch had brought about a newer, softer presence in her friend.

"How's the baby?" she asked, because that was something else that had changed in Rosa's life.

"Too well behaved. He barely cries, he sleeps most of the night, he watches everyone and *everything*, and he wears this serious expression on his face most of the time. I fear Lynch had more involvement in Phillip's temperament than I." Rosa's smile softened her entire face, however, for baby Phillip was the light of her life. "It's only now that he's reached his first birthday that I'm starting to see a hint of stubbornness about him. He tried to strangle his father the other day, and Lynch spent ten minutes telling him about the importance of cravats in a man's life, and how Phillip was to keep his chubby little fists off them."

"Did he listen?" A quiet yearning filled her. Ingrid adored Phillip, but it was a bittersweet sensation.

"He stuck the end of the cravat in his mouth, and Lynch just sighed." Rosa nursed her brandy, reclining in the chair like the Queen of Sheba. "So," she said, throwing down the gauntlet, "Malloryn tells me you're working with Caleb Byrnes again."

Which was the real reason that Rosa was making this early morning call. "Apparently I enjoy torturing myself."

"Really?" Rosa's dark eyes locked on her. "It has nothing to do with bets made and...not quite paid up?"

"I never should have told you about that," Ingrid growled. "And I paid what was owed. Byrnes should have been more specific."

Rosa's eyes narrowed. "How does *he* feel about this partnership?"

"Bloody ecstatic, by his own proclamations. I won't pretend that he's not interested in gaining some measure of revenge."

"Of course he is." Rosa sipped her brandy. "Byrnes lives for the hunt, and you, my dear, are the one that got away."

Which was nothing that she hadn't told herself. Ingrid threw back her brandy, then stalked to the liquor decanter to pour another. "Then he'll live to experience disappointment once again."

"Ingrid," Rosa warned. "You're upset. I can tell."

"That's because I was set upon by a vampire barely eight hours ago."

Rosa sucked in a sharp gasp. "What?"

And so Ingrid told her. As one of the councilors on the Council of Dukes, it wasn't as though Malloryn wouldn't have taken her into his confidence anyway, and she trusted Rosa a hell of a deal more than Malloryn.

All of the color had leeched out of Rosa's face by the time she'd finished. "You're certain there were four of them?"

"You're the one who taught me to count," she replied irritably. "And there's only three now."

"Three's enough." Rosa scrubbed at her mouth. "Hell. Vampires loose in London. I never thought I'd see the day."

"Well, they're not loose yet," she replied, softening a fraction. It was clear that Rosa was shaken. "And they're not quite in London. Ulbricht's manor was an hour's flight away. I'll let you know if I see them again though. Give you time to get Phillip out of the city."

"What about you?" Rosa asked.

Ingrid shrugged. "I survived one."

"Ingrid." There was that tone again.

"I'll be safe, Rosa. I promise."

Thoughts and plans raced behind Rosa's dark brown eyes. "I think you should—"

"Enough, Rosa," Ingrid said softly. "Enough. Let's speak of other things."

"Like Caleb Byrnes?" Rosa retorted, frustration twisting her mouth.

"Not like Caleb Byrnes."

Rosa crossed to her armchair, sinking onto the edge of it. "Fine then. No more talk of vampires or dangerous blue bloods. Come to dinner on Sunday," Rosa said, holding Ingrid's hands and squeezing them. "Promise me."

"I'll try," Ingrid replied. "It depends on this case. But I'll send a note if I'm not going to be able to make it."

"If you don't, then I'm going to think that something's wrong with you, and I'll only come looking for you again."

Ingrid rolled her eyes. "Was I ever this painful?"

Rosa reached down to kiss her cheek. "Yes," she said, "you were even worse. Remember when you threatened to skin Lynch alive if he broke my heart?"

But Ingrid smiled. Here, with Rosa, she *belonged*, and sometimes it was the only thing that made her feel whole. "I have no recollection of that at all."

Rosa drew away with a snort. "He does. Now the shoe is on the other foot. Be careful, Ingrid. I'll see you on Sunday."

CHAPTER TWELVE

A LONG FRUITLESS day of following up on smaller leads stretched behind Ingrid.

Jack had retreated to what they were affectionately calling the dungeon to attempt to decode the scrap of letter that she'd found; Byrnes was off at the guild, coordinating the use of Nighthawks in tramping all over the Venetian Gardens; Gemma Townsend was reportedly setting up surveillance on Lord Ulbricht; and Ingrid had snatched six hours of sleep before checking in on Ava to see if there'd been anything else from the autopsy or the Doeppler orbs connection.

Today had been a frustrating day. No results on any of the leads, but Ingrid knew from long experience that these hours spent laying down the groundwork often yielded a vital clue in the end. One of these leads would suddenly amount to something, and the entire case would open up.

She just wished it would happen sooner rather than later.

Ingrid dug her thumbs up under the arch of her brows to relieve the pressure in her aching head as she pushed aside her notes.

Footsteps echoed in the hall, along with soft feminine laughter.

"Are you coming?" Gemma Townsend called, popping her head in through the door to the library, where Ingrid had been meticulously going over her case notes.

"Coming?" Ingrid looked up distractedly. "Where?"

Gemma slipped inside the library, a fan dangling from one wrist and a rather daring ruby gown barely containing her figure. "Malloryn's letting us off the leash for the night," Gemma said, "while he sets his information networks to ferret out every secret Ulbricht ever owned. So a few of us thought we might as well see a bit of the town, get to know each other a little better." She shrugged one slim shoulder. "It's probably going to be our last chance for a while, for as soon as Malloryn discovers something, he'll have our noses to the grindstone. The man doesn't know the meaning of the word 'rest.'"

Time to get to know each other.... It wouldn't hurt. After all, these people might hold her life in their hands one day.

Ingrid looked down at the sheets of paper in front of her. *Ulbricht. Vampires. Venetian Gardens. Orbs. Connection?* She'd been staring at her notes for hours, and nothing was making sense anymore. Time away from this place would do her the world of good, and hopefully allow her mind to clear. "Who's going?"

"Charlie's leading the expedition—it was his idea, after all. And somehow he's talked Kincaid into coming. Something about gaming hells, I believe. Then it's just you, me, and Ava."

"No Byrnes?"

"No sign of him," Gemma replied with a cheerful shrug. "I think he's still at the Nighthawks Guild."

"Good." A weight lifted off Ingrid's shoulders. She needed a night away from him following the intensity of that kiss.

The man was dangerous to her senses.

"So... does that mean you're tempted?" Gemma asked.

"Be more specific," Ingrid drawled, crossing her arms over her chest, and leaning back in her chair. "Where, precisely, are we going?" A night out on the town could mean anything, from the fighting pits in the East End to the automaton theatres in Covent Gardens. And Gemma reminded her of Rosa in some ways; flirtatious, worldly, and cynical. She could be leading them anywhere. Particularly astray.

Gemma's smile was pure deviousness. "The Garden of Eden. Ava has an interest in plants and as soon as she heard where we were heading, she wanted to come and examine the... flora."

Flora. Ingrid's eyebrows arched. "She does realize that plants are hardly the draw card to the Garden?"

"Oh, I must have forgotten to mention that!" Gemma's eyes widened in mock surprise. "Want to come and watch her spectacles fog up when she realizes where she is?"

Ingrid frowned, then pushed her way out of her chair. "I'll come, if only to keep the rest of you from leading her too far afield."

"Excellent." Gemma spun toward the door, shooting one last glance back over her shoulder. "But I'm going to have to insist upon a dress, darling."

"Another?" Charlie Todd blinked as he leaned on the table and stared her down.

Ingrid allowed herself the faintest of smiles. "Give in before I drink you under this table."

"I can hold me drink...." He blinked again. "Hell and damnation, are you even feeling it? You look so bloody cool and collected."

"I'm verwulfen, Charlie," she replied, dragging her small cheroot case out of her reticule. "Alcohol burns through me like it's been set on fire."

"B-burns through me too," he declared, finding his feet and swaying a little. "But not that bloody quickly. Here. I'll fetch another bottle." He wove away through the crowd, swaying slightly, as he joined Gemma at the bar.

"Amateur," Kincaid sniffed, and threw back his glass. Considering the fact that he was purely human, his steadiness was impressive, as he wasn't far behind either her or Charlie. Seeing her considering look, and interpreting it correctly, he arched a brow. "Experience counts, love."

"There's experience," she countered, "and then there's the type of man who's drunk enough in his lifetime to earn some sort of immunity."

"Every man here's got his own demons," he said, stirring his finger through the sticky ring of brandy on the table. "And ways to deal with it. I had a few bad years a while ago."

"It's not going to be a problem, is it?"

Kincaid's blue eyes glittered as they locked on her. "Are you and Byrnes going to be a problem?"

Touché. Ingrid shrugged as she lit a cheroot, and breathed it in. The last thing she needed was Malloryn getting wind of this. She needed the money too much. "That's none of your concern."

"Not mine, no." His gaze slid sideways as the swish of skirts hurried up to the table. "But if I were a betting man, it might be someone else's."

Ava slid into the seat beside Ingrid, breathless in green silk. "Did you know that there are fire-breathers in the back room? This place is... extraordinary."

That was one way of putting it. At the front of the room, the crowd thinned as attendants wearing only tweed vests, tight pants, and bowler hats cleared some space. A sheet was dragged across the stage, but her attention was focused on Ava, and Kincaid's words.

She liked Ava. And she obviously wasn't the only one who'd noticed how the pretty laboratory assistant lit up when Byrnes entered the room, which left Ingrid feeling like slime coated her skin.

"Shadow Show's starting," Kincaid said, his voice like liquid velvet in the night, and again, they were on the same wavelength.

Ingrid had rather hoped Ava would stay enamored with the fire-breathers a little longer.

"Ladies and gentleman." A tall woman wearing a ringmaster's attire strode onstage as the lights dimmed, and instantly the room fell quiet. "The lovely Miranda and Cozette are about to begin their act. Do we have any volunteers to assist them?"

Over two dozen men threw themselves to their feet, waving their arms.

"Pick me, ma'am!"

"I volunteer!"

A chorus of enthusiastic cries rolled around the room, leaving only their table untouched.

Kincaid looked unimpressed and poured himself another brandy as a spotlight suddenly flicked on behind the sheet, highlighting a bed.

"You're not keen to volunteer?" Ingrid murmured.

"Do I look like I'm the fucking entertainment?" He held out his hand, and she passed him her cheroot, which he took a long drag from. "I prefer... something a little more private." His gaze lit on the long-legged beauty in the ringmaster's outfit.

"What must he do?" Ava asked, as a young man was helped onto the stage, thrusting a fist in the air in victory toward his rowdy table.

Ingrid looked at Kincaid. Kincaid looked back at her, and actually appeared to blush.

Coward. "He's, ah, they're going to engage in—"

"Oh, my goodness," Ava whispered, staring at the stage. "Are they...." Her mouth fell open as the shadows moved, and it became very clear that yes, yes they were. "Is that even legal?" she gasped, as the two curvaceous women dragged the willing young fellow behind the sheet.

Kincaid eyed the fellow's rampant excitement as one of the shadows pushed the fellow down on the bed. "Probably not."

Ava blushed to the roots of her hair, but tore her gaze away. "Oh, my goodness."

Ingrid shot Kincaid a look, who returned it steadily. Then he handed back Ingrid's cheroot and sighed. "Would you care to take a stroll in the gardens, Miss McLaren?"

"Is it going to be any safer out there?"

"Possibly." Kincaid's smile turned slightly evil. "But then, you'll be with *me*, so possibly not."

Onstage the female shadow crawled up over the ecstatic young volunteer, and Ava staggered to her feet. "Yes! Yes, the garden would be good."

"I deserve a medal for this," Kincaid murmured in Ingrid's ear as he rolled to his feet and extended an arm toward Ava.

"Be nice to her," Ingrid warned, and it wasn't entirely playful.

Kincaid rolled his eyes. "Virgins," he said, in some disgust.

And then they were gone.

Ingrid stayed to watch the show. A swift glance showed Charlie caught up at the bar, laughing at something that another young man was saying. The play onstage didn't interest her overly much, but if she closed her eyes and listened to the soft sounds of laughter and panting, then she could imagine she was elsewhere.

In Byrnes's bed, her thighs straddling him as she bent down to take his nipple between her teeth.

That got her going. Half memory. Half dream. Soft fingers of heat trailed through her abdomen and lower, leaving her wet as the man onstage gasped. *Then she was sliding lower, down the chiseled ridge of his abdomen, as Byrnes flexed beneath her, his wrists bound to the bed with her stockings.*

"Touch yourself," he rasped.

And Ingrid smiled, rearing up to tug at the ribbons on the chemise as they trailed between her full breasts. "Oh, Byrnes... who said you *were in control?"*

A shiver ran over her skin. A sense of foreboding. Ingrid stubbed her cheroot out, exhaling the smoke. She felt like she was being watched.

Opening her sleepy eyes, she had a moment of disorientation, as though she were in the dream again, reliving that memory. But as Byrnes prowled the edge of the room, his gaze locked on her, she realized it wasn't a dream. Nor a memory.

But the man himself.

Giving in to temptation, Byrnes trailed his fingertips along Ingrid's shoulders as he slid into the chair next to her, ignoring the stage with its enthusiastic noises. "Where was my invitation?"

"You weren't around," she replied, the sudden stiffening of her spine belying the easy way she'd been sitting with Kincaid and Charlie until he showed up.

And didn't that get to him.

Watching her laughing and drinking with the other men had set him close to the edge. Because she didn't behave like that around him. No, there was always some sort of tension in her whenever they shared a room.

It was his own bloody fault too. He'd not considered how frustrating this would be. Not so much in a sexual manner, though there was that too, but returning to Baker Street with the expectation of running into Ingrid and starting some kind of teasing debate, and then not finding her there....

"See something you like?" he asked, glancing toward the stage. There was not a chance in hell he was going to admit his conflicted feelings.

"Not yet," she replied.

"Liar."

She smiled faintly.

Despite the rowdy shouts throughout the room, and the ensuing climax onstage, they might as well have been alone. Byrnes reached out and traced his fingers down the back of her hand. She didn't pull away, but she didn't encourage it.

And he didn't know what to do about that.

Withdrawing his hand with a wry smile in her direction, he leaned his arms along the back of his chair and two neighboring ones, creating just enough of an illusion of distance to make her settle. There was an uncomfortable knot in his abdomen. He shouldn't have come. But the second Herbert had told him where they'd all gone, he'd wanted to. He'd even looked forward to it, to seeing her, taking some time to reconnect with her after a day apart. She'd enjoyed his kiss, but had it only been the heat of the moment?

"Find anything today?" he asked.

"Nothing," she replied, in a disgruntled voice. "And you?"

"Same."

Silence fell, and her gaze locked on the stage. Was this affliction something only he felt?

Suddenly he couldn't handle it anymore.

"I need some fresh air." The chair legs squealed on the floor as he stood.

Byrnes was halfway across the room before he realized he was being followed. Those sharp rapping heels alerted him to her identity, a second before Ingrid shoved him into a dark corner at the back of the room. "What was that?"

Byrnes glanced around. Nobody watching. "Nothing."

"You're the one who fled with his tail tucked between his legs."

That irked him. "Maybe I'm weary of being left out in the cold. You clearly didn't want my company. So I complied with your unspoken demand."

"I didn't want you to...." Ingrid pursed her lips together, then looked down, at the hand pressed against his chest.

"Didn't want me to what?" Byrnes captured it, and pinned it there, so that she could feel the beat of his heart. *Come on, damn you.*

Ingrid's eyes flared with heat as the pressure on his chest eased. "I shouldn't do this right now. I've been drinking."

"Don't go." He held her hand there, the words blurting out of him. At her arched brow, he cursed under his breath. "Nothing's going to happen tonight. Not if you've been drinking. I promise I won't touch you."

"How gentlemanly of you."

But she relaxed. And it felt like a kick in the guts.

"If you don't want this, Ingrid," he growled, "then tell me. And this ends. Now. Tonight. I keep thinking you're enjoying having me chase you, but then"—he let her hand go, gestured to her—"your spine practically acquires an iron rod whenever I walk into a room. And if I get too close to you, you push me away. If you don't want me, then say so."

Ingrid looked away. "You make me nervous."

Which was not what he'd expected her to say. Byrnes sorted through the words. Then again. And then a smile curved over his mouth as he began to understand them. "In what way?"

She buffeted him in the arm. "Stop smirking at me."

But all of the tension between them was gone.

Thank God. He wasn't the only one who was afflicted with this... issue. "That's not an answer."

Ingrid rolled to the side, resting her back against the wall and closing her eyes. "You make me nervous because I'm not entirely certain I trust your intentions."

"I—"

She waved his words away. "But I trust that you want me, more than you're willing to compromise that."

He brushed a strand of honey-brown hair behind her ear, resting the other hand on the brick wall behind her, near her hip. "Have I not proved that I'm willing to work with you? That I can compromise?"

Ingrid sighed. "That wasn't what I was referring to."

He examined her. "Then what—?"

"Forget it, Byrnes." She rested her head against the brick wall, looking up at him from beneath that fan of dark lashes. "Just forget it. It's the brandy talking."

Byrnes studied her, his thumb stroking her ear. He wasn't going to forget a thing, though he'd comply for the moment. "So… are you going to give me the second challenge?"

Ingrid considered it, then her eyes turned smoky with devilry. "Maybe."

"You've had time to think."

"Fine. Give me a present the likes of which no one's ever given me."

"Done." His smile widened, his thumb brushing against her cheek. Once. Twice. It didn't escape his notice that she was virtually asking him to court her. "And what do I get when I complete the challenge?"

"What do you want?"

Everything. "Don't tempt me," he whispered, leaning closer.

Ingrid's gaze dropped to his mouth, almost unconsciously. He wanted to kiss her, knew she wanted it too—but he'd promised.

Byrnes withdrew, just an inch or two. "I want… to pleasure you. I want… my mouth all over you."

Again that smile. "That sounds like a reward for me."

"Maybe it's a reward for both of us? You don't know how often I've thought of what happened last year, of how close we came…." He couldn't help himself. "Did you ever think of me?"

"Of course I thought of you." Her voice softened. "I'm rash sometimes, Byrnes. What I did that day—writing that poem and leaving it on your pillow, leaving you tied to the bed—it was not…. It was wrong of me, and I regret it."

Byrnes made a frustrated sound in his throat. This was not what he'd meant. "Are you *actually* apologizing?"

"Of course I am. I shouldn't have liked it if you'd done it to me. I was angry, and you were being your obnoxious best, and I lost my temper."

"Somehow I remember it differently."

"Really?" Her words came out more growl than speech again, but she did that when she was uncomfortable, he'd noticed, not just when she was angry.

He crossed his arms over his chest, considering his words. "It's entirely possible that I... deserved it. Sometimes I say things I don't mean." Clearing his throat, he added, "Lynch always tells me that pride will be my downfall."

"You're just saying that because you want to get under my skirts and get your revenge."

"Revenge has nothing to do with what I've in mind. I told you that."

"Oh?"

"Damn it, Ingrid. Is that all there is? All you've thought about me in the last year is regret about leaving me tied to my bed?" He reached out and rested his hand on the brickwork beside her head. "You didn't once think about what could have been? You didn't once regret the missed opportunity?"

Wary eyes gazed back at him.

"I've thought of you every day," he admitted, and that uneasy twisting sensation in his stomach made him pause. It was hard to admit this. Harder to let go of the secrets he kept hidden within him. But he needed to. "Every day." His voice softened as he saw that he had her attention. "And I looked for you. At first because, yes, I wanted revenge. Not in the way that you think. It was not your humiliation I sought, but you. What you'd promised. I wanted you. I wanted to kiss you, damn it, to taste your mouth again."

His gaze dropped to her lips. Those tempting plump pillows of rose. "I dreamt of that mouth. Of all the things it could do to me. I woke up with you tangled in my mind, but missing from my bed. A perfumed ghost. And you haunted me, day and night. You got under my skin and I... I don't even know how you did it."

Ingrid's heart began to race. Byrnes closed his eyes, leaning closer to her until their foreheads pressed against each other and his hands cupped her cheeks. Giving in to temptation, he stroked her silky mouth with his thumbs. "I hate it that you didn't think of me at all." Easier to admit when he couldn't see her looking at him. He brushed his mouth against her temple. "Not like that. I hate it that whilst you haunted me, I was barely a glimmer on your horizon, a port that you'd sailed from, without a single look back."

"I thought of you." She barely breathed the words.

Did you? His heart leapt at the thought.

"And then I thought that only madness came of following those thoughts, so I pushed you out of my mind." Her hands curled around his wrists, and she ducked beneath his arm, heat flushing through her cheeks. "How can I believe you? It sounds too good to be true. You're not the type of man to be tied down."

"Because I don't lie, Ingrid. You know that."

Those considering eyes killed him. But she finally nodded. "No. You don't, do you? Even if the truth is a blunt-edged weapon in your hands."

"Then hear this: this is my truth. I don't want revenge, Ingrid. I don't want forever. I just want you in my bed. I want to know what it feels like to explore that... that spark between us. I want to exorcise you from my mind, from my thoughts. That's all. I want to burn like the supernova that flames through my veins when you're nearby, and drown myself in these feelings until it's done. Until you're... extinguished from my soul."

Until I can finally forget you.

Ingrid's eyes grew dreamy, but the hesitation was still there.

"I want you," he breathed. "This needs to end between us, Ingrid. I need to burn you out of my blood, and the only way I can think to do so is to follow this through to its natural conclusion. *I will* complete your challenges." The words were a promise. "And you will end up in my bed. And then? Then I can forget you."

Ingrid watched him as he backed away, her eyes lost to the amber of the wild within her, her body frozen as if she both yearned to drag him back and push him away.

It was the first time he'd seen how haunted she herself appeared, and though he'd expected the sight to assuage something inside him, instead it did the opposite. The darkness within him rose, thick and choking, demanding that he go back to her.

But Byrnes turned away from it.

After all. He'd promised.

Somehow she'd gotten turned around.

Ava swallowed hard, her fingers clenching around her reticule's handle as she slipped through the shadows. The garden looked familiar. She'd been here before with Kincaid, she was certain of it. Just as certain as she was that she was travelling in circles. Damn it. Where were the others? She'd told Kincaid that she was heading to the ladies' refreshment rooms for a moment, but somehow she'd gotten lost.

A little chill ran down her spine, and her lungs squeezed tighter.

Don't panic, she told herself. *Don't make a fool of yourself when everyone's around.* The others were all clearly enjoying the night. She'd forced herself to come, determined to try and fit in with the rest of the group, no matter how badly out of place she felt. But the truth was that she'd perhaps pushed herself beyond her own natural boundaries.

Gemma teased her for being provincial, but it wasn't the worldliness of the place that had her out of sorts, but the fact was that she had rarely been out and about in three years.

I'm not ready for this.

There. That was the truth. The crush of people unnerved her, and the dark shadows and private grottos everywhere only added to her unease. Ever since she'd survived the ordeal that made her a blue blood, she'd been taking small steps back into a normal life, trying to pretend that everything was all right. The Nighthawks Guild had become a home to her, and in a way she'd thought she was getting better. She could manage small excursions away from the guild, could even view crime scenes, but the past few days at Baker Street had started the nightmares again, and desperate for some normality she'd thought that a night out with the rest of the company might improve matters.

She'd been wrong.

Instead, tonight had only revealed the truth. Whatever was wrong with her was not going to go away so easily. She was right back where she'd started during that first year with the Nighthawks, when every shadow made her jump and she'd suffered from her hysteria attacks.

A woman's laughter echoed nearby, and a man murmured something to her. Something explicit enough to make Ava blush. She stumbled away from them, trying to find the main pavilion. Even those shadow shows would be better than this. At least the others would be there.

A branch cracked beneath someone's foot.

Ava froze.

Then it came again, as though some large shape forced its way through the luxurious gardens.

Ava made an inarticulate sound in her throat and brandished the lacy parasol she carried. "S-stay back!"

The shadow stilled, fading into its surroundings, until she wondered if she were imagining things.

Ava swallowed, her pulse pounding madly in her ears and a rushing sound filling them. She was on the verge of a hysterical attack.

"It's only me," a deep, roughened voice said, and Ava nearly collapsed against the brick walls in relief.

Kincaid's hard face looked like it had been carved out of stone as he stepped out of the shadows. She'd never thought she'd have been so genuinely enthused to see him.

"Oh, this spot's already taken," said a pouty young lady, materializing at his side and practically wrapping herself around him.

Kincaid never took his eyes off her. Ava's corset laces dug in to her ribs, and she was fairly certain she was going to faint.

"Unfortunately, luv," he told the woman, "I seem to have remembered a prior engagement."

The woman gaped. "What?"

"Here's a monkey," he told the brunette, slipping her a five-pound note. "Drink's on me."

The brunette's lips thinned, and she said something as she strode away, but Ava was shaking too hard to hear it. *Don't do this*, she told her body desperately. *Not now. Not in front of him.*

Kincaid unnerved her. He was too large, too broad-shouldered, too... imposing. And there was never any kindness on his face, though she'd tried to steer clear of him at Baker Street.

"What are you still doing out here?" he growled. "Thought you were going back in to see Gemma?"

"I just came to... to take a walk, and I've lost my way—or maybe I deliberately wandered off the path, because I saw some sort of exotic greenhouse with these plants that I've never seen before, and I-I wanted to see if I could collect a sample. I collect ferns you see." Somehow her mouth was running away from her, all of the words spilling from her lips in a steadily rising stream, until she sounded almost hysterical. "And then I got turned around... and I couldn't find my way back, and now... now I can't... can't breathe..."

"You're safe now," he told her, watching her with those intense eyes.

"I can't... I c-can't...." *Not safe. Never truly safe again.* She knew the truth of that statement far too well.

Dark blue eyes smoldered down at her. She had to look away, but as she moved, his hands came down upon her shoulders and turned her around. Ava gasped. Her heart was racing, and she felt like she was about to fall face-first into the greenery.

"Here," he said, and brushed the loose curls at the back of her neck over her right shoulder. A second later there came a sharp tug, and then her bodice gaped.

"What are you doing?" She slapped over her shoulder at his hand.

"Unlacing your corset," he replied gruffly, and resumed his task as though she hadn't protested. "So you can breathe."

Another button popped loose on the back of her dress, and then rough fingers brushed against her exposed nape. Ava froze, only this time, it had nothing to do with fear.

The cold steel of his mech hand brushed her skin, and another button popped loose. Then two more. Ava was gasping by now, but somehow the touch grounded her, made her feel less and less like she was spinning out of control.

"H-how do you know... your way around a woman's undergarments so well?" she blurted, then instantly recoiled. Oh, goodness. She'd practically handed him a sarcastic rejoinder. Of course he knew what he was doing. The way he'd been watching those women behind the silk screen tonight had made her almost uncomfortable, and when he'd sensed her watching him, there'd been a knowing look in his eyes.

"I'm sorry." *Stop talking, right now.* But her mouth wouldn't listen. "Of course you know what you're doing. You were out here alone with that woman, after all. I'm sure you weren't just taking a stroll. Oh, God. Don't listen to me! I'm just.... I d-don't—" She clapped her hands to her mouth, silently praying for the ground to open up and swallow her whole. The movement made her corset and dress sag, and she clutched at them, realizing she could catch her breath now.

Even as she felt twice as vulnerable.

A warm coat slung across her shoulders. "Better?"

"No." She shuddered, and somehow her hand came up and caught his when he went to remove it from her shoulder.

She could sense the hesitation in him, the reluctance. "Please," she whispered. And then his other hand came down upon her left shoulder, and he squeezed. Ava let out the first full breath that she'd managed since this entire ordeal had begun.

"Sit," he suggested, and those firm hands guided her to the stone bench.

Long minutes ticked out as she sat there. At first Ava concentrated only on breathing, on trying to regain her equilibrium. Some part of her couldn't take her hand off his, even though it was made of metal.

"I'm sorry," she finally whispered. Those hands slipped from her shoulders, leaving her strangely bereft of his warmth, as he settled beside her on the stone bench.

"Happen often?"

"Sometimes. I thought I was past it. It's... being somewhere new, I think."

He stretched his long legs out in front of him, his hands resting on either side of his hips on the bench. Their shoulders brushed against each other and then his hand came to settle on hers again.

Ava looked down. His hand dwarfed hers, and his skin was so much darker than her own. He didn't speak, which made her feel both comforted and a little out of her depth, but seemed content to remain there.

She tugged the coat tighter around her bare shoulders with her other hand. What a mess she was, with her gown gaping and her corset awry, and her body starting to tremble as it came out of the hysteria fit she'd almost suffered.

"You don't leave the house very often," he murmured.

"It's safe there." The words came automatically, and she cringed. She couldn't speak of the horrors that she'd suffered through four years ago. Couldn't even remember them without dredging up the panic that she felt.

So she mentally began counting, going up in sets of prime numbers. And through it all, Kincaid simply sat there.

"I thought you hated blue bloods."

"I do."

Ava tugged her hand out from under his and clenched them in her lap.

"But you don't look like a blue blood," he added. "And you don't act very much like a blue blood. And I'm trying to come to terms with the whole bloody lot of you in the house."

"Language," she chided.

Kincaid arched a brow at her and withdrew a flask from his waistcoat pocket. Without the coat, he looked enormous, his shirt straining over those heavyset shoulders and the muscles in his biceps stretching the white cotton. He lifted the flask to his lips, then paused, staring at her.

"Please don't look at me like that," she whispered.

One of his eyebrows lifted. "Like what?"

"As though I'm some foreign object you're not quite certain what to make of." The same way that her father had looked at her when she'd vowed she wanted to enter the medical profession, or the way that her fiancé had looked at her when she'd tried to be more ladylike for him. And then couldn't resist speaking about stupid things that ladies did not speak of in polite company.

Kincaid lowered the flask. "I'm *not* quite certain what to make of you," he admitted, and then frowned again. "And you were looking at me."

Ava's shoulders sank. It was like Edinburgh all over again, like her father's home, like the entire rest of her life. The only place she'd ever belonged had been at the guild, and the only man who ever made her feel like a normal young lady had been Byrnes. He didn't care if she spoke too much, or had a peculiar interest in autopsies and the way the human body worked. He'd always been interested in what she had to say, as though she were nothing out of the ordinary.

And now he was interested in someone else.

Oh yes, she'd faded into the wallpaper the second Ingrid walked into the room at Malloryn's study, and she knew it. The worst thing was that Byrnes still treated her exactly the same, and in the past few days she'd come to the realization that whatever she'd thought had been going on between them had clearly only been in her mind. Not his.

"Here," Kincaid said, his knees spreading so that their thighs touched as he turned to offer her the flask. "You look like you could do with a little something."

The rich scent of whiskey hit her nose. Ava's mouth watered, but it wasn't just for the liquor. Something dark and heated flashed through her body as the *craving* awoke within her.

And wasn't that just the perfect end to the day.

"Sip?" Kincaid asked, offering her the flask.

She didn't want just a sip. She wanted to drain the whole bloody flask. "Bottoms up," she said cheerlessly, and set about doing precisely that.

"Hey, hey, easy now."

Strong hands caught the flask and for a moment she was half turned into his chest and the suddenly quite intriguing scent of his aftershave. Her vision changed, turning to little more than shades of black and white as the predator within her stirred. Suddenly she could see the minute hairs on the side of his jaw, the small abrasion from his razor... and the pulsing thud of his pulse through the vein in his throat. Everything inside her locked on that.

"Jaysus," Kincaid muttered. "Thought you was going to spit it all back out."

"My father's Scottish," she found herself saying as she stared at his throat. A part of her wanted to press herself against him, to push him down upon the stone bench, set her lips to his throat, and.... She blinked as a flash of image came to her; the rich, heated taste of his blood as she suckled at his skin. It was so intense that it took her breath away. "I grew up sipping whiskey."

It wasn't going away. Ava glanced up from beneath her lashes as Kincaid scratched at his jaw. Her vision locked on his fingers, on his throat, his pulse, his....

She thrust the whiskey flask at him and stood abruptly; anything to get away from him.

"Hell," Kincaid swore as the whiskey sloshed over his hand. "What are you about now?" He looked up, and then every muscle in his body stiffened as he saw her eyes. Something ugly crept over his face, and Ava lowered her damning eyes that were no doubt as black as tar.

"I think I'm having some sort of... out-of-body experience." She pressed her hands to her heated cheeks. ·

"You mean, you wanted my blood," he practically snarled, facing her like a spitting cat.

"Yes.... No!" She clapped a hand to her eyes, and hunched over herself. *Oh God, it won't go away.* "I do *not* want to drink your blood, like... like some sort of animal. I'm... a young lady. Not a monster." She patted her own pockets. "And I didn't bring my own flask." Why hadn't she brought it? She knew the risks. The formula must be taken at regular intervals, and she had at least another two hours until she needed to take it, but she was feeling not at all herself right now. Oh, she'd had moments since she was infected with the craving virus, but not like this. Ava gulped in a breath of air.

"Yeah, well, I only got whiskey, not blood."

"I wouldn't drink blood if you had it! I carry my own protein-enriched synthetic formula with which to sustain myself in the absence of blood."

"You're a blue blood and you don't drink blood?" Kincaid sounded incredulous.

"Not all of us like what we've become," she retorted, "and after the first few months I began dabbling with a formula to sustain myself. It's not the same, but I appear to be able to survive on it."

Those enormous arms crossed over his barrel chest and an evil expression touched his face. "Then what happened just then?"

"I momentarily forgot myself," she stammered. "And it's your fault! You... unlaced my gown! And you were touching me, and sitting so close to me... and sometimes I cannot help the way I feel, the thoughts I have! You don't understand what it's like!" She took a step away from him, for his cologne was beginning to distract her again. "What matters is controlling these urges when they arise. And not allowing them to overrule the senses."

Kincaid's brows slowly drew together. "You didn't just want my blood."

It wasn't what she'd expected him to say. "Pardon?"

"You said it was because I unlaced your gown and was touching you." One eyebrow went up. "So just what was going through your mind when you started looking at me like you wanted to strip me naked and eat me all up, princess?"

"I most certainly was *not* looking at you like that!"

He took a step toward her, and she took one back. They faced off, and a trace of heat crept into her cheeks.

"It's just... animal passions. That's all the craving is. Sir Richard Doyle presented a scientific treatise on the subject, about how blue bloods call it their 'darker half,' or the 'darkness' inside them, but...." He was stepping closer. "But it's just the primal side of one's nature, drawn to the fore... just.... What are you doing?"

"All them big words sound pretty, luv,"—he smiled—"but let's call it what it is. You feel the same itch as I do, as any man or woman does."

Reaching out, he caught both lapels of the coat she wore around her shoulders and tugged her a little closer to him.

"Now," he purred. "Look at that." Another tug jerked her against the wall of his chest, and then her hands were pressing there, and she couldn't stop herself from flexing them, and good God he was like warm steel, and—

"You're so firm," her mouth blurted, without any direct interference from her brain.

She made a sound, deep in her throat, as he took one of her hands and started dragging it down his chest, lower....

"It's even harder down here," Kincaid whispered, his gaze dipping toward his belt as if to point out the obvious.

I'll just bet it is. After all, as delightfully naive as everyone thought her, she was well aware of what had been going on behind that sheet. And of what, precisely, Kincaid referred to.

The thing that surprised her, however, was how tempting it was to let him keep dragging her hand lower.

He wasn't Byrnes. Indeed, she wasn't certain that she even liked him. But Kincaid was warm, and his body deliciously firm beneath her touch, and she was a scientist, after all.... Curiosity began to itch. And other areas of her body.

What would it be like, just once, to set aside all of that cursed thinking that constantly overwhelmed her and just feel?

Kincaid's pull on her wrist softened as her fingertips grazed his belt buckle. As Ava glanced up beneath her lashes, she saw the smile die on his mouth. The moment dragged out as he looked at her—looked *through* her—as though seeing every naughty little thought that was scampering through her mind.

"Bloody hell. You were thinking about it." He sounded almost as surprised as she felt, and not at all as cocky as normal.

Ava tipped her chin up as she took a step away from him. "I was not. And... and I am not giving your coat back! Not until tomorrow."

Then she fled.

CHAPTER THIRTEEN

THE MAN THAT answered to the name of Ghost lashed out with economical grace, the staff a whirling blur in his hands.

The lad facing him met the first attack with his own staff, then the second glanced off a hastily thrown defense. Ghost ducked beneath a blow and retorted with a sharp swing of his staff that swept Henrik's feet out from under him. As soon as the fellow hit the mats, Ghost drove the butt of the staff into Henrik's throat and held it there, not quite hard enough to crush the cartilage.

"You still expect me to strike at your upper body," Ghost told him. "Watch my hips and shoulders to see where the next move will come from."

Henrik gurgled and frantically caught the staff in both hands to alleviate the pressure.

"It makes you weak and susceptible to a strike at your feet or legs—" A disturbance at the door caught his attention. Ghost glanced up from beneath pale lashes and saw the man standing just inside his training room. He relented and stepped back, swinging the staff up under his arm as Henrik gasped for breath and touched the indentation in his throat. "Continue practicing with the others. You have a week to improve this flaw. The next time it happens in a spar, I'll kill you. Now leave us," Ghost commanded, and the pale youth scrambled to his feet and nodded respectfully to the man at the door as he hurried out.

"He's coming along," Obsidian murmured, tugging his gloves from his fingers one by one as the door eased shut. His silvery hair was tied back in a neat queue.

"They're weaker than we are." Ghost placed the staff in the wooden grooves where it usually lay, then swiped his shirt off the nearest chair and swung it around his neck, holding on to the ends. There was no sweat on his skin, but his muscles felt nice and loose. Henrik had at least taken the edge off him.

"That's to be expected," Obsidian noted. "We were the first, and without Dr. Cremorne to recreate the transformative elixir, we can only guess at the precise measurements required for it. They're still stronger and faster than a blue blood and that's what we truly require."

Ghost waved the conversation away. It wasn't important. The recruits were merely cannon fodder. He, Obsidian, and the other original four were the important ones. Sliding apart the pair of doors that led to his study, he strode directly for the blud-wein decanter in the corner and poured two glasses of it, though truly it was more blood than wine these days. "I didn't expect to see you until Monday." His tone held no disapproval, but Obsidian circled the desk warily and tugged a folder from under his arm.

"News."

Ghost offered him one of the glasses, and they chinked them together, then each took a sip. "Good news?"

"Our enemy is moving faster than we expected. Malloryn suspects something," Obsidian replied, taking a seat. "He's put together a special group, though I only caught wind of it yesterday. His Grace is remarkably difficult to follow for a duke. One would think he'd had *dhampir* training."

"We were warned that he wasn't what he seemed." Interesting, however, as Obsidian was one of Ghost's best agents, and if he was having trouble tracking Malloryn, then that meant something. Ghost sank into his own seat and flipped open the folder. There were sepia photographs inside. The top one displayed a man and a woman arguing in the street. The woman was tall and somehow vibrant, and the fellow had the look of a blue blood about him. A dangerous one. "Do we know them?"

"Part of Malloryn's taskforce. He's a Nighthawk," Obsidian replied. "Caleb Byrnes. She's verwulfen."

Ghost's eyes met Obsidian's, but he was curious more than anything else. "That shouldn't be a problem."

"They took out one of Zero's vampires at Lord Ulbricht's," Obsidian replied, and Ghost took a closer look. "Don't underestimate them."

"How?"

"Don't know. I wasn't there. But I saw the creature's body. Head shot with one of those exploding bullets that certain members of the population seem to be employing these days."

"Maybe someone got lucky." Ghost dragged the folder closer to him. That was interesting; certainly more interesting than biding his time and training the latest batch of inept recruits. "How many of them did the vampire kill? And what were they doing at Ulbricht's?" How had Malloryn's agents gotten a handle on that little plot so swiftly?

"No kills, I believe. The intruders escaped whole. As for why they were at Ulbricht's gathering, I don't know."

"Yet," Ghost said, and it wasn't a question.

"Yet." Obsidian frowned. "I know we were told to wait, but I don't see why we shouldn't simply kill Malloryn now. The Master might want to drag this out, but I'd much rather tie up loose ends. Malloryn already proves that he's no fool. The more chances we give him to ferret out what we're up to, the more chances he has to destroy this scheme. And if he already knows about the Sons of Gilead plot, then he's halfway there."

Ghost flipped through to the next sepia-toned photograph. "Dying is easy. The Master has a score to settle with Malloryn. He wants him to see the destruction first, to watch as his precious new empire is crushed beneath our heel. No, Malloryn shall be the last one to die. And the SOG are little more than one head of the snake. Losing a pack of puppets costs us little. They don't even know who's really pulling their strings, and they're only part of phase one. Who is this?" he asked, pointing to a heavyset man with a mech arm who was striding down the stairs of a house and settling his hat in place.

"A mech." Obsidian immediately dismissed him. "The others don't seem to like him very much, and he's easily killed. The younger fellow at his side is also unknown. A blue blood by the look of him."

Ghost glanced at the lad's colorless hair, pale eyes, and snow-white skin. "Clearly. Also clearly not someone from the Echelon." No, the young man had the look of a survivor about him from the way he watched the streets. Fancy clothes couldn't hide that.

"I'll keep an eye on them and try and figure out who they are."

Another photograph, this time of a pretty young woman with blonde curls and small half-moon glasses.

"Ava McLaren. She's a Nighthawk too," Obsidian explained.

"Then it's possible Malloryn is utilizing the Nighthawks for this?" That wouldn't bother him, though it gave his enemy more manpower than expected.

"Possibly, though it's not common knowledge, even among them. I broke into the Nighthawks Guild last night to confirm. Both Byrnes and McLaren are on a leave of absence. McLaren's a scientist, little more."

"That was a risky move."

"Nobody even saw me. You'd think for a building full of blue bloods they'd have some idea of when they were compromised. The problem is, they've accounted for both human and blue blood. They had no idea how to counter for something like *us*." Obsidian glanced away, tapping his fingers on the chair.

Ghost's eyes narrowed in on that betraying movement. His best agent was uneasy, an anomaly that he'd rarely seen in Obsidian. Ghost slowly turned over the last photo, and understood why.

Hollis Tremayne peered out of the window of the house. She was no longer blonde, and it took a moment to recognize her, but Ghost was immediately drawn back into the past, into Russia. He traced the glossy black curls and her pretty heart-shaped face before closing the folder. "So Hollis survived. What happened? You don't usually miss."

"I wasn't aware that I had, until yesterday," Obsidian replied in a chilly voice. "The last time I saw her I shot her point-blank in the chest and she fell into an icy river. She was human and she shouldn't have survived. There was no trace of the body, but I was badly burned, thanks to her. I barely managed to escape, let alone search for her."

"Is this going to be a problem?" he asked, sitting back in his chair. That entire mess in Russia had been catastrophic, and he'd nearly lost his best agent. Obsidian wasn't the kind of killer who had a weakness, but Russia had revealed it, and it owned a soft luscious mouth and a lying tongue.

"She calls herself Gemma now." Obsidian met his eyes. Not a muscle moved in his expression. "And no, it won't be a problem. It wasn't difficult to pull the trigger last time, but now.... When it comes time to finally set the next phase into action... she's mine, do you understand?"

"Understood."

Obsidian flowed to his feet. "I'll continue to keep an eye on the house, and on Malloryn. Permission to leave?"

"Permission granted." Ghost kept his thoughts to himself as Obsidian took his leave. Leaning over to the communicator in his desk, he pressed the buzzer that would summon Henrik.

It only took a minute. Henrik appeared, barely out of breath, his moonlight-blond hair wet from a bath.

"Yes, sir?" Henrik snapped to attention.

Ghost opened the folder again, and slid Hollis Tremayne's—or Gemma Townsend's—photo across the desk. "You've been granted a reprieve from training," he said. "I have a task for you. Find this woman. And don't come back until you've killed her."

CHAPTER FOURTEEN

INGRID WOKE UP with one hell of a headache. Grumbling to herself, she swiftly dressed and then made her way downstairs in the house at Baker Street. Malloryn had set aside rooms for all of them if they required, but this was the first time she'd actually stayed there.

"Breakfast, miss?" Herbert asked, appearing out of nowhere.

Ingrid's stomach growled. "If you find me breakfast, I promise I'll marry you. Herbert."

The tall, possibly-a-blue-blood smiled back at her. He was mostly invisible, but always in the background somewhere, she realized. "Not necessary, Miss Miller. But I'll keep it in mind."

In the dining room Gemma rested her head in her hands. Her usually neat hairstyle was missing, replaced by a messy chignon. "The next time I mention a night of debauchery," she pointed out, "remind me of this moment."

"You did seem to be having a rather lively discussion with Charlie when I left. You two still haven't decided what we're going to call ourselves?"

"A Company of Crackpots," Gemma replied with aplomb. "That's my vote this morning."

"Good morning," Ava said brightly, slipping into the seat opposite Ingrid and thanking Herbert as he brought her a tray of toast and warmed marmalade. "What are the plans for today, ladies?"

"Dying," Gemma groaned.

"Eating my way through this entire breakfast," Ingrid replied, reaching for the plate of fried beefsteak. "If anyone else wants some, I'd advise you take it now."

"Oh." Ava poured herself a cup of tea, blinking at them. "Both of you look half-dead. I've seen more color in the corpses on my examination table. You do realize what your livers probably look like this morning?"

Gemma paled. "Please. No mention of bodily organs. At least not until lunch."

"Well, look at the team," called a slightly amused voice as the baroness strode into the room, her red skirts swishing. "Busy night, was it?"

All three of them sat up a little straighter.

The baroness arched a brow at Gemma as she handed the woman a folder. "Malloryn's not going to like it."

"Well, Malloryn needs to locate a sense of humor," Gemma retorted, sipping her morning cup of blood. "I'd suggest he look inside the part he sits upon, to start with."

The baroness's lips twitched. "I'll pass that along to him when he arrives."

"You are prime evil, Isabella," Gemma shot back fondly. "No wonder the two of you get along so smashingly."

The baroness's sable eyebrow lifted. "Someone has to keep you rabble in line."

Gemma winced. "I'd continue sparring, but I don't think I have the temper for it this morning."

The baroness smiled, and Ingrid realized the two of them knew each other quite intimately. "Meeting in two hours," the Baroness said to Ingrid. "We need to discuss what to do about the Ulbricht situation."

"Kidnap him?" Ingrid suggested.

"Kindly ask him to provide more detail about this SOG?" Gemma added.

Ava frowned. "That sounds like torture to me."

"Ulbricht's a powerful lord," the baroness replied. "I'm not suggesting anything until Malloryn approves it." She glanced at Ingrid. "Do you know where Byrnes is?"

"Probably at the Guild."

"Then find him," the baroness said.

"As you wish," Ingrid muttered to her back. She looked around. "I suppose I've been given my marching orders."

"Good luck," Gemma called. "Byrnes looked like he went home in a hurry last night. Something you said?"

The last thing she needed was the rest of the company thinking there was something going on. Ingrid forced a smile. Malloryn would be certain to hear of it then. "Probably. But then, with Byrnes, it often doesn't take much."

He wasn't difficult to track from the Guild.

Blue bloods might have no personal scent, but they absorbed the scents surrounding them. Byrnes was leather, steel, and oil, with the faintest hint of the cinnamon he sometimes chewed. That scent was engraved on her skin, on her memory. Ingrid growled under her breath as she stared up at the building in front of her.

She'd never have thought it to be here.

Ingrid found him in the third room along the top floor of Miss Appleby's Home for the Elderly. Or more specifically, she tracked him there by his voice, which was strangely soft and lyrical, reading some sort of romantic comedy about a Mr. Darcy. She'd never considered his to be the kind of voice one could listen to for hours, but as she paused by the door she heard something there she'd never heard before. Warmth, perhaps. A trace of gentleness, as if he'd let down his armor, revealing hints of the man within. It reminded her of the way her mama had read to her as a child before she went to bed.

The door was cracked. She almost didn't hear the soft footsteps approaching until the door spilled open and Byrnes stared out at her, still reading.

Their eyes met, his blue and cool, and narrowing faintly. There was a much-loved book in his hands, and she couldn't stop herself from peering past him.

Ingrid caught a glimpse of blankets and a bed, and a frail hand resting upon the covers, and then Byrnes stepped forward, shielding the occupant from view.

"What are you doing here?" he whispered.

"I followed you."

"Clearly."

Frustration surged. "The baroness requested your presence for a meeting with Malloryn."

"Tell him I'm occupied." His mouth thinned to hard lines. "Go home, and—"

"Hello?" called a frail voice. "Hello?"

Byrnes paled and swore under his breath. Then he shot her a look so severe that she almost stepped back.

"Keep your voice lowered, and don't make any sudden movements. And for God's sake, if you tell anyone about this I will wring your bloody neck."

Swinging the door open, he gestured her inside. "My mother," he breathed, before raising his voice. "Moira?"

Mother? Ingrid's gaze shot to him in shock.

At first glimpse, the woman in the bed was much older than she'd expected. Long white hair streamed over her shoulders, and she wore a blank, faded expression, her mouth hanging slightly open.

"She doesn't like loud noises, or new experiences," Byrnes warned. "It scares her."

"Is she—?"

"Moira," he greeted, easing his hip onto the bed and taking the older lady's hand. "You have another visitor. This is my friend. Ingrid."

The very idea that sardonic, sarcastic Caleb Byrnes could be this gentle was like discovering that a vampire could tuck its child into bed tenderly. *Knock me over with a feather.*

Heart pounding in her ears, Ingrid summoned a smile. "Hello, Mrs. Byrnes. It's a pleasure to meet you."

The old lady gaped at her, and Ingrid realized that she wasn't that old after all. Worry had etched those sharp lines around her eyes, and her slack mouth spoke of an oft-broken jaw, not feebleness.

"She won't reply." Byrnes cracked the book open, finding the passage where he'd been reading and resuming in a soft voice that was almost hypnotic. "...I am perfectly convinced by it that Mr. Darcy has no defect...."

"Why don't you call her 'mother'?"

Byrnes scowled, thrusting his hands into the pockets of his coat as he stepped off the curb and negotiated the busy London traffic. "Quite frankly, it's none of your business."

Ingrid's lips pressed together, and he realized he'd made a mistake. Catching her wrist before she could turn to go, he stared down into those bronze eyes. "I don't like talking about her," he admitted, and even that admission scraped him raw. "Now come on, let's get this over with."

"Byrnes!" A hand reached for the edge of his coat.

He kept walking, but it came again, and reluctantly he stopped. He wasn't entirely certain why he felt so angry. Perhaps it was the reappearance of Debney into his life, scratching the scabs off old wounds and reminding him of a past best left hidden. Perhaps it was his mother's inevitable decline. She hadn't even recognized him this morning. He was losing her. Inch by inch, memory by memory. The nurses all claimed that his mother knew him, but every time he visited, his mother greeted him with a "Hello, dear," that sounded like a familiar greeting, until one realized she said the same thing to everyone.

Even him.

His mother couldn't remember his name.

Hesitant bronze eyes came into view, framed by wisps of hair that had fallen loose from her ruthless chignon. Ingrid. Who threw him into turmoil with just her mere presence.

It was all part of it; this maelstrom of emotion that knotted him up tightly.

"Fancy a walk along the Thames?" she asked.

"We have to meet with Malloryn."

She hesitated. "You're right. But we've got a half hour, and this won't take us too far out of our way. And I think this is important. You're not thinking clearly at the

182

moment. I know how it feels when emotion overpowers you."

"I'm not emotional."

"You're angry." Those dangerous eyes watched him, but there was no judgment there.

Byrnes swore under his breath, raking a hand through his hair.

"You need to have your wits about you if we're dealing with vampires and who knows what else. Come." Her fingers curled through his. "Come and walk with me."

And God help him, he went.

"I come here when I want to think," Ingrid told him, pausing along the banks of the ruins of Westminster and turning to face the Ivory Tower that ruled the city.

The marble gleamed in the weak morning sunlight, hurting Byrnes's eyes a little with its brightness. Once upon a time, it had been a symbol of brutish oppression, a sign of the power the prince consort had wielded over the humans, mechs, and rogue blue bloods of London. Now it was a sign of hope. Or it was supposed to be.

Byrnes felt nothing as he stared at it, but there was something about Ingrid's hushed confession that drew his gaze back to her. The light gilded her face too, but he had more interest in staring at the soft curve of her rosy lips and the honeyed slant of her cheekbones than at any stone monolith. "Why here?"

"It reminds me of them," she replied with a quiet yearning.

"Who?"

"My parents," Ingrid whispered, still staring up at the Tower, as if lost in memories from long ago.

And he was suddenly struck with a sense of uneasy kinship. Ingrid was verwulfen and of all the species that inhabited Britain, they had been persecuted the most, for they alone had the strength and power to overwhelm a blue blood. Hundreds of verwulfen had been slaughtered at Culloden by the Echelon's war machines, and they'd been kept as slaves or in cages as curiosities ever since.

He'd never asked where she came from, or what her life had been like. Ingrid never showed even a hint of vulnerability, but it was there now, and it made him uncomfortable.

"This was where the raiders who stole me from my parents brought me ashore," she told him, wrapping her arms around her middle. "I don't know how old I was. Rosa thinks that I was perhaps five, though verwulfen children grow larger than others." She glanced up at the Tower again, her voice lowering. "I just remember feeling terrified. I didn't know where my parents had gone, or why these strangers had taken me. They'd run me down in the snow near my home, and chained me, taking me aboard their ship and delivering me here. My father had been out hunting with me that day. I-I don't know what happened to him."

He felt ill. "Ingrid—"

"There was a market here," she said, gesturing about the stone cobbles. An Egyptian obelisk peered down at them. "They were selling all manner of things: screaming monkeys, beautiful macaws, parrots who swore like sailors, a pair of snarling baby leopards who smelled as terrified as I felt." With a swallow, Ingrid met his gaze, her own eyes suspiciously shining. "And I was in a cage right next to them. I kept stroking one of the leopards through the bars, for she was so scared. So little. I wanted to let her know that it would be all right, but it wasn't—"

"Ingrid."

"And that was when Lord Balfour appeared. He sat astride this enormous horse, and he peered down at me with such coldness that if felt like my heart stopped. And then he bought me for a hundred pounds." With a fractured laugh, her gaze danced to his. "I can remember every inch of what Balfour looked like that day; the imperious hook to his nose; those black, emotionless eyes; the cut of his black coat, and the gold serpents embroidered there. But I can barely recall my mother's face. I don't remember my father either—"

"Ingrid, stop." Byrnes caught her hands, stepping closer. He couldn't stand much more of this. Their eyes met. "Why are you telling me of this?"

There was a raw, hunted look in her eyes. "I took some of your privacy from you. And you were angry. I just thought... if you understood where I came from.... I would never cause any hurt to your mother, or—"

"I'm not angry with you." Byrnes's gaze dropped to the way his thumbs were stroking her leather-clad knuckles.

"You were."

"No. I'm just...." With a muttered curse word, he turned away, facing the Thames. "I wasn't expecting to see Debney the other night, and my mother's deteriorating, and... I can't do anything about it. Nobody can. The doctors call it dementia, and say that it's just age taking its toll upon her, but... it feels like I'm burying my mother, day by day." The words were raw, harsh. Their admission ripped his chest open. "Her body is still there. Her heart still beats, but my mother's gone. She's just a shell, a marionette now."

"Byrnes." A soft hand touched his back. A hesitant hand. "She's young to be suffering from dementia."

The words choked in his throat and died there.

"I could see the scars," Ingrid whispered, "and the lump on her jaw, and her nose—"

"That's enough." He burst away from her, breathing hard, as memory assaulted him.

"Don't you ever tell me what I can do to my own son," his father bellowed in his mind, as he lifted his clenched fist against her that last time.

If only Byrnes hadn't roused his temper that day. His mother would still be here.

No. No. He wasn't going there. Not today. With a hard swallow, Byrnes forced himself to turn back to Ingrid. "Her dementia is not natural," he finally said, when he thought he could control himself. "It's the result of years of being my father's punching bag. The last time he hit her... he did some sort of damage to her mind. The doctors didn't think she'd wake, but eventually she did, two weeks after she fell. They had to drill burr holes in her skull to remove the pressure, and... she was never the same. Not really. Sometimes you'd see her in her eyes, but most of the time she was a blank canvas, staring at nothing. It grew worse over time. Now she has no idea who I am, or where she is. Debney feels some sense of guilt, so he pays her upkeep. I wouldn't take a shilling from those pack of vultures, but damn it..." His nostrils flared. "They owe her. I can't give her back her mind, or all the years Lord Debney stole from her, but I can force them to acknowledge what he did to her."

"I'm sorry."

A hand slid over his. Byrnes looked down sharply, then up at her face. Those amber eyes had softened, and she stared at him with a haunted expression that made all of his insides knot up.

Without saying a thing, he squeezed her hand. And it felt so bloody right that he suffered a moment of doubt.

"Have you ever tried to find your family?" he asked, letting out another harsh exhale as the hard lump in his throat threatened to overwhelm him.

"I tried. Last year.... That's what I needed the money for, in that case we worked together."

It felt like a fist to the gut.

"I lied," she admitted. "I told Garrett and Lynch that you were no help in finding the Vampire of Drury Lane. I needed all of the bounty to purchase my passage to Oslo, and to pay people there for information." Her lips pressed tightly together. "It was wrong of me—"

"No." He cut her off with a tight wave of his free hand. "It was the truth. I let my arrogance and my competitive nature affect my case. *You* did all of the hard work. *You* found the bastard, and hence you earned the bounty."

"But your mother," Ingrid protested. "I saw the Home. It has to cost you a significant sum. I hate the thought that I took money you needed, for a fool's quest."

"Debney set up a trust for her years ago. Don't worry about it."

The cool breeze stirred strands of her honey-brown hair across her forehead, and for a moment he was tempted to brush them back behind her ear. "You look thoughtful," he said instead.

"I was just thinking that we seem to have a few things in common," she replied. "It explains a great deal about you."

"Such as?"

"Why you always seem so aloof," Ingrid said.

"I'm not always aloof." And now he was thinking of last night, of all the things he'd admitted to her. She'd been flushed with heat and relaxed, the smell of too much brandy on her breath. Ingrid in a state of flirtatious relaxation was a dangerous thing.

"True," she admitted. "Sometimes you play nice."

"When I want something."

"You're holding my hand right now, Byrnes, and I don't think it's because you want something." Her gaze turned thoughtful. "Why is it so difficult for you to admit to the gentler emotions?"

Hell. There was no answer to that. He'd shared enough today. And that itch was back: irritation making him shift. "It's not difficult," he argued. "But you seem to think that I've felt them before. And maybe I haven't?"

"Do you mean you feel them now?"

Instantly he realized his mistake. But it was too late. "Ingrid," he warned.

Ingrid turned into him, the angle of her body suddenly changing the way the wind brushed over them. She fiddled with the lapel of his coat, seemingly absorbed. Soft hair caressed his chin as the wind blew it.

Byrnes sucked in a sharp breath. Want kindled the fire in his blood. The urge to kiss her made every muscle in his body taut with need. "I wanted to kiss you last night," he told her. "But I was trying to be a gentleman."

"There's a first time for everything," she quipped lightly.

"Behave." He tapped her on the nose. "I'm trying to be nice."

The laughter in Ingrid's eyes made him smile. "Nice is overrated. Do you know what I think about sometimes?"

"What?" he breathed, leaning closer to her.

"About what it would be like if you *weren't* a gentleman." Her eyes told a thousand tales, all of them naughty, as she met his gaze.

He swallowed. Slowly the pad of his thumb rasped over her knuckles. Ingrid's dark lashes shuttered her eyes as she glanced down.

"I want to kiss you right here, right now," he said.

"And your challenge?"

"Curse the bloody challenge." He leaned closer, sliding his hand around her nape. "I want to kiss you, just because I can. Because we both want it."

"So you can burn me out of your blood?" she asked lightly, leaning up on her toes to brush her lips against his cheek.

Sheer idiocy. He wasn't entirely certain what he'd been trying to say last night. Only that she was tattooed under his skin, somehow. And leaning against him right now, her full breasts pressing lushly against his arm. Thought fled. The words he'd been meaning to say vanished.

"Do you do this to me on purpose when we're in public?" he growled, turning his face to brush his mouth against hers. Just lightly.

Her lips moved against his. "Of course. There's nothing to stop you from kissing me."

Only that pair of gentleman over there, watching them. His vision dipped into a chiaroscuro landscape as something dark within him snarled. What he had planned didn't bear witnesses. Byrnes's chest heaved. "You're doing this on purpose. Just to try and make me sweat."

One hand stroked down the hard planes of his abdomen. "I think I'm finally starting to work you out, Byrnes. That's all. I think you're... full of bluster. You say you want this to be over and done with, so that you can forget me." Hot lips scored his ear, her tongue darting out to lick his lobe. "Only... I don't think you're ever going to be able to forget me. No matter what happens between us."

Fuck. His cock leapt to ready attention, and he couldn't stop himself from picturing precisely what could happen between them. What he wanted to make happen.

"I am *this* close to throwing you over my shoulder and taking you somewhere where I can have my way with you," he growled. "Think that's bluster?"

The smile she gave him was completely mysterious and totally feminine: utterly pleased with itself. "You want me, Byrnes. You want me so badly you're burning with it. But I don't think you've entirely admitted to yourself why you want me. Or what you *really* want." Stepping back, she let go of his coat. "Don't look so surprised."

But he was. Because the words didn't feel like a lie. They had the ring of truth to them, and— *Hell.*

Ingrid tugged out her pocket watch. "We're going to be late for that meeting with Malloryn. Come on. Hurry up."

Bloody female.

CHAPTER FIFTEEN

GEMMA TOWNSEND FLUTTERED her fan as she moved slowly through the British Museum, keeping a surreptitious eye on Lord Ulbricht. He was pacing in front of the Elgin Marbles, and kept checking his pocket watch.

Stopping in front of an urn, Gemma opened the guidebook that she'd been pretending to peruse and made small notes in it. A bulky coat and a drab brown gown that was padded in certain areas to make her appear older than she was hid her figure. Her wig was a concoction of brown and gray hairs, and she'd carefully placed a much-loved hat on top of it. A pair of occipital lenses turned her pupils from blue to hazel, and the clever application of powders and a new set of eyebrows had aged her face a decade. Today she was Mary Halstead, reluctant spinster with an interest in Egyptian artifacts.

And Lord Ulbricht was meeting with someone.

A stranger appeared at the far end of the hall and strode directly toward Ulbricht. The stranger towered over Ulbricht, with graying muttonchops and a distinctly Georgian style of coat. Some of the older blue bloods remained old-fashioned, as the Echelon had always been shockingly resistant to change.

Gemma assessed the newcomer through the glass case. Clearly a lord, judging from the amount of gilt on his coat and the pompous way in which he carried himself. Could be a century or more in age, which meant he belonged to one of the Great Houses who ruled the Echelon. Though they might no longer have the influence they'd once had, thanks to technology's advancements and the revolution, some of them hadn't quite realized that fact.

"...this all about, Ulbricht? I don't have time for your nonsense." The stranger's voice echoed in her earpiece.

On her slow meander through the museum, Gemma had placed a communicator in the room Ulbricht currently lingered in, and scratching idly at her ear, she managed to tune her receiver.

"If you were wise, Sunderland, you'd make time."

Sunderland. Gemma's eyes widened. If she wasn't mistaken, that meant the stranger was the Duke of Sunderland, and he was over a century and a half old. This conspiracy went deep into the heart of the Echelon.

"I assume you're attempting to sway me from my plans." Sunderland sniffed. "You might have that pack of hounds baying at your heels, but I assure you that you don't yet hold enough to dictate the vote."

"Maybe it doesn't need to come down to a vote," Ulbricht murmured.

The duke laughed in genuine astonishment. "You're going to challenge *me*?" his hand slid to the rapier sheathed at his side, and he took a threatening step toward Ulbricht. "One of the premier swordsmen in England?"

Ulbricht's answering smile held sinister tones. "I guess we shall have to see. I was hoping you'd step aside and yield. I respect your work here. The Sons of Gilead would still be without a voice if you hadn't conjured up this idea and brought us all together in our unified cause. But your time is done, Sunderland. We need a new direction, a more emphatic voice. It's not enough for the SOG to merely mutter in the darkness. There's work to be done."

"Work is *being* done, you insolent little pup."

Ulbricht snorted. "Your rallies? The planned blockade of the Council? Please. The queen no longer respects us, nor our plight. Once we were kings, but this bloody revolution cost us everything, and if you're content to sit there on your ass and tug on her skirts in some vain hope for a crumb or two, then I'm not. I mean to see the queen and her Council of Dukes regret the way they discarded us."

"The meeting's tonight. Then we'll see who is fit to lead the Rising Sons," Sunderland hissed. "And it's not going to be you, Ulbricht. Not with your destructive plans, nor your liberal ideas! I've heard people are missing, and it's starting to be noticed. Did your whore take them?"

"That's none of your business, Sunderland."

"You're no better than that rabble in the White Tower. At least they're led by the queen, not your pale bitch. I am done with you!"

The duke turned away from Ulbricht, and Gemma straightened to attention as she saw the malicious glint in Ulbricht's eyes as he stared at the Duke's back and muttered. "Yes, we will see. By the time this week ends, Sunderland, it will be *explosively* clear who should lead."

The words sent a sinister chill down her spine, and she pressed the communicator tightly against her ear, trying to make out his mutters. Just what did he mean by that?

But Sunderland's heels clicked on the marble, coming directly toward her. There was no time to lose, nor time to get away. Gemma brushed a curl in front of her ear to hide her communicator, then lifted the museum's pamphlet as though she were perusing it. Two seconds later, Sunderland rounded the corner and bumped into her.

"Oh, I'm so sorry, sir!" she said, catching at his coat to stop herself from falling, even as she slipped a tracking device under his lapel. "I didn't see you there."

The duke frowned at her, but the disguise did its magic. All he saw was an aging spinster, one that was both unthreatening and undesirable. "Quite all right," he replied haughtily. "But you should watch where you're going in future."

Gemma straightened her hat as the duke strode away from her. Then she began to make her way back toward the entrance of the museum. Ulbricht had disappeared, but now she had another mark to follow.

Or did she?

A whisper of noise behind her made her pause.

Gemma glanced in a glass case, but could see nothing in the reflection. Still, her nerves were on edge. She'd always been a good spy, but after the events in Russia she'd been prone to these bouts of nerves. Russia had taught her that she wasn't invulnerable. It was one of the reasons Malloryn had retired her in the first place. She'd been a mess back then and she didn't blame him, but now he'd given her a second chance.

There's nothing there, she told herself. *You're only imagining things.*

Maybe it was only the words that Ulbricht had muttered? Setting her on edge with thoughts of conspiracies and explosions.

But... she'd long since learned to listen to instinct.

An Egyptian sarcophagus stared back at her, as Gemma flipped the small lady's pistol holstered at her wrist into her hand. "Hullo?" she called. "Is someone there?"

A servant drone suddenly wheeled into the room, steam hissing from its vents as its little brush swept up dust into a pan. The automatons had replaced the cleaning staff in most places in London, including here.

Fool. Gemma lowered the pistol. Just a drone. She was letting her anxiety get to her. To prove it to herself, she flipped the small pistol back into the mechanical wrist holder and let out a slow breath.

This time, she didn't even hear a thing. Only saw a blur move behind her in the reflective glass case.

A hand clamped over her mouth and hauled her back against a hard body. Her training kicked in and Gemma jerked her head back, hearing a resounding crack behind her as the base of her skull met a nose. Then a hard fist punched into her side, robbing her of her breath.

She caught the fellow's wrist and spun out of the way, twisting as she went... but it didn't all go quite according to plan. Gemma staggered, strength leeching from her body. What the hell was wrong with her? Another punch drove into her ribs, and cost her a lungful of breath as she staggered back into a glass case, smashing it into particles as she fell.

Whispers of darkness curled up from within her. Blood. She could smell blood. Or the *hunger* within her could.

As if the thought broke a glass wall between her and her body, pain came crashing down upon her. Bleeding.... She was bleeding. Gemma touched her side where the man had punched her, and her fingers came away wet.

"*Help,*" she whispered, crawling through the glass, its shards cutting into her hands. "Help!"

"There's no help here," came a cold voice, devoid of emotion. "This isn't personal, you know. Or at least, not for me. I'll make it swift, I promise."

A wave of dizziness washed through her head, leaving her tripping sideways as she tried to gain her feet, and she didn't have the strength to force the fellow away as he came for her again. Hard hands locked around her throat. As she went down, Gemma knew she was fighting for her life. Blue bloods were extremely difficult to dispose of. This wouldn't kill her. But it might render her unconscious, and once there, it would be easy for her attacker to cut her heart out of her chest. A pale face swam into her view as she gagged and punched up uselessly between his clenched hands. *No. Not like this.*

Gemma fought, using her knees and her fists, but a tide of blackness began to grow at the edges of her vision, and her lungs were heaving like a chest pump, robbed of air and sucking desperately for oxygen.

The last thing she saw as the world crashed down upon her was something moving behind her attacker's shoulder....

Obsidian stared down at the woman on the floor, his chest heaving with fury as his hand curled around the stone fossil he'd used to beat the man to death. There was nothing left of the fellow's head. Merely a bloody pulp. He couldn't even remember doing it. The last thing he recalled was Hollis flailing backward as Henrik's hands locked around her throat. And now he was standing here, Henrik was dead, and Obsidian's knuckles were cut from where he'd obviously punched his way through one of the glass display cases to retrieve the fossil.

What the hell had he done?

The lost time unnerved him. The sight of her unnerved him. It brought back a lifetime of bitter memories and unanswered questions, and he'd buried those doubts years ago. Or thought he had.

He dropped the fossil and backed away.

He'd lost control. That was clear. And dangerous. If anyone found out—if the man who called himself Ghost found out.... He should finish the job. Right now. This was his chance to take revenge for the way she'd double-crossed him in Russia five years ago. As his body had slowly healed from the burns she'd caused him, he'd had more than enough time to plot his revenge. And Ghost had sat by his bedside and told him that it was for the best: Hollis was a weakness, and the *dhampir* could not afford weaknesses.

Except she'd disappeared, her body failing to turn up after she'd gone into the river. Obsidian had been forced to realize that the cold-blooded bitch who'd betrayed him was gone, and there would be no reckoning. He'd been cheated. Even if the woman had haunted his dreams every night since.

And now Ghost had tried to cheat him again. Hollis's death was his. Obsidian knelt by her side. It would be so easy. But his fist trembled, and stayed clenched.

Hollis groaned. No, he had to stop thinking of her like that. Gemma suited her better, for Hollis reminded him of the cold Russian nights they'd shared, and the way she'd kiss her way down his throat in bed... the way that, for a moment, he'd begun to think dangerous thoughts about turning his back on those who'd broken him free of his incarceration, and simply running away with her.

God, she'd played him so well.

Far better for him to think of her now as Gemma, for that Hollis—the one who haunted him—had never existed.

Calling her Gemma reminded him of that.

He stared down at her for a long time, watching as she began to shift and groan, and then withdrew his knife.

Damn her. She deserved to die.

"My God! Scott, hurry and fetch the doctor, will you? Miss? Miss...."

Blinking in and out of consciousness, Gemma slowly found herself on the floor. Someone was patting her shoulder. She jerked and caught his wrist in an iron grip, then looked around. Blood. She could smell blood, and it called to the parasitic predator deep inside her.

"Get away from me," she snapped, scrambling backward on the floor.

The curator remained kneeling, his face white and his mustache quivering as he held his hands up in a sign of surrender. "Miss, I'm trying to help. You're bleeding."

Help. The poor man thought that she was frightened of him. If only he knew that Gemma was frightened of what she might do to *him* in this state.

"Just... give me some room to get some air," she told him. *And stay right where you are, with all of that tempting blood on your hands.* Her blood, she realized, and forced herself to take stock.

The man sucked in a sharp breath as he saw her eyes, and scrambled back.

"Don't move," she said, as the darkness inside her whispered, *Look how it flees us. Look how it runs. Like prey....*

Gemma squeezed her eyes shut and swallowed hard. She was in control of herself. Always. "Just don't move quickly," she repeated in a choked voice. "I need a moment to gather my... my wits."

The man swallowed. "As you wish."

Gemma let go of the breath she'd been holding. The world slowly receded in intensity as the shadows washed from her vision, and the staccato beat of his heartbeat grew quieter. A blue blood might pretend to be human, but what beat in their ragged hearts was anything but. And sometimes the chilling intensity of that darker part of herself bothered her. People were not *prey*. They were flesh and blood, with hopes and dreams of their own, but when the darkness washed over her, she couldn't see that anymore.

"It's all right," she told the curator, swallowing the saliva that had flooded her mouth. "I'm myself again. Just move slowly."

"Are you... unhurt?" His gaze dropped to the blood on her coat, but he kept his hands upright in the surrender position.

Gemma patted her side, where the knife had gone in. Her fingers came away wet, but she felt fine. The stab wound was tender, but not the sort of fiery pain that she'd expected. Her coat was tied neatly around her padded waist. How had...? The last thing she remembered was it being torn open... and the man with his hands around her throat.

And then the darkness.

Or no.... Had she seen someone else then? She winced. What had happened? There was no sign of her attacker, only a smear of dark blood on the floor, as if someone had hastily wiped it up. And it wasn't her blood. Hers was a richer color: a blue-red in tone, which was what had given the blue bloods their name. This was the blackest shade of red she'd ever seen.

What on earth...?

"Hold still, my dear. I'll..." The curator looked around helplessly, evidently unaccustomed to dealing with injured blue bloods. "I'll fetch a doctor."

Then he was gone, and Gemma carefully levered herself to her feet.

She had no intention of staying here. After all, someone had just tried to kill her, and although she'd blacked out before he could do so, clearly he hadn't just stopped out of the goodness of his heart.

She had to get to safety, before he tried again.

And then there was Ulbricht's comment to deal with.

CHAPTER SIXTEEN

INGRID'S NOSTRILS FLARED. "I smell blood."

She yanked open the front door just as Gemma staggered against the lintel.

"What happened?" Ingrid demanded, grabbing the other woman by the arm. There was blood on her coat, and her wig hung askew. "Ava!"

"Someone attacked me when I was following Ulbricht a couple of hours ago," Gemma said, looking pale. "I'm fine, Ingrid, I promise. Everything has healed, but I'm still a little weak at the knees."

Ava came out of the parlor, wiping her hands on her apron. "Oh, my goodness!" she said, hurrying to Gemma's other side. "What happened?"

Together they helped Gemma inside as she told them about it.

"You're certain the attacker was a blue blood?" Ingrid demanded, once Gemma had finished.

"It happened so quickly," Gemma replied, "but his skin was as pale as snow, and his hair so white it was almost translucent. He was definitely a blue blood. One quite close to the Fade, I'd expect, as his blood was almost black."

"But blue bloods don't have to deal with the Fade anymore, do they?" A few years ago, the Fade had been a blue blood's greatest fear; when the craving virus began to overwhelm them and their color began to fade, until they were slowly starting to transform into a vampire. "Isn't there that Distillation device, where they can counteract the CV virus in their blood? The Duke of Moncrieff designed it before he died."

"This way," Ava said, guiding Gemma into a chair. "Let me have a look at it."

"I don't know why my attacker's CV levels were so far advanced, but he was clearly at the higher end of the scale." Gemma shuddered and touched her throat as if remembering, her voice dropping. "He was so much stronger than I am."

"SOG Agent, do you think?"

Ava peeled the coat back and sucked in a breath. "Hmm. This is healed, but there's some unusual mottling here. Let me test your CV levels. Here, hold out your finger." She pricked Gemma's finger, and headed to the brass spectrometer to take her CV percentage rating.

"I don't know." Exasperation gained an edge in Gemma's voice as she glanced at what Ava was doing. "I'm usually more aware than that. I don't even know how they got the jump on me. They shouldn't have."

"The real question is: how *did* you escape?" Ava murmured, and the room fell silent as the brass spectrometer spat out a small curl of paper with her CV levels on it. "Or more to the point, what is wrong with you?" Ava frowned, examining the paper.

"Wrong with me?" Gemma sat up.

"They've gone through the roof," Ava said. "You told me you were in the low thirties."

"I am." Gemma held out a hand, and Ava deposited the reading there. "Oh, my goodness. They're eighty-three." She looked up, pale faced with fear. "What does that mean?"

"Let me test it again," Ava muttered. "That can't be right. The machine might need to be recalibrated."

Gemma bit her lip. "The stab wound *had* healed over before I even woke. And I couldn't have been out of action for too long. That's not normal. It should have taken two or three hours for the wound to seal over completely."

Ava held up a thermometer. "Open up. I want to check your temperature."

Ingrid paced. An attacker who was in the Fade.... She couldn't help but think of Ulbricht's mistress, with her silvery blonde hair and skin like bleached snow. "Describe the assault again," she said abruptly. "Every last detail. You thought you saw someone in the reflection, you said... do you think that someone saved you?"

"I don't know what to think," Gemma admitted around the thermometer, and it was clear that the assault upset her. But she went through the attack again, her voice clear and devoid of emotion, dealing out nothing but the facts. "But there's no other reason for him to stop trying to kill me. *Something* startled him, and he ran off."

"None of this makes sense," Ingrid muttered.

"You're telling me."

The brass spectrometer spat out a scroll of paper with little figures on it. Ava frowned as she held it up. "That's odd."

"Odd?" Gemma looked at her. "What do you mean odd?"

Ava lowered the piece of paper. "You're definitely at eighty-three." She poked the spectrometer. "Unless there is something seriously wrong with this device."

"Still?" Gemma swung off the table, and snatched the piece of paper off Ava. "Hell and bloody ashes. I don't feel any differently."

"Well, something healed that wound faster than it normally would," Ava said, fiddling with her microscope. "Sometimes a wound can exacerbate the amount of craving virus in the body. We call it the blooming, though I've only ever heard of rare cases. It's usually a grievous injury that sets it off, where the body can no longer fight against the craving virus *and* the injury, so it stops fighting the virus, we think, in order to save the person's life. The virus blooms out of control and the blue blood survives, but he's now prone to irrational hungers and dangerous side effects."

"I was stabbed in the side, Ava. It was hardly life-threatening. Or not like a knife to the heart, anyway. Would that cause this blooming?"

"I don't think so. But how else do you explain how you're healing so swiftly, or why your CV levels went through the roof," Ava pointed out. "Aren't you the least bit curious?"

"What I am," Gemma replied, pressing her hand to her temples as if expecting to find herself sweating, "is filthy and freezing cold. I need a bath, and a glass of mulled blud-wein to make myself feel quite human again. I am positively covered in grime. And no doubt Malloryn shall want a report on this, and... oh, hell! I meant to track Sunderland to this meeting with the SOG." She screwed up her nose, then winced as a sharp movement forced her hand to her side.

"You're not tracking anybody," Ingrid said.

"We cannot simply allow this chance to slip through our fingers! What if the entire membership is in attendance?"

"It won't," she assured Gemma. "I'll go. You do have the tracking device, don't you?"

Gemma handed it over.

"Not alone." Ava *tsked*. "At least let Byrnes know what's going on. And maybe take Charlie with you. You don't know how many blue bloods will be there, or what you'll be walking into."

"I'll go find them right now," Ingrid replied. Ava might be out of her depth in company, but she was rapidly becoming the mother hen of the group.

"As for you," Ava speared Gemma with her gaze, "I'm not going to stop digging into this. I'm going to get a second spectrometer, to make sure it's not the device."

"Dig away, my dear." Gemma headed for the door, rubbing at her arms. "I shall be upstairs, soaking in my tub."

And then she was gone.

Ingrid waited until Gemma was clearly out of earshot. "You're worried about something."

"It's nothing." Ava tugged her apron off.

Ingrid crossed her arms over her chest. "You do realize that you're the worst liar I've ever encountered?"

Ava sighed. "Have a look at this. I didn't want to show Gemma, until I work out what it means."

She gestured to her microscope, and Ingrid peered through it. A bunch of black-red sickle-shaped objects appeared, circulating among redder, rounder globules. "What is it?"

"It's Gemma's blood," Ava replied, and reached past her to replace the slide with another. "And this is what a blue blood's blood *should* look like. This is my sample."

There was definitely a difference. Ava's example was a paler blue-red, and the globules were rounder, like the others in the first sample, only there were no sickle-shaped elements. Ingrid jerked back from the microscope.

"Something happened to Gemma in that museum. Something healed her wound at an exacerbated rate, upped her CV levels, and set her body into some sort of fever. Which is virtually impossible for a blue blood. We don't fall ill. We don't *get* fevers, but I quite think she's succumbing to one, as her temperature has increased by three degrees. None of this makes any sense to me."

"I'm certain you'll figure it out," Ingrid told her. She frowned again. "There was something different about Ulbricht's mistress too. When she was unleashing the vampires from the device they were using to tear Debney apart, she pulled a lever down as though it was barely a nuisance. I could barely lower it, even with all of my strength, and verwulfen are stronger than blue bloods, especially when we're in the midst of the *berserkergang*."

"I fail to see the connection."

"Ulbricht's mistress looks like a blue blood deep into the Fade," Ingrid replied, thinking out loud. "And now Gemma's been attacked by a man who looks like he's well into the Fade too, and her CV levels have changed following their altercation. Then there are vampires afoot, when that is the natural conclusion to the Fade. Too many coincidences make me begin to wonder. What if Gemma got some of her attacker's blood into her wound? Would that make any difference? After all, sometimes blue bloods use their blood to heal wounds. What if this Fade blue blood had CV levels higher than Gemma's? Would that account for the discrepancy?"

Ava blinked. "Do you know, that is an entirely possible theory! His blood could have healed her." She paused in her mad rush for the spectrometer however. "Though the shape and color of the blood cells are unlike anything I've ever seen."

"Maybe there's some kind of change to the fellow's... craving virus? An abnormality?"

Ava looked up from the spectrometer. "Which means that we're not just dealing with one blue blood deep in the Fade. We're dealing with at least two, possibly more."

Hell.

"You called?" Byrnes said, flourishing the small note Ingrid had left on his pillow two hours ago.

"Gemma's found us a lead," she said, striding past him down the hallway of Baker Street. "Ulbricht met with the Duke of Sunderland today, and they mentioned a meeting of the SOG tonight. She's too injured to follow, which means it's in our hands. Charlie and us."

Byrnes fell into step beside her. He tucked the note back into his shirt pocket, along with her first one, feeling like an idiot for keeping them but unable to leave them elsewhere. If Garrett got wind of them, he'd never live this down, and the idea of burning them.... No. Just no. "Just how are you getting inside the Nighthawks headquarters?"

"Headquarters?" Ingrid paused in front of the main door. "Or your room?"

"Both. And what did you do in there? Your perfume was... everywhere."

On his sheets, on his pillow....

Stepping closer, she pressed her fingertips lightly against his chest and whispered in his ear, "Use your imagination."

Then she was through the door and striding in those ground-eating steps toward a steam carriage that idled at the curb. Charlie waved at him from the driver seat, wearing fingerless gloves and a bowler hat.

And then they were off, even as *"Use your imagination"* was still plaguing him.

Cursed woman.

Though he often preferred to work alone, Byrnes swiftly began to realize that he didn't mind working with others when they knew what they were doing.

Ingrid loped ahead of him through the fog that adorned London's rooftops like the icing on a cake, with Charlie at her heels. Taking off, Byrnes leapt across an alley and landed beside them as Charlie fiddled with the levers on a small brass box. Chittering noises came from within, as the locator tracked the beacon that Gemma had planted on the Duke of Sunderland.

"That way," Charlie murmured, and then took off, skating down mist-slick tiles then leaping to another row of rooftops.

With a grin at Ingrid, Byrnes launched himself after Charlie until it became almost a breathless race for the three of them.

Charlie paused in the shadows of a chimney, then pointed across the street to an enormous domed building that looked abandoned. "There."

"What is it?" Ingrid murmured.

The streets were silent, and someone had blacked out the nearby gas lamps. A pair of shadows shifted at the edge of the square. Byrnes frowned. "I'm not certain. But I can see lights within, and there are guards."

"Check it out?" Ingrid asked. "The beacon seems to think this is it."

Byrnes nodded, and they took off again, crossing rooftops until they could scale the walls of the seven-story building.

The enormous glass dome on the top of the building gleamed in the moonlight. Byrnes caught himself on a baroque pillar and peered through the dirty windows. Light glimmered below: a half dozen candles flickering as several people carried them in a slow circle.

"Think we can get closer?" Ingrid whispered in his ear.

Too many guards below. Albeit ones that were trying—badly—to blend into the shadows. "Got that harness?" he asked Charlie.

Whipping off the leather satchel he'd been wearing over his back, Charlie withdrew a pair of harnesses with various ropes and a winch device. The young man seemed to be prepared for anything. "Only got two."

The three of them looked at each other, and Charlie held his fist out. "Paper. Scissors. Stone."

The game was currently popular in certain areas of London, hailing from the Far East. Byrnes looked at Ingrid, then shrugged. They all held their fists out silently, Charlie ticking out the count of three with the fingers on his spare hand.

Ingrid lost, a soundless curse whispering from her lips. Then she turned without argument to set up the winch with Charlie, while Byrnes strapped himself into the harness.

When they were done, Byrnes cracked the seal on the nearest glass pane with his knife. Moving carefully, he opened the window to its full potential before slipping through the opening to the ledge beneath. Dust marked his fingers and a startled pigeon took one look at him before launching into space with thunderous affront. Byrnes pressed his back to the wall as he froze, prepared at any moment for the hue and cry below.

None came.

Then Ingrid peered down at him, pressing a finger to her lips.

It wasn't as though I knew the bloody bird was there, he told her with his expression.

To which she rolled her eyes. Of course she'd have known, if it were her.

Charlie slipped in beside him, and the pair of them turned around, resting their boot heels on the ledge and leaning their weight out over space. Below bobbed those flickering lights as the members of the SOG trooped down into the bowels of what appeared to be some sort of Roman-style theatre.

With a grin, Charlie leapt back into nothingness, a shadow that spiraled downwards, completely at ease with the fall. Byrnes glanced down, saw the endless darkness behind his boot heels, and suffered a moment where he nearly climbed right back out of there.

Ingrid clicked the winch out one inch, and his arms windmilled, before realizing he wasn't going any further.

Her eyebrow lifted. *Are you going? Or not going?*

Byrnes's gloved knuckles were tight around the rope. But he wasn't going to back out now, with both of them watching. Giving her a tight nod, he took a step back, and Ingrid let the winch out as the world dropped out from beneath him.

Jesus Christ.

The harness cut into parts unmentionable as his full weight tested its range. His fist wrapped around the cable, body swinging helplessly as Charlie silently laughed at him. Byrnes managed to return the sentiment, though his smile was somewhat tighter, with more teeth in it. He was also fairly certain he was going to choke on his heart.

Ingrid silently wound them down, with Charlie leaning back, peering at the world upside down without a care in the world. Byrnes endured. Those candles were growing closer. He could make out shapes now. Dozens of them, wearing dark-colored robes, with pale faces— No, not faces. Masks. Silver masks, with empty black holes for the eye sockets, and sewn-up lips.

Charlie flicked his fingers to catch Byrnes's attention. He didn't need to hear the words to know what the lad wanted. Down. Closer. Needed to hear what the masked men were saying.

Pointing a small crossbow-shaped device at a nearby column, Charlie silently shot a grappling hook up onto the spiral staircase, and used it to haul himself onto the railing, then to help Byrnes get closer. They both unhooked themselves from the main line before creeping closer to the main theatre in the grotto below.

Huge stone statues of Roman-style gladiators circled the small stage below. It was like no other theatre he'd ever seen, and the main stage was circled by stone seats. What on earth had this place once been?

"Gentlemen!" someone called, standing on the dais at the far end with a staff, which he thumped into the dusty floor thrice. "Shall we begin?"

"Begin," chorused several dozen voices.

Byrnes crouched above it all, at the last spiral of the staircase, his back pressed into the head of one of the gladiators as he swiftly counted. There were forty-seven figures below.

And one of them was the Duke of Sunderland. He swept his hood back, revealing his silvery muttonchops as he surveyed the gathering. "Come out, Ulbricht, you rotten cur. Come out and show your face. It's time to vote on who shall lead the SOG."

Laughter echoed through the circular chamber, strangely hollow. Byrnes jumped, though there was no sign of anyone nearby. Every man below began to shift uncomfortably.

"Who said we came here to vote?" Ulbricht's voice echoed through the room. "I said the Sons of Gilead needed a new master, and that this would be settled here tonight. I never said there'd be a vote."

The circular pit in the center of the room began to crack in the middle as both edges of the floor drew apart. One of the robed figures slipped through the crack and vanished with a howl that soon turned to a scream. Then all of the robed blue bloods began scrambling for the edges of the sunken stage as Byrnes finally got a good look at what was going on.

Not a stage. Nor an auditorium. A fighting pit, elegantly decked out for the elite to sit and watch their favorite sport, which had no doubt been closed shortly after the revolution, when pit fighting was outlawed. Thank God Ingrid wasn't here, for this was a place where her kind had been unleashed onto the sand below the retractable wooden floor to kill and maim each other for blue bloods to enjoy. For a moment he felt sick as the floors opened up, and then the blood drained from his face as he saw what was waiting within the fighting pit.

Another blue blood fell onto sands wet with dark blood as a pair of chained vampires launched themselves upon him and tore him apart as they'd clearly done to the first poor bastard.

"Ulbricht!" Sunderland howled, turning to look for a way out.

Others screamed as the floors kept parting, pushing their way to the edges of the sunken pit. A dozen men robed in scarlet appeared from doors hidden by the seating and stopped at the edge, pushing the terrified horde back down when they sought to escape. One of them kicked a blue blood in the face and he slammed back into his brethren, crushing them as he fell. Three of them vanished over the lip of the floor into the pit.

"Ulbricht! Mercy!" Sunderland screamed as he pressed against the walls, watching the floor vanish beneath his feet. "Mercy!"

The tableau ground to a halt as the floor stopped retracting, barely a foot from the stone walls.

"Mercy?" The word echoed through the room. Heads turned as people tried to see who had said it, and then a man in a shockingly scarlet robe appeared out of nowhere at the top of the stands. At his side was a woman gowned in charcoal gray, wearing a leashed vampire at her wrist.

Byrnes ducked out of sight with a flinch as Charlie did the same. Nobody had seen them yet, but who knew how well a vampire could smell? Neither he nor Charlie had a personal scent, but Ingrid's musky perfume would be on him.

"To those of you who joined the SOG thinking that you wished a return to the good old days, then I welcome you to my ranks. But know that it comes with a price. The SOG are going to take London back from that bitch queen and her cohorts! If you're with me, then be prepared for war and climb out of the pit. If not...."

Byrnes risked a look. Over a dozen bleating blue bloods scrambled out of the pit. Three remained by Sunderland, glaring mutinously at Ulbricht. Byrnes sank back down. *War?* He exchanged a glance with Charlie. That sounded ominous. But what precisely were they planning?

Gemma thought Ulbricht was planning something with explosives, but there'd been no sign of that yet.

"You turncoat!" Sunderland screamed.

"As for you...," Ulbricht said, and then the grinding noise continued as the floors evidently kept retreating.

Sunderland's scream cut off abruptly, and then a pair of growls choked the noise off. Byrnes swallowed. Hard. This was a slaughter, not a duel, and a part of that sat wrongly with him, but spoke to everything the Echelon believed itself to be. Entitled pasty-faced bastards who thought themselves beyond the law.

Charlie pointed up, and Byrnes nodded. Time to get out of here. They both scrambled into a low run, heading for the exit. They'd seen enough, and it wasn't as though Ulbricht was going to reveal more of his plan right now. At least they knew something was coming, and that the Rising Sons—this mysterious behind-the-scenes group—had taken control of the SOG.

"Hey! What are you doing here?" A figure in a red robe stepped out of one of the tunnels that branched off the spiral staircase. Byrnes barreled through him, slamming his shoulder directly into the fellow's chest, and tripping over him as he fell. Damn it.

"Someone's here!" the woman at Ulbricht's side called.

Ulbricht lifted a pistol and a shot rang out. Stone chipped off one of the columns as Byrnes ducked, then a second shot scored hot fire through his upper arm.

"Kill them!" Ulbricht yelled.

Another pistol echoed. Charlie ducked and wove, with Byrnes hot on his heels. They both slid to the marble floor, using the protection of the stone railing as gunshots ricocheted above them. Byrnes clapped a hand to his upper arm. Blood wet his fingers.

Charlie covered his head with his arms. "At least they're only shooting at us! It could be worse."

After all, there were vampires below. "Don't speak too soon." The room fell ominously silent. A faint fluting trill echoed up through the central core of the spiral, a sound that chilled his spine. "Run!" he snapped to Charlie, shoving the lad to his feet.

Then they were both sprinting up the curved stairs.

A blur of maggot-white shot into view behind him as he circled upwards.

Byrnes shoved Charlie in the back and launched after him, fists pumping at his sides as he sprinted for the rail that they'd climbed over. The ropes still hung there. He snatched a glance over his shoulder as they reached the edge of the spiral staircase, and saw that rocketing white blur hot on his heels. Byrnes ran faster, leaping up onto the railing and then launching his body out into air, reaching desperately for the rope.

The second he caught it, momentum carried him forward as a whisper of movement swept past his boots. A high-pitched scream of thwarted rage echoed up as the vampire fell below, vanishing into the circular depths of the tower. It landed on the bloodied floor of the pit and scrambled to its feet to stare up at him like a cat watching a ribbon dangle above it.

"So a fall won't kill it." Byrnes swung back the way he'd come, glancing behind to make sure it had only been one vampire. He yanked hard on the harness to signal Ingrid to haul them up, the bullet wound ripping through his shoulder as though the movement tore his battered flesh further.

"That was close," Charlie breathed hoarsely as the harnesses began to retract, dragging them higher.

"Closer than comfortable," Byrnes agreed, his heartbeat still racing. A figure was forming in the shadows, a hooded blue blood stepping to the edge of the rail he and Charlie had just vacated.

"We meet again," the woman called, turning her face up to the moonlight as her hood fell back just enough to reveal a smooth oval face framed by silvery hair. She watched as he and Charlie jerked higher.

Ulbricht's mistress.

And she was smiling faintly at him as if his appearance here pleased her.

CHAPTER SEVENTEEN

"HERE," INGRID SAID, handing him a flask as she pushed him back onto the bed in his room at Baker Street. "Drink this."

Blood. Byrnes set the flask to his mouth as she sat beside him. Charlie had driven them home from the pits, taken one look at the murderous expression on Ingrid's face, and said he'd tell Malloryn what they'd seen. Byrnes hadn't had a reason to argue. His arm hurt, despite the raging chill of the craving virus, and he was fairly certain that the bullet was still inside him.

Besides, he wasn't going to argue with her either. Not in this mood.

"What are you doing?" he asked. Ingrid tugged open his coat, unbuttoning it with crisp fingers. Then he realized. "It's just a scratch, Miller."

"I'll be the judge of that," she replied, pushing his coat off his shoulder and then gently touching the bloodied sleeve of his shirt.

Everything about her expression changed. He didn't have an answer for what he saw on her face. Stricken?

Perhaps stricken came closest. "The wound's healed around the bullet," she said. "I'm going to have to cut it out."

"Then do it." Feeling somewhat adrift, Byrnes tilted his shoulder toward her. Was this what had her so upset? The fact that he was injured? It didn't make any sense, as she knew he was a blue blood. "I've had worse."

"I'm certain you have."

"This is—"

"Byrnes. Please be quiet."

She was frighteningly proficient as she wielded the scalpel with a skill and grace that told him she'd done this before. Byrnes ground his teeth together as he breathed through the extraction. The bullet pinged as it landed in the tray.

It was as she cleaned the wound that her hesitancy came through. Byrnes watched her expressive face the entire time. When was the last time that someone had tended to him like this? He honestly couldn't remember. Perhaps his mother, bracing skinned knees. Or pressing cold meat to his face to still the heated echo of his father's fist.

That soured his thoughts. Instantly he was back there, slamming into the door in his father's study, too small, too weak, too pathetic to strike back.

Byrnes turned away from the memories, forcing them into that little locked box in his mind where he could pretend they didn't exist. He felt ill, as he always did when he thought of the viscount, but controlling it was easy. *Lock it away. Lock it up tight. Don't ever let it out.*

The guilt was not so easy to hide.

"Am I hurting you?" Ingrid's voice helped draw him into the present. She gently wound clean linen around the gauze that she'd packed over his wound. A chill told him that the craving virus was flooding back into the inflamed skin. By the end of an hour, there wouldn't even be a scratch.

Which made this a complete and utter waste of her time.

He said nothing though, because he quite liked those warm hands on his skin. "You're not hurting me."

The tension that had radiated through her shoulders seemed to ebb.

"Were you fretting?" he teased, then instantly wished he hadn't. Dark lashes fluttered down over her gorgeous eyes, but she couldn't hide how upset she looked in that moment. The bottom of his stomach dropped, much like it had when he rappelled down through the core of the staircase.

Because the answer was yes. And he didn't know what to do about it.

"Ingrid," he said hesitantly. "I'm incredibly difficult to kill. It's fine."

"I wasn't there," she growled, throwing the small scalpel aside and pressing her hands to her thighs. "And all I could hear was gunfire, then you and Charlie come bursting out, pushing at me to run and blathering about vampires, and you're bleeding, and you wouldn't let me see to it in the carriage—" She pressed her curled fists into her eyes, turning away from him.

It was the most extraordinary thing. Byrnes stared at her bowed back, thinking through a response. The most immediate one was another jest, but she was genuinely upset.

Nobody had ever been upset about his injuries before. Nobody had ever cared enough. There was a strange feeling in his chest, like a lump. Perhaps of coal, since he didn't have a heart. "Ingrid," he said, sliding down the bed toward her and cupping her arms from behind.

"Don't hold this against me," she growled, bowing her head lower. "I'm verwulfen. I can't help feeling this way, this—"

"Upset?"

"It doesn't mean anything," she pointed out.

Byrnes turned her around, holding out his arm. "See...." The scent of blood had vanished. "Just a scratch. Almost gone already, though I'll thank you for your ministrations. And I wouldn't hold anything against you. I like it when you get angry." Reaching out, he cupped her face in his palm. "I like the fact that you care enough about me to grow agitated when I'm injured—"

"Byrnes—"

"You care. Don't lie. It's written all over your face."

That didn't soothe the savage *wild* he saw in her eyes. Ingrid was close to the edge tonight, and one push would rouse her fierce verwulfen nature. Sliding his hands down her arms to soothe her, he instinctively kissed the tip of her nose. "After all, how could you not? How could you resist me?"

Ingrid couldn't fight the faint tug of her lips upwards. "I'm glad that someone thinks you're wonderful. Too bad it's only you."

He rubbed her arms, laughing under his breath. "You think I'm wonderful. Admit it, Ingrid. You wouldn't be in here fussing over me if you didn't."

"Arrogant fool." She set her hand to his chest. "And you like me fussing."

True. He smiled and tugged on a lock of her hair, which only earned him a swat with her hand.

"Ouch," he said, drawing his arm against his chest.

Instantly she was all contrition. "Oh, I'm sorry! Did I hurt you? Did I—"

He used the moment to capture her in his arms, dragging her half into his lap. "Yes, you did hurt me. Kiss it better?"

That earned him a narrow-eyed look, but she didn't push him away this time. Instead her fingers toyed with his collar and she glanced down. "I never thought you'd have this side to you," she admitted.

"Roguish?"

"Playful."

That made him thoughtful. He nibbled on her fingertips. This was more than pleasant. Seeing her eyes light up verwulfen bronze made his blood sing through his veins. Teasing her had begun to feel like the highlight of his day. But he wasn't about to admit that. "You should see me in bed," he told her instead.

Ingrid sighed. "You're the most frustrating man I know."

"That's unlikely to—"

The kiss took him by surprise. Her fists curled in his open shirt and her soft lips brushed his. Byrnes had missed the minute change in her expression that preceded this. He stilled, letting her draw back, and tasting the soft wash of her breath on his sensitized lips.

"Sorry," she whispered, glancing up at him from beneath those dark lashes with a teasing glow in her eyes.

"Liar. You're not sorry at all." Byrnes brushed his mouth against her cheek, nuzzling closer to her lips. "You do realize that's not going to end there."

He felt her smile. "Isn't it? Maybe I don't want it to."

For too long he'd been kept at arm's length, determined to be patient and outwait her. No more. Byrnes slid his hand up to caress her nape and drew her mouth to his. She tasted both sweet and sinful, her mouth opening to his as he deepened the kiss. The first lash of her tongue felt like it stroked along his cock. Byrnes slid his spare hand up her thigh, his fingers sinking in a little harshly as he fought to contain himself. Christ. His body ignited as Ingrid slid fully into his lap, straddling him. The kiss became hungrier. Deeper. Possessive. And it was moving in a clear direction.

Maybe I don't want it to?

The game slipped away, the challenge, the conquest.... He was surprised by how much he wanted this. Her. Just her. Hands hesitating on her hips, he drew back at the thought.

"I haven't been drinking tonight," she reminded him in a soft voice, as if she thought that the reason he'd withdrawn.

Well, now. He swallowed, every wicked little thought that had sprung into mind at the Garden of Eden echoing loudly in his head. He knew what she was offering. Everything. It lingered in her heated gaze, in the gentle way she traced the half-open collar of his shirt. Ingrid knew exactly what she wanted, and she was determined to get it.

And again he hesitated. What was wrong with him? There was a nervous pit in his abdomen, instinct whispering through him like it sometimes did when he knew he was in danger. But there was no danger here. Only Ingrid, with the candlelight turning her skin to molten gold, her natural perfume hovering in the air like a smoky lure and the shadows growing deeper, darker....

No danger. But he felt like he hovered on the edge of taking a momentous step forward, and he wasn't certain what that meant.

"You want me to tup you," he said, and his cock jerked at the words. As far as his body was concerned, it was all in. Who could blame him? Ingrid was absolutely gorgeous; all Amazon legs, generous breasts, and muscular litheness. A Valkyrie in human form. And all his...

"Maybe I'll tup *you*," she whispered, a palm pressing against his chest as he slid back on the bed, and she rose over him.

"What about our challenge?"

She kissed the words from his lips, her fingers trailing down his shirt and stroking the hard flex of his abdomen. "Maybe I changed my mind?"

He couldn't fight it anymore. His mouth took hers, hard and demanding. His fingers were in her hair, gently tugging the honey-gold locks from their braid and tangling the soft strands over her shoulders. He wanted to pause, to drink in the sensation of her hair against his skin, but Ingrid had him by the lapels. She muscled him back against the wall. The bronze ring around her pupils was heating, stealing through the hazel of her eyes, as if the berserker fury roused within her. Then she was nipping at his throat, tearing at the buttons there as if to get at his skin. Byrnes tilted his head back, one hand sliding through her hair and cupping her nape.

Sweet heaven. It had been an age since she'd been in his arms. Too long. Far too long.

He gave himself over wholly to her, and Ingrid yanked his shirt from his leather breeches. It was as if a dam had broken somewhere inside her.

And he liked it.

"Yes? Or no?" she whispered.

"Maybe," he breathed, to toy with her.

Firm hands pushed him down flat onto the bed and then a pair of hard-toned thighs straddled him. His back hit the pillows, her knees sliding deep into the coverlet on either side of his hips.

He certainly wasn't going to fight it. Byrnes curled a possessive hand around her hip, resting it on her arse. Their eyes met, and then she fisted both hands in the center of his shirt, and tore it clean up the middle.

"I'll buy you a new one," she whispered, a heated flash of her eyes sweeping over him before she leaned down and kissed the side of his throat. Her touch was ravenous as she slid his shirt off his shoulders, licking at his neck and then suckling hard.

Hell. His eyes rolled back in his head. Being ravished by Ingrid was definitely an experience he wouldn't say no to.

"That's okay," he breathed, a shock of feeling shooting through him as she bit him. His fingers curled into the flesh of her bottom, his hips thrusting up in reaction. "You can tear my shirt off me anytime you like. But don't think I won't be returning the favor."

The leather protective overcorset she wore was smooth beneath his hands. All of these fiddly straps and buckles. He wanted to explore more, but she was determined to have her own way.

Which was quite fine by him, to be honest, if only that little doubt hadn't reared its head again.

This wasn't surrender. This was Ingrid scratching a physical itch, and he had the sickening feeling that tomorrow she would buckle herself back into her protective corset-armor and lift her brow at him as if to say, *What?* Nothing would have changed. He'd have gotten what he wanted, she'd have gotten what she wanted... and yet the goal posts had shifted somewhere deep inside him.

Grabbing her by the wrists, Byrnes rolled them until he lay nestled between her parted thighs. They both panted, and Ingrid arched up beneath him as if to demand to know why he'd stopped. Part of *him* didn't know why he'd stopped.

"I've changed my mind," he told her. "This is cheating. I still have two challenges to go."

Only this time, winning his way into her bed wasn't the prize.

"Byrnes!" Her wrists lifted off the bed as she fought him, and she was very nearly strong enough to push him away.

But he kissed her throat, feeling the kick of her pulse against his lips, and trailed lower, lower, heading for the smooth slopes of her breasts. Perfect ground to wage his campaign.

"Ah, ah, ah," he told her, pressing her into the mattress and kissing his way down her throat. "I didn't say I intended to forgo the pleasure entirely. Just that I hadn't earned the right to fuck you."

"I don't care! Byrnes!" Ingrid writhed beneath him, then gasped as his lips nibbled over the soft fleshy curve of her breast. "This is ridiculous. I said yes!"

Not on her life. Stubbornness reared its head. He was going to win her over properly. As much as he desperately wanted to sink his cock into her wet heat, that would... not be right. Not yet.

"Tempting," he whispered, "but I think I enjoy torturing you. Call it payback." After all, he wasn't about to admit what had caused this little change of heart, at least not until he'd had time to examine the issue at leisure himself.

Ingrid pushed up onto her elbows stubbornly. "I'm fairly certain I could talk you into it." One hand slid between his legs and caressed the hard bulge of his cock through the leather as her eyes blazed with triumph.

Fuck. Byrnes swallowed. "I'm fairly certain you could." He bit the tip of her nose, teeth grazing lightly against her skin. "But what's the rush?" Trailing his fingertips down over her breast, he paid close attention to the soft leather covering her nipple. "Don't you want to have a little fun first?" He finally found the buckle at the side of her ribs that held her leather corset in place, and released it. "I do."

That caught her interest. "Define 'fun.'"

He smiled. "Off," he said, and Ingrid practically ripped her leather corset off and threw it across the room.

Frustration, thy name was verwulfen. Byrnes leaned closer, daring to meet that incinerating gaze. "I never understand you," she growled. "I practically handed you... *me* on a platter."

"I'm just slowing us down," he murmured against her lips. Such soft lips. "It *is* going to happen. One day."

"I think you enjoy torturing me. And yourself."

"Is this torture?" Resting on one elbow, he slid his other hand up the rumpled linen of her chemise, his thumb splaying into the groove of her ribs where her heart lay. The swell of her breast rode up, drawing his gaze. Then his mouth.

"Yes," she breathed, sinking her fingers into his hair as he kissed his way between her breasts. "Torture most profound. An ache so sweet that it's almost painful."

"Do you think that I don't feel it too?" He nosed aside the soft linen of her chemise. Her nipple sprang to view, rosy and peaked and aching for his mouth. His cock pulsed inside his pants. "Do you think that I'm not aching to be within you?"

"Byrnes!" She undid the buttons on her breeches, then wriggled out of them, revealing dangerously long legs encased in delicate stockings.

"Imagine," he breathed in her ear, as his hand slid down over the curve of her hip and began edging her chemise up, "what it's going to feel like when I'm finally inside you."

Ingrid moaned. "You talk too much."

"Oh?" He laughed and tugged her chemise lower, revealing the perfect arch of one smooth breast. More than a handful. "Didn't you know that anticipation is one of the greatest parts of seduction?" So saying, he tugged her chemise another inch lower, until the lace neckline hovered on the tip of her puckered nipple. "Now look at this," he breathed, brushing his lips over the lace.

Ingrid had frozen, barely daring to breathe. Her hips shifted restlessly but she didn't take her gaze off him.

"It looks… soft, and yet hard." Dragging the lace lower revealed her nipple, hardened into a bud. He blew over the tip of it, smiling evilly. "It looks… delicious."

"Byrnes, you—"

He closed his mouth around that aching bud and she gasped, her hands sliding into his hair. "Oh, oh God!"

Taking it between his teeth, he rolled it gently as Ingrid thrashed beneath him. Slowly his hand crept below the hem of her chemise, teasing at the flesh there. He was certain she'd stopped breathing.

"See what I mean about anticipation?" he whispered, lifting his mouth and blowing again until she arched her spine, silently begging for more. Byrnes let his fingers drift higher, back and forth, back and forth—

Until Ingrid grabbed his hand and slid it into her drawers.

"Demanding wench." He laughed softly, but he complied with her directive, brushed his thumb against her quivering clitoris.

Ingrid cried out, turning her head to the side. It was becoming harder to breathe himself, his body aching for its own release, but this… this was a moment to be savored.

"Wet," he whispered, tracing small circles there.

Ingrid whimpered, tossing her head to the side. "Byrnes—"

"Byrnes, you are an absolute master in bed," he whispered, sliding the tip of his finger inside her. "Say it."

She arched her spine as he stroked her deep inside, reaching up to grip the sheets with her hands. "Oh God. I'm not going to say that!"

"Aren't you?" He smiled, withdrew his fingers from her warm heat, and traced slick circles around her clitoris, just never quite close enough to scratch that itch.

Ingrid's body wilted. "Damn you, Byrnes. You are...."

"The handsomest, strongest, most intelligent and daring man you've ever met?" Reaching up with his hand, he licked his fingers as she watched him.

A hand slid down his bare chest, her finger tangling in the soft curl of dark hair just above his belt. Two could clearly play at this game. He smothered a grunt, but his hips flexed against her, his cock hard and demanding.

"You are," Ingrid whispered, her fingers tugging at the buttons on his breeches, "the most handsome rogue I've ever met." She bit her lip on a laugh, but it gleamed in her eyes. "You're the most dashing and daring blue blood I've ever had the fortune to get my hands on."

That hand slid between the gaping slit of his breeches and found him. Another growl echoed in his throat as she curled hard fingers around his cock, and gave way to a groan instead. "You're so big, and strong, and this"—her hand gave a slow thrust, thumb coming up to tease the slit of him—"makes me so wet."

Minx. Always a challenge, she was. "And I have the most wicked tongue," he told her as he breathed into the soft curls at her temple.

"Do you?" She dared him with her gaze. "I wouldn't know."

"Then I've been terribly remiss, my love." Byrnes slid down her body, his lips skating over the smooth curve of her abdomen. It ached to pull his cock away from that hand, but he had other plans. And if he were being honest, he was dangerously close to the edge himself. "Perhaps I'd best show you?"

"Perhaps." She let him slide his hands up the inside of her thighs and splay them wide.

Byrnes pressed a kiss to the inside of one thigh. Then the other. All the time, he stroked his hands up and down, up and down, teasing her. Making her writhe. Ingrid was panting by the time he tugged her drawers down.

"Byrnes!" A fist curled in his hair.

"Yes, love?"

"Kiss me," she gasped. "Please."

That was what he wanted to hear. Rearing up, he pressed his face under the hem of her chemise and found the slick heart of her.

The first taste was divine. Byrnes tortured her sweetly, using his hands and tongue until she was begging him. Gasping out the words.

"Byrnes... Oh, Byrnes... Please, please—"

He loved the sound of it.

She was nearing the edge, her hips bucking beneath him, her fist curling in his hair as she tossed her head back. And suddenly he didn't want her to go over that edge alone. He rose over her, taking his erection in his hand and pressing it against her wet sleekness, grinding the swollen head of his cock against her sweet clit, riding her until they were both gasping for breath.

"Yes!" she pleaded, spreading wide beneath him until his cock breached her opening.

He could have taken her. Could have thrust his way home. A vein throbbed in his jaw as he held himself back.

Instead he used his body to push her over the edge, watching as her eyes widened and her head and throat arched back as pleasure rolled through her.

Then he couldn't contain himself any longer. Thrusting high above her, he came with a hoarse cry on the smooth planes of her stomach. Nails sank into his upper arms, fire flashing through his cock and balls, leaving him utterly spent.

Byrnes collapsed upon her, the slickness of his pleasure pressed between them as he slowly came back to himself. He felt amazing. She felt amazing beneath him.

And more than that, he had this intense urge to sink his teeth into her throat right now and mark her.

Fighting against it, he buried his face against her throat, feeling the tremor work its way through her.

Ingrid caressed the back of his neck, making a contented growling sound in her throat. "You know," she admitted in a conspiratorial tone, "you just might be as good as you say you are."

Byrnes smiled as he stroked the bare thigh that cradled his hips. "You haven't even seen the best of me yet." He glanced down between them. "Sorry. I've made quite the mess."

Ingrid nuzzled into his throat in a move that left him utterly exposed. He blinked and looked down at her, at the way she curled around him. It felt strangely right. He wanted to nuzzle into her himself.

"It's quite all right," she told him sleepily, then whipped her chemise off and used it to clean herself up. "Here," she demanded, reaching out to him.

Byrnes scrubbed himself clean then tossed her chemise aside. "Move over," he told her, swatting her lightly on the backside.

"I don't recall this being part of the service," Ingrid replied, bemusement in her voice.

Byrnes slid in behind her, dragging her back into the curve of his arms. The bed was too small, not built for two large people. But she fit just right as she molded against him, and wasn't that a bloody thought?

"That was an excellent gift, Byrnes," Ingrid murmured sleepily. "But you still haven't won your second challenge."

"No," he murmured, snuggling his face into the back of her neck, and brushing a kiss there. "Not yet."

But he would.

CHAPTER EIGHTEEN

BYRNES STRODE into Lynch's dining room the following day, handing his hat and coat to the butler. He was tired of meetings, tired of talking about whether to arrest Ulbricht or not, and this note had arrived at a fortuitous moment. He'd taken two steps inside the room when Ingrid's scent assailed him. The hunger within him flooded upwards like a tide, his vision flashing to black and white before he swallowed and brought himself under control.

Ingrid looked up from the end of the ducal table, bouncing a chubby baby on her lap. Surprise gleamed in her bronze eyes, and her full lips parted slightly as she caught sight of him.

Ambushed.

"Byrnes," Garrett Reed, the Master of the Nighthawks, greeted, and Byrnes realized they were not alone. Garrett's wife, Perry, gently rocked one of her twin daughters at the end of the table, but the sight of Ingrid had shocked him enough to overlook them.

"What a surprise," he replied, meaning it, as he crossed to kiss Perry on the cheek.

"Buck up," Perry murmured in his ear, which was one of the reasons he liked her so much. "Rosa's on the warpath."

"Thanks," he replied dryly. "I hadn't guessed."

As Lynch rose and strode forward to shake his hand, Byrnes realized his old guild master was entirely complicit in this deception. After all, the invite had come from him.

"Anything I should be aware of?"

Those canny gray eyes gleamed with amusement. "Rosa's not entirely certain what to think of this entire affair. If she picks up her knife, I'd duck for cover if I were you."

"I always duck for cover when Rosa's giving me that look," Byrnes replied, accepting a glass of blud-wein from the butler.

It still felt strange to be invited into Lynch's inner sanctum here. Lynch had taken him off the streets when Byrnes's infection with the craving virus bloomed and given him a place in the world, but he'd never thought of the man as a father, like Garrett did. No, Lynch had been a mentor, one of the few people that Byrnes truly respected. They took dinner every now and then, and Byrnes knew he could go to the duke with a vexing case when he wanted insight, but Lynch's life had drifted away from the course of his own over the past few years. Though once reluctant to step into the duchy's shoes, now Lynch thrived on his involvement in politics and his busy little family's affairs.

"Byrnes," Ingrid greeted.

"Miller," he replied, his tone devoid of any emotion, as he circled the table and took a seat across from her. Being so clearly on display had his guard up, which wasn't entirely fair to her, especially not after last night. His tone softened,

"I didn't realize we were both attending tonight. Else I'd have offered you a ride."

"Likewise," she drawled, and turned her attention to the baby. Dinner was to be an informal affair then, if young Phillip was around.

Byrnes held little truck with children—until now, they'd never truly entered his life—but he was struck by how warm Ingrid's expression was as she burbled something to the baby, who promptly stuck her pearls in his mouth. She'd relaxed in a way that he'd rarely seen, and it troubled him.

Perhaps it was her confession the other day; she'd lost her own family as a little girl, and Rosa and her brothers were all she had. He'd known this. But the reality of the situation hadn't struck him until now.

Ingrid wanted children. She wanted a husband and a family of her own, and this was precisely why Rosa had wanted him to be here. To see it.

He met the duchess's dark eyes and felt like he wanted to be ill.

"So," Lynch said, leaning back in his chair, as if Byrnes hadn't just been struck by a revelation that made him want to bolt from the table. "Tell me about these Rising Sons. Just how dangerous do you think they are?"

It was easy to answer, to string sentences together, and put cold hard facts out for the duke's perusal, but a part of Byrnes remained aware of Ingrid, who was playing some sort of game with Phillip involving spoons. The baby was laughing.

A cold clammy hand gripped the back of his neck.

"Vampires," Garrett murmured, leaning back to rest his arm along the back of Perry's chair. "That bodes ill. How many do you think there are?"

"We killed one at Ulbricht's garden party, so there's at least three left."

Garrett and Perry shared a look.

"No," Perry replied firmly. "Don't even think it. I'm not leaving you here in the city to face a vampire alone. Or three."

"If trouble comes," Rosa chipped in, to prevent an argument and perhaps forestall Lynch on the topic, "then Perry and I will take the children out of London. But not yet, I think."

"Malloryn's passed along his findings to the Council of Dukes," Lynch said, looking at Byrnes, "but I wanted your take on matters first. The queen is uncertain whether to declare martial law upon the city, and if we're forced to take a vote on the matter... well, I'd like the facts, at least."

Martial law would send the Nighthawks out onto the street in force, which might be good for the case but would also cause panic among the citizens and lead to potential riots and outbursts in the streets. The revolution was still too raw in people's minds.

"I'd... wait," Byrnes said slowly. "So far these vampires seem to be under the control of Ulbricht's mistress. They're not rampaging through the streets."

"And by voting for martial law," Ingrid pointed out, "we're playing directly into the hands of whoever is behind all of this. Each event so far has been to provoke some sort of response in the populace. These people want the crowd to fear the queen, they want them to start thinking about what happened three years ago, and the second that starts, I suspect these events will increase in intensity. Right now there's a lot of behind-the-scenes work going on. Ulbricht and his crew are building up to something, but they're not there yet."

"You have the full cooperation of the Nighthawks," Garrett told Byrnes, which made something inside him spread its wings.

He'd been overlooked for the job of guild master when Lynch resigned, and had slowly come to terms with it. Garrett did a much better job than he ever would have. But it was nice to realize that his opinion was respected enough for Garrett to offer them to him without objections.

"Thanks," Byrnes said, just as the first course arrived. "We may just need it."

The Duchess of Bleight was not as easygoing as her husband, Lynch.

Byrnes heard the swish of fabric a moment before Rosa swept into view, bearing down upon him like a Dreadnought, its cannons raised. In that moment, he had a brief sensation of what the French might have thought at Trafalgar. *Oh, shit.* Just when he'd thought he'd escaped. Pausing in the entry, in the act of tugging his gloves on, he gave her a raised-brow look.

"A moment, Byrnes," she said, and her voice was deceptively casual. Her dark eyes, however, flashed fire. One might not think it to look at her in all of those green ruffles and pretty pearls, but Byrnes would rather face Lynch over weapons than Rosa. Anyday.

"Something the matter, Your Grace?"

"Don't you 'Your Grace' me. What are your intentions toward Ingrid?"

Byrnes's eyes narrowed. "None of your business, I believe."

She snorted, and a gloved finger stabbed into his chest like a chisel. "Ingrid belongs to me, and I don't like this at all. You're the last man I'd ever throw her to."

"Ingrid belongs to herself," he told her firmly. "Not you. Not me. As such she can make her own choices in life, regardless of what you think of me."

"I'll concede that point, Byrnes, and I mean no offense, but we all know what type of man you are. You're not the sort to dally with a woman past your interest in her. You don't have marriage written in your future, or children, or all of the things that Ingrid secretly craves."

No, he hadn't been that man. Ever. But last night something had shifted in his perception of what was happening between them. He just wasn't entirely certain what it was.

And he clearly wasn't hiding it well enough, for Rosa's eyes narrowed as she watched him. "What was *that*?"

"What?"

"That look," she said suspiciously.

"Dinner disagreeing with me perhaps." He turned toward the door, conversation over.

Rosa darted in front of him, and Byrnes stopped short just before he ploughed into her. They both looked down. He had his hands up as if to stop himself and they rested but an inch from a certain area of her anatomy that Byrnes generally pretended Rosa didn't have.

He jerked them out of range before someone shot him.

"That look," she said, highly amused by his panic, "wasn't just dinner disagreeing with you. You *were* considering something. What was it?"

Byrnes crossed his arms. Interrogation it was, then. Never let it be said that he was afraid to face the worst womankind could throw at him. "Answer me this first: why is she so frightened of rats?"

"This is not an exchange of questions."

"Rosa," he warned. "She practically leapt into my arms when a rat scurried over her foot. She was frightened, and she won't tell me why. I want to know."

Rosa paused. "What do you know of her past?"

"She was stolen from her family and sold to Lord Balfour," he replied promptly, "who by all accounts was a right rotten bastard."

"Well, that is succinct." With a sigh, Rosa continued, though hesitantly, "She's only ever spoken of this to me once, Byrnes, so consider this a matter she's extremely reluctant to deal with."

"I won't say anything."

"Imagine being a little girl, stolen from your family and placed on a ship by men who don't speak your language, and don't consider you even human. She wasn't the only child taken, either. There were two other girls in the hold, and a little boy in the cage next to her. His name was Viktor, and he'd sustained quite a beating in his capture. And, like most ships, there were rats."

Byrnes shifted uncomfortably. "What happened?"

"Viktor didn't survive," Rosa said, quite brutally. "You can imagine what the rats did to his body, and what she had to see. Ingrid would walk into a burning house to save someone she loved and not bat an eyelid, but rats... She's terrified of them."

"She's still looking for her family."

"Wouldn't you?"

He looked away. This was more complicated than he'd expected. "We have a... challenge set in place. If I win three challenges, she'll allow me into her bed. Those are my intentions. Now, if you'll excuse me, I have a vampire or two to catch."

"Byrnes." Rosa caught his sleeve as he opened the door. Those eyes were molten chocolate as she looked up at him.

"I'm not your husband, Rosa. I'm not going to fall for those innocent eyes. I know exactly who you are, and what you're capable of." He couldn't forget that she'd once been an assassin, despite the fact that Lynch seemed to be able to.

"But do you know who Ingrid is, and what she's capable of?"

"Rendering a man senseless, or tearing his head from his shoulders? She's verwulfen, Rosa. I know what she can do. I've seen her take on a vampire, after all."

"But do you know what it means, to be verwulfen?"

He paused then. There was something beneath the words that he couldn't quite identify.

Rosa took his hesitation as intended. "Verwulfen are passionate and loyal and completely enslaved by their emotions. The Scandinavian verwulfen often mate for life, and when their partners die, they rarely take another. They refer to marriage as mating, and when they do so, it is only ever once. Ingrid's wary when it comes to letting a person into her life, but when she does... it's forever. If she falls for you, then she won't let you go. Not in her heart, though she may watch you walk away. She has her pride, after all, and Ingrid has learned how to adapt to loss. Sometimes I fear that a part of her won't accept any man as her mate, for fear of losing him, but... I hope that one day she will find someone."

"And that someone is not me," he said coolly, his fists clenching at his sides, even though rationally he could admit that he agreed with the duchess.

"That someone is not you."

Byrnes looked away. It was one thing to know that she spoke the truth, quite another to... accept it.

"If you become her lover and you walk away, where does that leave her? Alone? Pining for someone who doesn't give a damn about her? She's lost enough in this lifetime, don't you think?"

"Who's to say she'll fall for *me*? After all, if it's not the first time she's been with a man…."

"This is not the same," Rosa told him firmly. "She won't speak to me about you. Just changes the subject. She's never hidden a man from me before, nor avoided me, which means that there's something different about you. I don't like this."

The floor felt like it tilted, just a little, beneath his feet. And the image of Ingrid bouncing that chubby child on her lap returned with full force, a gut punch that made his nostrils flare. What was he thinking? That he wanted her despite the fact that he would be the worst thing for her?

"What I am saying, Caleb, is that if you intend to pursue this, then step lightly, and be certain about your intentions. Because if you break my friend's heart, I'm afraid it will never mend, and then I shall make it *my* business to haunt you until the day you die. Do you understand?"

He stared at her for a long time. "Quite."

"You were quiet tonight," Ingrid said, gathering her skirts as she descended the stairs at the front of Lynch's house.

Byrnes paced in the driveway, staring at nothing. There was a remote set to his shoulders, as if he'd subtly withdrawn from the world. Or perhaps her. Ingrid frowned, her steps slowing. "Are you all right?"

"Just lost in thought," he said, and it felt like there was more distance between them than just a foot.

A chill ran through her.

Something had changed. She knew it, though she didn't understand it. "Rosa is just meddling. I didn't know that you'd be at dinner tonight. She's just trying to figure out what is going on between us. Don't pay her any mind."

"Ingrid," he said, peering down at her with some strange expression on his face. "Maybe you were right? Maybe the debris we'd leave behind wouldn't be worth the risk."

Her heart stuttered to a halt. She wasn't surprised. She couldn't be, as this was what she'd been trying to tell him all along. As much as the fire burned between them, ultimately they were too different to belong together. But she hadn't expected it to hurt quite as much as it did.

Nor had she expected it to happen so soon.

Rosa had done this. Her friend had swept from the room on Byrnes's heels, leaving Ingrid to try and disengage Phillip's fat little paws from her pearls.

"What did she say to you?" she demanded.

To his credit, he didn't bother to deny it. "The truth. That you and I come from different worlds, and that we have different futures in mind."

"So you don't want to complete your second challenge?"

Byrnes looked away. "Maybe tonight was a reminder that the stakes might be too high. We'd damage more than just ourselves if this ended badly. Jesus, Ingrid. I don't know."

"Then it's over?" Before it had even begun.

"Maybe... we'd best take a step back? Think things over before we go rushing into anything?"

Which meant it was over. Ingrid nodded, tugging her gloves into place. She didn't care, truly she didn't. This was nothing more than she'd expected. Why then was there a lump in her throat? "I'll hail the hackney then," she said, turning to lifting her hand to hail a steam carriage as she stepped out into the street.

And tried not to let her hurt show.

CHAPTER NINETEEN

IT WAS ONE thing to declare someone bad for you, quite another to make your body believe it. Especially when they were forced into close proximity with each other until this case was solved. All Ingrid could think about was the taste of Byrnes's mouth and how much she wanted to lose that bet. It even stole into her dreams at night, leaving her tossing and turning until morning.

Which was when Ava saved her with an invitation to go question a man about the Doeppler orbs. Henrik Doeppler was dead, but rumor had it that he'd once had an apprentice.

Ava caught her in the hallway. "I've found a lead, but I need someone to go with me to... to...."

"Intimidate the suspect?" Ingrid had replied, with a wolfish smile.

"Something like that," Ava answered, sharing a conspiratorial smile. "I've seen how Byrnes and Perry used to work together."

The once-apprentice, Bartholomew Hayes, owned a small shop near Farringdon where he catered to the stages in Covent Garden. Ingrid hopped down out of the carriage she and Ava had commandeered as it let out a hiss of steam. The windows to Hayes's shop were full of automata, as well as a range of devices she couldn't quite make out. He was no blacksmith of the Royal Academy, but he seemed to have managed to eke out a well-to-do living, judging by the sumptuous velvet beneath the displays.

"Hullo," Ava called as she pushed open the door and entered. The bell rang. "Mr. Hayes?"

A thin woman popped up from behind the counter, raking the pair of them with a sharp gaze that probably weighed them to within a pound of their worth. "Mr. Hayes is busy, ma'am, but I'm sure I can help you. Mrs. Hayes, at your service."

Ingrid leaned on the counter as Ava launched into the spiel of why they were there. There was a back room just off the counter, and it was filled with a listening silence. "So you see," Ava murmured, as she reached the end, "we would very much like to question Mr. Hayes about the orb."

"I can take a message, ma'am," Mrs. Hayes's smile held teeth. "But I'm afraid he—"

"Why don't you just fetch him out of the back room?" Ingrid broke in, eyeing the woman and letting the *wild* within her show. "He's standing right there listening to us."

Ava wanted intimidation, after all, and as much as a part of her hated to do this—to be what everyone in London suspected verwulfen were—they needed information.

Mrs. Hayes nearly collapsed a row of shelves as she scrambled away from the flare of bronze in Ingrid's eyes, her heartbeat rabbiting in her chest loudly. "What do you want with him?" she demanded shrilly. "My Bart has nothing to do with this... I see everything that runs through the books, I do!"

"Is that why he's sweating so badly right now, and his heart is pounding?" Ingrid inquired sweetly, before raising her voice. "I do hope he's not thinking about running. That would be a very bad idea. If I have to chase him down, well... I'll be most put out."

The curtains parted and a lean young man stepped through, his Adam's apple bobbing. "That's not necessary," he told her firmly, though the icy glaze in his eyes told another story. "Dolores, will you put the Closed sign up, and go see the butcher about dinner?"

Mrs. Hayes's lips thinned, but with a parting glance at Ingrid she complied.

Silence filled the shop, broken by the jingle of traces and carriage wheels outside. Several clocks ticked on the walls, and the eyes of numerous automaton stared blankly at her as Ingrid moved to tug down the small curtain over the door.

"What do you want?" Hayes demanded the second she did so. "I don't know anything."

"You *do* know how to make one of these," Ava told him, pulling the Doeppler orb out of her reticule. "You're possibly the only one who still knows."

He frowned, turning it over in his hands. "Yes, I made them." Handing it back, he met her stare. "Two months back. Three crates of them. Why?" Sweat darkened his upper lip. "They can't do anything dangerous by themselves."

"It's a gas-dispersing device, with a timer," Ava pointed out. "I can't imagine a good purpose this could be crafted for."

Hayes looked away. "They paid a small fortune. I-I—"

"You knew they were up to no good," Ingrid replied, strolling through the shop and running her fingers along one of the steel puppets, "but you didn't care because you wanted the money."

"Y-you don't understand." Hayes licked dry lips. "These men.... They weren't the type of men you say no to. I know times have changed—supposedly—but I still remember what it felt like when the Echelon were in charge. These... blue bloods...."

"Describe them," Ingrid suggested, leaning on the counter and peering at him. "And do try and remember everything."

By the time she and Ava exited the shop, they were convinced.

"Ulbricht," Ava murmured. "That name just keeps popping up."

"And now we have proof he was connected to the Begby Square disappearances, and a witness, and a reason to question Ulbricht." Ingrid cracked her knuckles then lifted a hand to flag down a carriage. "That should satisfy Malloryn's objections to bringing him in."

"I do hope that didn't sound like you mean to enjoy questioning him," Ava murmured.

"He tried to feed me to a vampire." A distinct thrill lit through her. Revenge. "There might be a small part of me that will enjoy it."

Ava shuddered as a carriage ambled to a halt at the curb. "You and Byrnes—you're terribly well-suited."

Hell. Ingrid slammed to a halt. The other woman's feelings were apparent to her, even if Byrnes was shockingly oblivious. "Ava, I'm.... I-I—"

"It's all right, Ingrid." Ava smiled sadly. "I'm not angry, or upset. You suit Caleb. I should like to see him happy with someone, and you... you get beneath that callous facade he wears so well in a way I've never seen anyone else do. He needs someone like that. Someone who makes him feel."

"I don't think he and I shall ever happen," Ingrid admitted as she tugged the carriage door open for Ava. "It would be very easy to begin to feel something for him. But I think you're misconstruing his attentions. It's just a game to him."

"I've known Caleb for nearly four years. Trust me, Ingrid. I wish he looked at me the way he looks at you. Don't give up hope just yet."

"You're taking this remarkably well."

Ava's blonde lashes obscured her eyes. "I've known for a while that nothing was ever going to develop between Caleb and I. The mind knew, even when the heart held hope." She swallowed. "And I think that you are a decent, kind person. Even when you want to break bones."

"Just Ulbricht's," Ingrid assured her as Ava stepped up into the carriage.

A sickly sweet scent caught her nose at that moment. Something familiar. Something strong enough to cut through the coal smoke.

"Are you coming?" Ava asked, peering out of the hackney.

"I'm just going to take a look around," she replied, nostrils flaring as she stepped back. "I think I can smell something."

Ava's green skirts swished out of the carriage, and Ingrid realized she intended to follow.

"Alone," she snapped, one hand to Ava's chest to hold her safely inside.

Ava's green eyes widened a little. "Is everything all right?"

"It's fine," Ingrid replied, cursing herself for her bluntness. "But I'm going to be moving quickly, and you yourself said that fieldwork sets your pulse racing. It's probably best if you take the information about the Doeppler orbs back to Baker Street."

For if she smelled that scent correctly... a vampire had recently passed through the area.

"If you see Byrnes, maybe send him this way," Ingrid said, still trying not to alarm the other woman. Regardless of her and Byrnes's not-quite-argument at the moment, she wasn't stupid enough to track a vampire alone.

She just wanted to see what it was up to. People spilled through the streets around them, children clutching their mothers' hands, and one even trying to ride a bicycle in the park across the street, guided by a man who had to be his father. This section of town was a bloodbath waiting to happen.

"All right," Ava concurred, closing the door and peering out of the window. "As long as you're certain you'll be fine alone?"

"Right as rain," Ingrid replied, and stepped back onto the footpath. Fog clung to the alleyways and the hair on the back of her neck rose, as if something was watching her from within, but she forced herself to wave to Ava as the carriage let out a hiss of steam and then burbled into the traffic.

It turned the corner and Ingrid let out the breath she'd been holding. Turning, she strode along the street, breathing deeply.

What was a vampire doing in this area of town?

Every person she passed only pushed her nerves right to the edge, as she couldn't resist glancing at their faces. A fat banker there, hurrying home to his wife and children perhaps.... What if he got home and found nothing but blood? Or nothing at all. After all, people were disappearing and they still didn't know why.

At least this was a bloody lead.

Thunder rumbled in the distance, and Ingrid looked up. Black clouds hovered on the horizon, but she still had some time before it rained.

A young governess looked both ways at the edge of the pavement, her hands clasped around her two charges' hands. Ingrid couldn't stop herself from taking the woman by the arm.

Startled eyes flew to hers.

"Take them home," Ingrid said curtly, trying not to frighten the young governess too much. "I'm working with the Nighthawks, and I'd highly recommend that you keep your charges inside today."

The young woman blanched, and Ingrid smelled panic. But the girl swept up the children and hurried them away. At least that might be two that she saved.

Children... everywhere. Ingrid's gaze locked on the grassy park across the street, her ears ringing with their laughter and screeches of joy. Indecision warred in her breast. Should she send them home? Or follow the creature to try and stop whatever it was up to?

Ingrid bit her lip, then started to run after the scent trail. There were simply too many people out, and if she paused here, then the vampire might start its killing spree before she got to it.

She was the only one who *might* be able to stop it.

Suddenly she realized where she was. Familiar streets that she'd only traveled herself a day or so ago. She began looking around, her steps slowing as the scent trail crossed itself. It had some sort of interest in this area. Where the hell was she? Why did she recognize—

That was when she knew.

"No," she whispered, "No, no, *no*." As she scrambled around the corner, she caught hold of the gaslight and stared up at the building across the street. Miss Appleby's Home for the Elderly.

Not coincidence. Not merely a chase. It had come here for a purpose.

Screams lit through the building. Ingrid was running before she'd thought about it. Byrnes had made her promise not to confront the vampire by herself, but this was no time to worry about breaking that promise.

Not when his mother was in that building.

Slamming through the front door, she saw the blood painted against the walls, one forlorn handprint splayed in wet vermillion before it slid in a splash toward the floor. A body lay there, throat torn out and eyes wide in horror.

Lightning flickered in the distance, highlighting the darkened entrance. Ingrid leapt over the body, seeing others in the halls, through the kitchen door.... Above her, noise thumped, and someone cried out in agony.

Upstairs. The bloody vampire was upstairs.

Moving quickly up the stairs, she caught its scent— that sickly sweet rot. This one was not as far advanced as the Ulbricht vampire had been. It had only just begun to stink of rot, not dripping in it like the house party vampire. That didn't mean anything. She had nothing to compare it to, as the Ulbricht vampire was the first she'd ever encountered. Who knew whether it was at the full peak of its speed and abilities, or whether it was only beginning to find its strength? Vampires weren't precisely a studied phenomenon. They were rare, and the usual way to deal with them was to exterminate them.

Following the muffled thuds and thumps, Ingrid took stealthy steps forward, one foot placed carefully in front of the other, both of her knives in hand and her heart thundering in her throat.

Right into mayhem. The creature was sitting at the end of the hall, glutting itself on a body. Others lay scattered and torn to ragged pieces. Ingrid froze, realizing it hadn't seen her. Its face was buried in the ravaged throat of what had once been a servant here, judging by the apron. Mrs. Byrnes's door was cracked open just across the hallway, faded sobs coming from within. Alive then. Perhaps it had focused on the maidservant in its grip, forgetting the other potential victims in here. Sometimes they did that, she'd heard.

She slid an inch toward Mrs. Byrnes's room.

Another inch gained, her heart pounding like it was fit to erupt through the cage of her ribs. How the hell the creature couldn't hear it was beyond her. One more step....

The vampire froze.

Ingrid echoed it.

Sniffing, the pallid face lifted like a dog's. Filmy glaze covered its eyeballs, turning them an eerie calcium blue. Right. It was blind. But it would smell her now, and its blindness would barely slow it down. She had to remember that.

A fierce, fiery cold began to creep through her veins, along with the faint tremble that preceded a fit of berserk rage. In the rage, a verwulfen man or woman was almost impossible to cut down. They barely felt pain or fear, or knew the cost of consequences. Nothing but brutal mindlessness and strength.

The unfortunate thing was that she was already quite afraid, and what she really needed to be was angry.

"Easy," she whispered, stepping closer to the door. "Easy there, lad."

Movement flexed in the vampire's hindquarters.

Ingrid twisted, driving the knife up as it launched toward her. Claws raked the hard carapace of her body armor, cutting through it like it was gauze, and then white-hot agony blistered through her abdomen. Oh shit. Ingrid forced herself to complete the blow she'd planned, her knife driving into the creature's eye, even as its teeth clamped down upon her shoulder. She had it by the throat with her other hand, but there was something there. A collar? Electricity zapped through her and she jerked her hand back.

A high-pitched roar of rage ripped from its throat. Ingrid punched it in the chest, earning a few precious inches. Rage burned in her blood, her entire body going ice-hot as she threw it away from her. Then she was through the door into Mrs. Byrnes's room, slamming it shut—

A weight hammered at the door, almost flinging her across the room. Turning, she set her back into it, knowing that this was the only barrier that might, just might, keep her alive. Byrnes's mother was huddled in the corner, her bare feet drawn up beneath her white night-robe. She stared at Ingrid with a childish expression of fear on her face, rocking slightly before burying her face in her hands. No help there.

Blood. Blood everywhere. On her shirt, on her hands, on her.... She saw the gaping mess of her abdomen, and instantly her body went cold. Shite. Her mind refused to deal with it, but the sight of the mess cost her the fury she'd been building. The *berserkergang* slid from her like a shroud, and Ingrid gasped as all of the pain came rushing back in.

Not now. Another blow almost broke the door in two.

"Help!" she screamed.

Claws scraped at the wood, slicing thick gouges of timber off it, she imagined. Blood. Pain. Shocking pain.

Ingrid's vision blurred. She couldn't breathe. Couldn't move—

The door rocked one more time. Her legs were about to give out. Then whistles broke out, high-pitched and stabbing through her ears. Nighthawks. She'd never been so glad to hear Nighthawks' whistles in her life. A fluting trill of notes sounded in response. Claws padded away from the door.

"Good boy," someone murmured, and a metallic clip snapped shut.

Ingrid slid to the floor, as footsteps vanished into the depths of the house. That awful clicking screech of claws on the floorboards echoed it.

Her abdomen was a hot, flaming mess of pain. God, what had it done to her? Tingles of heated numbness burned in her midsection, a sure sign that the loupe virus was hard at work.

But at least the bloody vampire was gone.

Static crackled in Byrnes's ear. Cursing under his breath, he stepped into the nearest alley and pressed a finger to the button on his communicator. He'd almost forgotten he was wearing it as he tried to track Ingrid, who'd asked for him, according to Ava. "Not now, Garrett."

"I've got an emergency at Clerkenwell. You're the closest Nighthawk—"

"Garrett, I'm busy." Ingrid wouldn't have wanted him if she didn't think she needed him, not after last night.

"Byrnes, it's a slaughter in there." Garrett's voice was on edge, even through the tinny speaker. "Sounds like your case."

Byrnes paused. "A slaughter?"

"One of the nurses escaped and bolted for the nearest Nighthawks garrison. They sent in a relieving crew, but nobody's answering. Craigmore went to scope the place out, and he says there are bodies everywhere. He hasn't been inside yet. Can see something moving in there, but he's waiting for reinforcements—"

"Where?" That cold feeling seeping through his veins unnerved him. No. Garrett had said Clerkenwell. That didn't mean anything. The borough was large. And there was no guarantee that this slaughter had anything to do with the vampire they were hunting.

"Miss Appleby's Home for the Elderly. It's on—"

"Grant Street," Byrnes said hollowly, his ears ringing as though all of the blood had drained from his extremities. His mother. "I'm on it. Get me reinforcements as soon as possible."

"Is anyone alive in there?" Byrnes demanded, frantically searching each window as he stepped out of the shadows behind Craigmore, a Nighthawk he'd worked with in the past. *Mother. No. Not this way.* After the life she'd led, she didn't deserve to die this way.

"I don't know, sir. I haven't seen anyone moving in the last five minutes. Earlier, yes, but..."

"Did—?" A hint of scent wafted past his nose, cutting off his next line of questioning. A scent he knew, musky and all woman. Nostrils flaring, Byrnes strode toward the building, a new fear rising in his heart. The scent was stronger here, near the door.

"Ingrid," he whispered, and everything in him went cold. What the bloody hell was she doing here? A new fear rose to choke his throat, because if Ingrid was here then she wouldn't hesitate to enter, not when she knew his mother meant so much to him.

Argument or no argument, he felt the darkness rise, the predator inside him just as frantic as he was. *Get to her. Protect her,* it insisted, locking bloodthirsty claws around him. The color in his vision vanished and blood pounded through his temples.

This case had already proven that neither of them was invulnerable when it came to vampires. *Jesus.*

"Sir, what are we going to do?" Craigmore sounded like a frightened little child behind him.

"Stay here," Byrnes replied, clamping down on the hot surge of emotion that threatened to choke him. "Guard the perimeter and wait for reinforcements. I'm going in."

CHAPTER TWENTY

BLOOD HERE. Blood there. The Home was a slaughterhouse.

Jesus Christ. Byrnes's mouth pooled with saliva, his nostrils flaring as he stepped inside. The *hunger* surged, sickening him. The men and women here were familiar. Not prey. It was the blood, overwhelming his senses and igniting the predator inside him.

He didn't force it down, however. He needed the predator. That was the only way he could imagine coming up against a vampire alone and surviving.

Ingrid, he whispered to himself, trying to refocus it. *Ingrid needs us.*

Above him, something clattered.

Byrnes froze, his gaze rolling toward the ceiling. Nothing moved. Only his heart, threatening to pound its way out of his chest.

More sound. A thud. Byrnes started for the stairs. Both pistols were in his hands. A faint, mocking flute sounded somewhere above, a sound that took him back to Ulbricht's immense gardens.

"Ingrid!" he called, reaching the top of the stairs. "Ingrid, where are you?"

Sound echoed behind him, and he spun, pistols rising instantly, only to see a startled cat flee past him. Byrnes let out the breath he'd been holding and eased both fingers off the triggers.

"Byrnes?" came a low, feminine cry.

Oh, thank God. She was still alive, and in his mother's room.

He strode toward it, body alert for the faintest shifts of breeze and shadows. The door looked like it had faced one of those hedge trimmers that were all the rage at the moment. Thick gouges marked its heavy surface and curls of timber lay abandoned on the floor beneath it.

"Ingrid?" he called, sheathing one of the pistols at his belt. "Is my mother there?"

"She's here."

Byrnes paused. Ingrid was breathing hard and something about her tone sounded strained. A faint note of panic crept down his spine. "Are you all right?"

"A scratch," she croaked. "I'll heal."

Something about that didn't sit right with him. "Where's the vampire?"

"Was here. A minute ago. Left with... the woman."

"What woman?" he demanded.

"The pipe-playing woman. Ulbricht's mistress, I think."

Her again. Byrnes looked around, but the house had an abandoned air. "Craigmore," he said, putting a hand to his ear to activate the communication device. "It's clear, I believe. Bring in the medics if they've arrived."

Holstering his second pistol, he tried to open the door, but there was something in front of it. Giving it a nudge revealed a long lean leg, clad in Ingrid's dark trousers. The second the door cracked open, the wash of blood stung his senses.

"Jesus Christ." There was blood seeping down her trousers. Byrnes pushed harder against the door, his breath catching. How bad was the wound? That was a lot of blood. "Can you move? Let me in, damn it. That's not a bloody scratch!"

Ingrid dragged her legs up to her body, then tried to move aside. And failed.

Shit. She was hurt. Badly.

Byrnes nudged the door open just enough to slip through. His mother rocked in the corner, but there was no blood on her, and though she looked terrified, she wasn't wounded. Ingrid was. It was a simple matter to prioritize. Simple to—

That was when he saw the damage.

Time seemed to freeze as his focus narrowed down to her. "Let me see. Ingrid, let me have a look."

Ingrid's hands were pressed against her abdomen, painfully pale against the mess of blood, and... other. Wide bronze eyes looked up, startlingly vulnerable, as he settled at her side. She was never vulnerable. It scared the piss out of him. "I-I can't."

"You're not going to bleed out." The skin was torn, a great, gaping wound. He didn't even know where to start. What to do. Reaching up, he pressed the comm at his ear. "Craigmore?" The word came out half-hysterical.

"Sir?" Came the static-crackled reply.

"Is Dr. Gibson out there yet?"

"Just arrived, sir."

"Send him up immediately. Room fourteen. I've got someone here who needs stitching and bandaging. She's bleeding badly. I don't.... Hell, just tell him to bring his entire kit."

"Will do, sir."

Byrnes shrugged out of his jacket, scrunching it into a pillow and pressing it behind her head as he laid her down. "Are you cold? Does it hurt?"

"Hot, actually." She was starting to shake now, her teeth forming an indentation in that plump lower lip. "Byrnes—"

"Hot?" A hand cupped to her forehead revealed the truth; blisteringly hot. He jerked his hand back in surprise before realizing. The loupe.

A hand caught his, wet with blood. Ingrid gasped for breath, as if she'd been running.

"Ingrid, can you breathe?" Panic lit through him like a struck match. He didn't know what to do. All of his medic training evaporated like smoke in his brain. Normal people didn't recover from wounds like this, but if she were a blue blood he wouldn't have been worried.

Don't be a fool. She's verwulfen. Nothing can take verwulfen down.

Except a vampire, came that little whisper.

Christ, what could she survive? The color of her skin scared the hell out of him, and the way she was panting.

"N-normal," she managed, grinding the word out between gritted teeth. Sweat darkened her hair. "Burning up... normal. B-breathing... like this. I'll fall asleep soon. Hard to... wake."

That eased his fear. Normal. This was normal. "Can you survive this?"

She managed to nod. *I can.*

"Good." Byrnes grabbed the sheet off his mother's bed and wadded it, pressing down over her abdomen to slow the bleeding.

Then he finally lost it.

"Why?" It was a hoarse demand. "Why the hell would you have entered this bloody place, knowing there was a vampire on the loose? Knowing you were alone? Why, damn it?"

"Your m-mother...."

Not his mother. She had done this for him. To save someone he held precious. Emotion knotted up in his throat, burning hot and heavy. For a second Byrnes was afraid it would spill out of him, that he wouldn't be able to choke it down.

"Don't you do this again," he snapped. "Promise me."

Ingrid looked startled. "I t-thought you... didn't care."

"I never said I didn't care," he snarled, pressing his forehead against hers so that he wouldn't have to look her in the eye. "Promise me you won't ever go off alone like this again."

"P-promise."

His hands were shaking too. "I could wring your bloody neck. You could have been killed."

"Byrnes," she whispered, weakly stroking his hand. "Caleb?"

That lump in his throat felt like a fist now.

"I'm all right," she said, watching him with wide, startled eyes.

He was shaking so violently he didn't know what was wrong with him. "You are *not* bloody all right—"

"Byrnes?" A sharp rap came at the door. Gibson. Thank God. "Am I right to enter?"

Byrnes yanked the door open.

In the medic van, Byrnes sat with Ingrid curled in his arms, wrapped in a blanket. Gibson had stitched her wounds closed and bandaged them, but Byrnes didn't have it in him to set her aside. Seeing Ingrid fade into a healing sleep as the loupe fired through her blood made every dark instinct within him rise.

"My mother?" he managed to ask.

"Garrett's got her," Gibson replied, watching him carefully. "He's taking her to the guild and making sure she's all right. He said to do what you need to; he's got your mother for now."

Byrnes relaxed an inch. He hadn't even noticed the guild master in the chaos, but there was no one else he'd trust with his mother's care. She'd been frightened and still rocking in the corner by the time Gibson had managed to sew Ingrid up, but she hadn't been injured.

Not like Ingrid.

"Like that, is it, lad?" Gibson reached inside his coat, tugging out a flask and handing it over.

Byrnes stared at it hollowly. "No. It's... not. It's—" He didn't know what it was. Or perhaps he had the slightest suspicion.... After all, he *had* run into a vampire-infested building after her, the very same idiocy that he'd accused her of. Not a moment of hesitation had afflicted him. All he'd known was that he had to get to her before something bad happened.

"Take a drink, boy. She'll steady your nerves."

"I don't *have* nerves," he replied flatly, though he took the flask.

Gibson merely looked amused. "Of course not."

Bloody rotting bastard. Gibson knew him too well. Better perhaps than he himself did, for he hadn't realized how he felt until this moment. Garrett was going to laugh himself silly. Of all the things to happen, falling for a stubborn verwulfen lass was the last thing Byrnes had expected.

But fall he had. The truth was unexpected, but how could he fight it? He felt like he wanted to squeeze her unconscious body against his chest, as if afraid she'd somehow be taken from him. That moment... the moment he smelled her scent and realized that she'd gone in there, alone....

Cold rushed through his body, as if he relived it. Byrnes took a swig and choked as whiskey burned down his throat. By the time he handed it back, Gibson merely looked old and tired.

"Not much for me to do there, lad. A bloody shame." Gibson upended the flask himself. "So many bodies."

"I thought she was going to be one of them."

Gibson made a clicking noise in his cheek. "Never had much to do with her type before, but by the look of it, she'll heal. You can't dwell on 'thought.' She's here now, and she'll be whole and hearty in no time."

Byrnes merely grunted. When he looked down, he found Ingrid's face tucked against his chest, her cheeks flushed with red, and the fingers of her right hand curled in his shirt collar as if she hadn't wanted to let go.

Realization was dawning upon him like a sun blazing over the horizon. This woman was precious to him. She was the strongest, toughest woman he'd ever met, but seeing her like this gouged out a piece of him inside.

He couldn't fight the truth anymore: Her smiles made him smile.

Her pain made an awful knot twist in his stomach.

Her anger and fear made him feel protective.

It was a textbook case of a blue blood claiming. Garrett had been just as irrational. Even Lynch had played the bloody fool, following around on Rosa's heels, and Byrnes hadn't understood then. He'd mocked the both of them, not even realizing how helpless one was against this emotion.

Swiftly, he ran their past few encounters through his mind, trying to work out precisely when it had begun.

Byrnes frowned, brushing a strand of sweat-slicked hair off her cheek. He couldn't think of a single moment that seemed to define this sudden momentous shift within him. Instead it had been a slow slide, taking him unawares, and it had begun the second he walked into Garrett's office a year ago and a pair of breathtaking bronze eyes had lifted to his as Garrett introduced his new partner.

"I work better alone," he'd promptly retorted.

"Afraid you'll be outclassed?" came the husky reply, and a part of him had known then that this woman was unlike any other he'd ever met.

In his arms, Ingrid gave a soft sigh and shifted in her sleep. And Byrnes couldn't stop himself from resettling her until her head rested against his chest where she'd hear his heart racing. What was he going to do? They wanted different things out of life, didn't they?

An image of baby Phillip shot to mind, dribbling on Ingrid's shoulder, and Byrnes panicked. Because he wasn't that man, he'd never been that man, and yet he didn't know if he could do the right thing again and walk away from her.

"Well and truly done in by the look of you." Gibson snorted.

And for once, he couldn't for the life of him disagree.

CHAPTER TWENTY-ONE

TWO HOURS LATER, Byrnes found himself at the guild.

A warm patient voice read some of Shelley's poetry in the guild master's office, and Byrnes eased the door open, slipping inside so as not to startle his mother. Garrett sat by the fire, book open in his lap as he read over the head of a sleeping infant tucked over his shoulder. His blue eyes flickered up and he nodded to Byrnes, then kept reading.

On the sofa lay his mother, her head resting against a pillow and her eyes sleepy.

"Hello," Byrnes said, kneeling by her feet and clasping her paper-thin hands in his. "Has Garrett been looking after you well?"

His mother smiled, blue eyes watery and distant. "H'lo, dear."

Dear. His chest squeezed.

A part of him wanted to say, "It's Caleb." But that wouldn't make any difference. In her mind Caleb was a young boy and she often worried about feeding him, or where he was and who was watching out for him. Just saying the name would rouse her panic as she tried to find her little boy.

She patted his cheek and Byrnes slid onto the sofa beside her, trying to move quietly. Having two of them in the room at once would agitate her a little, as if she couldn't quite pay attention to the both of them, so he simply held her hand and gestured for Garrett to keep reading.

It took almost another ten minutes for his mother to fall asleep, her head resting against his shoulder, and Byrnes stared into the flames in the grate until Garrett fell silent.

"Where's Perry?" he whispered.

"Coordinating the hunt," Garrett whispered back, setting the book aside and rubbing the back of his daughter. "I didn't want to leave your mother alone. She was quite settled with me sitting here, but when I tried to leave she grew upset again."

"Thank you." He knew how difficult it was for Garrett to let his wife coordinate a hunt for a dangerous vampire whilst he was forced to stay behind, especially now that Perry was a mother. But that was Garrett—he knew how to calm people, and listen to them, and charm them. There was no one else who'd have been able to keep Moira quiet. And Byrnes was fairly certain that Perry wouldn't be anywhere near the danger.

"There's word on the street that there's some sort of monster stalking the city," Garrett murmured, closing the book of poetry and setting it aside. "My Nighthawks have been dealing with hysterical people ever since. I know we said to wait…."

Byrnes eased the rug up over his mother's shoulders, then stroked his hand through her thin hair. "It's time to take action. We need to start hunting these creatures, and Ulbricht's mistress. It wouldn't hurt to have more men to help work out where they're holing up, if you're willing to send the Nighthawks into danger?"

"That's our job." Garrett sighed. "I thought that after the blood frenzy case I'd never have to deal with something like this again."

"You hoped."

"And how is Ingrid?"

There was a fist lodged in his chest at the mere thought of her, but he wasn't about to admit that. "Healing. She's lucky she's verwulfen."

Garrett considered him. "Gibson called in, after he'd seen to her."

"I'll just bet he did. And what did he have to say?"

"That apparently the mighty have fallen."

Byrnes cursed under his breath. Garrett had been waiting years for this to happen. Byrnes had thought it never would. "If you say one more word about it, I swear I'll strangle you."

Garrett's grin had something of the Cheshire cat about it. "What would I say? That Lynch owes me a bottle of his finest. Thank you, old friend." He clapped Byrnes on the shoulder as he stood. "Though it took you long enough."

"Nothing's happening."

"Are you fouling it up so badly?"

"I'm not—" Byrnes shut his mouth. "Get me something to drink." He glanced down as his mother shifted. "And lower your voice."

"At the risk of being told to go to hell, I'm not the one shouting," Garrett mock-whispered, then glanced at the baby on his shoulder as she stirred. "And I've learned the consequences of being loud. Here. Hold her while I get us a drink."

Byrnes found himself with a bundle of blankets and baby. Christ. Garrett rolled his eyes and helped settle her properly in Byrnes's arms.

"You're a natural," Garrett said dryly.

"Sometimes I wonder why I bother to visit you." He held the bundle awkwardly. "Which twin is this?"

"Ivy," Garrett replied. "Grace has been struggling with colic, so Doyle's pushing her in the perambulator to try and get her to sleep."

"Jesus." The Nighthawks had turned mad. He couldn't picture loud, swarthy Doyle pushing a perambulator. "It's probably a good thing I'm out of here."

"Whether you like it or not, we're all a part of your life, Byrnes. And Perry's adamant you're going to teach the twins how to use knives." Garrett poured him a glass of blud-wein. He cleared his throat. "Is there a problem? You couldn't take your eyes off Ingrid and Phillip the other day at dinner."

He wanted to bang his head against a wall. Garrett's instincts were too good. "No problem. Just... life is changing."

"Some of us have been through such a thing before. It's not all bad. Actually, its mostly rather wonderful, once you get through the confusion at the start. There's nothing like waking up—"

"Please. Don't." Byrnes curled up his lip. "Perry's like my sister."

"Which is precisely why I allow you near her," Garrett replied, and a flare of possessive heat filled his blue eyes.

"I seem to recall a moment where you thought I was a threat." That bought a touch of humor to the surface. "You thought there was something going on between us."

"I was an idiot."

"Well," Byrnes replied, "I'm not going to disagree."

"But now the shoe is on the other foot, and I'm not going to pretend I'm not enjoying the hell out of this. May I offer you some advice?"

"I'm fairly certain I'm going to receive it, regardless of whether I want it or not," Byrnes grumbled.

"You're a hard man to get to know sometimes, Byrnes. You've been with the Nighthawks nearly as long as I have, and I only found out your mother even existed two years ago," Garrett said, setting a glass down beside Byrnes and sinking into his own chair.

"Is there a point to this?"

"Yes, there is." Garrett eased back in his chair, looking into the distance of the past. "If you don't let Ingrid in, then you'll lose her, and trust me when I say that I've come very close to losing Perry in the past. I don't recommend it."

"I came very close to losing her today," Byrnes admitted, and a chill rose in his chest once more. "I don't.... This is not my area of expertise."

Garrett let out a snort. "Clearly."

"I'm not quite certain how I feel...." It scared the hell out of him. He'd had a vision of his life, and now it was completely in disarray. He'd never liked change, but if wanted to pursue this, then he would have to. Byrnes stared at the baby in his arms. Holding her was starting to grow awkward, but she smelled rather nice. "This was supposed to be just a dalliance with Ingrid. But it's very clearly not. Or perhaps I should say... it's rather rapidly leading in another direction. What if I can't feel the same way she does? What if I break her heart? Or don't want what she wants?" Rosa's words hammered doubt into his heart.

"Byrnes, I think the question you have to ask yourself is how you felt the second you realized she was in danger."

Terrified. He looked up. "Certain for the first time in my life that she was mine, and that I had to protect her."

"*Can* you walk away?"

"I tried that," he snapped. The baby shifted at the sound of his voice and he froze. "We weren't going to pursue this. But... Christ, I left her to work alone today, and *this* is what happened! She was injured because I'm too bloody scared of what's happening between us. I should have been at her side. I should have been there."

"You were there," Garrett said, "when she needed you. And this decision doesn't need to be made in a day. You have time to woo her, time to sort out your feelings."

"She wants children."

Garrett paused. "Do you?"

"I don't know. I've never really thought about it before, or about taking a wife." He looked down at the baby, feeling that age-old surge of panic light through him. First Debney pushing his way back into his life, now Ingrid.... It was easier not to have them there, easier to control all of the old feelings that Debney brought back into his heart if he didn't have to confront them, but the idea of pushing either of them away made him feel sick.

"And the darker side of your nature? What does it think?"

"The hunger *is* me, Garrett. I'm not going to pretend we're two separate identities, like you and Lynch do."

Garrett shrugged. "I know that. I also know that it represents everything primal about a man—or woman. If you want to know what you want, or what's happening, then it will know. There are no lies there."

He'd always been in control of himself, unlike a lot of other blue bloods. Lynch had praised him for it, but it was vexing now when all of these *urges* began to overwhelm him. He wasn't used to it. "It wants her. No, it's already claimed her, I think," he said, then cursed himself for an idiot for giving into thinking of this as the others did. "*I want her. I'm claiming her.*"

"Go back to her side then," Garrett suggested. "Work out where you want to go from there. You have all the time in the world, and frankly, Ingrid deserves a say in this too. It wouldn't surprise me if she's completely in the dark about what's going on in that head of yours."

"I told her we needed to take a step back and think about things rationally."

Garrett groaned and sipped his drink. "It's worse than I suspected then. She no doubt thinks you've given up on her or rejected her. Trust me. You don't want that to happen."

"Oh, shut up," he growled.

Garrett smiled. "Your mother is safe here, and I'll set Doyle to fluffing about her. There's nothing he likes more than mothering someone. She'll be drowned in vats of tea and buried in biscuits, and treated like royalty. Go tell Ingrid how you feel."

"Call me if she gets scared. She doesn't like new places. Or new people she doesn't know." Byrnes looked down at his mother as he stood and passed the baby back to Garrett. *I wish you were still there.* But she wasn't, and she wouldn't even notice if he wasn't here when she woke.

But Garrett was right. Someone else would.

"I will."

And he had a vampire to catch, a vampire who had just happened to attack the place where his mother was kept.

Coincidence? Byrnes didn't think so.

CHAPTER TWENTY-TWO

INGRID SLEPT THROUGH most of the night.

Byrnes sank into the armchair in the corner of her room and watched as the drizzle splashed against the windows.

There wasn't much he could do. Charlie and Kincaid had tried to track the vampire whilst he dealt with his mother and Ingrid, and both had returned an hour ago, claiming that the trail vanished in the sewers. The creature had glutted itself on blood at the Home then simply returned to wherever it was lurking, as if its purpose had been served.

Which made him wonder. What had been its purpose there? Anarchy? There were far more public places it could have attacked. And his mother was there. The link bothered him. The way that woman had looked at him bothered him.

Was this revenge for killing one of her vampires? Or something else?

A sharp rap came at the door, then Malloryn strode in, decked out in full opera regalia. A white silk scarf fluttered around his neck and he carried his top hat in his hand, but his gaze went immediately to the bed. "Just received word," he said, shutting the door behind him.

Byrnes tensed. The man didn't belong in here, not with Ingrid virtually unconscious. He looked up and Malloryn paused, as if aware that boundaries had been crossed.

"Long night?" the duke asked in a milder tone as he unfolded a newspaper from beneath his arm and tossed it at Byrnes. "How is she?"

"Healing," he replied. "It was... bad."

Malloryn crossed to the bed, staring down. "She's stronger than you think. There's not much she cannot survive."

"I'm aware of that." He scrunched the newspaper in his fist, his vision blanking for a second. Knowing the facts didn't make it easier to deal with, which was unusual. All he could see was— "The vampire gutted her. If I hadn't arrived in time...."

He didn't need to add anything else.

Malloryn turned to face him, his arms crossing slowly as he settled that piercing gaze on Byrnes. "This is new. I expected you to still be at each other's throats." He hesitated. "Do you think I should reassign you both? Partners with an emotional attachment don't work very well together, I've found."

Like hell. "You can try, but I'm not going anywhere." The words were soft with menace, and even he heard them. Byrnes shut his eyes, trying to get a handle on his emotions. The *hunger* whispered through his veins, resenting the other man's presence in Ingrid's bedroom. Possessive. Demanding. Looked like his decision had been made, and there was no point in fighting it anymore. "If she gets hurt again...."

"You're not the type of man who'd never forgive himself."

"You don't know me." He looked up. "But you're right. I'd never forgive you."

Malloryn's gaze narrowed to slits, and he seemed to be thinking about whether he'd want Byrnes as an enemy. "Then we shall leave the arrangement as it is. You're clearly not thinking straight. If I try and pair you with someone else, you'll be distracted and worrying about Ingrid. That might prove disastrous. I want you focused on the mission, Byrnes." For a moment incredulousness showed in the man's expression. "I used to think you a man after my own heart."

"What? That I had none? No man is invulnerable, I think. Even you might fall prey to the gentler emotions."

Malloryn didn't quite flinch but he turned toward the window, dragging the silk scarf from around his throat.

And suddenly Byrnes understood. "Who was she?"

"No one that you know," the Duke replied, peering out into the cold blustery night. "Take a look at the paper."

Confession time dismissed. Byrnes unfolded it. The headline screamed bold. *Bloody Rampage At Nursing Home! Blue Bloods on the Loose!*

"Hell," he said.

"That pretty much sums it up." Malloryn balled the scarf in his hands, looking vexed. "Someone's been busy at the printing presses all night. There was a newspaper lad right outside the opera." He cursed under his breath. "I thought we'd have some sort of lead by now. Whoever is doing this has to leave a trace somewhere. Somehow. They can't just simply vanish."

"Ava said that Ulbricht ordered the Doeppler orbs. We needed to run it by you, but we'd like to... ask him a few questions."

"Done," Malloryn replied, then frowned. "This doesn't feel like Ulbricht's style, however. It bothers me."

"I agree."

Malloryn looked at him as though he'd done something interesting. "Oh?"

"I think there's more to this than there seems. Every crime scene has been flawless. No clues, no trail to follow, or if there is one, it vanishes. Until the Venetian Gardens, where quite conveniently there is a Doeppler orb left behind. I've spoken to Ava—she said that Ingrid was unsettled outside Hayes's shop. She asked if Ava could smell something, which makes me believe that the vampire was watching the orb-maker, as if it expected us to go there."

Malloryn stared into space. "That seems quite a stretch."

"I'm an investigator. Putting impossible pieces together is what I do. Let's also look at the black flag, and the '0' that is the only blemish on an otherwise clueless case. Whoever is doing this wanted us to know that the Sons of Gilead had something to do with it. Why else would they paint those symbols? Why else would Echelon lords be walking around with it tattooed on their wrists? They're not hiding the symbols, not nearly well enough. So either they are ridiculously bold and stupid, or someone is setting them up."

"I thought there was some credence to the theory that some killers leave behind calling cards of some sort. Are the flag and symbol not just that?"

"Usually it's something bloodier—the same signature kill stroke. I just have this gut feeling...."

"Go on," the duke replied.

"Something's wrong. The vampire knew where to go. It stalked through an entire borough full of potential targets before choosing that one building in Clerkenwell, one with a connection to me."

"Byrnes."

"It followed me there when I was visiting my mother. It had to have. But why attack now? Why me? What the hell drove it there? Is someone watching us? Was it someone from Ulbricht's ball? There's coincidence, and then there's too many coincidences."

Malloryn looked disturbed. "That's impossible. Although... the vampire does almost seem as though it's taken a particular interest in you. Perhaps it knows you killed its... friend."

"Not the vampire," Ingrid whispered, and both of them shot to the bed.

"Ingrid," Byrnes said, his voice suffused with relief. "You're awake?"

She blinked sleepy eyes at him, frowning grumpily. Her hair was a mess. "Someone keeps talking. How could I possibly sleep through all of that?"

Byrnes curled her hand in his and squeezed it. She was alive and awake, and he hadn't realized until this moment how on edge he'd been.

"What did you mean about the vampire?" Malloryn pressed.

Dark shadows haunted Ingrid's eyes. "The woman. The woman's controlling the vampire somehow. And *she's* interested in Byrnes."

"That's impossible," Malloryn stated flatly.

"You keep using that word," Ingrid said with a yawn. "Right now, I believe that anything is possible."

"The flute." Byrnes chewed the thought over. "I think Ingrid's right. I'd never believe it if I hadn't seen it for myself now, but this is twice we've encountered a vampire that doesn't simply go off on a killing spree until it's cut

275

down. No vampire has ever walked past dozens of potential victims like that. It should have started killing the second it came into the streets, unless it was being controlled. These attacks are focused and planned. I think it's trained, somehow, which is the craziest thing I've ever said, but I cannot come up with another reason. And why is Ulbricht's mistress interested in me?"

"You killed her vampire, and tracked Ulbricht to his meeting. Maybe she wants revenge? Maybe she's impressed? I don't think she's his mistress either." Ingrid was fighting a losing battle against sleep. "And it was wearing some sort of collar too, now that I think of it. One that shocked me as soon as I touched it."

They had suspected that someone was pulling the strings of the Sons of Gilead, after all. Who better than a woman in control of one of its leading members?

"Maybe Ulbricht's not the danger?" he mused. "Maybe he's the distraction?"

"I'll see if any of my networks have anything," Malloryn said, watching Ingrid. "Byrnes, tomorrow you can work with Kincaid." Byrnes looked up sharply, but Malloryn held a hand up. "Until Ingrid is on her feet."

"I'm fine, Your Grace," she said stubbornly, pushing up onto her hands and looking surprised to find that they trembled.

Byrnes eased her back down. "No, you're not. And don't look at me like that. The sooner you get enough rest, the sooner you'll be on your feet. You're not ready. You'll only slow me down, and I need you at your best."

If looks could kill....

"I'll leave you to it," Malloryn murmured, and slipped through the door as if the sudden intimacy bothered him.

"I'm not an invalid," Ingrid growled the moment the door was shut.

Byrnes dragged the armchair toward the bed, then slumped into it. "Do we have to argue about this?"

"You're the one who started it!"

"Ingrid, I had to stuff your guts back into your stomach and hope to hell that you'd heal. There was nothing I could do. None of my rudimentary on-scene training...." Byrnes swore, looking away as the vision of it flashed before his eyes, taking him back to that moment. "I thought you were going to die." He broke off as that panicky feeling speared through him again. Only clasping his hands together helped. He could force the tremble down. "I don't think I could bear it, to see you hurt again so badly."

When he looked up, her eyes were wide and startled. All of her anger had leeched out of her and she turned her gaze to the ceiling, looking troubled. Candlelight warmed her features.

"I thought I was going to die too," she admitted in a quiet voice. "Just for a moment."

He swallowed the sudden fierce lump in his throat. "I'm not cut out for this."

Ingrid looked at him, but she didn't say anything.

Byrnes reached out slowly to curl her hand into his. Ingrid looked at it, then squeezed back gently. He sighed.

"Sleep," he told her. "You're safe now, and all bandaged up. You need to rest. And then you can work with me again."

An uncomfortable look crossed her face. "Promise you'll watch over me while I sleep?" Ingrid whispered, her eyelashes fluttering. "I can't keep fighting the loupe, and it makes me feel vulnerable."

Byrnes folded himself into the seat by her bed. "Promise."

And just like that, she stopped fighting the loupe and her own stubborn nature and her lashes fluttered shut.

CHAPTER TWENTY-THREE

INGRID WOKE because someone was trying to wear a rut in her floorboards.

Byrnes. She'd woken several times since the vampire tore her apart, and every time he'd been at her side in a heartbeat, demanding to know if she was all right, if she was in pain, hungry... what?

Ingrid didn't know what to make of it. She wasn't used to being fussed over, and if she were being honest with herself, Byrnes was fussing. He'd even fed her soup. Soup! And her favorite too.

How he knew this.... She suspected Rosa's help, which meant a conspiracy against her, but then again, who knew when it came to Byrnes? He was always watching. Always filing little pieces of information away in that brain of his.

It left her feeling distinctly uncertain about the way things were between them. They'd agreed, damn it. They weren't going to take that step forward, but it seemed that she'd missed some vital change of mind.

"Good morning," he said.

"Still here?" she asked, tossing back the covers and trying to stand.

She barely had a chance to do so before his lean body was pressed against her own, gently easing her arm around his shoulders as her legs wobbled.

"Byrnes." Her exasperation showed. "I'm not an invalid."

He sat them on the edge of the bed with his arm around her waist. "You've barely gotten your feet back under you. I'm not letting you out of bed until you're completely healed."

"I need some privacy, Byrnes."

"You can barely stand—"

"Byrnes," she growled, deep in her throat.

"Five minutes," he finally said, and then left the room so that she could take care of the necessities and then scrub her teeth.

Ingrid paused in front of the mirror, then rolled up her nightshirt, tentatively untying the bandages there. Smooth skin met her gaze. No sign of the vampire's attack. She touched the area lightly. "You survived," she whispered, meeting her eyes in the mirror. It didn't feel like it though. Not deep inside, where a part of her had met her own mortality head-on. She'd always been invincible. Or felt like it.

But this was the first time she'd borne such a grievous injury.

It left her feeling vulnerable in more ways than one, and Byrnes wasn't helping the situation. How could she deal with his sudden change of heart? What did it mean?

"Knock, knock," Byrnes called, and Ingrid jumped.

"I'm done," she called, scurrying back to her bed and slipping under the covers.

He entered briskly, carrying a tray. "I brought you breakfast," he said, as though she couldn't smell the beefsteak. "Jack told me you're not worth dealing with before you've eaten, after one of these episodes."

"I'm not hungry."

"Actually he *warned* me not to deal with you before then." Byrnes lifted the silver tureen off the self-heating platter. Steam wafted off it, and the smell hit her like a punch to the gut. Her stomach chose that moment to mimic the sound of whales mating. Loudly. Curse him.

"Pity," Byrnes said, wafting the steam toward her with the most evil smile she'd ever seen. "Herbert went to a lot of trouble to cook this up for you. Now what am I supposed to do with it? Hmm, there was this scrawny young cat out the back. I suppose I can just feed it to her."

Ingrid ground her teeth together. "There are times when I'm tempted to do... something to you."

Byrnes swung into the chair beside her bed, still fanning the steam her way. "Oh? Do tell? Something... wicked? Something involving the pair of us getting naked? Again?"

"Something permanent," she growled, and then took the plate off him, and the knife and fork. If she didn't eat then she was going to be too weak to get out of bed. It had nothing to do with him getting the better of her, and then acting all smug about it.

Besides, it felt good to have the fork in her hand.

Byrnes very subtly moved his leg out of the way when she glanced at it. Perhaps it was the way that her fingers curled around the fork? Or maybe the expression on her face?

"Just remember," he warned in a mild tone, "you like those bits of me."

"Do I? I find I can't quite recall why at the moment." Which was a blatant lie. She very much liked those bits of him, and her memory chose that moment to remind her in precise detail about what those bits looked like. What they felt like against her skin.... Ingrid smothered a groan, and stabbed the beefsteak instead.

It wasn't fair. Here she was trying to play by the rules that he'd invented—the rules that said that they couldn't do this—and he was doing his level best to dash all of her best defenses. Ingrid shoved a piece of steak in her mouth. She didn't understand any of it. She chewed thoughtfully. She needed Jack to talk to.

"Why are you here? Why are you bringing me breakfast? And why were you even sitting by my bedside at all? Don't you have a vampire to hunt?"

"Kincaid's waiting downstairs. I just wanted to see...." He paused then, and a half dozen expressions flitted across his face before he managed to soothe his expression back into a blank mask. "What do you remember?"

"I know that you didn't like seeing me like that." Byrnes hadn't been at all himself. There'd been a frantic energy to him, as if the blue-blooded predator within him lay very close to the surface. Ingrid frowned. "And I don't think you liked Malloryn being in here."

Which was a curious memory indeed.

Byrnes flicked a piece of lint off his arm, then shifted his gaze to the window. "I'm having a slight problem," he admitted. "I know what I should do. I know *why* I should do it." Those blue eyes locked on hers, spearing straight through her. "But I don't want to walk away from you, and to be quite honest, I am dealing with some complex emotions at the moment."

Ingrid stared back, working her way through what he was saying. "You don't want to walk away?"

Byrnes stood abruptly and began pacing. "I don't do this, Ingrid."

"Fetch a woman breakfast, you mean?" she asked, feeling a faint warmth wash through her, as if a part of her was starting to understand. She had to admit she liked seeing him so off-balance. Byrnes was always *too* composed.

"*That* too."

Ingrid swallowed another mouthful. "Are you trying to say that you have decided that we are going to pursue this little flirtation between us?"

"It's not a flirtation," he finally told her. "Not for me. Not any longer."

She nearly dropped the fork. Of all the things she'd expected him to say, this was not it. "But I... I... you...." Nothing. She had nothing to say.

Byrnes eased onto the edge of her mattress, clasping his hands carefully in his lap. "I've gone above and beyond to prove that you and I meant nothing, and it turns out I've been lying to myself all along." He hesitated. "I missed you during this last year, Ingrid. I couldn't stop thinking about you. And I said some stupid things about getting you into my bed and burning you out of my memory, but the truth is... I don't think I could ever forget you. You're one hell of a woman. And I don't know where this road will take us, or whether I can be what you want, but I do know that I want to explore that option."

"I wish you'd make up your mind," she whispered.

"It is made up." This time, there was no misjudging the expression on his face. "I am going to pursue you, Ingrid Miller, with the intention of never letting you go. So fair warning…."

Words died in her throat. This was supposed to be a chase, a game. Byrnes wasn't the sort of man that one started daydreaming about the future with. Except… that seemed to be his intention now.

"I understand that you weren't expecting this. Perhaps you don't feel the same way that I do. I don't know. We need to talk about this," Byrnes said, leaning in to kiss her gently, his hands cupping her face in a way that made her heart leap in her chest. "But this is not really a wonderful time, and I think you need some time to think. You keep making these incoherent noises." He grinned suddenly. "I'll take them to mean that you're flummoxed by my abrupt turnabout and not disgusted at all. Just know this: It's no longer about winning your body, Ingrid. When I finish these challenges, I intend to win your heart."

Withdrawing gently, he stood and stepped away. "Rest and heal, so you can join me as soon as possible. Kincaid's not nearly as pretty as you are."

And, after dropping that shocking statement upon her, he turned and left the room.

Locking away all of the doubts he felt about Ingrid and whether she felt even remotely the same way he did, Byrnes amused himself by toying with Kincaid.

"So you're saying that there's not a single positive outcome associated with a man turning into a blue blood?" he asked. "Just to make your statement clear."

Kincaid shrugged. "I don't know, bloodsucker. Is there?"

Stalking across the rooftop, Byrnes paused at the edge, then leapt down twelve feet to the next rooftop and looked up. "Well come on, then. We haven't got all night."

Kincaid examined the drop, then swung himself over the gutter and used his arm strength to lower himself a respectable distance before he dropped onto the roof at Byrnes's side. "Still can't see a benefit."

Byrnes examined his pocket watch. "I can. It's called efficiency. I should have brought Charlie. We'd be nearly there by now. You're slowing me down. And we have a vampire's trail to pick up."

"Malloryn's got him doing something."

"What?"

"How the hell should I know? I'm not his secretary."

"I'm faster than you," Byrnes pointed out. "I'm stronger than you. I heal from practically anything. And let's just say that when it comes to the ladies, I can go all night too."

"That's got nothing to do with being a bloodsucker," Kincaid spat back.

Byrnes grinned at him.

"So, I heard the chemicals in a blue blood's saliva can bring a woman to the edge of ecstasy," Kincaid said, casting him a sidelong glance.

"Your point?" Byrnes asked. "I assume you're not complimenting me."

"My point is, a real man don't need no *chemical* enhancements to satisfy a woman."

"Don't worry. It's not the chemicals in my saliva that leaves my women satisfied. Jealous?" Byrnes arched a brow.

"Is that why Ingrid's been casting big eyes at you—?"

Byrnes stopped in his tracks, his easy languor fading off him as if it had never been there. The hunger within him surged, shocking violence suddenly rising to the fore, and he realized that a part of it was due to his lingering uncertainty about what Ingrid's answer would be. "A blue blood can also kill you in a second and bury the body so deep that nobody will ever find it. And if you even breathe her name again," his voice dropped to a growl, "in a manner indicating anything less than utter respect, then I will take a lot longer to kill you than a second. I will make it last for *days*."

"You know... I were starting to wonder how deep you buried it. You're more in control than most of your kind, but it's still there, isn't it?" Kincaid stepped closer, eye-to-eye. "You're still ruled by it, itching to smear my blood all across this roof, ain't you?"

Itching to tear your throat out, at least. The pulse in his throat hammered. *Kill him*, whispered his inner darkness, his inner predator—the part of him that belonged in the shadows.

"No matter how deeply you think you've got that monster buried, it's still there, and one day it will hold the leash, not you."

Byrnes took a deep breath and swallowed it all. It was like flicking off a switch, like facing his father again and burying all of that rage, that fierce hissing need to kill deep within him.

"You have no idea," he told Kincaid, "how much I want to kill you right now. But the problem is, you're wrong. I am not and never have been ruled by the *craving*. I am also not very much of a gentleman, but in this instance, you crossed a line in mentioning her name."

Drawing his arm back, he punched Kincaid hard in the face before the man could even see it coming.

"Fuckin' hell!" Kincaid bellowed, clapping a hand to his nose and staggering.

Byrnes tugged his handkerchief from within his pocket. "No, I might have the hunger inside me, and the urge to make you little more than a smear on these tiles, but you're the one who can't handle your hate. Handkerchief?"

Kincaid pinched the bridge of his nose and tilted his head back. "Shove that up your a—"

"Stop your whining. I didn't break it. No matter how tempting it was. And you shouldn't bleed so enticingly in front of me." Byrnes smiled a nasty smile. "Who knows? I might lose control. I might let all of that *big, dark hunger* inside me overwhelm me, and then leap at you."

Kincaid wiped his sleeve across his face. "Anyone ever told you that you're a prick?"

"Frequently. Can you not see the tears of remorse in my eyes?"

Kincaid muttered something under his breath.

"See, if you were a blue blood, you would have seen that coming," Byrnes pointed out brightly, and stalked off backwards into the fog, watching his adversary just in case Kincaid decided to do something rash.

Kincaid muttered curses, wiping at the blood trickling from his nose.

"So," Byrnes continued, "what happened to you?"

"I'm fairly certain you punched me in the face," Kincaid growled.

"No, not that." Byrnes looked at the burly mech. "People don't just suddenly decide to hate an entire species. Something happened, something to do with a blue blood in your past. What was it? Did one of them kill your mother? Or a sister? Or a father? Drain all of the residents in your neighborhood?" He paused. "Steal your woman?"

"Go to hell."

"I'm sorry, I didn't quite hear that...?" He cupped a hand to his ear.

Kincaid glared at him. "You son of a bitch. It was my sister."

They both stared at each other.

"They took her," Kincaid continued, in a slower, quieter voice. "The Echelon lords. Took Agatha right off the streets and used her at one of their parties as some kind of bloodwhore for the night. Three days later she killed herself, because of those men. I was the one who found her hanging.

"And every time I look at you," Kincaid said, staring into Byrnes's eyes. "I see those men. Those monsters. And I see Aggie, staring sightlessly at the sky. Forever." He wiped at his bloodied nose. "That's what you are to me. But that's also why I'll work with Malloryn, because I remember what it was like before the revolution. I don't ever want to see my people, my friends, go back to that."

Silence fell. Byrnes actually felt a worm of guilt twist deep inside him. "I'm sorry," he said. He spread his arms wide. "Occasionally I can be an asshole. You get one free hit."

"What?"

"You mentioned my woman," he replied, "and I didn't like your tone. Now I've brought up your sister, and I was less than respectful too."

Kincaid mulled it over for all of a second, then swung. The full metal crunch of his mech fist slammed into Byrnes's nose. Byrnes fell onto the roof clutching at his face as pain speared through him.

"Bastard," he breathed, trying to blink through the ringing in his head. "Little bleeding pissant. You could have used your human hand."

"Leech," Kincaid replied, giving him an evil grin—and offering his hand for Byrnes to help himself to his feet. "What are you whining about? You're not even bleeding. And I'm only a poor weak human. I'm not as strong as you. Or as fast. Or as adept at healing. I can't even jump off a twelve-foot roof without risking a broken leg."

Byrnes tested his teeth as he grabbed Kincaid's hand and hauled himself to his feet. "Okay. Maybe I deserved that."

"*Maybe*?"

"That's as humble as I can be," Byrnes replied. He itched to touch his swollen nose, but wasn't about to give Kincaid the satisfaction.

Kincaid grunted under his breath. "Look, I'll deny this to my dying breath, and I still don't like you very much, but..." He looked pained. "You aren't entirely as bad as the rest of your breed."

"Did that hurt?"

Kincaid merely shook his head and walked on. "Smug bastard."

Byrnes laughed, but as he breathed in he got a trace amount of scent that slid through his chest like a stiletto. Instantly he turned, staring into the night, trying to smell the air. That scent came again, like sweet rot fresh out of a graveyard.

Byrnes shoved his hand out, slamming it into Kincaid's sternum. Kincaid grabbed his wrist, as if thinking it an attack, but Byrnes hushed him.

"What?" the mech murmured.

"Can't you smell that?" Then he realized. "No, of course you can't. I barely can, thanks to you."

"What is it?" Kincaid's nostrils flared.

Byrnes turned in a slow circle, examining the foggy rooftops. They'd been using them to hunt for the vampire's scent trail that Charlie and Kincaid had lost earlier. "You remember that thing we were hunting? Well, I think... we're not the hunters anymore."

A pistol clicked in Kincaid's hand. "Shit." Sweat sprang up along the man's temples. "Are you sure it's not the trail?"

"Not unless it's a fresh one."

A pale shape skittered out of the corner of his eye. Byrnes unholstered his own pistol and tracked the darkness, the sensation of a trickle of icy-cold fingers trailing down his spine. Kincaid's back met his. Both of them barely breathed.

Another sound whispered through the night, like claws scrambling on a roof. To the left. Byrnes swung that way, pistol raised, his eyes tracking the darkness. Kincaid was a wall of warmth at his back. A ghost whispered through the night to the right. Dashing close enough to be seen, then darting out of reach.

"They're playing with us," Byrnes breathed. *Sweet Jesus.*

"They?"

"Two of them, I think." Something else was moving out there, something that wasn't as albino pale as the vampires. "Why the hell aren't they attacking?"

"I don't like any of this," Kincaid muttered. "Vampires not going on a killing spree is unnatural."

"For once we're in agreement." He'd never thought he'd see the day where he wished for something uncomplicated like a vampire slaughtering its way through the population. But this made his skin itch. It wasn't right. It went against all of the natural laws. What if they'd... evolved somehow to start thinking like predators, rather than indiscriminate killing machines?

They'd be unstoppable.

A vampire's only weakness was its lack of rational thinking. The only way to get close enough to one to kill it was by waiting until it was so glutted on blood that it didn't see you coming.

A flute sounded.

And that's when the first vampire slunk out of the fog to pant at him, it's filmy eyes blank with blindness and its monstrously long claws skittering on the tiles. It hissed as it heard his sharp intake of breath and paced back and forth, looking hungrily at him, even if it couldn't see him. Byrnes lined it up in his sights, swallowing hard, but movement to his right made him hesitate and glance that way.

To where a tall, pale-haired woman stepped out of the shadows, outlined by moonlight.

"You," Byrnes said, lowering the pistol but not easing his guard one inch.

"Me," said Ulbricht's mistress, with a smile as sweet as a knife's edge.

CHAPTER TWENTY-FOUR

"WELL, IF YOU *were* a blue blood," Byrnes said to Kincaid, taking a stealthy step backward. "You might be able to survive the ensuing encounter. Me? I don't like my odds. Not against two vampires. You however, have no odds. Unless I take pity on you and decide to protect you."

"Do you ever bloody shut up? And nobody asked you for protection." Kincaid punched his mech fist against his thigh and a knife slammed through the gauntlet of steel that he wore as his hand. "I can watch my own back."

Ulbricht's mistress glided toward them, one hand patting the vampire's head at her side whilst its thin leash trailed up to a gold band around her wrist. Long silvery-white hair draped over one bare shoulder. It wasn't the coarse whiteness of age, but a spill of moonlight silk. A tight black corset spanned a narrow waist, with chains and a holster hanging stylishly from it. Everything about her was sleek. Even her black velvet skirts, which were embroidered in gold with a kraken by the look of it.

"How the hell do you move in that?" Byrnes asked. Their only chance of survival lay in getting her to start talking and keeping those vampires on their leashes. Kincaid's shoulder pressed against his own. Despite his words, the fellow's heart rate pounded like a train's engine fresh into the station.

The woman's leg thrust out through a well-designed slit in her skirts, revealing trim stockinged calves and heeled boots. The side lunge held traces of the martial art, batitsu, in it. He'd barely seen the movement, it had been so swift.

This was going to hurt.

"Christ," Kincaid said under his breath, his gaze locking on that leg.

Byrnes's smile held no humor. "Some vipers are pretty. Doesn't mean you take them to your breast."

As if he'd just graced her with the most delicious compliment, the woman's smile curved higher as she slowly undid the leash around her wrist and dropped it. "Oh, I do like you." Then she turned to the nearest vampire, and hissed, "*Stay.*"

Just smashing. There was a hint of insanity in those pretty blue eyes.

"May I have a name?" Byrnes asked, settling into a defensive stance as his gaze flickered between her and the now untethered vampires. "Or do I just refer to you as Madame Viper?"

"You may call me Zero, although once upon a time I was Annabelle Underwood." Her smile was dreamy. "I like this better. Much better. Nobody rips Zero's heart out of her chest—not like Annabelle's. Care for a dance, Caleb Byrnes?"

She knew who he was. His eyes narrowed to thin slits. "Is that why you're here?"

"No. I'm here to discover if you're worthy or not. You killed one of my vampires. Nobody's ever managed that before."

Worthy of what? But he thought it through. "You were watching. At the grotto."

Her smile sent tremors down her spine. "I could have killed you then and there but you caught my eye. I decided to spare your life so that I could learn more about you."

"Like what?"

"This—"

He barely saw her coming. The first kick took him in the shoulder as he twisted out of the way, and Byrnes stepped under her guard, slamming both hands flat against her chest. Zero staggered a step, then a knee drove directly for his balls.

Byrnes twisted, taking her knee to his thigh, barely managing to disengage. *Hell.* He winced as he put all his weight on that leg and felt that hard knot in his upper thigh.

Kincaid's fists were raised, but he hovered there, a constipated look on his face.

"What the hell are you hesitating for?" Byrnes yelled, ducking beneath a swinging kick.

Kincaid danced out of the way, his jaw tightening. "I don't hit girls."

Zero laughed, then spun and kicked Kincaid in the face. The second the kick landed, she jerked her knee back, and kicked him again in the throat. *Bang, bang.* The work of a second.

Kincaid went down. And stayed there.

Zero sneered. "Pathetic humans."

This was why he liked working with Ingrid. *She* wouldn't have hesitated. And now it was two vampires and one whatever-she-was against him. Smashing odds.

Launching forward, she lashed out with her other foot, and he caught it, locking her boot against his upper arm and clapping his other hand on her thigh. Zero's eyes widened as he spun, using a twist of her ankle to take her to the roof. They both went down, and he used his weight and his elbow to slam her back into the tiles before he disengaged and danced to his feet. The second she rolled onto her fingertips and knees, she launched toward him. Byrnes leapt lightly in the air, hammering a punch into her solar plexus the moment she came after him.

"Well, you're no gentleman." Zero pouted. Then tried to kick his feet out from under him.

"Take it as a compliment. Gentlemen get their throats ripped out in my world." If he let her get close enough to him, she'd take him down and make it hurt. That fall hadn't even winded her.

Another feint. Punches landed in a flurry of pain along his arms as he deflected them, and Byrnes used her momentum to head butt her. Zero staggered back, and for the first time in his life, Byrnes hesitated instead of going after her. She was dangerously faster than he was, and if that last punch was anything to go by, stronger. He might have years of training on his side—that was the only reason he suspected he was still on his feet—but something about the way she moved told him that she'd outlast him.

"What are you?" His breath came hard, and he lowered his hands a fraction, inviting her to talk.

Zero wiped her nose, sneering at him. "Haven't you worked it out yet? I'm the butterfly, you're just a caterpillar."

"I've been called worse." *Bastard* sprang to mind. Or *weak*. He'd hated that as a child, especially considering it came from his father's lips.

"You lack that one crucial element to your transformation. I could give you that element, the elixir. If you prove worthy to join my pets."

Elixir? Was this what that document in Ulbricht's cabinet had meant? He flicked a glance toward the patient vampires. "I've seen your pets. Thank you for the consideration, but I'm not really interested in being leashed like a dog."

"They're not my pets. They're the failures, the ones who didn't survive the transformation. They must earn back the cost of the elixir that was wasted on them."

"Lady, they're vampires."

"Precisely. How do you think a vampire is created?"

Byrnes paused. It wasn't something he'd ever thought of before. Most blue bloods lost control of their bloodlust once their craving virus levels reached 80 percent or so and the effects of the Fade set in. Then they began to devolve, their skin paling and their spines curving like a cat's until they loped along on all fours, stinking of rot. That was how a vampire came to be.

Or so he'd always thought.

Slowly, as if explaining herself to a child, Zero said, "You so-called blue bloods have never been what you were meant to be. A blue blood is the first stage of metamorphosis, and when your craving virus levels reach a certain percentage, you begin to transform."

"The Fade," he said.

"The Blooming," she chided. "Perhaps one in a thousand blue bloods survive the transformation without the elixir's help. Most don't. Most become a vampire, an abomination that was never meant to be. They're created when the creature dies during the end stages of metamorphosis. That's why they're weakened and crippled, with the personality of a vicious dog. Their brains suffer irreparable loss during the death stages, until all that remains when the virus reanimates them is the hunger."

Despite himself, Byrnes was fascinated. This was the ultimate mystery. He straightened, his fists lowering completely. "How the hell do you know that?"

"I know a lot of things." Zero stepped back, dragging her skirts with her. Fog swept around her legs and those brilliant blue eyes watched him from the shadows. "Such as the fact that Sir Nicodemus Banks brought the craving virus home from the Orient nearly one hundred and fifty years ago, but not the elixir guaranteed to evolve a blue blood as they were meant to evolve. He had stolen the virus from the immortal Imperial family of the White Court, and believed that by spreading the virus through Europe he took away some of their mythos, their power. He never asked himself why they allowed such a thing to happen: they knew that without the knowledge of the *elixir vitae*, they would never be threatened. Blue bloods, after all, are barely children in my world."

"Then what are you?"

Zero's smile grew as she swept up the vampires' leashes. They moved instantly, straining at her side. "Why don't you ask your good friend, Malloryn? After all, he knows more than what he's told you, doesn't he? You can tell him this from me: we are vengeance, pure and simple, and he will pay our price. We're here to watch the city burn, and to make Malloryn, the Duchess of Casavian, and all those who fought during the revolution bitterly regret their roles in it." Pressing her fingers to her lips, she blew him a kiss. "If you want to know more about what I am—what you could be—then you must prove yourself to me. Find me. Be worthy, Caleb Byrnes. And I might just grant you immortality."

With that, she took a step back and vanished off the rooftop, taking the vampires with her. Byrnes scrambled to the edge, but only fog greeted him. Nothing moved.

Zero was gone. The vampires had vanished.

And somehow she knew his name.

CHAPTER TWENTY-FIVE

"WE HAVE A problem," Byrnes said, striding into the house on Baker Street with Kincaid thrown over his shoulder. The bastard was out cold, and heavy as hell.

Ava looked up from the brass spectrometer she'd been fiddling with in the parlor. "You're bleeding." Her eyes widened when she saw Kincaid. "What happened?"

"Think you can pack his nose? It might be broken."

"I— Of course. My examination rooms, if you please." With a swish of skirts, Ava headed for the small room that she'd claimed as her own.

Fabric rustled. The baroness and Gemma Townsend both appeared in separate doorways, each looking extremely elegant. The baroness was clad in dark green, something sleek and luxurious with feathers and fur, and Miss Townsend wore a frothy rose monstrosity.

"What happened?" Gemma demanded.

"A little tête-à-tête with the enemy. She disapproved of Kincaid's manners. I tried to tell her he had none."

"Is that supposed to be amusing?" Gemma asked.

"Byrnes has the worst sense of humor," Ava muttered. "Put Kincaid down in here."

Byrnes complied, laying the heavy oaf down on Ava's examination table.

"That nose is definitely broken," Ava muttered, tilting Kincaid's chin to the side to examine the mottling bruise on his throat. Her fingertips were gentle as she made her assessment.

Byrnes looked Gemma up and down. "Are we going to a ball or something? I had the distinct impression that this was a house of spies."

Gemma peered down her nose at him. "Don't you pay attention to anything? It's Malloryn's engagement party tonight."

"Ah, the Hamilton girl." He shot a look at the baroness. "Why are you going?"

"It's not as though he loves the girl." The baroness snorted. "And please, Byrnes, we're all adults here. Miss Hamilton trapped him into a proposal. This is hardly going to be a marriage of like minds, but one of duty."

"Someone trapped Malloryn into marriage?" The thought actually amused him.

"He's been a proponent of the Thrall Bill, which enforces proper treatment of thralls and swift execution of those who think they can simply force a girl down and drink her blood." Baroness Schröder peered at Kincaid. "When Miss Hamilton caught him out in the garden with blood dripping down her throat and a sudden audience, it wasn't as though he could pretend it was a setup. Malloryn had to offer marriage or see the entire bill flung in his face. It was rather neatly done, actually. I'd commend the girl on her swift wits if she hadn't just earned herself a cold marriage bed and her husband's undying hatred."

"Wouldn't want to be in her shoes," he agreed. "I really need to speak to Malloryn. Right now, if possible."

Gemma blinked. "He's at his home."

"And the engagement party is...?"

"In his garden."

"You cannot just walk into an Echelon party," the baroness protested. "You smell like blood!"

"As if half the lords there won't smell like blood!"

"Yes, but they... they...." The baroness faltered, gesturing at him.

"You look like you kill people for a living," Ava supplied, peeling Kincaid's eyelid back and shining a bright light into his eye. "Most of the Echelon look like the only thing they've killed is a mink. Or a lemon tart."

"Why does everyone keep saying that?" He looked down at himself. "I'm dressed appropriately. I hardly look like some murderer."

"It's not the clothes, Byrnes," Gemma said. "It's your eyes. Or the look in them."

"Well, I'm not going there to make friends," he replied, circling the table. There wasn't much he could do about his eyes. "How's Ingrid?"

"She went out after you, but came back an hour ago," Ava said.

"What? You let her go out in *that* condition?"

Ava shot him a steady look. "It wasn't as though I could stop her. What did you want me to do? Arm-wrestle her into submission? And she's fine, Byrnes. Not even a scratch. She just went upstairs to clean herself up."

"And Kincaid?"

"His pupils are responsive, and his breathing is normal. I assume he'll come out of it soon, though he's going to feel rather sore and sorry for himself for a while." Ava winced.

"A wee woman in a very tight dress kicked him in the face several times."

Ava blinked. "A what?"

"Some kind of vampire, that isn't a vampire." Byrnes held his hand up to his chest. "This high."

"You found Ulbricht's mistress," Gemma Townsend breathed.

"She found us. And I'm absolutely certain Ulbricht's on her leash, not she on his."

"This will put Kincaid out of action for weeks! What were you doing at the time?" the baroness demanded.

"Getting punched. Repeatedly." He shrugged when he saw their faces, heading for the door. "What? She was fast. Did you not hear the part about her being some sort of vampire?"

"How did you escape?" Gemma followed him to the door.

"She offered me a promotion. I thought about declining, but decided she might tell me more if I played coy. Now, if you'll excuse me, I really need to check on Ingrid, then talk to Malloryn."

The baroness *tsked* under her breath. "The carriage is coming around in fifteen minutes. At least have a shave and clean yourself up. He'll be annoyed if you show up looking like this."

"I thought annoyance was Malloryn's general state of being."

"Oh, you've seen nothing yet," the baroness told him grimly. "Right now, he has a prickle in his drawers, and it's called Adele Hamilton. You don't want to cross him, Byrnes. Not right now."

In the end they wouldn't all fit in the carriage together, so Byrnes went on ahead, pacing outside Malloryn's as he waited. Although he didn't entirely approve of Ingrid's decision to come along, he had to trust that she knew her body.

And he strongly suspected he wouldn't have won the argument to see her stay behind anyway.

The carriage arrived, dispersing the baroness and Gemma, who gave him a wink, and then Ingrid.

Or someone who looked like Ingrid, wearing an enormous gown.

It was bronze silk, with black lace slashing across the bodice and a trim little black velvet jacket that showed off her divine curves. The color framed her eyes perfectly, and it wasn't too girlish. No, this screamed silk and sensuality, grace and elegance. A little black hat draped over her left brow, cocked on an angle, and a tumble of long golden-brown curls dripped over her other shoulder.

Quite frankly, Byrnes felt like she'd punched him in the chest.

"Will I do?" Ingrid gave a slow twirl, her skirts flaring out around her.

He could barely speak. This— Her— She was absolutely, stunningly beautiful. "You'll do," Byrnes replied, his words clipped. Then he looked away, out over the garden party at the back of Malloryn's house, searching desperately for some composure. Someone had stolen it completely. Or no, set it alight, and was stomping on the flames.

"I don't believe I've ever seen you speechless." Ingrid's laugh was breathy. Leaning against him, she fussed with his collar, for all the world like a society debutante. However, the look in her eyes as she glanced up at him from beneath her lashes was hardly innocent.

"You're enjoying this," he accused, leaning into her warmth.

"I enjoy anything that involves ruffling your feathers."

"Consider them ruffled." *I'm having a hard time not dragging you off into the house and having my way with you.* One glance down revealed that she was having difficulty with her breathing too. For quite a different reason. "Does this mean you're considering my proposal?

Ingrid hesitated. "We'll discuss it later."

He swallowed the flare of nervousness this statement wrought in him. "The bust doesn't seem to quite fit."

Ingrid rolled her eyes, tugging at the lace that barely hid her bountiful assets. "Of course you'd notice. It's an old dress."

"Perhaps I could help with that?"

Ingrid rapped his knuckles with her fan. "Not now," she cast over her shoulder, making her way down the stairs onto the lawn. "Malloryn."

Duty before pleasure. Byrnes followed at her heels.

"Let's separate," she said, twirling a finger. "All the quicker to find him."

"I'll take the left."

"Done." Ingrid sauntered toward a table loaded with sandwich platters.

Pasting a smile on his face, Byrnes tipped his head to some woman wearing a peacock on her head, then nearly collided with another young woman in gold.

"Pardon," he said, searching over her shoulder for the duke.

The pretty brunette gave him a curious look as he stepped past her, and the two men at her side were both clad in scarlet uniforms, shocked looks on their faces.

Two seconds later the baroness intercepted him. "Do you know who that was?" she hissed.

"No."

"The queen."

Byrnes looked back. "Well, what do you know? She's smaller than I expected." He wasn't the sort of person who had much truck with the elite. "Found Malloryn yet?"

"Good God, you're like a blundering ox. This way." They turned, then the baroness froze.

There was a young blonde wearing peacock blue in their way. "Baroness Schröder," she said, tilting her head like one adversary to another.

The baroness drew herself up. "Miss Hamilton. What a delight. Ah, this is my, ah, my—"

"You're not on the guest list," the young woman told Byrnes with a suspicious slant to her eyes. "In fact, I've never seen you before."

"How do you know?" Byrnes stole a glass of champagne for himself, and one for Ingrid. He couldn't see her anywhere.

"Because I wrote the guest list myself."

The bride. Just his luck. He was caught between two snarling felines, both aware of the tomcat caught between them, despite what Baroness Schröder had said. Girls of good breeding politely pretended that their fiancé's mistresses weren't their fiancé's mistresses. Unfortunately Miss Hamilton seemed to have missed that particular etiquette class.

"Long day?" Byrnes asked the young woman.

"It's the moment I've been waiting for," Miss Hamilton replied. "All my life."

Sounded like it too. "My commiserations."

The baroness sucked in a shocked gasp. "Byrnes!"

"Quick! I see Malloryn over there waving at us." He gave the baroness a little push in the back and she stumbled forward, blundering between two young lords in stockings.

Darting a glare over her shoulder, she took the opportunity he'd presented her with and disappeared.

Shrewd green eyes locked on him. "Who *are* you?"

"Someone who knows your fiancé well. Call me Byrnes. And this"—he finally spotted Ingrid's hat bobbing through the guests—"is Miss Ingrid Miller, my fiancée."

Ingrid summed the girl up in one glance. "Why hello, darling," she said, catching on swiftly, though with a slight questioning arch to her brow. "I found him."

"Ah, the happy bride-to-be." Malloryn appeared, his expression at odds with his charming words as he clasped Miss Hamilton's shoulders from behind. That icy blue-green gaze raked Byrnes over hot coals, as if questioning the fact they'd dared to show up. "Darling, the Reynoldses are with your mother. They're looking for you."

"Getting rid of me that easy, are we?" Miss Hamilton offered her cheek, and Malloryn dutifully brushed his lips against it. "I suppose I should have known both the baroness and I are disposable."

"Careful now," Malloryn whispered in her ear. "If you start rumors, I *will* finish them."

"Your friend here was just offering his commiserations. He seems to know you far too well." Offering Malloryn a challenging stare, Miss Hamilton moved away, her blue bustle swishing flirtatiously.

"My apologies," Malloryn said smoothly, watching her go with a decidedly hawklike expression. "It's been a trying day for Adele."

"No apologies necessary," Byrnes assured him. "I quite like her."

"Want to marry her?"

"I wouldn't want to deprive you of the pleasure."

Malloryn grimaced.

Both Byrnes and Ingrid exchanged amused glances, falling into place behind the duke as he swept them toward the house.

"My study," Malloryn said, shooting them both a look as he made smiles and nods to various people, all whilst propelling them toward the house. "I assume this is important?"

"You're certain?" Malloryn asked after Byrnes filled him in on everything.

"Well, yes," he replied. "She said her name was Zero, and that—"

"Not about that—about what she said about blue bloods being the first stage of the metamorphosis." Malloryn's expression was tight, and held the intensity of a man who'd just been told the entire kingdom was about to sink into the ocean.

"Is there something we should know?" Ingrid asked, picking up on the tension.

Malloryn's lips thinned. "You were right to come to me with this immediately. This.... Christ. We're in trouble."

"You know what she is." Byrnes was certain of it.

"I wish I didn't." Malloryn paced to the bell pull and rang for a servant. One appeared promptly. "Send for Lord Barrons and his wife—tell them it's urgent, and be discreet. They're in the garden somewhere. And bring us some blud-wein, brandy for the lady. Oh, you'd best postpone the cake too. I'm going to be a while. Make sure the guests have plenty of wine."

The servant vanished.

"Malloryn?" Byrnes asked.

"Wait," he was told by the icy duke. "This is something Barrons needs to hear."

And so they waited.

Barrons and his wife, the Duchess of Casavian, arrived promptly. If Byrnes wasn't mistaken the duchess was with child, though her midnight blue gown was designed carefully to conceal this fact. She was quite possibly the most beautiful woman he'd ever seen too, though in a cool, marble blue blood way. Not like Ingrid, who wore her passionate nature like a dress, or whose very touch seemed to burn him alive.

One glimpse at her husband revealed a dangerous man. Byrnes knew Barrons—had worked with him in fact—but never intimately. The Duke of Caine's heir wore a winking ruby dangling from his ear and was dressed in strict black, with a dueling sword at his hip. The first time they'd met, Byrnes had dismissed him as some peacock from the Echelon, but Barrons had earned his respect. This man had helped pull down the corrupt prince consort and now resided on the Council of Dukes with Malloryn and Lynch.

"Something urgent?" Barrons was straight to the point.

"My agents have discovered something about our nameless villain." Malloryn poured them all blud-wein, with a small glass of brandy for Ingrid, and dismissed the servants. "Tell them."

So Byrnes repeated himself.

This time he watched their faces. The moment he mentioned the metamorphosis, Barrons's gaze cut to Malloryn's. "Do you think it's possible?"

"Do you think *what* is possible?" Byrnes was tired of being kept in the dark. "Who the bloody hell is this Zero?"

Malloryn swirled his blud-wein, staring into its bloodied depths as though he could see the future within the liquid. "The question is not who is Zero? The question is, *what* precisely is Zero."

"Annabelle Underwood was a young woman who was sentenced to a mental asylum when she was barely sixteen," Barrons explained. "On the official register, Annabelle conveniently passed away at the age of twenty, following some sort of incident where she contracted the craving virus. According to a set of secret diaries *I* own, she was taken under cover of night and imprisoned in Falkirk Asylum, a private facility where she was under the care of a Dr. Erasmus Cremorne. She was the first of Cremorne's test subjects. Subject 0."

"Test subjects for what?" Ingrid demanded.

"What is about to be said does not leave this room," Barrons told them, and any sign of a cordial young gentleman vanished. This was a future duke, dangerous and powerful.

They both nodded. Byrnes would have promised the moon to discover *this* secret.

"Cremorne was testing a serum. An *elixir vitae* that he was trying to resurrect out of old documents from Tibet, the birthplace of the craving virus. They spoke of... creatures beyond a blue blood. Or, what a blue blood could have been. Our understanding of the craving virus has always been narrow. It was thought that the Fade led to a blue blood turning into a vampire, and following the Year of Blood, nobody allowed a blue blood to live through the Fade, so we had no means of discovering any different. However, Cremorne's experiments prove otherwise. Using the *elixir vitae* to control the metamorphosis, it appears that a blue blood does not revert to a vampiric state, but evolves into something more. Something faster, stronger, far more dangerous. We call them *dhampir*."

"Them?" Byrnes questioned. "How many are there?"

Barrons exchanged a look with his wife.

"Only one known," said the duchess, her hand sliding surreptitiously to her middle, as though she was worried. "Of the seven test subjects who survived the metamorphosis, it was thought that they had all died seventeen years ago in the fire that destroyed Falkirk."

"Who?" Ingrid demanded. "Who is the known *dhampir*?"

"The Duke of Caine," Barrons replied, with a mocking smile. "My father."

The Duke of Caine was a recluse, by all reports, and suffered from some sort of disease. "Bloody hell," Byrnes said. "What's his state of mind?"

"Normal," Barrons replied, "as far as we can tell. Or normal for him—he's still a cunning old bastard, meddling with people's lives, but that's not unusual. His appetite is increased, and he's stronger and faster than I am, but he doesn't appear to like leaving his house very often. Indeed, he seems to feel the cold more, and prefers to remain by his fire, in the dark. He cannot walk in sunlight the way we do, as it burns his skin and blinds him."

And they'd only seen Zero in daylight, Byrnes realized, if it were foggy.

"Both a blue blood's strengths and weaknesses are exacerbated it seems," Malloryn added, draining his cup. "They have the strength of a vampire, and the speed and healing, but are not deformed or blinded as a vampire is. And although a blue blood *can* walk in sunlight if necessary, the *dhampir* cannot. Interestingly enough."

"Not what I'd call it," Ingrid said gruffly. "Bloody terrifying is somewhat closer. After all, you missed the most obvious exacerbation—just how bloodthirsty are these creatures?"

"Very," Barrons replied, and set his cup down. "Almost vampiric."

Byrnes scratched at his jaw. "Zero said that a vampire was created when a blue blood in the Fade dies. That doesn't make sense. We've executed hundreds of Fade blue bloods over the years. One would presume we'd be swimming in vampires."

"Unless there's some kind of difference in the stages of the metamorphosis," the Duchess of Casavian corrected. "Maybe there is a certain point during the metamorphosis the blue blood must reach before they can make that leap?"

"We execute them when they reach 80 percent craving virus levels," Barrons mused. "So it must be a higher virus percentage."

"Hold on," Ingrid said. "So you're saying that Annabelle—or Zero—was one of the test subjects that you thought was dead."

"Yes," Barrons replied.

"Then what happened to the rest of them?" she asked. "You *say* that Caine is the only other one living. What if others escaped? What if there are more, just like her?"

A cold chill ran down Byrnes's spine. "She didn't say anything about other *dhampir.*"

"Then there could be others," Malloryn murmured.

"What does she want?" Ingrid asked, then turned and looked at Byrnes. "She said she liked you. That she might help you become what she is. Does that mean she wants to offer you the *elixir vitae?*"

"If I can find her and prove worthy, or some such nonsense." A cold hand curled around his heart. "And don't look at me like that. I'm not particularly interested in some mysterious potion. I like myself the way I am. No, she said her purpose was both vengeance and anarchy." He looked Malloryn in the eye. "Against you and the duchess in particular, and all those who fought for the revolution."

Malloryn leaned back in his chair, his gaze distant. "Why would she have such a personal stake in vengeance? She had nothing to do with the prince consort or his rule. Neither of us ever knew her."

"If her complaint is against you and me in particular," the duchess commented, "then it has to be something to do with the revolution. Very few people know that you, Barrons, and I practically ran it. It sounds like someone who was close to the Court, who might have been there when the prince consort was killed and knows what really transpired, might have some grievance against us."

"And the queen?" Barrons asked. "It was *her* revolution, after all."

The three of them looked between each other.

"See that the guard is increased," Malloryn finally said. "Perhaps move her to a different bedchamber. Cancel some of her engagements until we can discover more about this Zero."

"If someone wanted to make an attempt on the queen," Byrnes pointed out, "then she's downstairs in the garden. Supposedly along with half the people this Zero seems to want revenge upon. If I were her, I wouldn't attack the queen at the Ivory Tower, which is well guarded and practically impenetrable. I'd do it now."

Four sets of eyes locked on him.

And that was when the explosion sounded, the window shattering into thousands of glass shards that sliced through the air.

CHAPTER TWENTY-SIX

INGRID THREW herself at Byrnes, carrying him to the floor as glass spewed over them. Hot shards of pain lashed her thigh, weeping wet blood. What had happened? Where was—

Then she was being shoved, quite unceremoniously, onto her back. "Are you hurt?" Byrnes demanded, fingers tracing down the silk of her skirts. "I can smell blood."

"Saved by the bustle," Ingrid gasped, reaching down and dragging a thick spike of glass from her leg. Pain flared, but with it came the steady cold burn of the loupe. If not for the sheer volume of fabric, half her leg would have been shredded.

A thin runnel of blood in Byrnes's hair was his only sign of injury, and his face bore dark sooty marks. "Here," he said, picking several pieces of glass out in a peculiarly dainty way that wasn't at all like him. "Idiot woman. Diving atop me like I'm some kind of precious—"

"I'm fine," she said, sitting up. "Byrnes, I'm fine." *And you are precious. At least to me.*

"Is everybody all right?" Malloryn demanded, light on his feet like a cat. His coat was torn, and he'd lost his polished persona.

Leo Barrons helped the duchess to her feet. From the look of it, he'd borne the worst of the assault. Shredded strips of his coat hung off him, and blood dripped from his elbow. "Below," he gasped. "The queen."

"On it," Malloryn said, striding for the door. "Byrnes? Ingrid?"

"Coming." Byrnes tugged Ingrid to her feet, then stopped to check if she was bleeding.

"Go, you fool," she said, pushing at his chest. "It's naught but scratches."

"I'm not used to this."

And neither was she. But she kept her tongue as she pushed him toward the door, knowing that his fussing over her indicated the depth of his feelings. He wasn't the type of man to tease her with love words, and so she had to find them in his actions.

In the garden, everything was mayhem. People screamed, and here and there lay crumpled piles of silk like crushed butterflies. Smoke boiled from a pit in the ground. Servants were panicking, and none of the servant drones seemed to be working. Perhaps the explosion had fried their electrics?

Into the mayhem stalked danger. A vampire leapt onto the sandwich table, scattering trays as it hissed at the frightened party guests.

Ingrid whipped a silver sandwich platter off a nearby table and threw it like a discus at the creature. It launched itself over the tray and darted after a pair of screaming girls, hampered only by the panicked flight of the rest of the party guests. Too many people fled at one, distracting it as it looked for the weakest member of the herd.

"Watch my back." Byrnes vaulted over the table, knocking a dozen platters of sandwiches and cakes to their deaths on the tiled walkway.

"Byrnes!" Ingrid tried to follow and dragged two chairs with her. Bloody sodding skirts. With a slash of her knife, she cut away the offending lengths then went after him.

"This way!" Byrnes sprinted through the gardens with Ingrid on his heels.

The creature slid to a halt as the clouds suddenly parted and a wash of sunlight lit over the gardens. London's incredibly inclement weather was finally giving them a ray of hope, as it were.

It hissed as the sunlight burned its skin, and the pair of girls in front of it screamed. One of them was Malloryn's bride, holding a sandwich platter as a shield, as though that would do any good. The vampire darted into the shadows along the garden wall.

"Stay in the sunlight," Ingrid told Malloryn's fiancée. "And don't run."

A small package with brass springs and ticking clockwork pieces was attached to the vampire's back, strapped into place with a leather harness.

Ingrid's blood ran cold as she realized that it was ticking. "Byrnes! It's strapped to a bomb!"

Just one glimpse of his ice-cold blue eyes across the expanse of grass showed her that he was thinking the exact same thing as she was. *We need to get it out of here.*

Agreed.

There were too many people—too many innocents. But how were they going to lure it away?

Blood. They needed blood, something for the vampire to lock onto as prey. Ingrid slashed a thin cut down her arm, ignoring the flare of pain. Verwulfen blood was richer in iron than human blood, and according to most blue bloods, tasted better. Perfect.

"Ingrid!" Byrnes bellowed, seeing what she was about.

"Find me somewhere isolated," she shot back, darting close enough to flick her blood across the vampire's face. "Somewhere where we might be able to trap it, if that bloody thing doesn't explode!"

Then she was running before she could even look to see if it followed.

The shaking cold began as Ingrid darted out into the streets, the loupe firing through her blood and bringing with it the tidal edge of *berserkergang*. Fear washed away, leaving her buoyed with defiance and hungry for violence.

A fine edge to walk along. Push too far, and she'd be turning to face the vampire, careless of danger, fearless. Holding herself back meant that she wouldn't receive the burst of extra vibrancy, speed, and strength that she needed, just to stay in front.

A hack driver swore and those who'd turned out to see what all the fuss was about gasped as they realized what was behind her. Those gasps soon turned to screams, high-pitched enough to catch the vampire's ears perhaps.

"Don't run!" Ingrid yelled, but the lady in front of her snatched her little girl and darted down an alley. Ingrid cost herself a precious second in looking back, to see the vampire falter as it realized prey was fleeing from it. Instinct kicked in. It wanted to chase the slower, weaker prey.

Damn, and double damn. Ingrid's arm was beginning to heal now. She cut herself again, waving her arm in the air, and the vampire's head turned, blindly tracking her.

Byrnes met her gaze over the vampire's shoulder, lifting his pistol into the sky and then firing. The shot ricocheted through the streets, and screams echoed nearby.

What was he doing? Then she realized. Other streets would be just as clogged with people. If they heard the shots, maybe they'd have time to flee before she led the vampire directly toward them.

"Ivory Bridge!" Byrnes pointed toward the half-completed bridge arching up over the Thames, and fired his pistol into the air again.

Abandoned, thanks to the ongoing negotiations and workers strikes that had so fouled up river traffic and were causing endless headaches among the Council of Dukes. It just might work.

"Slow it down!" She took off running just as that ugly face tilted toward her again.

The Ivory Tower loomed in the distance; the heart of parliament, and the seat of London's power. Ivory Bridge speared out from its southern walls, the suspension bridge hanging in parts as cranes stood motionless.

"Come on, you ugly bastard," Ingrid muttered, leaping up onto the rail of the bridge and running along it.

Claws lashed through the remains of her skirt, and Ingrid leapt up onto the stone base of the tower, her fingers catching in the cranny between the slabs of stone. Lashing out with a foot, she managed to catch the vampire in the face and it fell, catching a claw on the base of the bridge, its body dangling over the dirty Thames.

Ingrid shoved upward, stabbing her fingers and shoes into the cracks as she climbed to the second span. There weren't a lot of options to take.

Behind her the vampire scrambled up the stonework like a rat up a brick wall, and Ingrid's blood froze. Looking around revealed only a thin iron span to use as an escape route, and she swiftly realized she was going to be trapped if she—

Something whizzed into gear on the clockwork package strapped to the vampire's back. Everything sped up, the *tick, tick, tick*, becoming more pronounced. The bloody creature fixated entirely on her, however, its teeth bared as it found the ledge she stood upon.

A shot ricocheted past, snagging the vampire's attention for all of a second. "Ingrid!" Byrnes screamed. "Get clear!"

Turning, she started to sprint along the narrow span, catching sight of a crane nestled on the battlements. Hissed breath stalked her heels, claws skittering over the iron. Jesus. She wasn't going to make it…. She wasn't— Ingrid leapt, snatching hold of the end of the crane, her body arching as the end of the chain swung wide, out over the water.

The vampire skittered to a halt as she vanished out of its reach. It spun, making high-pitched noises, as if to find another way to get at her, but she had reached the end of the arc now, and was swinging back round—

"Let go!" Byrnes yelled.

The water was a flat pane beneath her, brown and murky. Ingrid's blood ran cold. High. She was incredibly high, and her hands wouldn't unlock on the chain.

"Ingrid! It's going to explode!"

Taking a breath and forcing herself not to think, Ingrid let go. Gravity sunk its greedy claws into her, and she plummeted like a stone, heels held straight below her. Water rushed up, and then—

Everything went white.

She hit the Thames hard, tossed end over end, as the bomb exploded above. A sonic boom scraped her skin raw and left her floundering in churning water. Something slashed through the water nearby, trailing a wake of bubbles, and she could see fire blooming in the sky behind it as other various bits of flotsam and jetsam struck the river and slowly sank.

Another object cut through the river's murk, sleek and black, like a knife. Then hands were dragging her up. Presumably up. She didn't know anymore, but she couldn't breathe... she had no breath left inside her.

They broke the surface with a cough. Ingrid sucked in an enormous lungful of air, surrendering herself into Byrnes's grasp as he began to tow her toward the shore. Behind her, fire burned in patches on the river, and people were yelling and shouting as they streamed from buildings on both edges of the Thames.

"Guess that takes care of the workers strikes," Ingrid murmured, then rested her head on Byrnes's shoulder. So tired.

Lifting her in his arms, he waded ashore, and she didn't want to think about the stink of the river. All she could see were his eyes, wide and no longer icy, but very, very blue.

"The vampire?" she rasped, finally looking over his shoulder.

Most of the bridge was gone. Just gone. Sheared off like an enormous hand had reached out of the sky and torn away iron beams and rivets, leaving behind only the two stone towers in the center of the river.

"Apparently there is only one easy way to kill a vampire," Byrnes finally said, turning with her in his arms to stare at the remains of the bridge. "I wouldn't recommend it, however, and I'm fairly certain Malloryn's not going to be entirely pleased. He said to keep our heads down."

Ingrid simply stared. "Half of London probably saw that."

"Indeed."

CHAPTER TWENTY-SEVEN

MALLORYN WAS not pleased.

Fortunately, he had other matters on his mind and only gave them one snarled comment—*"could you possibly have found a bigger monument to destroy"*—before sending them off to tend to themselves. The fact that someone had tried to blow up the queen whilst she was at his engagement party seemed to be the bigger affront.

Ingrid found herself settled into a steam carriage driven by a member of the Nighthawks, who were now combing the garden at Malloryn's. She didn't care anymore. She'd done her bit, and now the loupe was demanding payment. The carriage rocked as Byrnes shouldered his way through the door, and then he was settling on the seat beside her.

"Zero was here," he told her, lifting up a note. "She had this delivered ten minutes ago by some street lad. It's to me."

Ingrid had just enough strength to lift her head to read. "Congratulations, Master Byrnes. You do prove resourceful—and somewhat vexing—though I do not care

318

for the company you keep. Never mind, I'm enjoying this game far too much, and people die—verwulfen die—such is life. We will meet again. Zero." She looked up, blinking through the heavy lassitude of the loupe. "She does seem particularly taken with you. Are you certain you didn't get up to anything I should know about?"

Byrnes looked affronted. "I've barely even met the woman!"

"Well, something made an impression. I'm not sure it's your charm."

"She's insane!" Byrnes screwed the piece of paper in his fist. "And she just threatened you."

With a laugh, Ingrid rested her head on his shoulder. "Don't get your drawers in a twist. She's not coming after me yet. Wake me when we get to Baker Street."

And then she stopped fighting the heaviness.

As evening drenched the skies, a swift knock came at Ingrid's door. Even before Byrnes opened it, he knew who was there. He'd recognize that scent anywhere.

"Rosa," he murmured, keeping his voice low.

Rosa peered past him. "Is she all right?"

"Apart from a few scratches, she's fine." He was not, however. Ingrid was going to be the death of him. Watching her on that beam, with the vampire at her heels.... "She's just tired. Hasn't woken up yet."

Rosa slid onto the bed, curling Ingrid's hand in her own. "She does that when she exerts herself immensely."

"Let's hope she doesn't fall asleep somewhere when she's not yet made it to safety then."

"She won't," Rosa said. "The fact that she's allowed herself to surrender to it means that she trusts you.

Byrnes... thank you. For looking after her, and guarding her back."

"You sound surprised."

Fabric rustled as the duchess smoothed Ingrid's hair off her head. "I'm not surprised you protected her. You're a Nighthawk, after all. I might be a little shocked to find you sitting here at her bedside, however. The Caleb Byrnes that I know is not the sort of man to hover at a woman's bedside."

There was a question in that.

"She asked me to stay the other night when she was injured. I don't think she likes to wake up alone in the middle of the night. I think—" He stopped in his tracks. Why the hell was he explaining himself to Rosa?

And the truth was, he was lying. He was here because he wanted to be here, and because he didn't want Ingrid to wake up alone in the dark and not know where she was.

Rosa saw it all, judging from her expression. "I thought we had an agreement?"

To hell with that. "I'm not giving her up, Rosa."

The duchess's lips thinned.

"I'm not," he told her firmly, standing and retrieving his coat. "Whether you like it or not." He slung his coat over his shoulders. "As Ingrid's friend, I respect your concern about our relationship, but this is between Ingrid and me, and I'll thank you to stay out of it."

Those dark brown eyes watched him as he headed for the door. Then she smiled, very faintly. "As you wish."

It was the smile that unnerved him. Far from looking like she was about to leap between them with pistols raised, Rosa seemed to be dwelling on some secret thought that amused her.

"I'll give you a moment alone with her," he murmured, slinking through the door and finding Lynch in the hallway beyond.

"You've just cost me one of my finest bottles of blud-wein," Lynch sighed.

It wasn't what he'd expected the duke to say. "What?"

"Garrett," the duke replied, sliding his hands into his pockets. "I should have known better than to bet against that bastard. Come. Walk with me."

Together they strolled into the garden at the back of the house. Fog lingered in the corners, and a single gaslight lit the yard.

"Should I be worried about Rosa coming after me?" Byrnes muttered, leaning against the wall.

"I think she's reconciling herself to the idea of welcoming you into the family."

That disconcerted him a little. Rosa as a sister-in-law. Jesus. Byrnes shifted. "Let's not get ahead of ourselves. Nothing's been decided, and... there are still some problems for Ingrid and me to work through, as soon as we get a chance to breathe."

"Oh?"

His first instinct was to clam up, but to hell with it. He couldn't do this alone any more. "She wants children. I've never— I didn't—" It was uncomfortable terrain for him to stare into a future he'd never examined before, never dreamed of. "I'm not good with children, and I've never wanted to be a father. I've never wanted to be a husband." Not until she'd walked into his life and turned it upside down. "But I cannot stay away from her."

"Mmm. This doesn't have anything to do with your father, does it?"

Byrnes shot him a shocked look.

"You've always been the one I worried about the most," Lynch admitted. "Emotion frightens you. It's never been a problem until now, but it always used to worry me that one day you wouldn't be able to control everything you felt, and... you'd do something stupid."

Byrnes swallowed hard as he rested his hands on the wall. "I'm not going to do anything foolish. It's just—"

"You see too much of your father in yourself when you get angry?"

Byrnes shoved away from the wall, pacing. "Christ. How do you do that?"

"I've made human nature a study of mine," Lynch replied dryly. "It's what made me a good Nighthawk."

"An excellent one," Byrnes replied grudgingly. Neither he nor Garrett would ever compare. Lynch could see right through a man, right through his motivations. Scrubbing a hand through his hair, he swallowed hard. Memories were starting to surface at the turn of the conversation: his father's swarthy face as he turned and spied a young Caleb Byrnes watching from the shadows as he took his rage out on Byrnes's mother....

"Is it the thought of being a father that concerns you? Or the intimacy implied in such a position?" Lynch asked. "Or does it have something to do with losing everyone you cared for at young age, and being afraid to be vulnerable again?"

A little bit of each. Anger throbbed through him. "If you think that losing my father bothered me, then you'd be wrong."

"I'm not speaking of losing your father." Lynch paused, a hesitation very much unlike him. "You do realize that I was the one in charge of his murder case?"

Byrnes froze. He couldn't help himself. Instead he saw it flash before his eyes again, the knife in his hands plunging into that bastard's chest again and again, until it was a wet pulp.

Lynch had never said anything. Instead he'd asked his questions about the incident, declared the case cold, and after the funeral had pulled Byrnes aside to offer him a position in the Nighthawks.

"I know you hated him. No, I was speaking of your mother's loss. Of young Debney." Lynch rested his hip on the window ledge, merely watching him come to the conclusion the duke had already reached. "Not the father you killed."

Byrnes pinched the bridge of his nose. "You knew."

"A crime of such passion? It was either you or your brother, or perhaps even the viscountess. Someone who hated him. The second I laid eyes upon you, wary and mistrustful, with your emotions so tightly locked away, I knew who'd done it. And then there was the fact that you were newly infected with the craving virus. You didn't come by that by accident."

"Then why did you let me join the Nighthawks? You should have executed me." The Echelon would have been baying for blood for the murder of one of their own.

"You were thirteen, Byrnes. And I considered it. The coldness you displayed unnerved me, but then there was the funeral and the way that you helped your mother hobble up to his grave to throw her flower on top of the casket, despite the fact you looked like you wanted to spit on it. You loved her. You were kind to her, and she was clearly a woman who'd seen the rough side of life. In that moment I realized that you weren't hiding some sadistic monster inside you. You were an injured wolf cub, lashing out, trying to protect the one thing that you cared for. You could have become worse," Lynch admitted, "without someone to guide your choices, and your control of the craving virus. You could have followed a dark path had I not taken the chance to help you. When I adopted Garrett into the Nighthawks—well, he was always easy to love, but you... you're the one I'm proudest of. The one who stood in the shadows and slowly hauled himself out of them."

Byrnes's back hit the wall and he half slid down it. He didn't know what to say. That young blood-soaked boy inside him, terrified, hurting, furious, and wild with emotion.... He'd spent so many years trying to bury him. And he'd succeeded in many ways. Succeeded in bottling it all up, locking it all away. Emotion and passion frightened him, because he knew what he was capable of. He'd seen the blood all across his hands as he slowly came back to himself that night and realized what had happened.

"I've spent so many years trying not to become him," he admitted in a hoarse whisper before meeting Lynch's eyes. "How could *I* be a father? Or a husband? I'm a good hunter, Lynch. I'm not afraid of the dark. I'm not afraid of the monsters, or of tracking them down, because I recognize that darkness inside *me*. How do I become something else?"

"No, it's not the shadows you're afraid of," Lynch said with a sigh. "But the light. And you're not seeing the situation clearly. I've seen you take care of Ingrid, Byrnes. I've seen you protect your mother. You're so gentle with her. There's another side to you that perhaps you need to explore." Lynch sighed. "Fatherhood scared me too, did you know? When Rosa was carrying Phillip... it was absolutely terrifying, for I've never been around children much. And then he was born, and it all became very simple." A faint smile quirked at his lips. "All of that worry for nothing. The second I held him in my arms, I knew I would shift heaven and earth to protect him."

It was easy for the duke to say.

"Did Ingrid tell you this?" Lynch asked. "That she wants children?"

"It was fairly obvious at your dinner. And your wife made some pointed remarks when she tracked me down."

"But Ingrid never specifically said it? Rosa's not always right. Though she's having a difficult time admitting it to herself. Why don't you ask Ingrid what *she* wants? She's passionate and rash, and living on the very edge of her emotions—in some ways she's your exact opposite. But I think that if there was anyone that could match the darkness inside you, anyone who could handle it... it would be her, Byrnes. The only problem is that in order to get what you want, you're going to have to expose yourself and risk the chance of losing her. You must face your own demons head-on if you want this."

Byrnes sank his head back against the wall. This felt like old times, the pair of them coolly analyzing a case. "Has anyone ever told you that your omniscience is annoying?"

Lynch smiled. "Rosa. And frequently."

The pair of them both relaxed, however, as if that one statement had defused the tension between them.

He would... deal with Lynch's assessment later. When he had time to pick it apart in his brain.

"So now that we've assessed your progress with Ingrid, tell me what else is bothering you."

There had never been any point in fooling the guild master. "You've heard?"

"About the assassination attempt?" Lynch arched a brow. "Malloryn held an emergency meeting of the Council two hours ago. We're aware of what's happened."

Taking the note from his pocket, Byrnes smoothed it out, then handed it silently to the duke. "The woman behind the explosion left this letter for me."

Once he'd read it, Lynch met Byrnes's gaze. "She's formed some sort of connection with you."

"It's the threat that concerns me. If she thinks that Ingrid stands between us...." He didn't bother to add more. They both knew that even verwulfen were no match for a *dhampir*. Not alone.

Lynch tapped the letter against his thigh. "Ingrid will be protected. I'll involve myself if need be, so set that from your mind. You're thinking like a newly mated male. Not an investigator. What else does this letter represent?"

That was the first time he'd ever been accused of sentimentality. Byrnes twisted the problem around in his mind, looking at it from another angle. "A chance," he said slowly. "If she's formed some sort of attachment or interest, or whatever the bloody hell she thinks it is, then I can use that to find her."

"She wants you to find her."

"And if I can find her, then I can cut the head off the snake before it becomes a problem. We can find the missing people, kill her vampires, and stop this Ulbricht scheme in its tracks." Byrnes shoved to his feet, his mind racing. "Keep an eye on Ingrid for me? There's a few things I need to see to."

Ingrid blinked sleepy eyes, smelling a familiar perfume. She turned, snuggling her face into Rosa's wrist, where their hands lay interlocked. "Rosa. What are you doing here?"

Rosa went to her knees on the floor beside Ingrid's bed, those serious dark eyes on a level with her own as Rosa rested her chin on her free hand. "Checking to see if my closest friend is all right." She blew a red curl out of her face. "Someone told me a rather statuesque young verwulfen woman blew up a bridge today."

Ingrid smiled faintly, even as she shut her eyes again. "It seemed like a good idea at the time." There was a certain absence in the room. That made her look up. "Where's—"

"Byrnes?" Rosa asked, in a dry voice.

Their eyes met. "It's not like that," Ingrid said quickly.

"Isn't it?" Rosa sighed. "He was sitting by your bedside when I arrived. I think he's scared of me. Lynch is talking to him."

Ingrid relaxed back down into her pillow.

Rosa settled her bottom on the edge of the bed. "Byrnes seems to be spending rather a lot of time at your side, lately."

"We *are* working together."

"Which explains why he was sitting here holding your hand."

"Rosa—"

"It's all right." Her friend smiled. "My concerns over Byrnes' feelings for you have been satisfied. He's clearly enamored."

Ingrid snorted. Then twisted her fingers in the pillow, plucking at it. *This time, I intend to win your heart...* She couldn't quite explain how that made her feel.

Nervous. Hopeful. Terrified.

Rosa's eyes narrowed. "Unless he's said something to the contrary?"

"No," she whispered. "He said he wants to... win my heart."

Rosa's skirts rustled as she shifted. "Hmm. That was not said in an entirely convincing tone of voice. What's wrong?"

Ingrid squeezed the bridge of her nose. "Nothing."

"Is it what you want?"

She looked up, and knew Rosa saw the panic in her eyes.

"Or are you afraid?" Rosa asked gently.

"What if something goes wrong?" she blurted. "What if he can't love me? What if..." She swallowed down the lump in her throat. "I don't think I could handle the rejection right now, if he decided he was wrong."

"If he cannot love you, then he's a fool. You're entirely lovable. And what makes now any different to any other time?" Rosa arched a brow.

Ingrid sighed and reached for her coat, which was hanging over the chair next to the bed. She tugged the small worn telegram from her pocket, and passed it silently to her friend.

Rosa read it. "Another dead end."

"Perhaps the last," Ingrid admitted in a small voice.

"Only if you stop trying," Rosa replied firmly. "Your parents are out there somewhere, Ingrid." She set the telegram down, her lips thinning with resolve. "And as much as this dalliance bothered me in the beginning, I see something there that wasn't there before. I never used to believe that Byrnes had a heart, not until I saw the way he looked at you. I think you're worrying for no good reason, but I can understand, given your past, why you're doing so." Rosa lay down on the pillow beside her, and turned her head so that their faces were inches apart. "I want you to be happy. I want you to be loved. And despite the fact that Byrnes has his flaws—many of them—I don't think he's the sort of man who would toy with your feelings. He simply doesn't have it in him to play pretend. Besides, if you never take the risk, then how will you ever know? He could be the love of your life. He might give you half a dozen fat little babies. Or what if he's a closet romantic, and plans to shower you with love and affection for the rest of his days. Maybe he's a poet at heart?"

Ingrid thumped her friend with her spare pillow. Rosa laughed, then hugged her. The pair of them fell into a breathy silence.

Ingrid bit her lip. "I'm scared."

Rosa snuggled in closer. "That's how you know it's real."

CHAPTER TWENTY-EIGHT

AS NIGHT FELL and the rest of the house on Baker Street filled with the others, Byrnes found himself chairing a meeting.

"You've looked better," Byrnes told Kincaid as the mech slumped into a chair at the table. Dark circles blackened both eyes, and Kincaid's nose was swollen and misshapen.

Kincaid's gaze darted to Ava, then away again. "She patched me up." He smiled menacingly. "I hear you've been blowing up bridges."

"Seemed like a good idea at the time."

"Aye. Wish I'd seen it." Kincaid's smile softened. "Bet Malloryn's having conniptions right about now."

Byrnes shrugged. "I think he's got other things on his mind. Someone did try to kill the queen at his engagement party, after all."

"Unsuccessfully," Ingrid added. "Thank goodness. Only a minor bruise or two, according to Rosa."

"So," Gemma Townsend said, lacing her arms across her chest. "Looks like the anarchists have kicked the hornet's nest. What are we going to do about it?"

"Are we waiting for Malloryn?" Byrnes asked.

"He's with the Council. Another emergency meeting. They're voting on whether to settle martial law over London," Gemma replied. "I doubt he'll be back before dawn."

"And the Baroness Schröder?"

"With Malloryn."

Byrnes stared around the table, meeting all of their eyes. "This began with the disappearance of forty people at the Venetian Gardens, but it wasn't the first time people have disappeared. We know who took them now. We know their purpose in doing so—to strike fear into the heart of the average Londoner, to encourage them to rise against the queen. It's quite clear that London is under attack by these *dhampir* and the SOG, we just don't know why."

"Or if those people are still alive," Ingrid admitted at his side.

There was silence then.

"Do you think they're feeding them to the vampires?" Charlie Todd asked, and his face was paler than usual.

"We don't know." The thought, however, had crossed his mind. "What we do know is that Zero wants me to find her. She's the key to it. Find her, find the vampires—and most likely find the missing people."

"And how do we do that?" Charlie demanded.

"We know the general vicinity in which they're operating," Ava said, tapping the map and drawing a circle with her finger from Clerkenwell to Barbican. Someone had speared little pins into every sighting.

"This is where we lost the trail when Kincaid and I tried to follow it from the Home." Charlie pushed a pin into the map.

Byrnes frowned. "This is the rough area where we lost it from the Venetian Gardens."

The two pins were within four streets of each other.

He added another. "And this is where Zero gave Kincaid a friendly love tap before she decided she wants to be wooed by me."

"Hell," Charlie breathed. "They're somewhere in this area."

Excitement flared. People always made mistakes, if you were patient. "What's in the area? I don't know it well."

"Two burned-out churches," Charlie replied. "A couple of weaving factories, one draining factory, an old asylum, numerous houses. It verges on Whitechapel territory, so I've patrolled it, but not well. I think there are a couple of abandoned train stations below that verged into Undertown once upon a time, but after Blade waged war on the slasher gangs that hid down there, we blew some of the tunnels so they couldn't get through."

"Are they all collapsed?" Byrnes asked. "Vampires like the dark."

Charlie's blue eyes met his. "Could be pockets, or caverns. Undertown always was a warren. I know people started living down there again in some places once the slasher gangs were gone and they no longer had to fear for their lives. It's not a nice territory, Byrnes."

"There's an old enclave here too, where they used to house the mechs before they freed us," Kincaid pointed out, tapping the map. "Been closed for three years."

"Lots of places to hide." But this was it. He felt it in his bones.

"So we spread out?" Kincaid demanded. "Try and find a vampire?"

"Or three," Ingrid muttered. "We don't know how many there are, and we also suspect there's at least two of the *dhampir* working against us, thanks to Gemma's attack at the museum."

Which sobered the entire group up.

"How quiet does this need to be?" Charlie asked. "Could we use the Nighthawks for manpower?"

"I'll talk to Garrett," he replied. "I think the cat's out of the bag, thanks to the explosion."

"We need bait." This time it was Ingrid who spoke up.

The room silenced as they all turned to look at her.

"You're not doing this," Byrnes growled, shaking his head.

"I wasn't talking about me," she said quietly. "This Zero is interested in you. She wants you to find her, Byrnes, which I think gives you the greatest chance to survive if you were bait. She doesn't want to kill you. Not yet."

"But what if she takes him right out from under our noses?" Kincaid asked, crossing his huge arms over his chest. "She doesn't need to keep the rest of us alive. All she needs to do is take him, and then how do we bloody well find him?"

"With Garrett and Fitz's tracking device." Byrnes's voice gradually strengthened as the plan unrolled in his mind. "Garrett put a tracking device on Perry years ago, following a case in which she almost died." He turned to Ava. "Do you think you can get it off Fitz?"

Ava nodded earnestly.

"When?" Byrnes asked, staring at Ingrid.

She considered the map. "Tomorrow morning. As soon as dawn breaks. We can't afford to do this in the dark, as much as I want to save those people. We don't have a lot of weapons against a vampire in the first place, but sunlight is our ally at least."

"And we need to let Malloryn know, and prepare," Gemma agreed.

Byrnes took a deep breath. "Dawn then."

CHAPTER TWENTY-NINE

"ANY REASON WE'RE heading down this street?" Ingrid murmured as she strolled beside Byrnes.

Midnight had come and gone, and they'd completed the list of tasks that they'd been given to prepare for dawn. The Nighthawks were ready and would meet them at the edge of the search area. Now she was tired, and wanted to snatch a few hours of sleep before she had to go vampire hunting.

Clearly not what Byrnes had planned.

He nodded toward the small set of rooms she'd leased. "I wanted to show you something."

"I'm fairly certain I've already seen it, Byrnes," she drawled.

"I'm fairly certain you haven't. I prepared it the other day, when you were recovering."

That caught her attention. What on earth was he up to? "At my set of rooms?"

"You'll see." Byrnes climbed the stairs to the front door, then leapt up and dragged himself onto the roof beside it, reaching down to offer her a hand.

"Now you've caught my attention." She let him help her up, and then he popped the lock on her window and slipped inside. "Just what are you up to?"

"Mischief."

"Well, that's nothing new." Ingrid slung her leg over the windowsill. There was an array of small tools laid on a strip of leather beside the skirting boards. "You fixed my skirting boards?"

"Oh, Ingrid." He pressed his ear against the wall, then frowned, toying with something in his belt. "I didn't fix your skirting boards. I promised to give you a present, something you'd never been given before."

Ingrid's gaze shot to his. She'd been expecting a gift-wrapped box when she set this challenge. Not a roll of tools on the floor. "What is it?"

He held out some sort of device to her. "Press the button."

It was a small brass box with a dial on the interface. Ingrid hesitantly pushed the ON button. Almost instantly she felt like she wanted to itch her skin. There was something whining in the walls, almost on the edge of hearing.

"It works somewhat like the Nighthawks' communicators," he explained. "A high-pitched frequency just enough to...." Taking the box, he fiddled with several knobs and the whine died down until it vanished, at least to her hearing.

"Just enough to...?"

A smile flashed over his face, that particular one that changed his entire aspect, like the sun creeping over the horizon at dawn and lighting the world. "It gets rid of vermin, Ingrid."

Surprise took hold of her.

"No more rats, Fitz assures me. They cannot abide the sound. He has something like this rigged at the guild."

Ingrid's mouth parted, and there was a suspicious warmth in her eyes. "You.... You...."

Byrnes waited, but she couldn't seem to put it into words. Or maybe there were none needed. That little smile was back, toying about his lips. "You're welcome."

This was a gift unlike any other, and she was so choked up with emotion that she couldn't quite use her voice until she swallowed it all down. It truly was the greatest gift he could have given her.

Except for his heart. Ingrid glanced away. She wasn't going to ask for that. She didn't dare. "And what reward do you want to claim for this challenge?"

Byrnes frowned, looking down at the screwdriver he'd picked up. "It's tempting...." He flipped the small screwdriver in the air, then caught it. "But we need to talk." He looked up. "I just want an answer. That's all, Ingrid."

Ingrid circled a chair, resting her hands on it before realizing that she'd deliberately placed a barrier between them. "About us?"

"About us."

Ingrid scowled. "I don't know what to think. One moment you want to earn kisses for challenges, the next thing you're telling me this is a bad idea, and then all of a sudden you're trying to charm me again."

"This has nothing to do with charm. I just realized what I truly want."

"Oh?"

Byrnes took a step toward her. "And it wasn't just you in my bed."

If he keeps up like this, I might almost start to believe him. "Stop saying things like that."

"Why?" Byrnes stepped closer, hovering but three inches away. "It's the truth, Ingrid. And I don't lie. Not about the important things."

No, he didn't. Sometimes the truth wasn't one you wanted to hear, but it was always true. "I thought you wanted to forget me." Her right foot stepped back, as if to flee, then she firmed. She wasn't retreating from anything, particularly him. Not anymore. "Burn me from your blood? Get your fix of me, so that then I could stop haunting you?"

"I'm an idiot."

"Are you trying to pretend that you didn't mean those words?" she scoffed, her heart starting to pound a little swifter in her ears. *No. No, it couldn't be.* She didn't dare believe it. "That you've been harboring some sort of secret tendre for me for the past year?"

Byrnes tossed the screwdriver aside and it slapped against the wall before dropping to the floor. She was fairly certain that she also heard some sort of growl deep in his throat, but then this was Byrnes. Caleb Byrnes, who kept his emotions locked away under lock and key.

"No, I didn't," he shot back. "None of this started with any romantic intentions. I'll concede that. Passionate ones, yes, but not romantic. You drove me crazy, Ingrid. You haunted me. And I wanted you. But I didn't want forever."

Her shoulders dropped, almost in relief.

Byrnes took another step toward her, closing the gap between them until the backs of his fingers brushed against her shoulder. "But I was lying to myself."

Ingrid's gaze shot to his in shock.

"I kept telling myself that sex was all this was, as if I could somehow convince the part of me that knew better." A hand reached out and pushed a lock of her hair behind her ear. As cool as marble, his hand curled against her cheek, cupping her face. "And I almost believed it. Until I found you nearly torn apart in my mother's room. Until I watched a vampire chase you out on a bridge with an explosive device strapped to its back. I can't pretend that this—what lies between us—means nothing to me. If I look at us from a rational perspective, this doesn't make any sense. We're a disaster waiting to happen." His face twisted as he grimaced. "But the idea of not having you... of not being with you.... I couldn't think of anything worse. And so I've tried not to be selfish. I've tried to step away and let you be, but I can't do it anymore." That hand curled behind her nape, dragging her closer to his body, until his forehead brushed against hers and his breath caressed her lips. "I want you, Ingrid Miller. And I don't know where this decision will take us, but I do know that I can't deny myself any longer. And if you think this is just about a bet, well... you'd be wrong. I want you, and I want all of you. And I don't know what to do with it."

Ingrid's hands curled into the lapels of his shirt as she held on for dear life, whilst everything she'd known shattered into dust.

Byrnes wanted her.

Not just for sex.

Forever?

"Say something," he murmured, drawing back just enough to look at her. "This is possibly the most terrifying moment of my life."

A shaky breath escaped her. She kept trying to sort out the puzzle pieces of their relationship, for it was easy to relegate it to little more than physical and not think anything more. Or no, not easy. Safer.

She didn't feel safe anymore. She felt like the ground had dropped out from under her feet. "Are you *serious*?"

She pushed away from him and paced past the window, dragging a hand through her hair.

"Deadly."

Ingrid swallowed. How could she do this? How could she risk it? "Damn you, I've lost everything. I can't—"

"I know you lost your family, Ingrid." He followed her. "I know I can't replace them. But perhaps we could create something new together."

Something new. It was so tempting.

"You're not the only one who fears the future." He laughed faintly. "Do you think that any of this was planned? Do you think that I'm not scared that I won't measure up? I know nothing of romance. I know nothing of being... being a husband. Even a lover. But I know that I want to try. I know that I can't walk away from you."

Ingrid swallowed. Those words.

"Give me your third challenge," he demanded, his words a rasp. A tremor ran through him, as though he repressed himself.

And suddenly, a part of her didn't want him to hesitate. Ingrid met his eyes, seeing the need in them, the fierce fury. All she'd ever wanted was to see Caleb Byrnes ruffled, to drive him to the point where he lost his mind.

And now she had it.

I'm scared, she'd once said to Rosa.

That's how you know its real, had been the reply.

And it was real. She couldn't stop running from this. Couldn't pretend that Caleb Byrnes didn't make her heart beat faster, and hope spread its wings within her chest. Here was a man that she... loved. A man that she could make a future with, if only she dared.

So be it.

Ingrid tipped her chin up, her decision made, and shrugged out of the navy velvet coat she wore. It hit the floor, and his gaze followed it then jerked back up to hers.

"The challenge is this: show me what it's like not to feel so alone," she told him.

She wasn't afraid anymore; Byrnes always spoke the truth. He meant this.

Ingrid took a step forward, sliding her hands up his chest and the sleek leather of his coat. "Fill up the empty spot inside me." Her lips grazed his ear and she bit his lobe. "Be mine, Caleb. For tonight, for all the nights that remain. Forever."

"Challenge accepted," he growled, and caught her by the hips.

Their mouths met as Ingrid locked her long legs around his waist, her arms sliding around his broad shoulders.

God, he was strong. She clasped the back of his muscled neck, her tongue darting against his as he strode toward the side of the room. Byrnes kissed her back as though he thought she was going to be taken from him; as if this spell could break if they had a moment to think it through.

She didn't need that moment. And this spell was hers, damn it, her dream to take in both hands. Nothing would deny her. Not anymore.

I love you. She said it with a kiss, not quite daring to put it in words. And he answered in kind, his mouth a harsh, desperate claiming. *You're mine*, his lips told her.

Byrnes set her on the vanity, wedging his hips between her thighs. Rough hands slid up her corseted waist, the pads of his fingers grazing the smooth slope of her upper breasts. "Jesus," he rasped. "How's a man to think...?"

"That's the point." She nipped at his mouth, kissed him again, harder, her hands stripping his coat off his shoulders. "You're not supposed to be able to."

His coat hit the floor. Byrnes's lips slid to her jaw, the rasp of his stubble grazing her throat as she tilted her head back. A shudder ran through him. "I'm a blue blood, love." His hands stilled on her waist. "The second I stop thinking is the second all the darkness runs to the surface." His lips nuzzled at her throat, sheer want shuddering through him.

Ingrid paused. She knew what he was suggesting. "You want my blood."

Those fingers curled into iron claws as he grasped her hips. "It's not that simple." The breath exploded out of him as he tore his face from her throat. "It seems to be more of an urge to mark you... as mine. I've never drunk from the vein before. Never really wanted to."

A little thrill tore through her, and her nipples hardened into points. It took all of a second to make her decision. Byrnes wanted this, but feared the loss of control. And she found she rather liked the idea of him marking her. "Do it," she whispered.

He hesitated.

"Do you think I can't handle you at your best?" She curled a fist in his hair, and forced him to look at her.

Those icy blue eyes were glazed, pinpricks of darkness growing in them. "I know you can handle me, anytime you want." Then Byrnes turned those clever fingers to her armored corset and the thin chemise she wore beneath it. "Stop me if I hurt you."

A shiver ran through her as he kissed his way down her throat, pausing at the lace edge of the chemise. "You won't hurt me."

Then he was dragging her chemise up, tugging it over her head until her breasts were free, round and heavy, swollen for his touch.

"Jesus." He curled his hands around them, filling his palms with her breasts. "I forget how beautiful you are sometimes. And then it takes me by surprise all over again."

Ingrid dragged his mouth to hers. He might claim he knew nothing of romance, but his blurted truths filled her heart with joy. She arched into his touch, the sensation of his hands on her whispering through her blood. Then his mouth was there, sucking gently on her nipple. Ingrid groaned, sliding her hands through his hair.

"Yes. Please." She bit her lip. "There."

Byrnes knelt and stripped her trousers from her legs, tugging them down over her sensitive feet. Ingrid thrust her foot against his chest, pinning him there as he looked up with blackened eyes. The hunger had him in its grasp, but he smiled, as if challenging her to relent. And she did.

She wanted this too much. Her breath came hard and fast, wetness slick between her thighs. "Do it," she whispered. "Take me. Claim me. Make me yours."

Byrnes pressed forward, her knee caught up between them. Suddenly he was the one in charge, locking her knee against his chest as he dragged her other leg around his hips. The heat of his erection rasped against her drawers as he showed her in no uncertain manner how much he wanted her. "As my lady wishes."

Then he tugged his knife from the sheath at his hip. It kissed her throat so lightly, so sweetly, that she barely felt the sting. And then his mouth locked over the wound, a gentle suckling sensation that swiftly turned to fierce desire.

Ingrid cried out as that sensation speared right through her core. Jesus. She hadn't expected this. It was like lightning through her veins, like setting fire to oil, as each suck of his mouth pulled directly on the heated flesh between her thighs. The connection between them was intense. She felt like she truly belonged in that moment, belonged in his arms, belonged with this man.

And suddenly, it wasn't enough to be merely marked like this.

"I need you," she gasped, and thrust her hand between them, finding the buttons to his tight trousers. Byrnes made a grunting sound deep in his throat, as he swallowed her blood.

"Yes," he breathed as she tugged them open.

His cock surged into her hand, hungry for attention. Ingrid curled her fingers around it and squeezed, then she was guiding him between her legs, tearing the slit in her drawers apart. Feeling the blunt head of his cock slick through her wetness.

Byrnes sucked hard at her throat, and Ingrid threw her head back. Everything ached. A bittersweet sensation that blew her mind. She felt like she was going to explode.

Then he was pushing his way inside her, inch by heated inch, working into the tight slickness of her sheathe. "Please," she found herself saying. "More."

The first full thrust took her by surprise. Sweat gleamed on her skin, and her muscles locked tight, as though she never wanted to let him go.

"Oh," Ingrid gasped, her nails curling into his upper arms, as the storm beneath her skin threatened to tear her apart. "Oh, my God!"

She had forgotten the rumors: the chemicals in a blue blood's saliva could sometimes bring a woman to orgasm. Another hard suck at her throat brought her to the edge, hovering there, on the precipice of the fall. Byrnes thrust again, and it was enough to shatter her.

Ingrid gasped, bucking in pure bliss, her sheath tightening around him and clamping down hard as she came. It exploded through her as though she'd been struck by lightning, until she was nothing more than wild abandon, pure need.

"Ingrid." Byrnes thrust hard, lifting his face from her throat as she dug her heel into the cheek of his arse as if to urge him deeper. "Jesus. I can't—"

And then he lost control himself, one hand clamping the back of her neck, the other her hip, as he pounded himself into her.

It was wild and furious, and she reveled in it. The vanity beneath her hammered against the wall until Byrnes caught her up with a growl and half spilled her onto the bed.

"Mine," he growled, thrusting home and filling her.

"Mine," she corrected, and he seemed to like that even more, as he captured her mouth in one final, fierce coupling of tongues.

She dug her nails into his spine, clenching all of her inner muscles around him. Byrnes growled. Their eyes met, and then he gasped as he came inside her. One last final thrust and Byrnes's head dropped, his forehead resting against hers. "Jesus," he breathed harshly. "You... You're amazing."

Ingrid collapsed against the sheets, gasping, her entire mind a white blaze of sensation as they shuddered together. Destroyed. Utterly destroyed.

She had the vague feeling that she was still half wearing her drawers, and Byrnes's leather trousers were around his knees. They were a mess, the both of them. Sweat-slicked and breathing hard. Ingrid laughed as she met those startled eyes, unable to stop touching him, each stroke so gentle that he half collapsed on her again.

"When I was dreaming of this," he told her with a groan, "I thought I'd last longer than a green lad on his first tup."

A smoky laugh shivered through her as Byrnes curled against her, his chest heaving as he sought to regain himself. "Oh, Byrnes. Whoever thought that Mr. Control would lose himself entirely when it came to the deed?"

Byrnes lifted his head, that evil glint back in his eye. "Is that another challenge, Miller?"

Ingrid stroked her fingers down his chest in lazy abandon. She felt like purring. "Think you're up to it, Sir Leather-britches?"

This time the growl in his throat had nothing to do with claiming her as he slid between her parted thighs, his cock growing hard against her leg. "Ingrid Miller, I think we need to prove just who, precisely, has no control...."

His mouth slid down her skin, his lips capturing one peaked nipple between them. "Starting here, I think."

Ingrid shivered as he suckled hard. Her eyes rolled back in her head in pleasure. "Challenge accepted."

As the moon slid across the sky, Byrnes simply stroked his hand through the cascade of honey-brown hair that smothered his chest.

It was surprising to realize how enjoyable this moment was. Ingrid was heat and warmth in his arms, soft curves pressed against him, and her breath whispering over his bare chest. He knew she was awake. Occasionally she shifted a little, but there was joy and peace in the silence between them. At least there was until she broke it.

"What did you mean, that you're afraid to think of the future?" Ingrid murmured.

Byrnes's hand paused in her hair, his throat growing tight as she threw them straight into the conflict that he'd been putting off. *Coward.* "I was speaking of the unknown."

"Of me?" Her voice dropped to a mere whisper, and he heard doubt there.

God, no. Byrnes shifted until he lay on his hip and shoulder beside her with her head nestled in the crook of his arm. Bronze eyes looked up, met his. "Not of you. You're the one thing I don't doubt." He kissed her mouth, a gentle caress. Then paused. "I never thought that there would be someone for me. I never dreamed of what that would be like, or the complications involved."

"Are you saying I'm a complication?" She arched a brow and bit the skin covering his biceps, and relief filled him. No doubt in her eyes. Not anymore.

Byrnes rolled over her slowly, resting on his forearms as he looked down at her. Time to plunge right into the heart of this. "You want children."

Ingrid froze and glanced up from beneath dark lashes. "And you don't?"

"I don't know what I want. I don't know... if I would be a good father. It's as I said. I never looked down this road."

There was a subtle withdrawal as she stared past him, toward the ceiling. "I never looked down this road either," she admitted, but it sounded sad.

"You've dreamed of it though," he pushed. "I could see it in your face when you were holding Phillip that time at dinner."

Ingrid bit her lip and turned back to him. "I never used to dream. Not when I was trapped in the cage, because if you dared to dream, then you would dare to hope. And nothing hurts more than having that crushed and thrown in your face."

A fierce, bloody desire filled him, and he kissed her mouth. "I sometimes wish Lord Balfour hadn't died in the revolution. Then I could take him apart with my bare hands for you."

"So do I." No smile, no regret from her. Only bloody violence gleaming in her eyes. "I never dared to dream when I was trapped under Balfour's hand. But when we escaped from him, life changed. It was still hard, don't mistake me. But... we'd escaped Balfour. That was all I'd ever wanted. I grew into a young woman in Undertown, because it wasn't safe for a free verwulfen to be seen above ground, but I was out of the cage. The dreams that I'd never dared dream came true. And something else began to grow in my chest, in my heart. A sense of something missing. Then three years ago we won the revolution, but it always felt a little hollow for me, because"—she looked away—"that something was still missing."

"Your family."

She shrugged, as if careless of her feelings. Or perhaps trying to dismiss the depth of them. "Maybe I'll never find them. I think that sometimes in the middle of the night. And... I might not have dreamed of children before, but if you asked me if I wanted them? Then yes, yes I think I do. Holding Phillip fills that hole inside me. Not all the way, but for a moment I belong."

"Trust me." This time his tone was dry. "You belong to Rosa. And her brothers. I've learned that in the last week."

"And Rosa belongs to Lynch," she said with another careless shrug. "Jeremy's been walking out with young Evelyn, and even Jack's been making calf eyes at Debney."

Byrnes reared back. "What?"

She rolled her eyes. "Right under your nose. You call yourself an investigator."

He frowned.

"I belong to them," she continued in a softer voice. "And I always will, but it's not the same. Because they all have that someone else, and I will always remain the interloper."

"No, you're not. Don't ever stop dreaming of that, Ingrid." He wanted to curl her in his arms, take away the hurt he saw deep within her. It became a physical ache in his chest. "Dream that dream. You deserve it."

Ingrid looked up at him, resolve firming in her eyes. "Then I will. I want a family of my own. Just as I suspect you don't."

He shifted. "It's not that easy."

"I thought we were being honest with each other?"

"I am." He rolled to the side again, landing flat on his back and staring at the ceiling. "It's not that I don't want children. It just... scares the hell out of me."

Ingrid rolled over him, kissing his shoulder, but she never took her gaze off him. "Why?"

Why? He stilled, and knew she felt it. There was a knot growing hard in his lower abdomen. A knot of hard emotion, of things felt but never admitted to. The only person who had ever gotten close to seeing it had been Lynch, and even then the duke had only skimmed the top of it.

He didn't want to speak of it.

But he had promised her honesty.

Byrnes cleared his throat. "What if I'm terrible with them?"

"What if *I* am? Sometimes I fear I'll drop poor Phillip on the floor. He's so... squirmy."

He looked at her. Really looked. "What if I'm a danger to them?"

Ingrid sobered, then the bronze rings around her pupils seemed to intensify, as if she understood what he wasn't saying. "Why would you think that?"

Another hesitation. *Hell.* "I'm a bastard, Ingrid. But if you were to line me up with Debney and my father... then you'd think *I* was the heir. I look at myself and see him sometimes." And there was nothing he hated more.

"You never speak of your father."

"That's because I killed him."

Silence.

He waited—waited for her revulsion, or something else to come. But Ingrid simply rested her head down upon his shoulder and slid her arm across his chest. It shook him all the way through and he caught her hand in his and clasped her fingers in silent relief. Maybe Lynch was right. Maybe Ingrid was the only woman who could ever handle the darkness within him.

"Did he deserve it?"

"Yes." That one word nearly overwhelmed him. All of it began to come back to him. The hatred, the rage, the shame, and worst of all... the helplessness. He swallowed it back down, but it sat like a hot coal in his chest, threatening to choke him.

And she knew. Another kiss touched his shoulder. A confirmation. "What was he like?"

"There was a darkness in him that scared me. A darkness that was nothing like the hunger of the craving virus, though he was a blue blood. He liked to hurt people. He enjoyed it. I don't know why, but it gave him some sense of power. H-he's the reason my mother is the way she is. He hit her one night because he thought he could— she was just a servant in his eyes, just his mistress—but this one time, she fell and hit her head on the fireplace. And she was never the same."

Ingrid's hands squeezed his. "He doesn't sound very much like you at all, Byrnes."

"When I was a little boy, I was terrified of him, but I would have done anything to keep my mother safe. I could fight and be beaten bloody myself, or I could rage and scream, but nothing helped. Indeed, it only worsened the situation. My father would say, 'Are you angry, boy?' and I would nod, and then he would strike her down, then come back to me and say, 'That is what your anger has earned your mother.' He would say, 'You made me do this. Do you want to make me do more?' If I tried to stop him, or grew angry, he would hurt her again. And again." Byrnes took a deep breath, burying his face against Ingrid's abdomen. Hands slid through his hair, and just that simple touch eased the pressure inside him, the raging emotion that he couldn't quite contain. "There was nothing that I could do to stop him. I didn't dare let my anger rule me, or my fear, or sadness. Eventually I learned to bury all of my emotions so deep, until it felt like they were not there anymore. And that last time he hit her, I was so numb. I kept waiting for her to get up. But she didn't. If I had stopped him—"

"He sounds like the kind of man who could not be stopped," Ingrid said softly.

Byrnes looked up and fell into the bleeding compassion in her eyes. Grabbing her hand, he kissed her knuckles. "But I did stop him in the end. I killed him," he whispered. "It just... happened. I lost control and I had a knife, and I wanted to kill him. I wanted him to die for what he'd done. And I can't remember all of it, but afterwards... Christ, afterwards I looked up into the reflection in the window, and there he was. In me. I thought it was a ghost at first, but then I realized I was covered in blood. His blood." He could see it all over again. Lived it. "There's a darkness inside me that is capable of anything. *Anything.*" Emotion washed in upon him. Byrnes sucked in a breath, but it suddenly felt as though there was not enough oxygen in the room. "I... I—"

Warm arms slid around his shoulders. "Just breathe," Ingrid told him. "In and out, Byrnes."

And so he did. Ingrid became his lifeline in a sea of darkness, and as his breathing began to match hers, he realized that although he'd never looked down this road before, suddenly he didn't think he could see himself doing anything else.

She was his future.

She was his meaning in life, the reason to keep on fighting, keep on breathing. And if she wanted children, then he would stand by her side. Together they could achieve anything. He firmly believed that.

"That's how I became a blue blood, actually." Facts were easier to deal with, than the complex emotions filling him. "There was so much blood, and that's when Debney found me." There was a vile taste in his mouth. "The look on his face—he was shocked. And I just lost it. 'Why didn't you stop him?' I screamed. I told him that it was his fault, because I knew it was mine, and I couldn't bear to feel that way."

"It was your father's fault. Not yours. Not Debney's. Don't take your father's guilt away from him. He sounds like a monster. And you're not him. I've known monsters in my time, Byrnes, and you're nothing like them. The fact that you're even worried about it should tell you that."

Byrnes buried his face against her throat and sucked in a long, slow breath.

"I know how you feel," Ingrid whispered. "Sometimes you make yourself so hard that nothing gets in. Nothing can hurt anymore, because you know you've reached the limits of what you can endure." Her hand stroked down his back. "If you stop caring, then it can't hurt anymore. It's a shell, something that words and blows just glance off, but something I learned, Byrnes, is that the shell is brittle. It will break, eventually."

It took a long time to be able to find the voice to answer that. "You sound as though you speak from experience."

Ingrid shifted. "We all have our breaking point."

"What was yours?"

"My family," she admitted, tracing small circles on his chest with her finger.

"That didn't sound very hopeful."

"I'm not going to find them, Byrnes." Ingrid's eyelashes shuttered her eyes when she saw him looking. "I think I know that, deep inside, but if I'm still trying...."

"Why don't you think you'll find them?"

"Because I've spent years searching for them." Her fists clenched, frustration flooding through her and tears hovering on the edge of her eyelashes. "Years, and so much money, and... nothing. Going to Norway didn't help. I've travelled through towns all along the coast, but I could walk past them and not even recognize them. Last year was my fifth voyage. I don't remember enough to help me, and Balfour was the only one who kept any records of my sale, and he's dead! I'm trying to run an investigation with no clues, and no matter how much money I promise, too many girls went missing during those years thanks to English raiders. I can't stomach it anymore. The families... coming to me, hoping that I belong to them and then discovering that I don't. And worse than that are the people who see the reward I'm offering for information and pretend to be something they're not." Ingrid covered her face with her hands.

This time it was his turn to drag her into his arms, wrapping them around her as if he could hide her from the world, from her pain. "Don't cry."

"I'm not crying."

His chest was wet, but he didn't call her on it.

"This one time," she whispered, crying silently against his shoulder, "...there was a couple who seemed so perfect. Everything fit. *Everything*. I truly thought that I had done it... and then the woman slipped up." A long sigh went through her as her body softened.

"It's all right, Ingrid." His throat burned with the ache of all she'd lost. "You're not alone. Not anymore."

She cried for a long time as Byrnes simply absorbed it.

It took him a long minute to realize that she was asleep, worn out by her grief and her confession. Byrnes continued to stroke her hair, then looked down at the honey-colored head resting on his chest.

He didn't dare move, just in case he woke her, though he couldn't stop stroking his hand through that mess of hair. There was a fist lodged somewhere in his chest that felt like something he almost recognized. A little fist of hurt and worry and protectiveness that wasn't going to shift.

This. This was what it felt like for the ice around his heart to melt. It felt like he was taking his first breath in years, through a raw, bloody throat. It was terrifying and yet exhilarating. "Ingrid," he whispered almost soundlessly, and that simple name turned the key, unlocking something he'd thought long buried.

He'd spent so many years feeling nothing, or not understanding what he did feel. Aloof, watching the world around him, fitting together the pieces. It was what made him such a good investigator, but the lack of those emotions was what stopped him from being truly brilliant.

And a plan formed.

"If there's one thing I don't do—it's give up," he whispered.

Byrnes could find anything. It was what he did. The very thought of it made him nervous—this was no simple pledge, and there were stakes here that could rip a woman's heart from her chest. A woman who had slowly, somehow, curled her own fist around his long-frozen heart.

"I'll find them, Ingrid," he whispered, pressing a kiss to her hair. "No matter how long it takes me. I promise I'll find them for you."

But not yet. Now he had a group of vampires and anarchists to discover.

CHAPTER THIRTY

DAWN GLOWED GOLDEN on the horizon.

Finally.

Byrnes waited as Jack inspected the small cut on the back of his head where he'd inserted the tracking device an hour ago. It had already healed, thanks to Byrnes's CV levels, but they were taking no chances that Zero would smell any blood on him.

Jack began to clean his instruments, as Debney paced the room. Byrnes hadn't been entirely surprised to see him here. Not after Ingrid's little revelation about the two men, but the pacing was getting on his nerves.

"Heavens sake, would you sit down?" he growled. "You're making me dizzy."

Debney promptly sank into a chair, knotting his hands in his lap. "I'm sorry."

It took the edge off his words. "Don't you think you ought to go home? Get some rest?"

"I don't think I can," Debney muttered. "Ulbricht's still out there somewhere, and... well... You're going to be careful?" Debney asked, and the words were so perfectly pronounced, that Byrnes hesitated.

Flippant words died on the tip of his tongue. He eyed his brother. Was Debney *actually* worried about him? "I'll be careful," he promised.

Debney let out a slow breath.

"Ingrid will watch his back," Jack added, resting a hand on Debney's shoulder and squeezing. "Nothing's going to happen to him."

Their eyes met, and Byrnes found himself in the middle of a moment that was awkwardly sweet. He stepped out of the way before Debney tried to do something ridiculous, like hug him.

There *were* limits.

Heels clicked on the hallway floor.

"Slight problem," Ingrid said, sailing into the parlor. She wore her protective armored corset over a loose white shirt, and a tight pair of leather pants that showcased those Amazon legs to perfection. He couldn't stop himself from looking, remembering them wrapped around his hips.

Malloryn followed on her heels, slipping his embroidered coat from his shoulders. "I'm a problem now, am I?"

That tore Byrnes's attention off her legs. "I thought you were in meetings?" The last thing they needed was the duke getting in the midst of all of this. Malloryn pulled strings. He didn't prance into vampire dens.

"They're over. Martial law has been declared. Nobody is allowed out after night falls, and the Nighthawks are going to flood the streets."

"Have you thought about this, your Grace?" Byrnes asked him. "We're going into vampire-infested tunnels. It's possible some of us might not return."

Malloryn settled that unsettling blue stare upon him. "Do I look like I need you to hold my hand, Byrnes?"

"I've never seen you fight. This won't be a duel, your Grace."

"Oh, good. I'd best leave my rapier behind then," Malloryn replied, tugging off his cravat and then piling his rings in the mess of his coat. "Someone fetch me one of those armored waistcoats."

"As you wish, your Grace," Jack murmured, and shot Byrnes a steady look as he left to find Malloryn some protective gear. Debney continued trying to fade into the wallpaper.

"And stop treating me like I'm going to be bloody underfoot," Malloryn bellowed, so that Jack could hear it. He glanced at Byrnes. "Problem?"

Byrnes crossed his arms. "You can come on one condition. You're not in charge of this mission. You don't have any experience in the streets, or beneath them. I do. Ingrid does. Even Charlie knows what he's doing. So order of command goes like this: Me, then Ingrid, then Charlie. If all three of us are down, then, and only then, do you get to take charge. One hint that you're not listening, and I will personally truss you up and deliver you to the Nighthawks until all of this is done, do you understand?"

A slight smile crossed Malloryn's lips. "I think I can manage not to get myself killed. You're in charge. So let's get this briefing underway, shall we?"

In a way, Malloryn actually helped. The borough was quietly cleared by the Nighthawks, and a troop of the metal Cyclops suits that the humanists had created to overthrow the prince consort were supplied to help clear any tunnels.

Charlie enthusiastically claimed one of them, strapping himself inside the heavy metal suit and tugging the harness into place.

The entire thing was unnerving, but Byrnes had to admit that the enormous steel automaton would prove handy if they needed to clear tunnels or take on a vampire. It clomped along at his side, pistons hissing as Charlie worked the gadgetry inside it.

"If all goes well, Zero will kidnap me off the streets, you'll track me to her den, and then you can come in guns blazing and we'll take down the entire nest of vampires in one fell swoop." The plan pleased him, but he had to admit there was doubt there too. It knotted itself in his stomach like a leaden weight, and the cause of it tilted almond-shaped eyes up to his. "Ingrid," he murmured, capturing her hand. "Don't do anything stupid, and stay safe. You're lucky I'm letting you do this."

"Letting me?" she replied, in the kind of tone that was the exact reason he hadn't bothered arguing against it.

This was one fight he wouldn't win.

"Zero's made a threat against you," he pointed out, and caught Charlie's eye over her shoulder. They'd already had a quiet little chat, man-to-man. But the last thing he wanted was for her to know that. He squeezed her hand and dragged her closer, his voice lowering. "If anything happens to you…." This was unfamiliar terrain.

Ingrid's gaze softened. "I'm not the one walking into a vampire den unprotected," she pointed out.

"Then you know how I feel."

Ingrid toyed with the lapels on his coat. "I know how you feel."

Their eyes met. Byrnes squeezed her waist. He'd never gone into battle like this—worried about anyone else's safety, or even his own, now that he had a promise to fulfill.

"Are we quite done with the sweet nothings?" Malloryn asked, striding back to the group and priming his pistol. Sunrise turned his brown hair coppery.

Byrnes stepped back from Ingrid and cleared his throat. He'd never been one for public displays. "Time to see if she takes the bait."

Ingrid grabbed him by the lapels and hauled him against her. Clearly she disagreed. Their mouths met, fast and furious, and saying more than words.

When she let him go, Byrnes cupped her cheek in his hand. So many emotions raced through her bronze eyes. He knew how much she'd lost, and how much she feared the idea that he might not return.

"I'll come back to you, I promise. And I always speak the truth, Ingrid." Then, giving her one last kiss, he turned and walked away.

He went ahead alone.

Ingrid bit her lip, pacing in the shadows as Byrnes's lean form slipped into the fog... then disappeared. She ached to go with him, to guard his back, but this task needed to be undertaken alone. Even if it felt like she was cutting her heart out of her chest.

"He'll be all right," Charlie murmured. He'd managed to discreetly give them both some privacy by turning his face away and studying the wall as they kissed, but she didn't think much slipped past Charlie. Despite his youth, he wore the weight of the rookeries on his soul. "Byrnes knows what he's doing."

It wasn't so much doubt about Byrnes's abilities that made her fret, but the fear that she'd never see him again. She'd tried so hard to keep him at bay, and yet in true Byrnes fashion he'd pushed his way into her life, aggravated her, argued with her, seduced her... and then stolen her heart when she wasn't looking.

Now she finally knew what it felt like to have something that she could lose. That certain little something she'd been missing from her life had come from an unexpected direction, but she couldn't fight the fact that she wanted it. Wanted him. A future with him.

And it was only now, standing on the precipice of losing him, that she could see that.

"What if Zero doesn't decide to keep him? What if she sets her vampires upon him? Anything could go wrong." She could almost see it.

"I know how you feel—"

"How I feel?" she retorted. "How could you? You're just a boy."

"I'm old enough." Shadows darkened those brilliant blue eyes as Charlie's entire demeanor changed. It happened so quickly that she realized just how much of a facade that cheerful mask was. "You're afraid because he's walking into danger, and there's a chance—just a slim one—that something bad might happen and you cannot protect him. That's the worst part of this, the fact that there's not a damn thing you can do to help. The lack of control.... You just have to hope for the best."

Shame washed through her. She was taking her emotions out on him, and it was clear from Charlie's tone that he had someone he worried about too. "I'm sorry," Ingrid said gruffly. "I'm on edge, and—"

"Don't worry about it." Charlie flashed her a smile. "You're not the first verwulfen I've ever dealt with."

Ingrid realized she was pacing and stopped, brushing her knuckles restlessly against the seam of her pants. "Who is she?"

"Who?"

"The girl you were speaking of; the one you worry about."

The humor dissolved off his expression. Charlie glanced down, thick blonde lashes hiding the slither of a blue blood's *hunger* as it flashed darkly across his irises. "Who said I was speaking of any girl in particular?"

"Your tone. Your voice. The fact that you cannot control your *hunger* when you think of her. It shows in your eyes." As Charlie fell into stillness, she added, "You don't have to tell me."

"Helps take your mind off matters, doesn't it?" Charlie sighed, then glanced at the tracking device that he held in his hand; the one they would use to hunt Byrnes down if he didn't rendezvous with them at the appointed time. "Her name is Lark. And she hates me."

"Why?"

"I did something reckless during the revolution, and the man she thought of as a father died because of it. He took a bullet that was meant for me." Charlie's voice broke, and he fiddled with the tracker in his hand, his agile thumb toying with the small compass arrow that was pointing due south. Toward where Byrnes had disappeared. "Lark's barely spoken to me since that day. That's one of the reasons I took this commission when Blade told me about it. I just... I needed to get out of the rookeries for a while."

"I'm sorry."

A translucent smile darted over his face, bittersweet and half mocking. "That's why you should be careful with Byrnes's heart, Ingrid. You just never know when you might lose such a thing—"

The compass arrow suddenly jerked. Both she and Charlie leapt to their feet, staring down at it.

"Why did it do that?" Ingrid whispered.

Charlie's face paled. "Something happened."

Something... Byrnes....

She started to run, but Charlie nearly jerked her off her feet. "No!" he told her fiercely, his hand locked around her wrist. "No, we can't just rush in there looking for him. Zero might not kill Byrnes, but she'll cut you down without a second's thought."

Ingrid glared at him. "That's why you're here, isn't it? To stop me from—"

"Doing something reckless." Charlie's grip on her arm slackened, but didn't disappear. "He wants to keep you safe. He told me about the threat against you."

A growl sounded in her throat. "And what about him? Who's going to protect Byrnes?"

"We all are," Charlie replied. "Time to bring in the others. Zero's taken the bait."

A whirring sound stopped her tirade in its tracks. Ingrid's gut plummeted through the soles of her boots.

The arrow was spinning.

A hand reached out and jerked the black hood off his head.

Byrnes flinched as light stabbed his sensitive eyes. He scrambled back, but his hands were bound to the chair they'd thrust him into and the chair only scraped on the stone floor. Zero circled him with slow sideways steps, wearing a set of black leather breeches similar to the Nighthawks uniform and a burgundy-colored coat made of velvet. Her silvery hair curled over her shoulder in loose waves, and kohl darkened her eyes.

Rather than finding it enticing, his blood chilled. Four maggot-pale vampires lolled around the room, resting on the rug in front of the fireplace like hounds. Each of them wore a thick leather collar with metal coils and wires through it.

"Looks like you found me, after all." Zero smiled, and somehow Byrnes forced himself to drag his gaze back to her.

"Looks like I did," he replied, swallowing his fear and distaste. "Now what?"

"Now," she whispered, straddling his thighs and curling a hand around his neck, "*my* friends take care of your friends."

Byrnes's blood ran cold. "What?"

"Oh, Byrnes," Zero crooned, tugging at his shirt collar and fiddling with it flirtatiously. "Please tell me you didn't think I wouldn't notice a half dozen Nighthawks wandering around my asylum? And your pretty little friend... the verwulfen bitch. She looks lonely—" Lifting a small flute, she blew out a series of notes. "I think she needs someone to play with, now that you're mine."

Several chitters echoed out of the shadows of the room as all four vampires sprang to attention. Zero lifted a small control box with an antenna on the end and smiled at him as she pressed the button.

Electricity buzzed, and two of the vampires sank back down, resting their heads on their claws as static crackled over their collars. One of them had clearly been a woman, with sagging teats and straggly white hair that hung in clumps from its skull. The other two headed for the door as Zero played the same set of notes on her flute.

Byrnes tried to struggle, but it was no use. Zero's weight and the manacles were too strong for him.

"Go and glut yourselves, my pretties," she hissed behind her to the pair of vampires that slunk out through the door, before wrapping her arm around his neck playfully and crooning, "After all, we wouldn't want to be disturbed. Would we?"

CHAPTER THIRTY-ONE

"AN ASYLUM."

Of course. The map showed that Byrnes's beacon signal was coming from the abandoned St. Mary's Home for the Criminally Insane.

"Makes sense," Charlie replied, taking a step in the heavy Cyclops suit that he wore. Pistons hissed as he knelt to peer through the opening that he'd just made using the Cyclops to tear down half a brick wall. All Ingrid could see through the glass slits in the Cyclops's headpiece was his pale face with that mop of blond curls. "They'd have cells here to incarcerate their vampires when they weren't using them. Or to hold people perhaps. And they're sitting right on top of this abandoned section of Undertown. Nobody would even see them coming in and out."

"Plus the asylum's reputation would keep most curious onlookers at bay," Garrett noted, running a hand down the stone wall. The Nighthawks guild master insisted upon coming along and bringing two of his men. Something about a debt he owed Byrnes from a few years ago.

Water dripped in the darkness through the hole Charlie had just made, but apart from that, all was silent. The smell, however....

"Jesus," Garrett muttered.

Ingrid had smelled death before. "That smells like old death," she told him. "Something's been dumping bodies just through here." One of the EMLEDs in hand, Ingrid crept through the hole in the wall onto a ledge, and looked down. The Electro-Magnetic Light Emitting Device would be one of their greatest weapons this morning.

The room fell away into a pit with a narrow pair of boards stretched across it. Ingrid squatted on the plank and then activated the EMLED, dropping it down into the hollow below.

The light tumbled end over end, then splashed to a halt far below. Something looked up and hissed, it's eyes shining blue-white with cat shine, and then the shadowy creature fled into the darkness. And that's when Ingrid began to make out the bodies.

Bone gleamed as the EMLED burned like phosphorus. There were the ragged remains of clothes and misshapen lumps of rotting flesh. She didn't need to see more.

"Vampire below," she murmured over her shoulder, looking into the darkness where the planks stretched. "I'm guessing this is where they dump the bodies. You're going to have to leave the Cyclops suit here, Charlie. The plank won't sustain the weight."

"Kincaid," Charlie murmured, touching the communicator in his ear. "Can you hear me?"

A static buzzing sounded, and Charlie's shoulders eased in relief. "We've got something here," he said. "Found a vampire, and maybe a way into Zero's holdout.

She's been using the old asylum as a vampire den. Ingrid and I are going in."

Static crackled, and Charlie smiled as he let go of the button. "I think he's actually starting to come round," he joked quietly. "Even wished us luck."

"Really?" Garrett arched a brow.

"Well, it was more like, 'Go kill them bloodsuckers, and don't get bit, 'cause I ain't comin' in after you.'"

Ingrid had to grudgingly admit that Charlie gave an impressive impression of Kincaid. "You coming?"

"Of course," he replied, pressing something that made the chestpiece open on the steel suit. Charlie looked strangely vulnerable as he stepped down out of it.

A vampire couldn't gut a Cyclops, but it might do so to him.

"Kincaid's going to enter the asylum from the north with Malloryn and Gemma," he said, touching his earpiece again. "Ava's coordinating the Nighthawks and will have them slip into place surrounding the asylum so that nothing escapes. It's up to us to get Byrnes out."

In one piece. Ingrid swallowed. "Let's go then."

The two Nighthawks that Garrett had brought scrambled over the planks, running low with their weapons raised. Flanders, the one in the lead, pressed his spine to a crumbling brick wall and cocked his head to listen before flicking two fingers. The other Nighthawk, Nicholson, vanished into the shadows in response.

"It's clear," Garrett said, and urged her and Charlie forward into the darkness.

She quite enjoyed working with people who knew what they were doing.

"Anyone think that this seems a little easy?" Charlie whispered, swallowing hard as they hurried through the abandoned tunnels.

"What do you mean?" Ingrid asked.

"Not a single guard, or a vampire sighting," he pointed out.

Which was troubling.

Nicholson returned from ahead, appearing out of nowhere. "We've reached the bottom level of cells," he murmured. "It's quiet."

"Too quiet," Garrett added grimly, then gestured them on ahead. "Expect anything. This is starting to feel like a trap."

"How would she know we were coming?" Charlie whispered.

"Maybe she saw us?" Ingrid replied. "Flanders, take point. Nicholson, cover the rear. Everyone, weapons out." She tipped her head toward Garrett, gesturing him to slip in behind Flanders. "I've got your back."

"Thanks," he murmured, unholstering his enhanced pistol.

They all carried firebolt bullets, which could take off a vampire's head if necessary.

The phosphorus glow from the glimmer light in the headset around Flanders's head provided just enough light to see by as they wound down, through half-used tunnels filled with rot and mud and the filth of this part of London. All of them were preternatural: they could see with the faintest of lights, and light made them a target in these tunnels.

The vampire tracks they were following led to a half-rotted door set into stone. Up, then. The scent through here was stronger, and bones lay scattered around. Ingrid's eyes watered, as her sense of smell was the strongest, and she took a moment to wipe them as the men fanned through the room and down the two tunnels spearing out from it.

"There are people in here," Charlie whispered, slinking back along the corridor from a small excursion. "I can hear them."

People? Ingrid went to the first cell and peered in. A pair of children scrambled away from her, curling into their mother's arms. An old man lifted a piece of chair and waved it threateningly. "Stay away from us," he rasped.

Jesus. The stench hit her again: unwashed bodies, blood and old death, mixed with a strong presence of *eau de vampire.*

"Sir," Garrett called under his breath. "Sir, I'm with the Nighthawks. I'm not here to hurt you."

Relief dawned on the man's face and the woman started sobbing. The man grabbed the bars, desperation plain on his face. "Please! Please let us out!"

"Who are you?" Garrett asked, looking around for a key. "What happened?"

"I don't know," the man gasped, gripping the iron bars on the cell doors as if afraid that they would leave him here. "Something rolled into the room of my house and started hissing gas. The next thing I knew, I woke up here with Verna and the children." The man swallowed. "There's vampires here. You can hear the screams at night, when they come and drag some of us away. They don't come back." He started sobbing. "They took my son three days ago, and they didn't bring him back."

Garrett came back out of the shadows. "No keys."

Ingrid slid her hand inside one of the pouches on her belt and withdrew her lock pick set. As much as she was frightened for Byrnes, she couldn't leave these people here in the dark.

She knew all too well what it felt like to be locked in a cage.

"A woman after my own heart," Charlie said as she set to work.

"Stop flirting, and keep an eye out." The lock was old, but it gave an appreciable click. Ingrid listened intently, but it seemed there were no guards on duty who'd heard the small noise.

The door was another matter. It groaned on its hinges, and she cursed under her breath as the old man yanked on it.

"Quiet," she hissed, holding the door firm. "You'll have to slip through the gap. And don't make any noise."

"Hullo?" someone called from further up the passage. "Hullo, is anybody there?"

She exchanged a look with Garrett. More prisoners. "Keep them quiet."

Garrett nodded and slipped into the darkness with the two Nighthawks following him.

The cell door opened and Ingrid helped the old man out. His wrist was shockingly thin, and the children were crying silently as their mother carried them out. Ingrid took the small water flask from her hip, wishing she had more as she shared it between them.

"Where did you live?" Ingrid asked, stroking the dirty hair out of one child's face.

"Begby Square," the man replied. "This is my neighbor, Anne, and her children."

"My husband?" Anne pleaded, grabbing hold of Ingrid's hand. "Please, my husband! They took him three weeks ago. Are there other cells? Other people?" She looked frantically back down the hallway where Garrett and the Nighthawks were freeing other hostages.

Three weeks ago. Ingrid swallowed, for the only answer she suspected she had was not one the woman would want to hear. "It's a warren down here. We'll make sure they all get out," Ingrid said soothingly, "but we need to get you and your children to safety first. I'm sure if your husband is down here, we'll find him."

The old man exchanged a look with her as he tried to help Anne to her feet. "I'll make sure she gets out," he said, and Ingrid saw in his eyes the same thoughts that lurked within her. Anne's husband wasn't going to be found. Not alive, anyway.

This then, was what had happened to all the people who went missing. Someone had taken them, both in order to cause chaos and for far more practical reasons. After all, what could you feed to vampires?

It made her furious, and all of the hairs along her arms rose as the *berserkergang* fired within her. People weren't objects, and they weren't food. They didn't deserve to be locked in cages. Like she had been.

Zero had done everything possible to make this personal. Ingrid ached to smash her face in.

"Easy," Charlie muttered. "Save your anger for the one who deserves it."

"Oh, I will," she snarled, standing and glaring up the passage. "I'm going to make that bitch rue the day she ever set eyes on Begby Square."

"But first, we need to get the prisoners out," Charlie said.

Garrett came out of the darkness, a little girl wrapped in his arms and a trail of sobbing people hobbling behind him. His expression looked as haunted as her heart, and she realized that the little girl in his arms was only a year or so older than his twin daughters. "I'll get them out," he promised. "I've sent Nicholson back for more Nighthawks. You two go on ahead and rendezvous with Kincaid and Malloryn. We can't risk this bitch taking her anger out on Byrnes."

"It will be my pleasure," Ingrid growled, as she let the fury spill within her. She'd never let the berserker part of her nature have free rein before, but now wasn't the time to play nice.

CHAPTER THIRTY-TWO

"FANCY A LITTLE music?"

Zero moved to the cylinder phonograph in the corner and set it to playing. A faint waltz echoed through the brass horn. Instantly the two vampires' eyelids began to lower as firelight flickered over the gaunt bones of their spines. Two hounds at rest by the hearth.

Somewhat sickening.

"Did you know," Zero murmured, watching them with a faint smile, "that they can be trained? It interests me. That one can be taught to react to something in association with... the same kind of stimulus. For example, they hear this music and they know that I am pleased with them, and that it is time to sleep."

Byrnes wriggled against his chains. "Fascinating." The daft woman was scratching one of the vampire's heads as though it were a hound. And he could swear that one of them was making some sort of purring sound deep in its throat.

"Do you wish to know how I discovered this?" Zero asked.

Why not? Anything that made vampires sleepy was possibly a good thing to know. "How?"

"I was once interred in an asylum by my husband." Her smile remained just as bright. "And I use the term 'interred' deliberately. He meant for me to die there. One of the things I learned is that sounds bring certain associations to mind. Even now the mere scrape of a key turning in a lock makes me feel ill."

He didn't want to sympathize with her, but it was all too easy to imagine what had happened to her. "How did you escape the asylum?"

"Oh, I didn't escape. I seduced one of the other inmates' visitors—a baron—and became infected with the craving virus. After I tore out my handler's throat, the governor of the asylum took note. It's not the sort of thing one wants to have whispered about their facility, you see. Blue blood lords taking advantage of the patients. Tut, tut. What would the papers say?" She swirled in a slow circle as the phonograph played a couple of piquant notes, holding on to her skirts as if it were a waltz. "The next day a pair of red-liveried servants arrived to take me away. At first I thought it was Nigel—my baron—but I soon learned he'd forgotten me. Fickle man. No, these servants belonged to the Duke of Lannister. And they took me to Falkirk Asylum, which was masquerading as another treatment facility."

Falkirk, which had been owned by the Dukes of Lannister, Caine, and Casavian. He sensed where this was going.

"That was where I was reborn." Zero swirled to a halt near the table and opened a small case. He craned his neck to see what was inside it, but the curve of her body hid it. Zero held something up and flicked her nail against it. "I went into Falkirk as Annabelle, victim of a half dozen men and their whims, and I exited it as Zero, who can be judge, jury, and executioner."

"I won't argue that you've been poorly done by, but the people from Begby Square did no wrong by you. The guests at the Venetian Gardens had nothing to do with your incarceration. So why hurt them?"

Zero laughed. "Oh, Byrnes, I thought you were an investigator. That party belonged to the Earl of Carrington. Do you know who was on the guest list?"

"Nigel? Your baron?"

Her smile softened. "I almost began to doubt you, but you *are* just as clever as I had hoped. Poor Nigel's still alive, by the way, but I bet he wishes he wasn't. Did you know that blue bloods can survive almost anything? And they might be able to heal, but they can't actually regrow limbs or organs... or eyes."

"And what about Begby Square?"

"My husband lived there. Unfortunately, Thomas didn't last long enough to see my justice." Her face flattened as she strode toward him, holding something low against her skirts. "But his cow-faced mother did. And his two sisters. And all of their families, and the neighbors who sneered at me. Who is sneering now?"

A chill ran down his spine. What the hell was in her hand? "Possibly no one. You don't have to do this. I'm no threat to you—"

"Relax," she said, holding up a syringe. "I don't mean you harm. You're going to be one of my allies, Byrnes. This will hurt a little—the first time is always the worst—" She suddenly giggled. "That's what men always say, isn't it? But once it's done, you'll be on the first step toward your new transformation. I do hope you'll be strong enough to survive it."

A bubble of fluid wept from the top of the syringe. Byrnes's gaze tracked it warily. "I think I'd like to know a little bit more about this... ah, transformation before we go ahead with it. Is it reversible?"

"Oh, no." Zero tore his sleeve clear up the middle, revealing the muscle in his upper arm. "Once it begins you must continue it, or else you'll end up like my failures."

Byrnes's gaze shot toward the vampires reclining on the floor. "How many treatments?" Hell, where was Ingrid? She should be here by now, and if she didn't come quickly, it was going to be too late. His gaze narrowed on the syringe needle.

"Seven treatments, provided all goes well. They shall proceed a week apart. Any closer together and your brain might trickle out of your ears." Zero rubbed a spot on his upper biceps, crooning a little under her breath. "You need to stay nice and relaxed, otherwise you'll hurt yourself. Don't worry. We've refined the formula since Dr. Cremorne used it upon us. The failure rate has gone down significantly. Only three in ten die now."

"Us?" He seized on the word, trying to crawl through the chair as she inched closer. "Who's us? Am I joining some sort of... elite brotherhood, hmm?"

Zero paused, glancing up from beneath her silvery lashes. "They're of no concern to you or I," she finally said. "You're mine. I'm tired of being told what to do and kept on a leash. I want my own fun, my own allies."

"Who's holding the leash?"

"You wouldn't be trying to get information out of me, would you?" Zero went very still.

He'd taken a slight misstep there. Byrnes summoned every ounce of arrogance that he could muster. "Of course I am. If there's someone running this entire coup, then I want to know who. I'm about to become what you are. Do you think I want to walk into a trap where there's a leash around my throat too, without at least knowing who it bloody well is? What if I take this leap and end up as slave for some despot? That's not me, princess."

"That's not me either." She seemed delighted. "I hate playing by the rules."

"You and me both." He made himself smile. Bloody hell. "Do you know what I like? I like puzzling out the answer to mysteries. And this is the greatest mystery of all. I won. I found you, so that we could be together. Don't I at least get my prize?"

Zero nibbled on her lip. "You could help me remove the leash," she whispered, as though thinking about it.

"Who do we have to kill?"

A slither of darkness slid through her pale blue eyes. "My brothers. We were born in a trial by fire, and since then we've only been able to rely on each other. Ghost is the problem. Without him, the others would leave us alone to do as we wished."

"Who's Ghost?"

"The first," she whispered. "The first one who survived the transformation. He thinks that gives him the right to lead us."

"And how many others are there?"

"There were six of us altogether: Ghost, me, Omega, Obsidian, Sirius... and X. Omega died in the fire. The rest of us fled when Falkirk went up in flames, and took new names to represent our rebirth. It took a while to... come to terms with being free. Ghost took control because he said that we couldn't simply slaughter our way through the population, or they'd turn on us." A snarl curled her lips. "Why should we care? We're better than them, all of them. But he said that even we should fear the people, and the way technology has provided them with a means to hunt us with their spitfires and Cyclopses."

"So Ghost is making the rules," he said, watching her face. "Kill him, and... we're free?" Why the hell did this Ghost have something against Malloryn?

Zero seemed to come back to herself. The distance faded out of her eyes and she turned that direct look upon him. "Try to kill Ghost," she told him, "and he'll make you eat your tongue for breakfast. If it were so easy, do you not think that I'd have done it by now?"

"You don't seem to care for your brothers very much."

"There is no blood between us. Only a shared experience, and they consider me to be the weak one." Hatred ignited on her face. "I'll show them weak. I'm the one with the vampires."

Byrnes eyed the nearest creature. Its head had jerked up, its nostrils flaring wide.

"What are you—?" Zero followed his gaze, her cool smile vanishing as she too saw the intensity in the creature's frame.

Please don't be Ingrid. Or no, please be Ingrid. Byrnes strained against his ropes, but it was hopeless. There was no escape.

Footsteps pounded along the hallway, and gunfire suddenly burst out in a sharp staccato.

Both vampires perked up, like hunting hounds sensing prey. It would be a slaughter if he didn't warn them.

"Vampires!" Byrnes bellowed, knowing that he'd blown his cover. "There are two vampires in here—"

A fist slammed into the side of his head. Byrnes spat blood, trying to blink through the dizziness.

"So...."

The look on Zero's face boded trouble. "You lied to me," she said, and the way she said it was so eerie that all of the hairs on the back of Byrnes's neck lifted.

"No, I never meant to—"

And Zero slammed the syringe into the muscle of his arm and injected all of its contents into him with a vicious look upon her face.

The first scream tore through the asylum.

Ingrid had never heard anything like it. She froze. "Byrnes." There was no way to guess how she knew it was him, but something about that animalistic sound shivered down to the very core of her.

"Ingrid! Wait!" Charlie snatched at her sleeve, but she wasn't listening.

All that she knew was that her man was in danger. The world vanished as blood rushed through her veins and she tore ahead of Charlie, Malloryn, and Gemma, just as a pair of vampires came out of nowhere.

One of their heads exploded like rotten melon as someone shot from behind her. The other one launched itself toward her, claws raking the air, and its lean body twisting catlike as she threw herself beneath it, rolling in a ball as it flew over her—

Ingrid came up and hit the door with her shoulder. It jarred the whole way through her. She caught a glimpse behind her of Charlie and Gemma parting around the vampire, moving with blue blood grace as they lashed in with knives. Another scream echoed from within, and Ingrid slammed into the door again.

Malloryn withdrew a hollow-looking rifle from inside his coat. It looked somewhat similar to a grappling gun.

The second he had an opening he fired, and a silver-tipped net shot out, trapping the vampire inside.

"Go," he called, catching her eye and jerking his head toward Charlie.

The vampire's high-pitched scream of rage pierced her eardrums as she took out her pistol and shot the lock off the door. Slivers of wood erupted from the timber and Ingrid flung her arm up in front of her face. The second it had settled she burst through the door, looking for Byrnes. He strained in a chair, blood dripping from a mark on his arm and the muscles in his biceps standing out in stark relief as he screamed again. There were chains bolted into the floor, holding him there.

The sound shocked her. Not pain. Not fear. That was rage she heard in his voice.

"Byrnes?" she whispered, sliding to a halt.

No time to follow up. Zero came out of nowhere, swinging some sort of staff, with a pair of vampires at her heels.

This time Ingrid didn't hesitate. She ducked below the staff and came up with her fists clenched. Her first punch smashed into Zero's face, flinging her back onto the table.

Bitch. Ingrid grabbed a chair and swung it. Zero rolled off the table a second before the chair hit it and came apart at the legs. Then she darted forward, low enough to hit Ingrid around the waist. They both went down with a crash, one chair leg remaining in Ingrid's hand.

"Fancy seeing you here," Zero spat, locking her hands around Ingrid's throat as she crawled up over her body.

Ingrid tried to twist free, her air cutting off. She outweighed the woman by a decent portion of solid muscle, but the *dhampir* was strong. "You've... got something... belongs to... me."

Zero's eyes narrowed and she leaned close enough to whisper, "He belongs to me now."

What had she done to him? Ingrid drove her knee up between the woman's legs and tried to fling her aside, but something crashed nearby and then a weight hit Zero, flinging her off Ingrid with ease.

Charlie. He stood over her with his gun held low as he tracked both the vampires and Zero. "It's clear!" he called.

A pair of vampires circled them, crouched low and snarling.

The others came in firing, and Zero darted into the shadows. She shot Ingrid and Byrnes one last furious look, then turned to her vampires. "Come!"

One of the vampires followed her as she vanished behind a tapestry hanging from one of the walls. The other's gaze locked on Byrnes's arm and the single drop of blood there. Only the fact that there were five of them in the room seemed to confuse it.

"Got it!" Gemma said, and clipped it with a bullet.

"Byrnes!" Ingrid took her chance and slid to her knees in front of him.

Byrnes strained in his chains, his fingers curled into claws and bloodied froth spilling from his lips. The *berserkergang* died down a little as she saw that. Suddenly she was swimming up through the tides of the fury, her speed and strength ebbing as uncertainty overtook her.

"Byrnes?" What was wrong with him? His shirt was torn, and a faint bloodied circle marred the muscle in his upper arm.

Somehow he ground his teeth together, every cord in his throat standing out in sharp relief. His black eyes met hers, every trace of the man she knew washing away until all she could see was the *hunger* overtaking him. "Run!" he screamed, and his forearms flexed as he tore at the chains. The steel links stretched, then one tore apart with a clink.

"Ingrid." Charlie dragged her back out of the way. "He's not himself at the moment. He might not recognize you."

"What's wrong with him?"

"I think she gave him the elixir," Charlie said.

"We've got to get him out of there." Ingrid strained against his hold on her.

"We've got other concerns first," Charlie retorted, and jerked her back sharply as the vampire skidded on the rug nearby, narrowly missing Gemma.

Bullets retorted behind them as Malloryn spun to track the creature, firing five times as the white blur bulleted around the room. "Stand still, you bastard." He clicked empty, and Gemma rotated in front of him, a pistol in each hand.

BOOM. BOOM. BOOM.

The way they moved showed an old partnership, as Malloryn swiftly reloaded then rotated back to point the second Gemma ran dry. Tracking the vampire with the pistol, he let it get dangerously close to him before he shot it point-blank in the face.

The head exploded. Black blood spattered across Malloryn's chest, but he let out the breath he'd been holding and lowered his pistol.

The second he did so, Byrnes broke the second chain pinning him to the floor, his black gaze locked on Charlie. "Mine," he snarled.

Charlie's face paled as he dragged her away. "Whatever it's done to him, it's unleashed the *hunger* within him. He might not be able to separate friend from foe at the moment."

"He knows who I am," Ingrid replied incredulously. This was Byrnes. *Control* was practically his middle name.

Byrnes darted toward Gemma and snatched her back against his chest, hissing at Malloryn over Gemma's shoulder as he curled his hand around her throat. Gemma froze, her hand locking on his trembling arm and her gaze meeting Ingrid's pleadingly.

"Byrnes!" Ingrid called, stepping forward with a placating hand. She forced herself to be calm. "Let her go."

"Jesus," Charlie muttered.

Byrnes dragged Gemma back a step as the three of them fanned out, flanking him.

Malloryn lifted the pistol, aiming it directly between Byrnes's eyes. Then he hesitated. "Ingrid?"

"Don't shoot!"

Byrnes grabbed a fistful of Gemma's hair and tilted her head forcefully to the side.

"No!" Both Ingrid and Gemma yelled.

"Talk him out of this, Ingrid!" Malloryn's pistol never wavered.

"Don't hurt her!" Ingrid took another step toward him, meeting those all-black eyes and trying to find any hint of the man she loved. "You don't want to do this, Caleb. We're your friends. *I'm* your... your lover. This is just the elixir running through your veins. Zero did this. She infected you with whatever she herself is infected by. Focus on her. Not on us. Use that rage against her to take control."

Byrnes paused. "Zero," he said in a shockingly hollow voice.

Gemma squeaked, and went up on her toes as his fingers tightened on her throat. "Malloryn—"

Malloryn visibly steeled himself. "Ingrid. It's for the best. There's no coming back from this."

"No!" Ingrid smashed into his side as the pistol retorted.

An enormous chunk of brick wall shattered into powder. Byrnes flinched and Gemma tore free, throwing herself into Charlie's arms. Byrnes turned swiftly and then he was gone into the tunnel after Zero, moving like liquid night itself.

Ingrid wasted no time. She wasn't about to lose him.

Not now.

CHAPTER THIRTY-THREE

INGRID LOST BYRNES in the space of five minutes. Scrambling through narrow tunnels, she finally came to a halt in a larger cavern, following the scent of Byrnes's aftershave.

"Byrnes?" she called. Not a cavern, but an abandoned underground train station. Which meant she was somewhere below the asylum now, and the room where she'd first discovered him.

And, as she turned in a slow circle, she began to realize that she wasn't alone. Ingrid jerked around as an ethereal ghost stepped onto the platform, the hairs down her arms rising.

"So," Zero said, her boot heels ringing on stone as she settled into an aggressive posture. "We meet again. The beauty... and the beast. May the best woman win."

Ingrid glared back at her, bringing up her hands in a pugilists position. "This is not a competition."

"Oh, it is," Zero purred. "You're the only thing stopping him from being mine. Once you're gone, he'll accept the transformation."

Ingrid took a step toward her. "You're mad as hatters. Byrnes is not some prize to be won. And you've effectively poisoned him. What if he doesn't survive?"

Zero's smile faded, and her black eyes glittered. "I'm not mad," she stated flatly. "And if he doesn't survive, then clearly he wasn't worth it after all."

Ingrid sidestepped the other woman's sudden lunge, her heart pounding. It wasn't much, but the sudden rage in Zero's eyes hinted at a weakness to exploit. What was it? The reference toward madness? Had to be... and they were standing beneath an asylum, which Zero seemed to know all too well.

Warily they circled each other.

"Your kind are filth," Zero spat.

"As opposed to vampires?"

This time there was no avoiding the blow. A fist hammered toward her face, and Ingrid barely deflected it, taking the blow to the shoulder. She retaliated with a brutal elbow as she ducked beneath Zero's second swing, and they came together with a clash. Fists punching, arms flailing... it wasn't pretty, and she couldn't avoid every blow. One slammed into her face, sending her sprawling to the ground, but as Zero leapt upon her, Ingrid kicked up with her feet into the *dhampir's* midsection and sent her crashing off to the side.

Ingrid flipped up onto her feet just as Zero tackled her. They hit the platform hard, and then they were rolling, each fighting for the upper hand. Ingrid landed flat on her back, the other woman getting in a glancing blow across her cheekbone. Pain exploded through her face and ear and she tried to lock her legs around the other woman's hips.

They rolled, end over end. Ingrid felt her fury growing. "You poisoned him!" She slammed Zero's head into the floor. "You bitch!"

"Maybe he wanted it? Maybe he was tired of smelling your rank scent?"

"And maybe," Ingrid rasped, her hands closing around the other woman's throat, "he just pretended to be interested in you so that we could find you? You do realize there's a tracking device on him?"

That sent her sprawling as Zero's eyes narrowed and she renewed her efforts. A knife flashed and Ingrid scrambled to grab Zero's arms as the woman stabbed down with it. Ingrid's arm trembled, and she grimaced as Zero forced the knife closer to her throat. *Christ*, the woman was strong!

"Just die," Zero hissed.

"N-never." Ingrid shoved her face to the side as she let go of Zero's hand. The knife sparked as it hit the stone beside her ear, and Zero lost her balance just enough for Ingrid to throw the *dhampir* clear.

They scrambled to their feet, both of them panting.

One thing was becoming abundantly clear: she would need every trick in the book to win this. Zero's strength superseded her own.

But then, Ingrid had grown up in a cage. She'd been used as a child to test Lord Balfour's men and their strength. Balfour had pushed her into cage matches at the age of ten, sending his men in with steel against her to prove their worth. Verwulfen strength might be an arsenal all in its own, but it wasn't the entirety of what she had. Ingrid knew what it felt like to fight men or women stronger and faster and bigger than she. She knew how to push through pain and focus on winning. And she'd been doing it since she was a child.

"What did they do to you?" Ingrid asked. "Lock you up in here? Why? Why are you doing *any* of this?" It made no sense. Why attack the Council of Dukes, or the queen? What did the queen have to do with Zero?

"None of your bloody business." Zero circled her.

"Was it the Council of Dukes who put you in here?"

Zero launched into a flying flurry of kicks. Ingrid blocked each one, taking one retreating step after the other. Finally the other woman let up, as if catching hold of herself.

But something about what Ingrid had said had pushed her over the edge.

"Is it Malloryn?" she asked. "Did *he* put you in here? He doesn't remember you."

"Not Malloryn!" Another blow.

Ingrid stepped aside, locking her arm up under the other woman's as Zero's arm reached the end of its extension. She shoved a hand into the woman's back and wrenched her shoulder back as they both spun. Zero slammed into the wall, face-first, and Ingrid dug a knee into the back of Zero's, forcing it to bend as she pinned her there.

"Then what the hell kind of grudge do you have against Malloryn?"

Zero laughed, the sound echoing through her entire body. "You stupid bitch. I've never even met him. Malloryn's the target."

"The target?"

"There's a price on his head," Zero ground out. "But the Master doesn't want him dead. He wants him destroyed. We're just the catalysts to do it."

Zero slammed her head back into Ingrid's cheekbone. She staggered back, taking another blow to the ribs. Then a glancing one off her shoulder as she recovered.

The Master? Who the hell was that? Was this all a ploy? One hand pulling the strings of both the Sons of Gilead, and… Zero?

No time to think on that though.

She wasn't going to win this by strength or speed, and Zero healed faster than she could inflict enough damage. Which meant smarts. Zero knew how to fight, but she fought without a care to her body, as though she knew she could survive practically anything. Ingrid had once felt that way too, until a vampire showed her just how mortal she could be. Ingrid glanced around at her surroundings as Zero wiped blood from her nose.

"Time to finish this," the *dhampir* told her, and strode forward.

Precisely what I had planned too. Ingrid's eyes narrowed and she ripped a strip of rusted iron from the wall where it had been holding a section of boards in place.

Zero rolled her eyes. "Really, you just get more pathetic as you—"

Ingrid plucked one of the EMLED orbs from her belt. "Surprise," she said, then twisted the two halves so they popped open.

Zero's gaze shot to the orb just as a flash of intense light emitted. Ingrid looked away at the last second and tossed it toward the other woman, the orb making a high-pitched noise. Then she swung the strip of iron low, aiming it at the woman's shin. Zero screamed as she went down, an audible crack filling the air.

"Heal that," Ingrid snarled, and scrambled atop the woman, shoving her onto her face in a wrestling move and yanking both of Zero's arms behind her back. Reaching for the strip of iron, she dug a knee into Zero's back and used sheer force to bend the iron around Zero's arms. Rust flaked her hands. "Now who's pathetic?"

Zero screamed deep in her throat, a sound of thwarted rage. The second she fell silent, she also stopped struggling, then made a low whistling noise in her throat.

Ingrid froze, then glanced up into the darkness as something scrabbled behind the boarded-up passage she'd just ripped the iron bar off. In the thin slit between boards a pair of filmy eyes gleamed.

Jesus. A vampire.

Move. Or die.

The sound of the EMLED was like a stab wound to the ears, but she snatched it up as that high-pitched wail began to fade. They had two minutes on them. How long had it been alight for? She reached for the other one at her belt as she started sprinting along the platform toward the boarded-up tunnel at the end, but her hand snatched at nothing. Must have lost it in the scuffle. *Hell.* The second the EMLED in her hand died, there was going to be nothing stopping that vampire from coming after her.

"Hello? Can anyone hear me?" Her communicator was gone too, presumably when Zero punched her in the face, but surely her voice would drift through the tunnels. There had to be dozens of Nighthawks in them. And just where had Malloryn and Kincaid gotten to? Or even Charlie? "*Hello!*"

Zero began to laugh as Ingrid sprinted, the sound echoing hollowly through the tunnel.

The EMLED began to sputter, and she picked it up, swinging it around as the shadows pressed in upon her. Something hissed in the darkness, but the claws scrambled away from her as the EMLED pulsed in her hand.

There was an explosion of sound behind her as she reached the boarded-off tunnel, and a swift glance showed a maggot-pale body smashing through onto the platform, pausing to sniff at Zero where she lay on the ground.

"After her," Zero rasped, and the creature's head lifted unerringly toward Ingrid.

She yanked one of the boards off the timber frame, breathing deeply. The stink of rotting vampire wasn't as strong here, so hopefully she'd made the right choice. The EMLED sputtered again, its light pulsing as though she was running out of time.

"A few seconds more. Come on." She could feel the vampire watching her. Waiting. Yanking at another board, she managed to slip through, cursing her broad shoulders. Timber stabbed into her shoulder and she ground her teeth together and shoved through, taking the EMLED with her.

In the distance, light gleamed. It wasn't much, but it lifted the swell of hope inside her.

She started running just as claws scrabbled at the boards behind her. That inspired a surge of speed, but she tripped on the rail line, staggered forward, kept tripping—

The EMLED's light flickered, and Ingrid threw a glance over her shoulder as a pale shaped rocketed toward her. It squeezed through the hole she'd made.

"Charlie!" she screamed.

Light pulsed. Flickered once more. Then began to fade. Ingrid threw herself toward the light at the end of the tunnel, but a blur of movement caught the edge of her vision and then something catapulted into the vampire just as it leapt for her.

Claws lashed through her calf, and Ingrid hit the floor. She screamed in pain as she landed on the steel train tracks, kicking back and twisting, trying to break free—

But the vampire was gone, rolling end over end with a figure in black as they tore into each other.

Ingrid scrambled backward, reaching for the flickering EMLED. There might not be much life left in it, but it was better than nothing.

The scuffle lasted half a minute, shadows telling the tale on the walls around her as two creatures snarled at each other and blood spilled. Pain flared through her calf as she tried to crawl away. *Come on... you can do it.* Ingrid thrust the EMLED up behind her as the snarls died down, and silence fell.

The figure in black froze, kneeling over the vampire's body, and Ingrid's heart kicked as she recognized Byrnes. His eyes were nothing but pools of shadow in the darkness. Shadows darkened the hollows of his cheeks, turning his face from one she knew to that of a predator stalking the depths of the tunnel system. There was a head in his hand, which he dropped.

Ingrid hesitated.

"Caleb," she whispered, clutching at her bleeding arm.

But those eyes held no sign of her lover as he straightened from the vampire's headless corpse, his hand dripping black blood.

CHAPTER THIRTY-FOUR

BYRNES PACED BACK and forth, as though considering her.

Clamping a hand over her bloodied arm, Ingrid hopped to her feet and immediately staggered as an icy burn went through the back of her calf. "Byrnes?"

He took a step toward her, black eyes narrowing.

"It's me," she blurted. "Ingrid! Or Miller. You know me."

Those eyes slid to the blood dripping down her arm, and his nostrils flared. Ingrid froze. "I've captured Zero," she said, anything to get him thinking, get him to talk. "And we've rescued the people from Begby Square. You did it. We did it. We found Zero's nest."

No sign of recognition in his eyes.

Ingrid swallowed hard and stepped toward him, her leg giving way just enough that she nearly fell. Byrnes caught her, the reflex dangerously fast. "Byrnes," she whispered, looking up into his eyes as the EMLED finally died. The last thing she saw was the predator looking back.

"Caleb," she whispered in the darkness. "I've often wondered if you'd mind if I called you that?"

"Miller," he breathed, as if the word meant something to him.

"Ingrid," she corrected, resting a hesitant hand on his arm. "It's me, Ingrid. The woman who… who loves you. And I know you love me too, even if you've never said it. You wouldn't be thinking about a future with me if you didn't. You wouldn't hover at my bedside, or feed me soup, or create a way to keep rats from my room if you didn't. Who knew?" Ingrid reached up onto her toes, her heart hammering in her chest. "Caleb Byrnes has a heart, and it's all mine."

And then she kissed him.

The first touch of her lips to his was hesitant. Byrnes captured the back of her neck, however, and dragged her against him like a drowning man searching for oxygen. The way he kissed her, the way he touched her, was rougher, more urgent, than he'd ever been before.

Ingrid gasped for breath, and then he picked her up under her thighs and wrapped her legs around his hips. Another kiss stole her mouth, and her back hit the brick wall of the tunnel. Ingrid gasped as pain flared through her. Byrnes froze, letting her slide back down his body again.

He growled deep in his throat, his hand coming up to cup the nape of her neck as he turned his face into her throat. Ingrid froze.

A fierce trembling shivered through his hard body. "You're hurt," he whispered, his voice raw. She'd never heard him sound like that.

"A little." Ingrid shivered. The loupe was beginning to take its toll. She was exhausted and almost at the point where her body was beginning to shut down in order to repair itself.

"Tell me again," he said as a shudder ran through him.

"Tell you—" And then she knew. "I love you."

He shuddered as she stroked the back of his neck, holding him against her.

"I love you too," he whispered, pressing his cheek against hers like a cat. "You're everything to—"

Noise echoed through the tunnel—the sound of voices. Byrnes lifted his head sharply. She realized she could just make out the edge of his jawline in the dark.

"He went through here!" Malloryn yelled.

Oh, no. Stillness slid through Byrnes's body, and the sinister way he turned to survey the tunnel sent a chill through her.

"Byrnes," she whispered. "They're friends. Our friends."

A hand shoved her behind him, and she nearly went down again as her calf betrayed her. Only a snatch at his coat saved her.

As lights bobbed toward them, revealing the outline of four men and one lumbering spitfire automaton, Ingrid intensified her hold on his coat. She couldn't hold him. Not like this. And he was dangerous at the moment. If not to her, then to their friends.

"I'm sorry," she whispered, reaching for the hemlock darts at her belt that Ava had doctored to have enough strength to take down a vampire.

Byrnes's head turned back to her.

And then she jammed the hemlock dart into his gut, and hoped it did the job.

CHAPTER THIRTY-FIVE

"WHAT'S WRONG WITH him?" Ingrid demanded, pacing the room as Byrnes snapped and snarled from the examination table he was strapped to. It had been a long trip home, despite the way Kincaid pushed the carriage horses.

Ava lifted her head from the microscope. "His blood's beginning to change. It's full of blacker, sickle-shaped globules, and they're overwhelming his... craving virus cells."

Ingrid strode toward the microscope and peered through it. Ava was right. "Like what happened to Gemma's." Hope flared. "There's a chance that he'll return to normal then?"

"Ingrid." The tone of the word said too much.

"Gemma's levels are still dropping."

Ava began rolling up her sleeves, preparing an injection of hemlock to subdue Byrnes. "Gemma absorbed some of the *dhampir's* blood, and it sent her body into a fever state, increased her craving virus levels, and then healed her. Byrnes received a full dose of this elixir that they use to transform a blue blood." Ava hesitated. "I don't know enough about what's happening, but the way he reacted... it's nothing like how Gemma did. I don't know what's going to happen to him."

"No," Ingrid snarled, raking her hands through her hair as her verwulfen temper unleashed. "No! I've only just found him." This couldn't be happening to her. Dare to dream, and then someone stole it from you before it could come true. She should never have risked it. Never have believed in it. Ingrid curled into a hunched position as the *berserkergang* flushed through her, her fists throbbing as she squeezed them. "I can't lose him," she whispered hopelessly.

Ava went to her knees beside her and clasped her hands. "Ingrid, I won't let anything happen to him if I can help it. He's important to both of us."

Ingrid nodded.

"If there's any chance at all, I'll find it," Ava promised, then helped her to her feet.

"Thank you." She staggered back to Byrnes's side, touching his hand gently. The thrashing stopped, as though her presence bought him peace. "You had better come back to me," she whispered in his ear. "Because you promised you would never leave me alone. You're failing your third challenge, Byrnes."

Byrnes's fingers twitched as if he heard her, and she swallowed. "He's coming around."

"Hold him still," Ava said, tapping the syringe.

"I will." Ingrid leaned on his shoulder and arm. "Trust me," she whispered, when those black eyes locked on hers. "I won't let anything bad happen to you. I'll protect you, Byrnes. We just need to make you... relax."

Malloryn strode in through the door, waving a leather-bound book in his hands. "Got it!

"Got what?" Ava asked, finding the vein in Byrnes's arm and injecting more hemlock to keep him temporarily paralyzed.

"Dr. Cremorne's journals," he replied, peering down at the patient as the tension flooded out of Byrnes's body. "Here's everything we need to pull him through this." That all-seeing gaze locked on Ingrid. "You look like hell."

She glared at him.

"She won't let me see to her leg," Ava admitted, pressing gauze down over the injection site as she removed the syringe from Byrnes's arm. "And I've got my hands full."

Traitor. Ingrid bared her teeth at both of them and paced, trying not to limp.

"And that pacing is distracting me," Ava warned, giving her a dire look. "Ingrid, he's fine for the moment."

Surprisingly, it was Malloryn who caught her by her arm and dragged her toward the door. "I'll see to it."

"If you want to keep that hand, I'd suggest you remove it," Ingrid growled, peering through the open door as Ava opened the journal.

Malloryn sat her down in the parlor, then went to one knee in front of her. "Temper, temper, Miss Miller. Tell me what happened down there," he said, and began gently tugging at her boot.

This was for the best. It had to be. Ingrid spared the examination room one last glance, then told Malloryn everything.

When she got to the part about Byrnes coming out of the darkness and killing the vampire with his bare hands, she began trembling.

Shaking, she bit her lip as she looked up at him, the loupe threatening to override her. "P-promise me.... Promise m-me you w-won't kill him. No matter... w-what."

Malloryn's lips thinned. "Ingrid, he's been injected with the *elixir vitae*. Whatever happens to him, it's out of my hands now."

She curled her good hand in his shirt and yanked him closer. "If you kill him, I will hunt you down."

Lightning flashed in Malloryn's blue eyes, but he caught her wrist and arched a brow. "I'm not going to kill him. Not unless it becomes necessary. To be honest, I actually rather like the bastard. And...."

"And?" She wasn't certain she liked the way he said that.

"Think about it. If he survives, then that means that we have our very own *dhampir*," Malloryn muttered, sliding her bloodied stocking down over her foot. "One that can stand against a vampire and survive."

"You cold bastard." Ingrid winced. "You mean to use him."

"Someone has to make the hard decisions, Ingrid. And that someone is usually me." Malloryn's brow furrowed as he pressed gently against her calf. "The bleeding's stopped, but the skin still looks raw. How does this feel?"

She gasped as he probed it. "As though you just set fire to my leg."

Malloryn eased back, then stared at her. "It looks fine. You'll heal, and I'm no surgeon. But judging from the way you're shaking, you need to sleep and let your body heal."

"I'm not... leaving him...." Sweat dripped down her forehead, her entire body beginning to convulse as the loupe fought to drag her under.

"You might not have a choice. I'll sit with him," Malloryn promised, his face gentling. "At least until you're on your feet again. I swear I won't let anything happen to him."

Because Byrnes's potential *dhampir* state made him valuable. Ingrid hated to admit it, but her eyelids were so heavy. "Wake me if he snaps out of his fugue."

"I will."

The following evening, Ingrid blinked her eyelids as the chill of the room began to wake her. Her head slipped off her hand, and she almost thumped her chin into the arm of the armchair as she came fully awake.

Where was she—?

It all came flooding back. Byrnes. Zero. The elixir. And finally falling asleep in the armchair that Malloryn dragged into the examination room for her.

"Awake?" whispered a soft, sensual voice.

A head turned, and then Byrnes stared at her with those all-black eyes, his wrists and feet manacled to the table and steel bands snapped tight over his throat and waist.

"Byrnes?" she breathed the word, then found her feet. Before remembering that he wasn't quite himself.

His nostrils flared at the sight of her hesitation, and he flexed his wrists inside the steel manacles. "I'm... myself again. Hungry as all hell. But... in control. I think."

"Oh, thank God!" She hurried to his side, reaching out to caress his face. "You gave me one hell of a fright."

Byrnes turned his cheek into the caress, the tension washing out of him, as though her touch settled him. "I can imagine. I just... keep seeing that creature diving for you over and over again...." He shuddered, his lip curling up in a snarl that he fought down. "And I lost myself. God, you don't know what it feels like. I've known the *hunger* all these years but this.... It's like a black wave washing over me, and

I lose all sense of rationality. Nothing but primal instincts remain. You. Me. *Mine*." The way he snarled the word was most unlike him.

"Do you remember?"

"Enough." His gaze slid unerringly to the jug of chilled blood on the vanity. "I need to feed, before the urge overwhelms me."

"Let me undo you," she whispered, turning for his wrist.

Byrnes froze. "No. No, Ingrid, leave me here." He swallowed hard, his hips flexing almost unconsciously. "I'm in control, but I can't say how long that will last. The slightest things drive me under the darkness again. Perhaps... just unlock the band at my throat. So I can drink?"

She unlatched the steel band and then cupped his head to lift it to the jug. Byrnes drained the entire thing, the bands of muscle in his throat working greedily. Finally he slumped back down, and she wiped his mouth with a clean cloth.

Ingrid dragged a stool to his side. "Ava's working on reading Cremorne's journals, so that she can perhaps reverse the process—"

"No." The word jarred the quiet of the room. He looked at her. "There is no way back. Zero told me that, right before she injected me with the serum. If I stop now, then I'll die." He shuddered again. "Worse than that; I'll become a vampire."

Ingrid couldn't resist sliding her fingers into his. "Then we'll work out a way forward."

"There'll be another six treatments, each a week apart," he told her, squeezing her hand back. "Zero said the first one was the worst. Maybe... maybe I won't react as badly next time."

"Did it hurt?"

"Still does." His voice was raw. "I can feel my body changing. Ingrid...."

"Yes?"

"If you can't deal with this, then you let me know," he said. "While I'm still lucid." That stark gaze locked on hers. "I won't blame you if you call an end to us right now. I don't know what the future holds—"

"None of us do," she replied fiercely, leaning down and pressing her lips to his. Just lightly. Need almost overtook her, but it was the sudden rush of hot tears to her eyes that burned the most. "And I'm not leaving you, you fool. I'll sit by your side through all of this. And I'll be there waiting for you at the end, when it's safe. I know that you think that I'm yours, that you have some claim on me. And it's true, but so is this: you belong to me too, Byrnes. And I'm not letting go. You're *mine*."

She was no longer afraid of surrendering herself to him, of taking that risk. Losing him in this way was a far worse alternative. And just like that, all of her earlier hesitation had vanished.

"I remember what you said, in the tunnel...."

She remembered too. "I meant every word."

As if the words overwhelmed him, he kissed her back fiercely, his tongue thrusting into her mouth and his need overwhelming her. It was a long time before she came back up for air, but the passionate rage inside her was strangely assuaged.

Mine. She liked the word. She liked the claiming of it. For too many years there'd been a hole—a longing—inside her, but as she drew back and smiled at him, she realized that there was no gaping emptiness inside her. Not anymore. That place had been filled. And regardless of what happened in the future, she felt oddly at peace.

And half tempted to take advantage of the situation.

Ingrid made a purring sound deep in her throat as she dragged her nails down his abdomen. "This reminds me of a promise I made, once upon a time, that went unfulfilled."

"You fulfilled your promise to the letter," he breathed, heat filling his expression. "And I'd love to take you up on that offer, but I think"—he squeezed his eyes shut and breathed in deep—"that we'd be best to stick to something less overwhelming."

Instantly she eased back onto her chair. "Lust is a consuming thought?"

"Anything primal," he admitted, with a faint mocking smile. "I'm holding on to the thought that when I finally get a hold on this, I get to have you all to myself. I'm planning everything that I'm going to do to you. In exquisite detail." He swallowed again.

"I'd best make sure that the house is empty when that happens," she teased, but only lightly.

"And perhaps reinforce the bed."

"Well now." Ingrid smiled.

"Read to me?" he whispered, turning that all-black gaze on her one more time.

Ingrid took a deep breath. "What would you like to hear?"

"*Pride and Prejudice*," he said, then shrugged when he saw her eyebrows arch. "What? It's my mother's favorite."

"And of course, you don't see anything of Mr. Darcy in yourself?"

"Are you calling me proud?"

Ingrid laughed, then pressed a kiss to his forehead before she went in search of the book. "It's one of your most frustrating traits, yes. But Byrnes," she paused in the doorway with a flirtatious smile, "I still love you, despite it."

Love you.

Byrnes breathed in the words, feeling them flood through him, a light to sway the darkness. Ingrid didn't know how close to the edge he still was, but everything she'd said gave him hope—a means to fight this.

He'd spent years in perfect control of his craving virus and his emotions. He could win this battle. And he would.

Because he had one hell of a prize waiting for him when he did.

"Seven weeks," he whispered, as a promise to himself. "You can do this."

Because her love was worth the fight.

Zero strained at the manacles binding her, feeling them give, just slightly. Malloryn might have her trapped in this godforsaken little dungeon, but if he thought steel could keep her here, then he had another think coming.

The first thing I'm going to do is kill that cold bastard, she told herself as she felt the steel link stretching on the chain that pinned her right hand. *Perhaps I'll even make him eat his own tongue?*

Footsteps whispered in the hallway outside. Zero looked up, holding still.

A key rattled in the lock, and a chill ran through her, taking her back years and years to that first asylum. Zero fought to remain calm. Everyone who'd ever hurt her was dead. Malloryn didn't scare her. And she was Zero now, not Annabelle. She was prepared for anything. No doubt it was merely Malloryn, that smug bastard, back to question her or to gloat some more.

"I'm not telling you anything else!" she snarled.

And then the door opened and a figure stepped inside, easing it closed behind him.

Zero's resistance faded as she caught a glimpse of that moonlight-pale hair, her shoulders slumping into the seat. "It's about bloody time. I thought you were never going to come."

"Have you told them anything?"

Zero paused. "Of course not."

But she knew he'd caught the pause.

Obsidian stepped closer, tugging off his gloves, one finger at a time. His face remained implacable. "I'm not telling you anything... else," he repeated. "Which means you told them something."

A mistake. *Oh, hell.* Zero wrestled with her chains. "I meant... Caleb Byrnes. That bastard tricked me. I thought I had him captured and I *might* have mentioned one or two things about *dhampir*, but nothing else. I swear it, Obsidian!"

Thick blond lashes obscured his eyes. "You mentioned nothing about the Master?"

If she could have sweated, she was certain she'd be doing so right now. "Of course not! Do you think I'm stupid! If Malloryn gets even a hint of what this is all about—"

A single slashing hand stopped her. "Good. The Master is not happy. You've made one mess too many, Annabelle. You were warned to follow your orders and not draw too many eyes to the moves behind the scenes, but thanks to your arrogance, Malloryn is now aware of things he shouldn't know yet. You got sloppy."

"Don't call me that," she whispered, suddenly furious. "Annabelle is dead!"

And then he looked at her, just looked, and she knew why he was really here. There would be no chance to talk her way out of this. The Master had been her judge and jury, and now Obsidian was here as his executioner. "You treacherous—"

A hand clapped over her mouth and Zero sank her teeth into the flesh there. Then heat exploded behind her eyes, and her head rang.

"I'm sorry. This is not something I wish to do," he whispered, withdrawing a small syringe from his inner pocket as she struggled to blink through the dizziness of his blow. "But you have done this yourself. You were warned, damn you. Warned to keep yourself under control."

She tugged her face aside from his controlling hand, just for a second. "No! No," she whispered, kicking and scrambling to break free. "You bloody little lapdog! Did you kiss his feet when he demanded this of you? Do you think that he won't d-do the same... to you—"

The needle slid into her throat and icy cold spilled into her veins. Zero jerked. "No! N-no, please...." She was suddenly frightened. She didn't want this to end. She didn't want to be alone. Not again.

"I'm sorry," Obsidian said. "But there is no other way." He moved to step back from her.

"D-don't... leave... me," she managed to gurgle as pain lit her nerves on fire. "Please...." Her eyes rolled up in her head as her feet and body began to jerk uncontrollably.

A moment passed, as if he hesitated. Then a pair of strong arms went around her, and for the first time in a long time, Annabelle felt like she wasn't alone. She jerked as fire flooded through her chest, narrowing in on her heart.

"Shush," Obsidian whispered, pressing a kiss to her temple and ruffling her hair. "It will be over soon. And I won't leave you until it's done. The same way that I wouldn't leave you back then. I'm sorry."

It lasted minutes. It felt like hours. And through it all, Obsidian rocked her, even when she began to weep tears of blood.

And then the fire exploded in her chest.

Gemma paused in the doorway to her room, feeling a breeze slip over her skin. Just that, but it was enough for her to draw the small pistol at her side.

"Hullo?" she called, pressing her back to the wall and waiting for her eyes to adjust to the darkness.

The last time she'd left her bedchamber, the window had been closed.

Now the sash was lifted and her curtains fluttered in the slight breeze. Gemma swept the room, but there was nobody there.

"Maybe I left it open after all," she murmured, then frowned. She was fairly certain she hadn't.

Instinct drove her back out into the hallway. Slipping quietly through the house, Gemma made her rounds. She was being silly. There was nothing here. Just—

The door to Zero's cell was cracked open an inch. All of the hairs on Gemma's arms lifted, and a chill ran down her spine. Maybe she wasn't imagining things, after all? She sidled closer, her gaze raking the darkness, and her heart suddenly thundering to a crescendo. And then she eased open the cell door with a steady hand and stepped inside, her pistol swinging to track each shadow.

Only one shadow remained in the room. Zero, slumped silently in the chair and chains where they'd put her.

"Are you awake?" Gemma whispered as she crossed the room, though she was fairly certain that she knew the answer to that.

Zero didn't move. No breath lifted her chest. Gemma swallowed and tilted the woman's head up.

Black blood dripped from her eyes and her ears. Her skin looked like a thousand small bruises had erupted, as though her capillaries had burst in a hundred places.

Gemma staggered backward, trembling badly.

What was the first rule of espionage? Leave no comrades behind. Sometimes that was due to the fact that in dangerous cases, you only ever had each other to watch your backs. The more sinister reason was so that your enemy couldn't use them for information.

A floorboard creaked behind her.

She spun, the pistol tracking... nothing. There was nothing there. But as she swallowed, she was fairly certain that there had been.

"Who are you?" she whispered.

For there was but the faintest scent left behind in the air, a peculiar sweetness that she'd only smelled one time before.

In the museum, when someone killed her attacker.

CHAPTER THIRTY-SIX

THE BLOOD WAS sweet as Byrnes stared out through the window in Malloryn's study, watching rain drip down the windows of the new house that they'd moved to the second the old one became compromised. Ingrid had sought their bed, but something was bothering him. A weight upon his mind.

Now that he had it back.

The door opened and Malloryn strode in, scraping his wet hair back off his head. The instant he realized that someone was in the study, his hand dipped, coming up with a knife.

"It's only me."

Malloryn's hard gaze flattened and he vanished the knife as swiftly as it had appeared. "That's an easy way to get yourself killed. All I saw was your bloody pale hair. I thought it was one of the... others. What are you doing in here?"

"Waiting for you, actually." *Others.* Other *dhampir.* Byrnes twitched a little. The changes to his physique were coming swiftly. He'd shaved off his hair the second the roots of it stared to grow in silvery, and his eyelashes were already lightening. His hair was an inch long now, changing his appearance significantly. Ingrid said it didn't bother her, but looking in the mirror was like looking at a different man.

And maybe that wasn't all bad. He no longer saw his father, at least. Perhaps this could be a fresh start? A rebirth?

Even if the weight of the hunger remained constant and his moods more mercurial.

"There's something that bothers me." He couldn't stop his gaze from sliding to the wrapped package under Malloryn's arm. "Light reading before bed, your Grace?"

"The Cremorne diaries," Malloryn said, holding the book-shaped package aloft. "Ava's finished with it, now that your treatments are well on the way." Those mercurial eyes examined Byrnes. "What is it you wished to speak of?"

"Ulbricht's gone to ground, and Zero is dead," he said. "Someone broke into the house and killed her. And you haven't found them yet."

Malloryn sidled around the desk, looking thoughtful. "Yes. I'm assuming it was one of her *dhampir* brethren. What surprises me is that I didn't wake up with a slit throat. Or not wake up, as it were."

"Maybe they're not finished with you yet," Byrnes suggested. "Zero said they wanted revenge upon you for the revolution, and if I were planning revenge, I wouldn't want it to be too easy. I'd want you to suffer."

"Remind me not to get on your bad side."

Byrnes smiled. "One could say the same, your Grace. Though it would be interesting to see who wins."

Malloryn poured himself a glass of blud-wein and then topped up Byrnes's. They chinked their glasses together. "If we went to war against each other, it would be... bloody.

And you're not that type of man. Neither of us likes disorder, or mess. And sometimes the mystery of not knowing the answer is more intriguing than the knowing."

"Besides, if you won, you'd have a furious verwulfen breathing down your neck."

"There is that," Malloryn conceded with the faintest hint of amusement. "So enough games. What's bothering you?"

"I've had a lot of time to think lately. This whole thing," Byrnes said, "from the Sons of Gilead to Zero herself, was merely... puppetry. Zero's dead, her vampire stable burned, and the missing people were found, but I don't feel like this is a victory at all. Ulbricht's still out there somewhere, with his Rising Sons. There are at least four other *dhampir*; this Ghost, Sirius, Obsidian, and X. It's a mess of threads, but none of it makes any sense."

"Yes. One would almost think that someone was pulling all of the strings." Malloryn lifted his own glass in a kind of wry salute, then tipped the glass to his lips. "This 'master' that Zero spoke of."

That was when Byrnes realized that Malloryn didn't look shocked. "You knew."

"I suspected." Malloryn shrugged, and for a moment looked younger and weary as he stared at the desk surface, or perhaps beyond it. "It's been clear to me for a while that someone is manipulating events."

"Who?"

"If I knew that"—Malloryn's eyebrow quirked—"then there wouldn't be a Company of Rogues."

"The others have settled on the name then?"

A touch of humor softened that hard mouth. "They have. Young Todd made an impassioned debate of it." Malloryn stared at his blud-wein, then drained what was left of it. "It's the first time in my life that I've ever been called a 'rogue.'"

"The boy means no offense." Rogue blue bloods were, after all, the scum of the blue blood world.

"None taken. I've never truly considered myself a part of the Echelon, or that world."

No, Malloryn had always been the puppet master, working behind the scenes for the queen. "How *did* you ever form an alliance with Her Highness? Or why?" He'd been born into a world where he should have had it all. Why would Malloryn give a damn about the working classes, or the way blue bloods had killed and slaughtered without repercussions?

Malloryn's smile died and his eyes glittered as he poured himself another drink. "A long story, Byrnes. And one not commonly shared."

Silence. Byrnes didn't pretend to be affronted, even though his endless curiosity bit deep. After all, where was the fun in simply being *told* the answer? But that was for another day. Something Malloryn had said bothered him. "You knew that someone was behind it all. That's why you set us on this course. Not to find those people. Not to hunt Zero or any of the others, but to flush out your true quarry. After all, you could have used your spy network, or the Nighthawks. But no...." He thought it through. "You wanted to set a trap for him—or her—a challenge. To see if he'd take the bait and come after us."

Malloryn merely tipped his head to Byrnes.

"If we'd known that," he pointed out, "then we might have come at the answer quicker. And you might have gotten some of us killed."

"I ask you to take no risks that I won't take myself," Malloryn pointed out. "I don't have to be hands-on here."

Byrnes whistled under his breath. "You *are* cold."

Malloryn leaned forward to refill his glass. "Coming from you, that almost sounds like a compliment."

"Almost," Byrnes warned. "I have a stake in this now."

"I don't intend any harm to come to any of the Rogues. There are plans in place in case the danger gets out of hand."

"And there's no point in throwing away good operatives."

Malloryn looked a little unsettled at that. He tapped his fingers on the desk. "I have to be cold to survive this world. I learned that in the womb." He hesitated. "The Rogues' usefulness isn't the only reason I would prefer you stay alive. Contrary to popular opinion, I'm not *that* ruthless."

"You did try to shoot me in the tunnels below the asylum. Twice."

"The first time I was protecting Gemma. The second... well, you *were* about to try and rip off my head, I believe."

Touché. Byrnes considered it, then let it go. It was interesting to come up against a mind quite like his own. "We're even. But what are you going to do about this mastermind?"

"Nothing." Malloryn slumped back in his chair, looking entirely relaxed. "Except watch. And wait."

"And discover if they will play their hand. Very *good*, your Grace. And you say you're not ruthless."

"'Not *that* ruthless,' was the precise term I used."

"Doing nothing might gain you a name in the end," he pointed out, "but it puts all of us at danger, and paints a rather large target on our backs. You might not be pulling the trigger, but you might get us killed all the same." Leaning forward, he pointedly set his glass down and stood. "Maybe that is 'that ruthless.'"

Malloryn toyed with his glass, looking distant. "Maybe it is." He smiled sadly.

"Sometimes I have a hard time seeing it anymore. Which means you should keep your mouth shut, and keep an eye on your fiancée."

"Fiancée?" It was clear he was being dismissed, but that word still shocked him.

"If Ingrid doesn't belong to you, then she can be taken," Malloryn said, sleepy-eyed but no less dangerous. "I assume that's the direction this matter is taking."

"It is, but not because I'm afraid to lose her. Not like that." Snagging his hat, Byrnes offered a respectful nod to the duke. "The others are my friends too. Ingrid's not the only one who means something to me. And we should mean something to you too. The way you're headed.... It's a difficult thing for a man to stand alone, and it turns you hard. I should know. I've been there. You need someone to be your conscience, if nothing else."

"It seems I have you," the duke replied dryly.

"I'm not enough, and Lord knows my sense of boundaries is not exactly trustworthy sometimes. If it cannot be one of us—for obvious reasons—then maybe you should look elsewhere."

"I have someone to warm my bed."

"I'm not just talking about your bed. The reason Ingrid and I work so well together is because she's not afraid to tell me the truth whenever I cross the line." Byrnes crossed slowly to the door. "Think about it, at least."

"Byrnes"—the duke settled that glittering gaze on him—"there are more than enough females in my life trying to tell me what to do."

Sensing that he'd pushed far enough, Byrnes opened the door and smiled. "You mean Miss Hamilton?"

Malloryn shook his head. "Go play with Ingrid. My relationship with Miss Hamilton is none of your business. And you're starting to sound like your new romantic entanglements have warped your brain."

"It's everybody's business," Byrnes countered, holding onto the doorknob. "Haven't you heard? This *is* a company of spies, after all. Gemma's running a betting pool on whether you're going to get the bride to the altar, or whether one of you will cry off first or kill each other."

"Byrnes, you're a menace." Malloryn sounded disgusted. "And it sounds like none of you are busy enough. I can fix that."

"You don't even know who I'm backing," Byrnes protested.

Something was lobbed at the door—the crumpled piece of paper off the desk. Byrnes slammed the door shut just before the paper hit, laughing to himself as he hurried along the corridor.

Malloryn had one thing right: going to play with Ingrid was precisely the destination he had in mind.

EPILOGUE

Two years after all is said and done...

THE TABLE WAS crowded, full of old friends and new and their offspring. Ingrid sat in the guest of honor's position with Rosa's youngest son, Emery, on her lap.

"I hope you had a wonderful birthday," Rosa said, leaning down to kiss her cheek as Lynch and Garrett retired to the duke's billiards room to discuss business. Or more likely, to rest their eardrums. Perry and Garrett's twin daughters, Grace and Ivy, had declared war over dessert upon Phillip, the ducal heir. Baby Emery had joined in by squealing every time they caught his brother.

Perry went after her children with an aggrieved expression as the trio took off through the house.

Thank goodness. The noise had been overwhelming.

"It's not really my birthday," Ingrid protested. She couldn't remember which day she'd been born on, only the month. Rosa had insisted she pick a day years ago, and so she'd chosen the twelfth of June. Today.

It still didn't quite feel right though.

"Hush." Rosa's frown scolded her, but her smile looked far too pleased. She was up to something. "Just enjoy the day. And now, I do believe your husband wanted you in the library." This was accompanied with a slightly arched brow and a knowing smile as Rosa took young Emery off her hands. The boy had his mother's eyes, her personality, and her deviousness, and even though he was only one, he grinned at Ingrid over her shoulder as if he were in on the conspiracy. "I'll go rescue Perry."

Ingrid snatched up her glass of dessert wine and drained it. She enjoyed the revelry—it reminded her of what she'd missed out on growing up—but there was definitely a limit to the amount of hours she could sit through it.

The noise and light died down as she went to find her husband. He'd vanished sometime during dessert, but she'd been so distracted that she hadn't noticed his removal, only his absence.

"Caleb?" she called softly. There was light limning the door of the library, and the faint fragrance of roses. With a brief knock, she pushed inside.

Her husband was pacing in the middle of the room, carelessly crushing the red rose petals beneath his boot heels. Byrnes turned at her entrance, hands clasped behind his back and his expression arrested. His appearance never failed to light her up inside. Here was her other half, the one person in the world who understood her and her need for independence. She spent most of the day with him at their leased apartments where they ran the private detective agency they'd formed a year ago, but she never grew tired of his presence.

One look at the rose petals crushed all over the floor and the champagne bottle in its ice bath, and she arched a brow. "Rosa?"

His mouth stretched into a smile and Byrnes cracked the champagne bottle with a pop. Bubbles frothed over his hand. "You doubt me, darling?"

"I know you," she admitted dryly, crossing the room to take the glass he handed her. He'd only ever told her he loved her three times. Byrnes was never careless with such words, nor was he prone to romantic notions. Every now and then she wished he might be a little more romantic, but that was what made those three little words so cherished when they came. "Roses and champagne aren't your style."

He chinked his glass against hers. The smile faltered. He actually looked nervous for a moment, then recovered admirably. "Ah, but I'm quite happy to claim someone else's efforts."

Ingrid enjoyed the first sweetly bitter mouthful, but she couldn't take her eyes off him. "You're up to something."

Capturing her fingertips, he drew her into his arms, setting his glass down on the nearest table. The swish of her green skirts pressed against his thighs. "You look beautiful tonight," he told her, turning serious again.

"*And* you're trying to distract me."

"You accuse *me* of being unromantic," he quipped back. "Can't I compliment my wife?"

Firm fingers took her champagne glass and set it aside too. Then his hands cupped her face and drew her closer. Her entire body pressed against his, and Ingrid breathed in the subtle scent of his aftershave.

"Of course you can," she whispered. "But don't think I'll forget that you're hiding something."

Byrnes smiled, his pale eyes growing lazy. "Always a challenge, Ingrid. Obviously I'm not trying hard enough."

The kiss took her breath away as he caught her hands and wrapped them around his waist. Then his own hands captured her face and he drank in the taste of her breath, every soft gasp... turning her into a molten puddle of quivering need.

Yes, romance definitely seemed like a suitable distraction.

Ingrid slid her hands inside his coat and pressed him back against the desk. Byrnes caught her wrists. "Ah, ah, ah." He murmured, withdrawing from her. "You are *not* going to ravish me on Lynch's desk."

She bit her lip, her gaze lifting to his. "Do you think he'd notice?"

"Undoubtedly." Byrnes put a finger to her lips. "Later. You're not going to distract me from my purpose."

Ingrid bit his finger. "I could."

There was that smile, there and then gone again. "This is important."

Ingrid rested her hip on the desk and folded her palms in her lap. "You have ten seconds to convince me it's interesting. Then I want my present." A darting glance toward his erection told him precisely what she meant by that.

"Maybe this *is* your present," he replied, leaning his hands on either side of her hips and pressing closer.

"Continue."

"You know I've been distracted lately."

Ingrid hesitated. Of course she'd noticed, though she'd thought it the residual effects of his mother's passing last year. "Ye-es...."

"I've been working on a gift for you," he said, and the laughter vanished from his face, leaving him darkly serious.

Once upon a time, she would have thought that she'd done something wrong when he looked like that. She understood him now, however. That closed-off expression and the tight way he pronounced his words meant that he was emotional and trying to rein it in.

"A gift?" she teased, to lighten the mood.

"It's been perplexing me since the day we married. I wanted to do something for you, but it hasn't been as easy as I'd hoped it would be. In my arrogance I assumed I would be able to present you with this gift for our anniversary. Let's just say, it took a little longer than expected. Come." He took her fingers and drew her to the polished walnut secretary, where he gestured her into the seat. There was a creamy envelope on the secretary, as well as a box somewhat larger than a book. It smelled like paper and ink and the faint chemical tang of photographs.

"What is it?"

"Not a puppy," he replied promptly. "Or a diamond ring. Or all of the other foolish ideas Rosa presented me with. I wanted to do something special for you."

Ingrid looked up and he brushed his mouth against her cheek. "It's the reason I disappeared for two weeks last month, darling. I didn't go to Edinburgh with Garrett for that Ripper case. I lied about that, but I hope you'll forgive me."

"Byrnes." Her voice lowered, her heart starting a rapid pitter-pat. She didn't know why, but she was suddenly nervous. As was he. She could see it in the tense line of his body. "I thought we promised not to lie to each other."

"I didn't want to get your hopes up." Then he let out an exasperated breath. "I didn't want to get *my* hopes up. Do you know how frustrating this case has been? I honestly didn't expect this lead to go anywhere, as all the others haven't. And if I'm being honest, this was a promise I made a long time ago to you."

"Case?" Her spine straightened. "You were working a case without me? And what promise?"

"Bloody hell, Ingrid. Just open the envelope."

Shooting him a sidelong glance under her lashes that promised future retribution, she obliged. A pair of first class tickets aboard a steamer fell into her hand. "Oslo? But why...?" And then she stopped speaking. She was fairly certain she also stopped breathing. Her heartbeat echoed in her ears.

Byrnes pushed the package toward her with a faint, nervous smile. He rested his hip on the desk. "I found them for you."

"Who?" she whispered, but she knew.

"Your family, Ingrid. I found them."

The world fell apart. Tears blurred her vision, and she froze, unable to so much as speak.

Byrnes's hand clenched around hers comfortingly. "Your legal name isn't Ingrid, which has been the bother all along. It's actually Britta Ingrid Apslund. Your Aunt Kristina, however, decided you were most certainly not a Britta when you were a one-year-old. They called you Ingrid from that moment until your fourth year, when you were taken by the English raiders. It's all there in the package. I have photographs of your family. I have your birth documents, your... your bill of sale. I even met your mother. She's still alive, after all this time, and looks remarkably like you. You have aunts, uncles, sisters, nephews and nieces—"

Ingrid couldn't bear to hear anymore. All this time.... With trembling hands, she opened the box and lifted a pile of photographs out. The top one showed a smiling woman resting a baby on her hip whilst another child clung to her skirts. The man beside the woman was tall, with dark hair and light-colored eyes that—even through the sepia portrait—she knew were bronze. The image seemed to suddenly open up a previously locked box in her memory.

She could almost hear his voice in her mind, reading to her before bed. A deep, patient voice, and her favorite book, *The Snow Queen*.

With a gasp, she clapped a hand to her lips, but her tears were more difficult to contain. "My father."

"Yes." Byrnes kissed her forehead. His voice lowered. "He was killed by the hunting party that took you. Your mother searched for you for years, but there was nothing to find. The English raiders were good at their job, and some of them were even rogue blue bloods. They didn't leave any scent, or any trail. She never knew what had happened to you, but she never gave up hoping."

She couldn't stop herself from crying harder.

"Ingrid?" Byrnes gathered her into his arms, where she sobbed against his chest. "You're starting to make me nervous. You're happy about this, yes?"

In response, she simply nodded wetly against his shoulder.

"There's nothing I wouldn't do to make you happy, darling." His strong arms drew her tight into a hug that shielded her from the world. "I would even resort to flowers and poetry if I thought that would put a smile on your face."

She couldn't help laughing at the thought. Dashing the tears from her eyes, she pushed away from him just enough to try and gather herself. "I should make you write me a poem, just to see if you would."

He grimaced. "I'd pay Garrett to do it. He's better at that sort of thing than I am."

"I don't want empty words, Caleb." Ingrid tugged at his lapels, trying to compose herself. "Just you. Always you. You always know exactly what I need."

Gruff, and slightly embarrassed, he couldn't quite hide his pleasure as he cleared his throat. "I love you, Ingrid.

They're the only words that I know, and they're not empty." Pressing her hand to his chest, he gave a faint smile. "They fill me up, in here. I never knew there was so much emptiness inside until I met you, but you fill me up. You make every day a revelation."

Ingrid gave a hiccupping laugh that was filled with more tears. Her family.... She still couldn't believe it. "Thank you."

"I thought we could take an extended honeymoon," he suggested, offering her his handkerchief. "Since we missed out on our first one, thanks to that debacle at Malloryn's wedding."

"A honeymoon?"

Fingers tiptoed down her bodice, pausing at the lace along her décolletage. "We leave in two days time. So you'll have to pack. But that's unimportant. I believe you were saying something about another type of present?"

Ingrid curled her fist in his collar. "Come here," she growled, and hauled him against her for a kiss.

Lynch's desk be damned.

If you enjoyed *Mission: Improper*, then get ready for *The Mech Who Loved Me*! Book two in the Blue Blood Conspiracy series, it features Kincaid and Ava, and continues the mystery of figuring out just who is the figurehead behind the *dhampir* and SOG. If you want to know more about its release date, cover reveals, and pre-order links join my newsletter at www.becmcmaster.com

THE MECH WHO LOVED ME

COMING 2017

The Sons of Gilead are rising, threatening the very heart of the Empire: the Queen herself. Only a secret handful of people dare to stop them, though they may be risking life and limb—and even their hearts—in the process.

Freed from the grips of a madman, Miss Ava McLaren has had a difficult time fitting back into the life of a gently bred young lady. Stricken by the craving virus, she found solace in the laboratories of the Nighthawks trying to create a synthetic solution for blood, until one day a strange missive arrived, asking for her help in thwarting a plot against the Queen.

Thrown into the Company of Rogues, Ava finds herself intimidated by the dangerous men and women who form the core of the group, particularly the brutish mech, Kincaid. The man's a devilishly handsome rake who barely notices that she's even female. Indeed, he considers her blue blood status a personal insult and makes it clear he'll never trust her.

Until an assassination attempt proves that Ava's experiments just might have caught the attention of the Sons of Gilead. Kincaid's the only one who can protect her from the dangerous anarchists—and together they are forced to discover just why Ava is suddenly the most sought-after bluestocking in London...

ABOUT THE AUTHOR

Bec McMaster is the award-winning author of the London Steampunk series. When not poring over travel brochures, playing netball, or cooking things that are very likely bad for her, Bec spends most of her time in front of the computer. A member of RWA, she writes sexy, dark paranormals and adventurous steampunk romances, and grew up with her nose in a book. Following a life-long love affair with fantasy, she discovered romance novels as a 16 year-old, and hasn't looked back.

In 2012, Sourcebooks released her debut award-winning novel, *Kiss of Steel*, the first in the London Steampunk series, followed by: *Heart of Iron*, *My Lady Quicksilver*, *Forged By Desire*, and *Of Silk And Steam*. Two novellas - *Tarnished Knight* and *The Curious Case Of The Clockwork Menace* - fleshed out the series. She has been nominated for RT Reviews Best Steampunk Romances for *Heart of Iron (2013)*, won RT Reviews Best Steampunk Romance with *Of Silk And Steam (2015)*, and *Forged By Desire* was nominated for a RITA award in 2015.

In 2016, she debuted the *Dark Arts* series with *Shadowbound*, and the second *London Steampunk: The Blueblood Conspiracy* series with *Mission: Improper*.

For news on new releases, cover reveals, giveaways, and special promotions, join her mailing list at www.becmcmaster.com

ACKNOWLEDGMENTS

The storyline in *Mission: Improper* first began to rear its head in *My Lady Quicksilver* (book three in London Steampunk). We were rapidly heading toward the revolution, but what happened next? After all, there were a lot of threads to tie up, a few characters who needed to find their HEA, and just how well was the Queen going to rule now that she was out from under the grip of her tyrannical husband? One of the things I liked exploring in this book is the fact that not everything is perfect. We like to pretend that when we overthrow the villains, the world is suddenly sunshine and roses. But mistakes get made, and sometimes those changes don't just happen in the blink of an eye. London is now changing, but slowly, my friends. Slowly. And we've got a bit of a ways to go yet.

I enjoyed every second of writing this novel, but as with every project I take on, I couldn't have done it without a lot of help from these amazing people:

I owe huge thanks to Jennie Kew and Kylie Griffin for the beta read–who else highlights every cat reference in somebody's manuscript? *grin*–to Olivia from Hot Tree Edits for all the editorial efforts on this project, my wonderful cover artists at Damonza.com for that glorious cover, and to Allyson Gottlieb and Marisa-rose Shor from Athena Interior and Cover Me Darling for the print formatting.

Special thanks go to my very own beta hero, Byron–who encourages and supports me every step of the way–and to the Central Victorian Writers Group, for all of the tea and chocolates consumed at our meetings/brainstorming sessions.

And to everyone who read/loved/reviewed/ or talked

about this book, you guys are awesome! And yes, Charlie is coming! He just has a little bit of growing up to do. I hope you enjoyed Ingrid and Byrnes's HEA!

35761135R00241

Made in the USA
Middletown, DE
08 February 2019